S0-AHP-651

Bay County Library System

This book has been placed in your facility as part of the Outreach Services Collection of the Bay County Library System.

Happy Reading!!!

**Outreach Services
893-9566 ext 2111**

UNDAUNTED HOPE

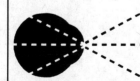
This Large Print Book carries the
Seal of Approval of N.A.V.H.

UNDAUNTED HOPE

JODY HEDLUND

THORNDIKE PRESS
A part of Gale, Cengage Learning

Farmington Hills, Mich • San Francisco • New York • Waterville, Maine
Meriden, Conn • Mason, Ohio • Chicago

GALE
CENGAGE Learning®

Copyright © 2016 by Jody Hedlund.
Scripture quotations are from the King James Version of the Bible.
Thorndike Press, a part of Gale, Cengage Learning.

Thorndike Press® Large Print Christian Romance.
The text of this Large Print edition is unabridged.
Other aspects of the book may vary from the original edition.
Set in 16 pt. Plantin.

LIBRARY OF CONGRESS CATALOGING-IN-PUBLICATION DATA

Names: Hedlund, Jody, author.
Title: Undaunted hope / by Jody Hedlund.
Description: Large print edition. | Waterville, Maine : Thorndike Press, 2016. | © 2016 | Series: Beacons of hope ; book 3 | Series: Thorndike Press large print Christian romance
Identifiers: LCCN 2015044986| ISBN 9781410487780 (hardcover) | ISBN 1410487784 (hardcover)
Subjects: LCSH: Large type books. | GSAFD: Love stories. | Christian fiction.
Classification: LCC PS3608.E333 U53 2016 | DDC 813/.6—dc23
LC record available at http://lccn.loc.gov/2015044986

Published in 2016 by arrangement with Bethany House Publishers, a division of Baker Publishing Group

Printed in Mexico
1 2 3 4 5 6 7 19 18 17 16

*To women everywhere who have
experienced helplessness and hurt*

May you find courage to face your fears
and walk through to the other side.

CHAPTER 1

Eagle Harbor, Northern Michigan
September 1871

"You're not the new teacher," the bald, round-faced man said again in his childlike voice.

"But I am," Tessa Taylor insisted. She pushed the wrinkled letter toward the proprietor of Cole Mine Company Store and Office.

The man's chubby cheeks were flushed red. His eyes shifted in distress toward the shop door. And he refused to so much as glance at the official document she'd carried over the past week, her beacon of hope, her only escape from the past that haunted her.

"The new teacher is supposed to be a man," the storekeeper said. "And you're a woman."

She braced her hands on the spotless glass countertop and leaned across it, taking in

7

the name badge he wore pinned to his vest. "Listen, Mr. Updegraff. I'm T. Taylor, which stands for Tessa Taylor. I'm the new teacher for the Eagle Harbor School. I'm sorry you thought you were getting a man, but lucky for you, I'm worth ten men."

At the sight of her hands on the counter, the man shook his head and made *tsk*ing noises at the back of his throat. When he reached beneath the counter, Tessa jerked her hands off the glass and took a quick step back.

She'd heard tales about the wild, untamed regions of upper Michigan, of the brawling, drunkenness, and lawlessness that were rampant. It would be just her luck if he pulled out a gun and shot her on the spot.

She could see the headline in the *Detroit Free Press:* Town Demands a Man Teacher, Shoots All Women Who Apply for the Job.

As Mr. Updegraff lifted his hand, Tessa started to raise hers in self-defense, but then stopped. It wasn't as if she could catch the bullet if he decided to shoot her.

To her surprise, he plopped a frayed rag onto the glass and began to swirl it in circular, squeaking motions in the very spot she'd touched. His brows puckered, and his flabby jowls shook at his exertion.

Behind her, the store was deserted except

for one woman with a baby propped on her hip and two children running around her in circles and tangling in her listless skirt, one giggling and the other crying. They were racing awfully close to the glass jars of pickled beets that sat on a low shelf.

For all the noise the children were making, the mother didn't seem to hear them. Instead she let her dirt-encrusted fingernails trail over a grain sack of potatoes marked with a crude sign that read *Two dollars a bushel* in sticklike elementary handwriting.

Next to the potatoes stood barrels of apples, turnips, melons, cucumbers, cabbages, and carrots — apparently the stock of local farmers. But the prices on each of them were outrageously high.

"I don't suppose you take arms and legs in payment for the fresh produce, do you?" Tessa couldn't refrain from muttering.

But Mr. Updegraff was too focused on removing her fingerprints from the glass to pay attention to her sarcasm.

The shelves along one wall were stocked with flour, sugar, beans, tea, coffee, and rice. Another set of shelves running down the middle of the store revealed more practical items like lard, tallow, clothespins, baking powder, and condensed milk. A large portion of the store, near the back, was

9

overflowing with kegs of powder, fuses for blasting, hard hats with candles, drills, sledgehammers, along with numerous other mining supplies she couldn't begin to name.

It hadn't taken Tessa long during her four-day voyage on the *Temperance* to realize the steamer was loaded with barrels and crates headed to Copper Country in preparation for the harsh winter that would soon cut the mining communities off from the lower part of the state.

The idea of being trapped in the north for the winter had given Tessa pause for only a moment before she'd cast it aside. She was going on an adventure, she'd reminded herself. And adventures always had an element of danger to them. That's what made them exciting.

She drew in a deep breath of the strong odor of salt pork that mingled with the spiciness of tobacco. Even if she'd already run into the first major roadblock of her adventure, she wouldn't let a little thing like a mix-up in her gender stop her.

"If you'll point me to the schoolhouse," she said.

"You just go on and get out of here," Mr. Updegraff said, almost petulantly still rubbing at the glass. "We've never had a woman

10

teacher, and we're not about to start having one."

"Let's call a gathering of the school board and parents and let them decide."

At a crash of glass, Mr. Updegraff's head snapped up. His eyes rounded at the sight of the rapidly spreading pool of purplish liquid on the floor amidst shards of glass and lumps of beets.

The woman with the baby on her hip yelled at the two children who'd stopped running to stare at the mess.

"Uh-oh, uh-oh," Mr. Updegraff said as he fumbled for a cornhusk broom in the corner, his worried eyes never once leaving the puddle.

For the first time since Tessa had embarked on her journey, she experienced a real pang of worry. Would she be out of a job before she even began? "Mr. Updegraff, please listen —"

He strode around the counter, broom in hand wielded like a warrior charging into battle. "Go home, lady. I won't talk to you anymore."

As he waddled with single-minded attention toward the broken jar of beets, Tessa released a whistling sigh and glanced out the grocery store window to the other businesses that lined the main street of Eagle

11

Harbor — the smithy, several boarding-houses and taverns, a carpenter shop, livery stables, and the spire of the Methodist church rising beyond a smattering of identical-looking log cabins.

With firm, decisive steps, she crossed to the door, opened it, and stepped onto Center Street. The thoroughfare was little more than a dirt path engraved with wagon ruts.

She lifted her face, first to the thickly wooded hills that bordered the eastern edge of town, and then to the wide expanse of Lake Superior that hemmed in the west with its bald, rocky bluffs and fierce coast-line. She drew in a breath of the September air that already had a nip to it.

Everyone had warned her that she was moving to the frontier, that life in the far north was more rugged than out west. But their warnings had only fueled her desire to travel to the Upper Peninsula all the more. It was the perfect place to distance herself from her past and to start life over with a clean reputation, where no one would ever have to know about her past mistakes.

She let her sights linger on the hundreds of gulls perched on rocks in the bay. Their calls were muted by the waves crashing against boulders. The constant roar even

12

drowned out the shouts of the *Temperance* deckhands as they began unloading the cargo onto one of the two docks in the harbor where it would be transported and stored in the warehouse built near the shore.

Her faded orange carpetbag sat where she'd discarded it on the long wooden platform.

She might as well retrieve her bag and check into one of the boardinghouses. Then she'd at least know where to have her personal trunks delivered once they were unloaded from her berth.

With a bound to her step, she headed back to the harbor, the path growing gradually sandier as she neared the water. If the town thought they could get rid of her so easily, they were in for a surprise. She usually got her way, and she wasn't about to let that change now. She'd simply have to convince everyone that she was the right person for the job — even if she wasn't the man they'd been expecting.

"Why are men always deemed more worthy?" she muttered, thinking of the struggle her older sister, Caroline, had experienced when she'd wanted to become head lightkeeper of Windmill Lighthouse near Detroit. Even though she'd been more experienced and competent than most men, she'd faced

13

discrimination simply because of her gender.

Tessa's gaze slid to the lighthouse perched on a bluff overlooking Eagle Harbor. The side of the redbrick keeper's house was attached to an octagonal brick tower that was rather short. She guessed it to be around forty feet in height. But what it lacked in height it seemed to make up for in girth. With the pounding of the wind and waves, as well as the harsh winters, she had no doubt the tower had been built to withstand the elements rather than win prizes in beauty contests.

"But I don't care," she said, focusing on the dock and her bag. She'd vowed to herself that once she left Windmill Point, she'd never step into another lighthouse as long as she lived.

She was done with lighthouses. Forever. And she wanted nothing to do with the sea either. If she'd had her choice, she would have traveled overland instead of by steamer. But since sailing through the Great Lakes to the north was the fastest option, she'd grudgingly done what she needed to.

The truth was that she'd never be able to forgive the sea or lighthouses for all they'd taken from her.

Turning her back on the tower, she found

14

herself facing several deckhands rolling barrels along the dock. As the only woman on board, the captain had kept her under close supervision during her voyage out of Detroit and then out of the locks at Sault St. Marie. Now that she'd reached her destination, he was too busy to chaperone her.

She moved out of the way of the crew, stepping to the side of the dock to let them pass. As they neared her, she tried not to think about the fact that she was utterly alone in the world. That she was, for the time being, without the job she thought she'd secured. And that she was also homeless.

The first deckhand eased his barrel to a stop next to her. He gave her a smile, revealing yellowing teeth that contrasted with the dark scruff on his face. "So what does our pretty little miss think of Eagle Harbor?"

Pretty little miss? Was that what the crew was calling her behind her back? She didn't return the man's smile. "As a matter of fact, the place is . . ."

She glanced to the sprawling town set amid stumps of trees that had been cleared to make room for the mining community. Under the gray sky, the log cabins appeared shabby, the laundry swinging in the breeze dingy, and the coastline sharp and impos-

15

ing. Distant wisps of smoke rising from the hills signaled the mine buried somewhere beyond the town.

"I'm sure the place is charming," she said, adding cheer to her voice, trying to ignore how deserted everything looked. A few young children played in a heap of rocks and dirt that stood between cabins, and a haggard-looking woman with her hair covered in a scarf faced a pot that hung over an open fire pit. She stirred the contents slowly without bothering to look at the newly arrived steamer, the sailing vessels apparently an everyday occurrence here.

On the shore nearby, a lone fisherman in waders stood up to his knees in the water, reeling in his line. His two husky dogs lay patiently on the beach behind him. As if sensing her attention, the man touched the brim of his bowler hat in greeting.

"Maybe the pretty little miss is having second thoughts about staying." The deckhand grinned over his shoulder at the two men behind him. "Maybe she'd like to stay aboard the ship with us, eh, mates?"

They nodded their agreement, looking at her with an interest that made her want to wring their necks.

She'd been told there weren't many single women in the north, mostly mining wives.

16

And she'd been fine with that, had decided it meant less worry about wagging tongues gossiping about her. Perhaps it also meant she'd have to spurn unwanted attention from the male species. After all, she hadn't come seeking a relationship. She'd come to teach, and she didn't want or need to be distracted by romantic notions.

She gripped the handles of her carpetbag more firmly and started to step down the dock toward shore.

The deckhand quickly moved in front of her and blocked her way.

"Excuse me," she said, pulling back. "I must be on my way."

"Can't you stay for just a minute?" The man's grin turned hard, and his attention focused on her mouth. "And give me and my mates a kiss good-bye?"

"Absolutely not." She narrowed her eyes at him in what she hoped was a withering stare, but inside her stomach churned. Had these men learned about her reputation? Is that why they were being forward with her? "Now, if you'll kindly let me pass."

She moved to the side, hoping to slip past him. But he sidestepped with her and continued to block her path. "Just one little kiss," the deckhand insisted, "right here on my cheek." He tapped a finger against his scruffy face.

She stiffened her shoulders and bit back a slew of caustic words that begged for release. She decided instead on a different tactic. Hoping to keep the sarcasm out of her tone, she said, "As tempting as the prospect is, I really must decline. I'm a teacher, and there are rules against teachers engaging in unseemly conduct."

"This won't be unseemly," he said, lowering his voice and winking. "I promise."

She was tempted to slap him across the face, but she'd learned to control her impulses over the years of having to ward off inappropriate advances. Her best course of action was to bolt past him and run back into town. He surely wouldn't attempt to accost her in the middle of Center Street.

She jolted forward and slipped past him as fast as a fish angling out of reach of a net. She only made it two paces when his rough fingers circled around her upper arm, jerked her to a halt, and spun her around.

She squirmed against his hold and dropped her carpetbag for more leverage. But he yanked her closer so that his hot breath fanned her face, and the sour stench of his sweat swirled around her. There were several small mackinaw boats tied to the dock and bobbing in the waves. Could she

18

break free and jump into one?

"Let go of me this instant!" she shouted, stamping her heel into his boot.

The man only laughed.

"I think you better do as the lady said" came a voice from the shore.

She turned her head at the same time as the deckhand to the sight of the fisherman nearby. He was still up to his knees in water and was in the process of casting out his line again calmly and steadily, as if he hadn't a care in the world.

"Stay out of this, mate," the deckhand called. "This isn't your business."

"With the way you're treating the lady, you've forced me to make it my business. Mate." The fisherman watched his line arch out over the water and then sink beneath the waves.

"I suggest you keep out of things or you'll force me and my mates to make *you* our business." The deckhand grinned at his friends as if pleased with his comeback. It was likely the cleverest thing the man had said all year — or perhaps in his life. Nevertheless, Tessa was tired of his antics. It was time to put an end to the situation once and for all.

Before she could knee the deckhand or bite his hand, the fisherman gave a short but piercing whistle between his teeth.

At the sound, the two dogs behind him bolted up. Their pointed ears perked, their snouts lifted, and their eyes riveted to their master. At their full height, with their silver-and-black markings, Tessa could almost believe the dogs were wolves. But their build was stockier, their coats thicker.

The fisherman cocked his head at the deckhands, and the dogs started toward the wharf, baring their teeth and growling.

"Oh, so he thinks he can frighten us with his puppies," the deckhand said with a guffaw toward his friends.

At the sight of the dogs moving toward the wharf, looking like they would rip flesh from bones, the other two crewmen had lost their grins, deserted their barrels, and retreated back to the steamer.

The fisherman didn't say anything further. Instead he reeled in his fishing line as unperturbed as before. Underneath the brim of his hat, Tessa caught a glimpse of a handsome face, but that was all she had time to see before her captor yanked her forward and positioned her so that she was acting as a shield between himself and the dogs.

Low to the ground, ears back and fangs exposed, the dogs continued to advance. If she'd been a timid woman, they might have frightened her. Yet all she could think about was devising a strategy for freeing herself from the deckhand so the dogs could charge in and chew him up like a piece of rawhide.

Out of the corner of her eye, she glimpsed the mackinaw. She'd break loose and leap into the swaying boat. It wasn't much of a plan, but at least she'd be doing something more than standing here and allowing herself to be manhandled.

Before the deckhand knew what she was doing, she bent her head and bit the fleshy part of his hand between his thumb and forefinger.

He yelped and his grip slackened.

She didn't waste any time. She wrenched away and leapt toward the edge of the dock. To her dismay, her feet landed in a wet spot. She skidded and tried to stop, but she found herself tumbling over the side of the dock not even close to the mackinaw.

She hit the icy water with a splash. The sharpness immediately took her breath away. She spluttered as murky waves battered her mouth and nostrils. The water wrapped around her, saturating her heavy linen overskirt along with the fuller underskirt. The weight of the wet material dragged her down, submerging her under the waves.

As she sank, her legs tangled in the floating linen, and she couldn't get the momentum she needed to kick and force herself back to the surface. She flailed with her arms, but the pounding of the waves refused to release her.

Her lungs burned, and she had to resist the instinct to open her mouth for the air that wouldn't be there. Darkness swirled around her. Suddenly all she could think was that her adventure had hardly just begun and she was about to die.

CHAPTER 2

She was going to die a watery death. Just like her father had.

Even though her father had known how to swim, and even though he'd taught her and her siblings to navigate in water almost as well as a fish, sometimes swimming wasn't enough.

She'd learned that all too well.

The sea had already taken so much from her, and she wouldn't let it defeat her today. With a desperate lunge, she grabbed at her skirts, trying to free her legs. Her chest seared against her rib cage with the need for a breath as she struggled to push herself up.

At a splash next to her, she reached out, groping, hoping to find help. Her fingertips grazed something. Then a hand shot out, gripped her arm, and heaved her upward until her face broke through the surface. She gulped in air, choking and spluttering as another wave hit her.

Strong arms slid around her waist and hoisted her above the waves, and she found herself staring at the fisherman. He'd discarded his hat and was now as drenched as she was. His hair was plastered to his head, and water trickled down strong Nordic features — a perfect nose, a strong angular jaw, and a chiseled chin that had the beginning of a dimple in it.

To say he was handsome was an understatement. In fact, she could quite confidently say he was one of the handsomest men she'd ever seen. More than any other feature, his eyes were beautiful. Not only were they wide and framed with thick lashes, they were a startling blue, like Lake St. Clair back home when it was calm in the morning with the sunlight brightening its surface.

"Are you all right?" His brow creased over those mesmerizing eyes.

For a split second she was tempted to answer him, *No, I'm drowning in your eyes.* But then she thought better of it and decided such forwardness wouldn't put her off to a good start in Eagle Harbor — not that she'd gotten off to a particularly good start anyway.

Instead she sucked another gulp into her

24

air-starved lungs. "I've never been better. Such a friendly welcome."

One of his brows cocked.

A wave splashed into her face. At the icy touch against her already cold skin, she couldn't contain a bone-jarring shudder. To her dismay, neither could she keep her teeth from chattering.

"Well," he said, "as much as you're enjoying your welcome, I'll have to insist on putting an end to this party and getting you back to dry land."

She smiled, realizing it was the first real smile she'd managed in days. She could appreciate quick wit when she heard it, which wasn't often.

He tugged her forward, his hands still on her waist. She realized then that he'd been treading water, keeping them both afloat, and that now he was guiding her toward the shore.

Her legs were too stiff from the cold to be of much use. She imagined she was double her normal weight with her skirts and bodice having absorbed at least half the water in the harbor. But he moved effortlessly as if she weighed nothing more than a baby bird.

"Put an end to the party?" she said. "So I take it that in addition to fishing, you have

25

the occupation of being the local spoil-sport."

This time he grinned. It was a lazy kind of smile that showed off even teeth and made him more handsome — if that was possible. Her stomach did a funny flip.

"If you stay in Eagle Harbor long enough," he said, "you'll learn that I have a reputation for boring people."

She highly doubted he bored anyone, but before she could toss out a witty retort of her own, her feet grazed the rocky bottom of the lake. Soon she was standing, the water up to her chest now.

His hands fell away from her waist, and he straightened to his full height. She could see that he was no longer wearing the coat and shirt he'd had on while fishing. He was donned only in a thin cotton undershirt that was stuck to his chest, leaving nothing to the imagination. Every rippling muscle and taut bulge was visible. As he stepped forward, his entire body exuded vitality and power.

Close your mouth and stop drooling, she scolded herself. She attempted to follow him, but her legs were weak and the stones sharp and slippery, causing her to stumble.

At her splash and cry of frustration, he spun. He took one look at her half-submerged form and retraced his steps.

"You wouldn't happen to know how I can walk on water?" she asked, hoping to cover her embarrassment at her bumbling and gawking. "That might be an easier way to get to shore rather than making a fool of myself slipping over these stones."

"I know an easier way." Before she could protest, he scooped her up and cradled her in his thick arms against that muscular chest of his.

For once in her life, words deserted her. She could only stare at his chin, not daring to drop her eyes any lower.

He strode through the rolling waves with ease. When his feet finally reached land, he lowered her as gently as a rare piece of porcelain.

On her feet again, she stared down at herself in dismay. Her lovely emerald skirt with its layers of ruffles was a soggy mess, with some of the lace having been torn and now hanging loose. She smoothed down the short-waisted basque bodice, noting a missing button near the frilly bow at her limp collar, which had been so crisp and white earlier when she'd dressed in her best outfit in hopes of making a good impression her first day in Eagle Harbor.

The fisherman took a step back, and she

could feel his gaze upon her, as if he expected her to crumple at any moment.

"Don't worry," she said, peeling a strand of her dark hair from her cheek and tucking it behind her ear. "I'll be fine in a minute." If only she didn't look like a limp rag doll that had just washed ashore.

A breeze swept off the lake and brought the nip in the air she'd felt earlier. It seemed to blow right through the wet layers and into her skin, so that her body began to shake.

The fisherman watched her for only a second before bounding toward the place where he'd dropped his fishing pole. He grabbed his discarded coat and shirt from among the rocks.

She could only stand and watch, huddled in a freezing mass of wetness, shivering uncontrollably and hugging her arms in a useless effort to warm herself.

He trotted back to her, his brow once again crinkling with worry. "Where are you staying? I'll help carry your things there."

"I'm homeless for the time being." She tried to make her tone light, but a sudden heaviness began to weigh upon her. She'd come to Eagle Harbor hoping to make a new start to her life, but so far nothing had gone any better than it usually did.

He moved behind her and draped his warm wool coat across her shoulders and over her arms, tucking it under her chin before stepping away and putting a proper distance between them.

She wouldn't have guessed a brawny man capable of such tenderness. No one had treated her so kindly in a long time. "Thank you." She met his gaze and then wished she hadn't when the blue of his eyes captivated her again.

"You're welcome," he said and crossed his bulky arms over his incredibly attractive chest.

"And of course, thank you for rescuing me." She hoped he couldn't read her thoughts, yet she had the feeling he could from the way his brow quirked.

"It was my pleasure." His lips rose in a half grin.

She wished she could have met him when she was at her best rather than her worst. Forcing her attention anywhere but him, she turned and found herself taking in a scene that made her burst into laughter. There sprawled on the dock was the deckhand who had accosted her. The dogs were perched on his arms and legs, pinning him down. He lay absolutely still, paralyzed with fear. Every time he so much as twitched,

29

one of the dogs would bare its teeth and growl at him.

"It appears as though I owe my gratitude to your dogs too, Mr. . . . ?"

He followed her gaze to the dogs and nodded. "Bjorklund. Alex Bjorklund."

"Mr. Bjorklund."

"Just Alex."

"Then I'm just Tessa."

"Tessa." The way her name rolled off his lips, as if he were tasting a savory piece of cake, made her insides warm. "Very pleased to make your acquaintance."

"I'm the new teacher." She waited for him to say something about the fact that she was a woman and how Eagle Harbor hadn't hired a woman teacher before.

"Actually, you already know me. I'm the local spoilsport."

She laughed with relief. Maybe not everyone was as opposed to having a female instructor as the store clerk. Perhaps there was hope after all.

"I suppose you could call your dogs off the man before they give him a heart attack."

"I suppose I could," he replied, his eyes narrowing at the deckhand. His companions had long since escaped into the safety of the steamer. "But I'm leaning toward let-

30

ting my dogs scare him for a few more minutes just to make sure he learns his lesson good and well."

"And what lesson are you hoping to teach him? How to play dead perhaps?"

"No, I only want him to learn to keep his hands off pretty women."

Ah, so he did think she was pretty. A measure of satisfaction wafted through her. "Maybe I should start keeping a pack of dogs with me to ward off unwanted attention."

"Sounds like a good idea. I'm sure you get a lot of attention."

The satisfaction swelled. She liked a man who knew how to flatter, and it was clear Alex was quite adept at it.

"I tell you what," he said. "Come spring, I'll give you the pick of the litter."

She started to shake her head, but his smile stopped her words — and her heartbeat.

"Purebred Norwegian Elkhounds. You couldn't ask for a better dog to protect you. They're fiercely loyal."

"Yes, they do look fierce."

"Don't tell me they scare you too?" he teased.

"Of course not —"

His short whistle cut off her words. The

31

dogs perked up their ears and turned their heads toward him. "Come," he commanded. At once, the dogs released the deckhand and scampered down the dock.

At the sight of the two husky dogs bounding toward her, Tessa tried not to cower. Like their master, they were powerfully built. Yet as they neared Alex, their curly tails began to wag and their tongues lolled from their mouths, which were tipped up in what could almost be called a smile, if it was possible for a dog to smile.

They halted at Alex's feet, sat and peered up at him with adoring black eyes.

He tilted his head toward Tessa. As if on cue, both dogs swiveled to stare at her.

"Tessa," Alex said, "meet Wolfie and Bear."

She wasn't exactly sure how one went about talking to dogs, but she had the distinct feeling she couldn't ignore the two pairs of eyes gazing up at her so intently. "Um. Hello?"

Their tales waggled in unison.

"Wolfie and Bear are nice names," she said to Alex. "Original."

"Are you mocking my dogs' names?" His voice contained the hint of a smile.

"I'd never do that," she replied with mock horror. "Not when they've obviously been so carefully chosen."

He gave a low chuckle.

The clatter of a wagon drew their attention to a well-worn dirt road that had been cut through the spruce on the edge of town. A double team of oxen strained to pull their heavy load out of the forest and down the gently sloping road that led to the shore. The man guiding the team was hunched beneath a coat that was covered in a dark-red dust. His face and hands were covered in the same.

Tessa guessed the barrels in the back of the wagon were filled with the copper that had attracted fortune hunters to Eagle Harbor and the Keweenaw Peninsula for the past two decades — the copper that had earned the peninsula the nickname Copper Country.

Another gust of wind swept off the waves and knocked into her. In spite of Alex's coat, she'd grown cold again. Seeing her shivering, Alex retrieved her carpetbag. She located her heavy cloak, and Alex insisted she put it on over his coat to add extra warmth. Once she was bundled, he accompanied her along the path toward town. The rocks gave way to pale sand. After dragging her feet through the sandy drifts, she was breathless by the time she reached town but was warmed a little from the exertion.

At the sight of a man on horseback riding down Center Street straight toward them, she stepped aside into the tall yellow grass and wild pink roses that grew among the lichen-encrusted rocks.

"T. Taylor?" the man said, reining his palomino so that he faced her. Attired in crisp pinstriped pants and a matching vest and waistcoat, he appeared to be a businessman of some sort, certainly not a miner like the man driving the wagon. His face was smoothly shaven except for a thin well-groomed mustache that might have been black at one time but was now threaded with hints of silver. His features were suave, made almost handsome with the age lines that crinkled the corners of his eyes.

"I'm T. Taylor," she replied. "Tessa Taylor, the new schoolteacher for Eagle Harbor. Who are you?"

"I'm Percival Updegraff." He tipped up the brim of his hat and smiled. He was almost old enough to be her father. "I'm your new boss."

Her new boss? She straightened her shoulders. Her letter of acceptance for the position had told her to report to the Cole Mine Company Store and Office. She'd assumed the clerk there was the one who'd hired her.

"I already met Mr. Updegraff at the store."

"That's my brother, Samuel."

Alex came to stand next to her. While she'd just met him, there was something comforting about having a man of his strength close by, there to help her if she needed it.

"I'm chief clerk of Cole Mine," Percival Updegraff said. "I do all the hiring and firing in Eagle Harbor."

"Your brother attempted to fire me because I'm a woman teacher. I hope you don't share his unfortunate sentiments."

Mr. Updegraff's smile widened. "Rest assured, I hold none of his prejudices against women."

Even though Alex wasn't touching her, she could feel him stiffen at the chief clerk's words.

"You'll have to pardon my brother," Mr. Updegraff continued. "He's a simpleton and has the mind of a child. Everyone around here knows it, but they also know I won't tolerate anyone trying to take advantage of him."

At Mr. Updegraff's explanation, she finally made sense of the store clerk's unusual mannerisms. "Very well, Mr. Updegraff. I have no intention of taking advantage of him or anyone else. I simply want to know

35

that I'll be allowed to have the teaching position I was assured would be mine."

"There was a mix-up," he explained. "We saw T. Taylor and assumed you were a man."

"As you can see, I'm very much a woman."

"Indeed. And you're a fine-looking woman, Miss Taylor." When he perused her, she wished she'd bitten her tongue and kept silent. Somehow his compliment felt entirely different from the one Alex had given her only minutes earlier.

Alex took a step forward. The lines in his face had grown hard, and the muscles in his jaw flexed. His eyes had turned an icy blue with nothing even remotely welcoming in them.

If Mr. Updegraff noticed Alex, he certainly didn't bother looking at him, but instead went on addressing Tessa as if the two of them were having a private conversation. "You have to realize we've never had a woman teacher at our school."

"A fact your brother made quite clear."

"And for good reason," Mr. Updegraff said. "The Keweenaw Peninsula is not an easy place to live for a hardened, seasoned man, much less a frail dewdrop like yourself."

Frail dewdrop? She had the fleeting thought of showing him her dewdrop fists.

36

When she finished with him, he'd drop. Instead she forced herself to remain calm. She couldn't afford to alienate her new boss.

"I'm stronger than I look," she said.

"Then it's a good thing you are. We're at the edge of civilization. And once winter settles in, we're cut off from the rest of the world until the spring thaw. Supplies dwindle. Tempers flare. If the cold and snow doesn't kill you, then the isolation just might."

Was he attempting to scare her into leaving? Maybe he didn't want her there after all. "I'm not attempting to scare you away, Miss Taylor," he spoke again as if reading her mind. His expression softened for an instant. "I just want you to know the reality of the situation you're getting into before it's too late."

"You don't need to worry about me," she said, hoping her voice contained more confidence than she felt. "I'm able to fend for myself."

"She needs to get into some warm clothes." Alex finally broke into the conversation. "I was just taking her to one of the boardinghouses to get a room."

"She can't stay in a boardinghouse, Mr. Bjorklund," Mr. Updegraff said testily. "They're full of single miners. And she won't be safe even behind locked doors."

"Maybe she can live with the Rawlings family," Alex suggested.

"She can stay in my house and board with my housekeeper." Mr. Updegraff spoke with finality and glanced toward town at the biggest house that rose above the rambling shacks. It was made of clapboards and painted a fresh coat of white.

Alex took another step forward, this time positioning himself between her and Mr. Updegraff. "Miss Taylor will stay at your house over my dead body."

CHAPTER 3

The low, menacing growl in Alex's tone reminded Tessa of his dogs, who had followed them up the path and were now standing straight and stiff next to their master.

It was becoming increasingly clear that Alex and Mr. Updegraff weren't the best of friends and that the situation was quickly escalating. "How would Mrs. Updegraff feel about having another mouth to feed?" She addressed Mr. Updegraff as she attempted to sidle around Alex. "Perhaps you should check with your wife before you invite me into your home."

"No need to worry about what my wife thinks. She's living down in Detroit with the children on all the handsome paychecks I send her." There was the flash of something in his eyes before it disappeared. Was it loneliness? "I've insisted that she and the children stay in civilization where it's safe. I wouldn't have it any other way."

"Surely it can't be that uncivilized here," she started.

Mr. Updegraff cut her off curtly. "If you stay, I insist that you live with me. I reside in the company house, which is quite nice. I'll be able to make sure you're well protected."

His sincerity was difficult to refuse. Nevertheless, Alex's renewed murmur of protest spurred her to reject his offer. "Mr. Updegraff, I'm sure you can understand that staying under your roof without the presence of your wife would put my reputation in jeopardy." It was already in jeopardy, but she prayed he'd never learn that.

"If we can't come to terms upon a safe living situation for you," he replied smoothly even as his gloved grip on his horse's reins tightened, "then I'm afraid I won't feel right about allowing you to remain in Eagle Harbor."

Tessa stared up at the man who claimed to do all the hiring and firing in Eagle Harbor. From the steely way he held himself atop his gelding and the hard set of his mouth, she suspected he was accustomed to giving orders and commanding unquestioning obedience in return.

A warning bell in the back of her mind

told her she couldn't accept Mr. Updegraff's offer of hospitality, which was really more of an order than offer. Even if he was trying to look out for her best interests, she couldn't take any chances on tarnishing her reputation.

"She can stay with the Rawlings," Alex insisted. "They have the next biggest house in town. I'm sure they'd appreciate the extra income from having a boarder."

"Yes, I'll stay with the Rawlings," she agreed, not caring or knowing who the Rawlings were. She wasn't ready to be kicked out of Eagle Harbor yet. But could she make Mr. Updegraff understand her dilemma without angering him and getting herself fired for the second time in one day?

"I'll take her to the Rawlings myself," Alex said, hooking his hand through her arm. "She's drenched and freezing and needs to get warmed up before she takes a chill."

Mr. Updegraff didn't say anything for a moment. When he finally spoke, the terseness in his tone set her on edge. "Bjorklund, I'll hold you responsible if her living arrangements don't work out."

Alex didn't respond and instead urged her along at a pace so fast she could hardly keep up. He didn't stop until they turned the corner at the livery.

41

"Are you all right?" He finally slowed.

"Mr. Updegraff is quite the character," she said. "Apparently he thinks he's king over this town?"

Alex nodded. "Unfortunately he *is* king, and there's no one to stop him."

"Looks like you stopped him well enough, or at least saved my reputation."

Alex released her arm and glanced into the open double doors of the livery. Seeing the deserted entryway, and with the faint ring of someone hammering in the back of the barn, he lowered his voice. "No one dares to talk about it, but it's no secret that Percival's housekeeper doubles as his mistress."

"No-o-o," she whispered harshly.

"Yes."

Maybe she should start thanking God for bringing a guardian angel into her life the moment she stepped into Eagle Harbor. Without Alex, she'd either have drowned or gotten herself trapped into boarding with Percival.

She shuddered.

Alex's brows came together in a worried frown. "Let's get you to the Rawlings." He started forward, but she stopped him with a touch on his arm.

"Have I said thank you yet?"

"No thanks is necessary."

"You've saved my life twice in one day. Of course thanks is necessary."

He rubbed his hands over his bare arms. He was as drenched as she and yet he hadn't issued one word of complaint.

"What can I do to repay you for your kindness?" she asked. "Bake you a pie? Maybe an apple pie from overpriced apples?"

"I mean it," he insisted, moving down the road again. "You're not indebted to me. There's such a thing as helping a neighbor in need without expecting anything in return."

She hurried to follow after him, liking him better by the minute. She had the impression he was the kind of man who'd help anyone, no matter their predicament.

Alex turned onto a side street, and they passed a dozen or more of the identical log houses. Alex answered her questions as they walked, and she learned that the small log houses were owned by Cole Mine and rented to the miners with families. The one-room cabins seemed hardly big enough to house a single man, let alone an entire family.

"William Rawlings is a mine engineer and mechanic," Alex said as they reached the

43

front door of a large frame house. The paint was peeling around windows that were so grimy, Tessa wondered how anyone could see through them. The yard was littered with stumps, discarded toys, and an assortment of rusty tools and steel mechanisms that looked like they had once belonged in the mine.

"The Rawlings family are good people, honest and hardworking," Alex continued with a firm rap on the door. "You'll be safe with them."

At his proclamation, the door swung open and a ball came flying through, hitting Alex in the chest. He caught it in one hand without so much as a blink. In the next moment, two small boys flew against him and grabbed his legs. They shouted and chopped at Alex's legs with sticks.

She raised her brows at Alex. "Safe? Really?"

His grin inched up on one side. "You're not going to let a couple of little boys scare you away, are you?"

Before she could quip back, he scooped up both boys, one in each arm. He lifted them and blew noisy bubble kisses into each of their bellies, earning giggles.

She guessed the children to be about two and four. Alex held them in his thick arms with such gentleness that Tessa's chest expanded with unexpected warmth.

"Did you bring Wolfie and Bear?" the older child asked, peering over Alex's shoulder.

"Of course I did." Alex lowered the boys back to the ground and tousled their hair, which probably hadn't seen a comb in days if not weeks. "I wouldn't dream of coming to visit you without bringing Wolfie and Bear. They'd be mad at me if I didn't let them have the chance to play with a couple of their favorite pals."

The boys scampered outside toward the dogs waiting in the yard. When they jumped onto Wolfie and Bear, tackling them and rolling with them on the ground, she expected Alex to tell the boys to be more careful. But he only watched with an affectionate smile.

"I'm sure Wolfie and Bear would be terribly disappointed to miss coming here," she remarked.

"They're having fun," Alex said. "Can't you tell?"

The dogs lay on their backs and let the boys crawl all over them.

"*Fun* isn't exactly the word I'd pick."

"Now who's the spoilsport?"

She laughed. She hadn't met many others

who could match her wit, but Alex was coming close.

His hair was beginning to dry to a shade of pale wheat. The wind teased the strands, giving him a boyish appeal.

Her stomach did another strange but pleasant tumble. As much as she wanted to deny the effect he was having on her, she couldn't. Not only was he good-looking, he was also sweet and funny. A remarkable combination.

"Alex?" A woman crossed the darkened front room of the house, moving toward them and dodging toys and clothes scattered on the floor. With a fussing baby on her hip, she sighed wearily as she approached.

"Good morning, Nadine," Alex said with a bright smile.

Nadine gave Alex a small smile in return. She jiggled the crying baby absently and at the same time raised a hand to swipe a loose strand of graying hair off her face. At the sight of the woman's cracked, dirty nails, recognition dawned in Tessa.

This was the woman she'd seen in the company store earlier, the one whose rambunctious children had broken a jar of beets.

Alex continued, "I'd like to introduce you

to Eagle Harbor's new teacher, Tessa Taylor."

Nadine didn't look at her. "I saw her at the store, and Mr. Updegraff told her loud and clear that she weren't to be the teacher here." The woman spoke with a heavy English accent.

Tessa searched for animosity, for the sign that once again she was to be disregarded and shunned simply for being a female. But the woman's face reflected neither acceptance nor dislike. Only resignation, as if she were accustomed to having everything about her life ordered by someone else.

"Samuel was mistaken," Alex explained. "We discussed the matter with Percival, and he's agreed to allow Tessa to remain and teach."

"That so?" Nadine examined her closely now, her eyes lighting up with something akin to interest.

"Mr. and Mrs. Rawlings have three children in the school —"

"Only two now. Edward went to work in the mine a week ago."

"I'm pleased to meet you," Tessa said. "I'm sure I'll enjoy teaching the two who remain."

"If I can get Josie to go," Nadine remarked loudly over her shoulder, toward the door

47

that revealed the kitchen. "She's been saying she don't need any more schooling."

"How old is she, Mrs. Rawlings?" Tessa asked.

"Fifteen. But she thinks she's twenty, that she does."

Familiar guilt nagged Tessa. Even after five years, shame always came rushing back when she thought of her obnoxious behavior toward her older sister. She'd always believed she was mature and ready for more than she really had been. She knew now that she'd been a foolish young girl. The least she could do was make sure that other young girls didn't make the same mistakes she had.

"Don't worry, Mrs. Rawlings," Tessa said. "I'm sure I can be a good role model and provide wise counsel to your daughter."

"I thank you for your offer." Nadine released a long sigh that said she'd all but given up hope. "But I won't hold you to it."

"Tessa needs a safe place to board," Alex cut in. "And I thought you might be willing to let her stay with you."

Nadine shifted her fussing baby to her other hip and continued to jiggle her. She studied Tessa for a moment, taking in her wet garments and hair. Then she began to shake her head. "I don't —"

48

"Of course, she'll pay a fair rent," Alex said hastily.

Tessa joined in the battle. "Maybe that will allow you to buy a few more items from the store without having to chop off your limbs to pay for them."

Nadine didn't smile at Tessa's attempt at a joke. Instead she pursed her lips as if thinking about the fresh potatoes and melons she would be able to buy.

"And besides, I'm sure Tessa will be good company," Alex said, flashing Nadine another one of his devastating grins. "With all the little ones, having another woman to talk to will be like a little bit of heaven."

At the sight of Alex's grin, Nadine didn't quite smile, but her lips curved enough for Tessa to know that Alex's charm had indeed worked.

"I suppose she could stay up in the attic room with Josie," Nadine said slowly.

"How does that sound to you?" Alex turned his winsome smile upon her. She wasn't sure how anyone could say no to him, even if they wanted to. The prospect of living in an attic with a fifteen-year-old didn't sound too appealing, but neither did the prospect of living with Percival Updegraff.

"I'm sure we'll get along just fine." She

49

squared her shoulders in determination. The home with its obvious neglect wasn't the ideal place to live, but perhaps God had brought her to Eagle Harbor to do more than change the lives of the children in her charge. Maybe He'd brought her to bring hope to poor, tired women like Nadine as well. She could instruct the adults and help them better themselves so they wouldn't always have to live in such squalor.

A renewed sense of purpose filled Tessa. She'd surely suffered the worst by nearly losing her new job and almost drowning. She was confident things could only get better.

Alex strode along the bluff path with Wolfie and Bear trotting behind him. The spruce trees nearby provided a protective hedge from the rocky cliff that dropped dangerously down into the lake. Though he couldn't see the water, he could hear the waves roaring and crashing against the jagged boulders below. In fact, the sounds of the waves and the wind were almost identical today.

To say he'd had an interesting morning was an understatement. Like the other men, he hadn't been able to stop staring at Tessa Taylor the moment she stepped off the

50

steamer's gangplank onto the dock. In her lovely green skirt, she looked like the first buds of spring arriving after a long winter. Her dark hair and creamy skin had contrasted with the green, and there was no hiding her womanly figure beneath the frills and lace of her garments.

Even if she hadn't been a beautiful sight to behold, he likely still would have stared. Single women were rare in these parts, rarer than a warm day in winter.

He breathed in a deep lung-cleansing breath of air, a damp mixture of sea and pine. It was a scent he'd fallen in love with when he moved to Eagle Harbor five years ago with Michael.

It was one of the many things he loved about northern Michigan and Lake Superior. He loved the ruggedness of the coastline here. He loved the boundless supply of whitefish, trout, and herring. He even loved the snow that winter brought, because it meant he could hitch his elkhounds to the sleigh. He wasn't sure who enjoyed the sleigh rides more, the dogs or the children.

From the way it looked, not only would the dogsledding keep him entertained all winter, but the pretty new schoolteacher would liven up their community too.

He smiled just thinking about her sassi-

51

ness. Even drenched, she'd shown a vivacity that enthralled him. He'd reacted strongly to her, so strongly that he was still surprised by it. He couldn't remember a woman affecting him so deeply — not since Jenny.

Alex's steps slowed. His wet trouser legs chafed his skin, and he stifled a shiver that rose in his chest, which was covered only by his damp undershirt. Over the past five years, he'd tried not to think about Jenny and all he'd lost. It was too painful. He hadn't much considered the possibility of finding another woman. Until today . . .

When he'd scooped her up into his arms and carried her to shore, something fierce had loosened inside him. He wasn't sure what it was, but he'd wanted to protect her, make sure she was taken care of and respected.

Wolfie trotted next to him and nudged his hand with her wet nose. He scratched behind one of her ears. "What do you think, lass?"

She licked his hand as if to encourage him.

"Oh, so you want me to win the new teacher's affection, is that it?" He rubbed at Wolfie's neck, digging his fingers into her thick fur and giving her the scratching she liked. "Don't you think it's a little soon to think about wooing the lady? We just met."

Wolfie licked his hand again.

Alex chuckled at his conversation with the dog. Sometimes he was glad for the isolation of his work and life. He didn't have to worry about others seeing him talking with his dogs like they were people and thinking he was addled in the brain.

He strode forward again and whistled a made-up tune. He'd sacrificed so much for so long. Was it time to start thinking of his future again? Could he ever entertain the thought of loving someone else, someone like Tessa Taylor?

His feet picked up speed around the last bend, and then he was in the clearing.

He stopped to take in the sight. There across the rocky tip of the peninsula, with remnants of wild rye and switch grass growing among the gravel, stood the gem of the whole bay — the Eagle Harbor Lighthouse.

Along the rocky shoreline was the red-brick keeper's house and the connected tower, which was red brick on the side adjacent to the house but painted white on the side facing the lake. Waves crashed against the stones, their foamy fingers rising up, slickening the ledges and turning them cobalt.

The lighthouse against the backdrop of the lake was breathtaking. He never tired of seeing it. The view out over the lake was even more spectacular from the tower, especially at sunset on a clear night when every hue of red, orange, and blue mingled together in the sky and upon the lake.

He was glad Michael had given him the first shift in the tower every night. Of course, as assistant keeper he didn't have quite as many duties or responsibilities as Michael, yet he worked just as hard.

When they'd first arrived, he wasn't sure he'd like living at a lighthouse and being an assistant keeper. But after five years, the job had grown on him. The truth was, even if he wanted to move, he wouldn't. He'd never desert Michael or leave him to fend for himself. He hadn't five years ago and he wouldn't now, especially when Ingrid needed surgery.

But was there the possibility he could find a woman who would join him in the life he'd made for himself at the lighthouse?

The image of Tessa's face filled his mind again.

Wolfie nudged his hand with another wet lick.

"All right, young lass." Alex rubbed the dog's nose. "You've convinced me. I'll win her over."

CHAPTER 4

Tessa peered into the cracked mirror she'd hung on the attic wall next to the only window in the low-beamed room. The early morning light illuminated her wide eyes, revealing the nervousness that was tying her stomach into knots for her first day of school.

She smoothed her hair back, making sure each strand was in place. At a pinch on the back of her neck, she swatted the spot. She wasn't sure if it was really a bedbug or if her skin was crawling at the mere thought of encountering another one.

In the two nights she'd spent in the attic, she'd killed nearly a pint of the little biters. She'd slept fitfully, wondering how she'd ever get a good night's sleep when she was waging war every time she climbed into bed.

"You sure do look pretty," Josie said from where she lay tangled among the sheets.

"Thank you." Tessa glanced at the girl

through the reflection of the mirror. Josie had been talking endlessly since the second she'd awoken. She'd gossiped about everyone in town while Tessa had dressed and readied herself for school.

At fifteen, Josie clearly thought she was an adult, but her body was still flat like that of a young girl. Her long hair was straight and a plain shade of brown. Her bluntly cut bangs hung across her forehead and made her look even more like a child.

"Remember," Tessa said, "you promised you'd come to school today. So I'll hold you to that promise."

Josie yawned. "I don't need any more learning. Not when me and Robbie are planning to get married just as soon as he saves up enough money to pay the rent on a cabin."

Tessa swallowed a sarcastic remark, knowing it wouldn't help Josie. The girl needed her gentle encouragement, not the hard fist of discipline. She already got enough of that from her mother.

Even two stories below, Nadine's voice was loud and shrill. From what Tessa had gleaned during her short stay so far, Nadine's primary method of discipline was yelling. And since her children were always

56

getting into trouble, Nadine was always yelling.

The waft of burnt toast did nothing to comfort Tessa's rolling stomach. Nadine had proved as poor a housekeeper as she did disciplinarian. The food she served for meals consisted of stale molasses, dry bread, and butter that was so dirty it looked like it had veins of copper running through it. They'd also had trout for one meal, along with a few potatoes and carrots.

Tessa couldn't understand why Nadine didn't have her own vegetable garden so that she could have a bounty of produce to store up for winter. Then she wouldn't have to rely upon the overpriced mine store.

Tessa had determined that in the spring she'd help Nadine and the other women in town plant gardens. It was one of many ways she could help them better themselves.

She let her fingers stray to the driftwood cross she'd set out on the attic ledge that served as a narrow shelf for her few belongings. She traced the two pieces of wood that had come from a shipwreck years ago. The lone survivor of the wreck had fashioned the cross from a piece of the ship as a reminder not to give up hope. For the past few years she'd cherished the cross, praying and hoping for a fresh start in life. Now she

57

was finally getting that chance.

With a final check of her hair, Tessa reached for the straw hat that sat on top of her trunk and positioned it on her head. The blue-and-white-striped ribbon on it matched the pattern of her bodice and the blue of her bustled skirt. She was probably overdressed for her first day of school, but she wanted to make sure she was the epitome of a good example for her students.

Tessa descended through the busy household, thanked Nadine for the toast, though she was too nervous to eat it. A brisk half-mile walk through town brought her to the schoolhouse. Thankfully, the structure was built of clapboards rather than logs and had several large windows of glass.

She pushed open the door, which squeaked on its hinges, to reveal a classroom filled with rudimentary rows of benches. There were no desks for the students, but a narrow teacher's desk sat in one corner, covered with the books, tablets, maps, and other supplies she'd unpacked yesterday.

A blackboard covered the front wall. A wood-burning stove sat at the back of the room with an empty woodbox next to it. A board of rough pegs had been nailed to the wall to serve as coat hooks for the students.

After hanging her coat, she made her way

to the front, her footsteps clicking hollowly against the floorboards. The excitement that had been building inside over the past week swelled with each step.

Her first day of school of her first head teacher's job. She was almost giddy enough to twirl a full circle. She picked up the piece of chalk she'd placed in readiness on the ledge of the blackboard and wrote the words *Welcome* and *Miss Taylor.*

When the students began to arrive, she greeted each one with a smile and tried to learn their names along with a little bit about their families. But as an endless stream of students continued to enter the one-room schoolhouse and cram together on the benches, she lost track of which name belonged with which face.

She was squatting and in the middle of speaking with several siblings when the outline of a man entering the schoolroom caught her attention. The striking man with the sandy hair belonged to Alex, the one who'd rescued her the day she'd arrived in Eagle Harbor. She couldn't keep from pausing and staring, causing several of the students to turn and stare too.

During her exploring around town yesterday, she hadn't seen Alex, although she hadn't searched particularly hard for him.

Nevertheless, she wondered where he'd disappeared to and why she hadn't seen him. She'd told herself that she wanted to see him again because she needed to return his coat, and that was all.

But now, seeing him again in all his magnificence, her stomach fluttered with anticipation.

He scanned the classroom until he spotted her, and then with a wide grin he started toward her.

She rose to meet him, smoothing her skirt and trying to slow her heartbeat.

"Miss Taylor, it's nice to see you again. You look so . . ." His eyes swept over her, and she was glad she'd taken extra care with her appearance that morning.

His eyes matched the cobalt blue stripes of his hand-knit sweater. They were swoonworthy, and she had to fight hard not to actually swoon. Instead she waited for him to finish his sentence with a word like *beautiful* or *stunning* or something else flattering.

"You look so dry," he finished. "And warm."

"I've been called many things in my life, Mr. Bjorklund," she said wryly, "but no one has ever paid me the high compliment of calling me dry and warm."

"I don't go around paying such lavish

compliments very often, so count yourself privileged."

She couldn't contain her smile of appreciation at his easy comeback. "Very well. Since you're flattering me so wildly, I suppose you deserve a compliment in return."

His eyes widened in expectation.

She could feel the attention of her students, each of them watching her interaction with Alex. She lowered her voice in mock conspiracy and said, "You have nice shoes."

He glanced at the scuffed, worn leather of his brogans and broke into a hearty laugh.

"Hey" came a small voice behind him. "You're shaking me."

Alex glanced over his shoulder.

Tessa followed his gaze and was surprised to see a little girl clinging to Alex's back. His body had blocked her, but now Tessa could see that he was holding the girl up with both of his arms crooked behind him like a saddle.

The girl was petite, her arms and legs as thin as those of a newborn colt. Her face was sweet and pretty. Her long blond hair looked like it needed a trim, or at the very least a brushing and then plaiting. But it was the girl's blue eyes that startled Tessa. The blue was the same shade as Alex's.

61

"I'll take care of Ingrid now," said a boy who'd been standing behind Alex.

"Are you sure?" Alex said.

The boy nodded.

Tessa was speechless as she took in the boy's appearance. His blond hair and blue eyes resembled Alex's. Even more astonishing was the stocky shape of the boy's body. He was a miniature Alex. It was almost as if Tessa was getting a glimpse of what Alex had once looked like as a child.

Were these Alex's children? Mortification spilled through her, and she spun toward her desk. She felt her cheeks flush. Had she been flirting with a married man? In front of her entire class? On her first day of school?

She fumbled blindly for the paper that contained the list of students who'd come so far that morning. Part of her wanted to sink down into a crack in the floorboards and disappear into the crawl space under the building. Who cared if there were rats and spiders down there? She'd rather face them than have to face Alex again.

But another part of her twisted with frustration. If he was married, he should have known better than to flirt back. Even as she tried to direct her anger at him, the accusing finger only swung around and pointed right back at her.

If anyone was to blame for the impropriety, it was her. She knew she shouldn't flirt. She'd known it would only get her into trouble. Besides, flirting was entirely inappropriate if she wanted to remain single-minded in her devotion to her position as a teacher. After all, the teaching contract she'd signed just yesterday stipulated that *"Teachers will not marry or keep company with a man friend during the week except as an escort to church services."* In fact, the contract had gone so far as to say, *"Women teachers who marry or engage in other unseemly conduct will be dismissed."*

The rules weren't new. They were standard, the same she'd had in Detroit as an assistant teacher. It's just that now she actually had a chance of being taken seriously, of proving herself without her past creeping in to undermine her efforts to better her life.

Behind her, Alex spoke gently with his children, getting them situated on one of the benches. Then there was a long pause, as though he were waiting for her to turn around and say something more.

She pretended to be writing something on the paper. "What are their names and ages, Mr. Bjorklund?"

63

"Gunnar is eighteen, aren't you, old fella?"

The boy laughed. "No, I'm eight."

"Oh, that's right." Alex's voice was filled with adoration. "And Ingrid is sixteen —"

"I'm six" came the more practical, no-nonsense voice of the girl.

Tessa knew that she couldn't keep scribbling on the paper forever, that she had to turn around and face them again sometime. So with a steadying breath, she forced herself to pivot. Gunnar and Ingrid were sitting on the front bench, with Alex standing next to them.

She decided the safest course of action was to focus on the children. "Well, Gunnar and Ingrid, I'm Miss Taylor. And I'm most definitely one hundred and ten years old."

They awarded her with smiles. She didn't look at Alex to gauge his reaction, but his low chuckle told her he'd liked her banter.

This time, his pleasure only irked her. How dare he laugh and tease and act like everything was perfectly normal? Just then another family of children entered the classroom, and she used it as an excuse to make her escape from Alex.

As the morning progressed she was too busy to think of anything but the roomful of children before her. By the time the last of the students straggled in, her attendance sheet numbered fifty-two. With so many children needing her attention, she didn't know where to begin. She was more than grateful for the mother-helper, Hannah Nance, who took charge of the younger children.

Tessa spent the morning attempting to get an idea of each student's progress. She could tell that the previous year's teacher had set a solid foundation, for which she was grateful. Nevertheless, many of the children lagged far behind where they should be.

At lunchtime Tessa plopped down into her chair and released a weary breath.

"Are you tired, Miss Taylor?" the little girl in the front row asked.

Tessa glanced up, surprised to see that Ingrid Bjorklund hadn't budged from her spot. Gunnar was at the back of the room, retrieving a tin pail that probably contained their lunch.

Ingrid's thin face was pale with a smudge of dirt on her nose. She watched Tessa expectantly and much too seriously for a girl of six.

Tessa gave the girl a smile. It wasn't the child's fault that her father was a shameless flirt. And it wasn't the girl's fault that she was overwhelmed with the mammoth job of teaching so many children.

"I'm not sleepy tired," Tessa said to the girl, "but after being on my feet for the past few hours, I'm ready to sit a spell."

"You did a good job," Ingrid offered.

"Thank you."

"I was too young for school last year," Ingrid continued. "But Gunnar didn't like the old teacher. He said that Mr. Chaws liked to box ears better than anything else."

"Well, you needn't worry," Tessa assured her. "I don't box ears." In fact, Tessa wasn't a believer in corporal punishment in the classroom. She preferred a gentler approach.

Gunnar strode back to his sister, swinging the pail.

"I could tell right away that you're going to be much nicer than Mr. Chaws," Ingrid said. "The very first second I saw you, I knew you were going to be the best teacher Eagle Harbor has ever had."

"Well, I certainly hope I can live up to your expectation."

"You will, Miss Taylor."

Gunnar picked up a carved stick from underneath the bench and held it out to Ingrid. "Come on, Ingie. Stop pestering Miss Taylor."

Ingrid took the stick with a frown. "I'm

not pestering her. She likes children. I can tell."

Gunnar shot Tessa a glance as if to apologize for his sister's brazenness. Then he took hold of Ingrid's arm. "C'mon. It's time to go and eat our lunch."

Ingrid slowly rose to her feet. When she was standing, she swayed and would have fallen if Gunnar hadn't had a tight grasp on her arm. Ingrid lowered the stick and used it to balance herself.

When Ingrid managed one stiff step forward, Tessa saw that the little girl was crippled with one of her thin legs turned in at an odd angle. How had she missed seeing it earlier?

Of course, Alex had carried Ingrid into the classroom and placed her on the bench, and Ingrid hadn't risen from her spot all morning. Even so, Tessa should have noticed the twisted leg and the makeshift crutch.

"I don't suppose you're married, are you, Miss Taylor?" Ingrid asked.

Tessa decided the best thing to do was to act like she wasn't surprised by either Ingrid's condition or her forward question. "No, Ingrid," she said, "I'm not married." Although she'd come close once.

"Do you ever want to be a mama, Miss Taylor?" Ingrid asked.

67

"Ingie," Gunnar whispered harshly. "Let's go. Leave the new teacher alone."

But Ingrid stayed put, hunched on one side. "I don't have a mama."

In the same instant that Ingrid spoke, understanding rushed through Tessa. Alex was a widower. His wife had obviously died and left him alone with the two children.

"I'm sorry you lost your mama," Tessa said. "That must have been very hard."

"I don't remember her anymore. She died giving birth to my baby brother when I was only one."

Five years ago. Alex had lost his wife five years ago. That would explain why he'd flirted with her so effortlessly now. He'd moved past the time of grieving.

"My baby brother died too," Ingrid said, ignoring Gunnar's tug on her sleeve. "And Daddy has been really sad ever since then."

Sad? Tessa hadn't gotten the impression that Alex was sad. But maybe he was different at home. "It's hard to lose someone you love. I know because I've lost both my parents and my little sister."

Ingrid searched her face. "You don't look as sad as my daddy."

"I'm sure his sadness just means that he loved your mother very much."

Gunnar stared at his feet and twisted the

68

tip of his shoe, obviously embarrassed by his sister's boldness. "Can we go eat now?" he whispered.

Ingrid nodded and took a wobbly step forward, using her stick to compensate for her misshapen leg.

Gunnar started to release a breath, but before he could get it out completely, Ingrid stopped and spoke again. "I hope my daddy learns to love someone else now." Tessa nodded, but before she could respond, Ingrid rushed on. "Maybe he'll learn to love you, Miss Taylor. Then maybe you can become my new mama."

Without waiting for Tessa's reaction, the girl limped away, clutching her brother's arm with one hand and her cane with the other.

Speechless, Tessa could only stare at them as they exited the schoolroom.

CHAPTER 5

Tessa closed the schoolhouse door and smiled at the boy who'd asked if he could help carry her books home.

"I'm perfectly fine carrying them on my own, Henry," she said to the gangly boy waiting for her outside. His white-blond hair was clipped almost to his scalp, likely an attempt by his family to control the lice, a prevalent problem among her scholars. His nose still contained a smattering of freckles he'd gained over the short summer, during the days of fishing and swimming in the lake. Although there was still a boyish fullness to his face, at eleven he was her oldest male student.

Josie was her oldest female student, a fact Josie never failed to complain about each morning when Tessa prodded the girl awake and elicited a promise that she would attend class.

Tessa had learned that most boys started

working in the mine when they were ten. Some of the girls went to work too, hired at the boardinghouses as housekeepers, cooks, or washerwomen.

The classroom was primarily populated by young children who weren't conscripted yet into the drudgery and danger of the mines. She'd been told by the mother and helper, Hannah Nance, that there were enough children in town to fill the school to overflowing. "Over one hundred," she'd said.

Tessa couldn't imagine teaching more than the forty or fifty who had shown up for class the past two weeks. Even with Hannah's help, she struggled to listen to everyone's recitations, give spelling lists, and drill on math facts. So many of the students needed individual attention, and no matter how hard she worked to get around the classroom, she could never seem to reach every student.

She was in short supply of McGuffy Readers, North American Spellers, slates, slate pencils, and an assortment of other supplies. Already she'd had to find creative ways for the children to share the meager resources they had.

Even with all the shortages and challenges of her new position, it still troubled her that

71

the older children who most needed an education were missing out.

She stood on the lone wooden plank that served as a step and stared at the wisp of smoke that rose from the stamp mill. The brick building was just down the road at the base of the hill that ran down the one-hundred-fifty-mile length of the Keweenaw Peninsula. It was the hill that held the vein of copper a dozen or more companies were mining.

The children had been a wealth of information about the mines and had answered her questions with more knowledge than any child should have about mining operations. She'd learned that the fissure deposit at Cole Mine was massive, dropping some thirty levels and over three thousand feet straight down into the earth.

She could only shudder at the thought of men down that deep in the bowels of the earth. But young boys? Like Henry Benney? It was scandalous.

She'd also learned that most of the miners had emigrated from Cornwall, England, when the tin and copper mines there had reached a peak of production. With their knowledge of copper mining, the Cornish had become invaluable assets to the copper industry in the Midwest.

In the late September afternoon, the sun had disappeared behind a band of clouds. The air was cold and damp with the threat of rain. She thought she heard the faint rumble of thunder, but realized the sound might also belong to a load of rocks being dumped out of the mine into a chute that would carry them down the hill to the stamp mill.

Henry waited for her on the rutted wagon path. He was the last of the students to leave the schoolhouse every day. After she dismissed everyone, he always came up to her desk with numerous questions about his assignments. She relished his eagerness to learn and didn't mind staying late to tutor him.

She fell into step next to the boy. "I just wish more boys your age would attend school, Henry. Perhaps you can talk with them and encourage them to come."

"Lot of my friends don't care about any learning," he said, lengthening his stride to match her pace. "But my father, now he's a good one. He keeps saying he wants me to have something else to do with my life besides working in the mines like him and his father before him."

If only more of the fathers felt the same way. But sadly, most of them were stuck in their old ways of doing things. They'd lived and died as miners in Cornwall, and most of them planned to live and die as miners in Michigan. They had no other aspirations.

"All week I've been thinking about what I can do to help educate more of the students who work in the mines," she said as they walked toward the main business district of town, "and I've decided I'm going to start holding evening classes."

"That so, miss?" Henry said.

"Yes. What do you think of the idea? Do you think I'll get the older children to attend?"

Henry shrugged. "Can't rightly say. Maybe some."

Teaching evening classes would make for long days. Over the past couple of weeks that she'd been in Eagle Harbor, late in the afternoon, utterly exhausted, she'd trudged back to the house where she was staying. She'd wanted only to flop down onto the bedbug-infested mattress in her attic room and sleep, but she'd had lessons to plan and assignments to grade.

How would she manage teaching all day *and* all evening? Especially after she'd already promised her younger students that she'd hold extra spelling classes for those who wanted to participate in a spelling bee contest.

She forced the negative thoughts out of her mind. She'd come to Eagle Harbor to teach, but now that she'd realized God had bigger plans for her here, she needed to trust that He would give her the strength to do whatever He called her to.

"Maybe you could open the class to parents too," Henry suggested. "If the fathers are learning, I bet they'll be more keen on their children learning."

"You're brilliant, Henry." She stopped and smiled at the boy. "That's an excellent plan."

He beamed at her praise. "I know my father always talks about how he wished he'd had more learning when he was a lad. He'd be mighty happy to get the chance now."

"Of course he would. Most of the parents would." Why hadn't she thought of including them earlier? If the parents were educated, they'd be more supportive of educating their children. Perhaps there would be fewer dropouts. Then the community as a whole would have the tools to improve themselves rather than being at the mercy of the mine and its owners.

She let her gaze linger on the look-alike

log cabins that housed the miners' families. Now that school was out for the day, the yards were dotted with young children helping with the endless chores and some laughing and playing in spite of their dismal existence.

"I'll start a class next week," she said more to herself than to Henry.

"Will you ask permission of Mr. Updegraff first?" Henry's young face took on a shadow of worry.

Percival Updegraff had left the day after her arrival for a trip downstate, or so she'd been told. Josie had speculated that the superintendent of Cole Mine had gone to see his wife and children one last time before winter locked them in and stopped navigation on the Great Lakes.

Whatever the case, Tessa hadn't seen him since the day she'd signed her contract. "I don't think Mr. Updegraff will mind if I start an evening school," she said. "I don't see how he could object. Not when it would be a huge benefit to the town."

Henry glanced around and then lowered his voice. "My father says Mr. Updegraff likes to know everything that's going on. He says a man can't relieve himself in the woods without Mr. Updegraff hearing about it."

Tessa bit back a laugh. "I can't imagine he'd concern himself with what I do or don't do with the school."

"Oh, he'd concern himself, all right."

Before she could say anything more to ease Henry's mind, a child's voice calling her name came from the direction of the bluffs that ran along the bay.

She turned to see a blond-headed boy trotting toward her. The stocky build and proud stiff hold of his shoulders belonged to Gunnar Bjorklund, Alex's boy.

"Miss Taylor," he called again with a wave.

She lifted her hand in a return greeting, trying to ignore her pleasure in seeing the boy again. Even though she'd just said good-bye to Ingrid and Gunnar a short while ago, she couldn't deny that she enjoyed their company. They lingered briefly with her in the classroom at lunch instead of rushing outside with the other children. She'd found their sweetness endearing, even if Ingrid was slightly overbearing in the questions she asked.

Of course, Tessa hadn't been able to avoid seeing Alex when he dropped the children off for school each morning. And she hadn't been able to shake the awkwardness in knowing he'd once been married, had lost a wife, and had children. She still wished he'd

77

said something about it earlier. But how did one go about divulging such personal information? She didn't suppose he could have saved her from drowning, carried her to the beach, and then made the declaration, *I'm flirting with you. By the way, I'm a grieving widower with children.*

She almost laughed aloud at the absurdity.

Gunnar didn't stop running until he was standing in front of her panting like one of Alex's dogs. He bent over to catch his breath.

"Is everything all right?" she asked.

He shook his head, but didn't meet her gaze.

Something in his manner set her on edge. "What's wrong?"

He held his side, still gasping for breath.

Her mind flashed with the picture of Ingrid having fallen and hurt herself. "Is it Ingrid?"

Gunnar nodded. "She asked me to come for you," he managed to say. Guilt rippled across his face before he could hide it.

But Tessa was already turning to Henry and sending him ahead without her to the Rawlingses with instructions to carry her books to her room in the attic where they'd be safe from the younger boys of the household who tended to be destructive.

78

With Henry scampering off, Tessa took Gunnar's arm. "Take me to Ingrid," she said, trying to keep the anxiety out of her tone. She wanted to assure Gunnar that he had nothing to worry about, that she was only too glad to help, and that everything would be fine.

But as they hurried along, she grew breathless in her attempt to keep up with the boy. She had no time for conversation, to discover what had happened. She had no care about where he was leading her either. Her only concern was getting to Ingrid just as fast as she could.

Her shoes slapped the path and her chest thudded. Even so, she could hear the crash of the waves growing stronger as they ran. When they broke through the wooded bluff into a clearing, Tessa stumbled at the sight of a lighthouse straight ahead. It was the same lighthouse she'd seen from the harbor the day she arrived. From a distance it had seemed rather plain and unassuming. But now up close, she could see the keeper's house was actually quite large and solid.

"Don't tell me the two of you were playing where you shouldn't have been," Tessa said to Gunnar, who was now at least two body lengths ahead of her.

He didn't respond except to pick up his

79

pace and sprint the last distance to the door of the keeper's cottage.

"You do know that a lighthouse is federal property," she said, coming up behind him, heaving and hot from the exertion. "You shouldn't enter one without permission from the keeper, especially if he's not available to give you a tour."

Gunnar and Ingrid's misdeed reminded her of something her twin brothers would have done in their younger days. They'd always gotten into one kind of trouble after another. And since she'd been the only mother they could remember, she'd been the one to rescue them from death-defying incidents.

Gunnar didn't stop to make sure she was following him. Instead he barged into the cottage as if accustomed to doing so. She followed him inside, praying the lightkeeper wasn't at home. She didn't want to bring trouble upon herself or the children for breaking and entering into a house that wasn't theirs.

She followed him down a hallway past two closed doors she assumed to be bedrooms. He led her to a parlor near the back of the house, which was across from the kitchen. A big picture window overlooked Lake Superior. Maybe the men who'd designed the house had put the parlor at the rear of the house with the thought of providing the family with a view of the lake. She supposed to anyone else, the rocky ledge below with its crashing waves and endless lake beyond offered a majestic sight. But she cringed at the thought of having this view every day.

She wanted to yank the curtains closed, but instead she focused on the rest of the parlor. It looked as though it hadn't been cleaned in weeks. Clutter was piled on end tables, balls of dust crowded the edges of the wooden floor, and blankets were tossed haphazardly across armchairs.

She'd grown up in a nearly spotless keeper's dwelling, always living with the fear of a surprise visit by an inspector. Keeping the cottage clean had been one of her most important duties. Lighthouse officials expected the keeper's house to be as perfectly clean as the lighthouse.

What had happened here?

"Miss Taylor?" came Ingrid's muffled voice beneath a scattering of knitted afghans on the sofa.

With a start, Tessa rushed across the room to the little girl. "Ingrid?" she said, kneeling beside the sofa and tugging back a blanket to reveal the girl's flushed face. "Whatever is the matter? Are you hurt?"

Ingrid nodded and pointed to her neck. "I have a scratchy throat."

A scratchy throat?

The girl peered up at Tessa and batted her eyelashes over her baby-blue eyes. Her expression was one of such innocence that Tessa could almost believe for a moment the girl really was suffering.

But then Tessa glanced over her shoulder at Gunnar, who stood in the middle of the room staring down at his feet and shuffling them. The guilt she'd observed earlier was now plastered all over his face.

Tessa turned her attention back to Ingrid, her mind spinning as she tried to make sense of the situation. Ingrid was clearly not hurt. And Tessa couldn't be sure she had a sore throat either. But for some reason, the little girl had wanted her attention, apparently badly enough that she'd cajoled her brother into coming after her.

Tessa lifted a hand to Ingrid's cheek and brushed back stray strands of her hair. While the girl's cheek was warmer than usual, Tessa guessed the overheating had come from covering herself with too many blankets rather than sustaining a fever.

For an instant, Tessa debated scolding the child for playacting and deception. But when Ingrid sighed a contented breath and leaned her cheek further into Tessa's hand, a sweet ribbon of pleasure wrapped around Tessa's heart.

She lifted her other hand to Ingrid's forehead. "You do feel warm."

"Yes, I think I'm running a fever," Ingrid said hastily.

"Perhaps if I sit here for a few minutes and hold your hand, you'll feel better?" Tessa reached under the blankets and folded her hand around Ingrid's.

The little girl smiled and nodded. "I'm already feeling better, Miss Taylor."

"What if I tell you a little story?" Tessa asked. "That might cure you altogether."

Ingrid sat up straighter. "Oh yes. I'm sure that would work."

"And Gunnar, why don't you join us . . ." Her voice trailed off as she turned to look at Gunnar and instead found herself gazing upon a bare-chested Alex standing in the opposite parlor door. One of the bedroom doors they'd passed on their way into the house now stood open behind him.

With one hand he slipped a suspender over his bare shoulder, and with the other he rubbed his eyes as if he'd just awoken. When he gave a big yawn and stretched out his arms, Tessa couldn't keep from staring at the muscles of his bronzed chest, everything perfectly chiseled. On the day of her near-drowning, she'd thought his thin undershirt had left very little to the imagination. Well, she'd been wrong.

He was a beautiful specimen of manhood. She honestly had no desire to take her eyes off of him, even though she knew she was ogling inappropriately in front of the children.

"Why, Miss Taylor," he said, his voice hinting at humor, "I wasn't expecting you or I would have made sure to strap both of my suspenders."

She wasn't sure if she could get her voice working, but somehow she managed, "Yes, if you could please cover yourself with the other suspender, I would appreciate the modesty." The moment she looked into his face, she regretted the move. His lopsided smile nearly took the breath from her lungs.

"So what brings you here?" he asked. "I'm guessing it wasn't to get a peek at me half clad, although I wouldn't be surprised if that was your ulterior motive."

She had to pull herself together and stop allowing him to fluster her. He was deriving too much satisfaction from her reaction. "I actually came to check on Ingrid —"

"I wasn't feeling good," Ingrid interrupted, sitting up and throwing off the

84

blankets. "But I'm doing better now."

Alex studied her and, seeing nothing amiss, raised one of his brows.

"We shouldn't have bothered Miss Taylor," Gunnar said, toeing his boot into the area rug that needed beating and airing.

"I don't mind being bothered," Tessa started, then stopped and glanced around again as understanding dawned.

The lighthouse was their home. And if the lighthouse was their home, that could only mean one thing. Alex Bjorklund was a lightkeeper.

Chapter 6

Tessa took a rapid step backward as if she'd been struck. For a moment, Alex thought he glimpsed horror in her eyes before she averted them.

He stepped to the sofa and retrieved a shirt from a pile of discarded clothes. His fingers fumbled to get the garment turned right side out. He hadn't meant to offend her. But he supposed he had overstepped the bounds of propriety with his remarks. The moment he'd noticed her, he should have immediately donned a shirt.

But her brazen and appreciative stare at his bare chest had sent a jolt of heat through him, and he wasn't able to resist teasing her just a little.

He stuffed his arms into the sleeves and bit back a mutter when the fabric stuck at his bicep. It wasn't his fault that he'd stumbled into the parlor without his shirt on and she was there. Usually he tried to make sure he was up to greet the children when they arrived home from school. But some days, after a particularly stormy night like last night, he overslept. Thankfully, Ingrid and Gunnar were old enough now to occupy themselves for a short while, and they usually didn't get into too much trouble.

Though the opening of the front door had awakened him, it was the strange voice that dragged him out of bed. He stumbled toward the parlor and certainly hadn't expected to find Tessa Taylor kneeling next to the sofa and smiling down at Ingrid with such tenderness it had nearly broken his heart.

"Please forgive me, Miss Taylor," he said, jerking the shirt up to his shoulders. He cringed when he heard a sharp rip. "I've behaved like a complete idiot."

She glanced around the room again with a wildness that said she couldn't wait to escape.

He hadn't meant to drive her away.

"It's my fault," Gunnar said. "I'm the one who asked Miss Taylor to come." He exchanged a glance with Ingrid, one that told Alex the two had been up to something.

Ingrid shook her head, her eyes flashing a warning.

But Gunnar continued anyway, always the more forthright of the two. "I'm sorry, Miss Taylor."

Tessa took a breath, seemed to push aside her own reservations, and then looked at Gunnar. "You needn't ever feel bad about coming to me. That's what I'm here for. But now that I know you're in good hands, I'll be on my way —"

"Don't leave yet, Miss Taylor." Ingrid slid off the sofa, reached for her cane, and hobbled toward Tessa. "Please stay for a few more minutes."

Tessa didn't resist when Ingrid grabbed her sleeve. Instead she pressed a hand to the girl's cheek as Alex had seen her do when Ingrid was on the sofa.

The adoration in Ingrid's eyes pinched Alex's heart. She'd gone far too long without a woman's touch. Now that she had it, she was basking in it.

"I can't stay, Ingrid," Tessa said gently, lifting her gaze and meeting Alex's with a mixture of pity and sorrow.

Was she feeling sorry for him?

"Perhaps your father will allow you to participate in the special spelling classes?" Tessa directed her question to him. Arched with long lashes, her luminous green eyes were as irresistible as Ingrid's.

88

"Well?" she said, waiting for him to give permission for Ingrid to take part in the spelling classes.

"I don't know . . ."

"Maybe you'll allow Gunnar to join the classes too?"

Wait a minute. Alex glanced first at the eagerness in Ingrid's expression and then at the guilt that still shadowed Gunnar's. Did Tessa think the two were his children?

He almost grinned at the realization. Of course she'd think Gunnar and Ingrid were his; they shared the same family name. He brought them to school every morning. And they all had the Bjorklund Finnish looks.

Maybe that was why she'd been aloof with him. With her polite façade in place, he'd decided she was simply trying to stay as professional as possible around her students, and he'd attempted to respect that.

At the thump of footsteps in the other bedroom behind him, Alex couldn't contain his smile, relishing the shock Tessa was about to get. "I'm not sure I can give my permission," he started.

Frowning, she said, "Mr. Bjorklund, I assumed you were the kind of man who took the education of his children seriously."

Behind him the door opened, and the stomp of footsteps drew closer.

89

"I do take the education of my children seriously, Miss Taylor. The only problem is that I don't have any children."

Confusion creased her forehead, and her lips stalled around an unspoken word.

"Who's here?" Michael asked in a groggy voice behind him.

Alex stepped out of the doorway and allowed Michael to enter the parlor and stand next to him. Of course, his older brother was fully attired and had even managed to comb his hair. Michael was a couple of inches shorter than Alex and had a leaner, thinner body. But otherwise he and Michael, though four years apart, looked a lot alike.

Tessa's eyes widened at the sight of Michael.

"Miss Taylor, if you'd like to get permission for Gunnar and Ingrid to attend spelling classes, then you'll have to ask their father for yourself."

Her attention bounced back and forth between Alex and Michael.

"Daddy!" Ingrid called, leaning closer to Tessa. The girl's eyes sparkled. "Daddy, this is our new teacher, the one we've been telling you about."

Next to him, Michael stiffened and raised a hand to his hair to comb it again even

90

though every hair was already in place. He cleared his throat. "Pleased to meet you, Miss Taylor."

"And I, you, Mr. Bjorklund," she said hesitantly. "So Ingrid and Gunnar are your children?"

"Yes." Michael's voice squeaked, and his features became a tense mask of nervousness.

Alex stared at his brother's strange reaction. What reason could Michael have for being nervous around the new schoolteacher?

"They talk about you all the time," Michael continued.

"They're delightful children," Tessa responded by smiling at Ingrid in spite of having been completely surprised by the situation. Then she turned narrowed eyes upon Alex. "Now, your brother, on the other hand, I'm not quite sure *delightful* would be the word I'd use to describe him."

Alex chuckled. There was something about the spitfire in her attitude that never failed to humor him.

At their exchange, Michael's forehead wrinkled.

"Daddy," Ingrid said, "isn't Miss Taylor the most beautiful woman you've ever seen?" Ingrid was peering up at her teacher with such adoration that once again Alex's chest ached. It hurt to see her so desperate for a woman's attention.

He'd thought he and Michael had done okay raising the children together. He'd assumed the attention they gave Ingrid and Gunnar had been enough. The children had two fathers instead of one. Two really good fathers, if he could say so himself.

But perhaps two adoring fathers could never take the place of one loving mother, no matter how hard they'd tried.

"What do you think, Daddy?" Ingrid insisted.

Michael peeked again at Tessa, and much to Alex's amazement, his brother's face turned bright red. "She seems like a very nice lady," Michael mumbled.

Gunnar was blushing too.

Like father, like son. The two were enamored with Tessa Taylor and too shy even to look her in the eyes. Alex would have to tease them mercilessly later.

For now, however, someone needed to take charge of the situation. He turned a bold gaze upon her. No one could ever accuse him of being shy. "I think we all agree that your new teacher is very pretty."

He regarded her appreciatively. She was wearing the same green skirt and matching bodice she'd had on the first day she arrived, only this time it was dry and sewn together. The color served to highlight her creamy complexion and bring out the brightness of her eyes. At his perusal, some of the strain eased from Tessa's features, and a smile almost made it to her lips.

So, she liked compliments? Well, he liked giving them.

"Mr. Bjorklund," Tessa began.

Michael lifted his face and responded with "Yes" at the same moment as Alex.

Tessa glanced between them, her smile widening.

"You're more than welcome to call me Michael," Michael said shyly.

"Then Michael it is," Tessa said, giving Michael a smile.

When Michael returned Tessa's smile, Alex could only stare. His brother hadn't smiled at another woman since his wife had died.

"Would you be willing to allow Gunnar and Ingrid to attend my special spelling classes?" Tessa asked. "I'll be hosting a spelling bee this winter for all those who participate in the class."

"Sure. They can attend," Michael said readily. From the puppy-dog look on his face, Alex had the feeling his brother would agree to anything Tessa requested, even if she asked him for half his worldly possessions, which unfortunately wasn't much at the moment.

Ingrid gave a small cheer of happiness, hobbled over to Michael, and hugged him. Tessa watched the interaction between father and daughter with a wistful smile. Then she glanced around the room again unable to hide a shudder as she stepped toward the kitchen door.

He tried to view the room as she saw it — the mismatched and worn furniture, the faded carpet, and then the miscellaneous tools he'd stacked on one of the end tables.

They'd missed earning the superintendent's Efficiency Star this past summer because the house had been "too disorganized and unkempt." Alex couldn't understand why the inspector didn't put more weight on the things that mattered, like a flawless record of lighting the lantern, or their above average lifesaving rescues.

Every time the inspector visited, the older man shook his head at the condition of the keeper's dwelling and told them he could dismiss them for not keeping the house cleaner. But one look at Michael and the children always softened the inspector's heart. He knew they were bachelors trying

94

to raise two children on their own. So he always left with the same warning to do better the next time.

Now they had no choice. They *had* to do better the next time. If they had any hope of raising enough money for Ingrid's surgery, they needed the bonus that came with the Efficiency Star.

"I really must be going," Tessa said, but then she stopped as her attention caught on a wooden crate sitting next to the sofa. Her eyes rounded and she sucked in a breath.

She went to the box, knelt next to it, and peered inside. "Oh, heaven," she said, stroking one of the spines reverently. She whispered several of the titles. "*Alice in Wonderland, Little Women, Great Expectations.* Where did you get all these books?"

"The Lighthouse Tender Crew brought them the last time they delivered supplies," Alex answered.

"Since when do tender crews deliver books?"

"Apparently they're trying something new with the books. They hope to start a lending library of sorts that's passed from lighthouse to lighthouse for keepers and their families."

"Amazing," she said, fingering another book. "My favorite, *The Courtship of Miles*

95

Standish."

"I suppose the Board has decided if they can keep their staff from getting so bored during the winter, they'll have less turnover."

She lifted one particularly thick book from the crate and traced the silver-embossed lettering engraved on its black cover. "So you'll have this precious supply of books all winter long?"

Alex nodded. "They're for Gunnar and Ingrid to read."

Tessa looked at him sharply. They both knew that Gunnar and Ingrid weren't proficient enough to read the thick books in the crate. "*You* and their father will need to read them to the children, Mr. Bjorklund."

Alex didn't dare look at Michael. He had the feeling his brother's face had flushed with the same embarrassment that was swirling through him. How could he respond to Tessa without coming across as the complete dolt that he was?

"They won't be able to read them to us, Miss Taylor," Ingrid said.

"I'm disappointed with such news." Tessa leveled a censuring look at him.

He lifted his shoulders in question. Why was she singling him out? Why wasn't she bestowing her wrath upon Michael too?

"My daddy and my uncle never read to us," Ingrid said.

Alex shook his head at his niece, warning her not to say anything else. But she lifted her chin almost defiantly and continued, "But it's not because they don't want to. It's because they don't know how to read."

Tessa sat back on her heels and stared between him and Alex with widening eyes.

Michael ducked his head.

Alex had long ago stopped caring about the fact that he'd never had but a rudimentary education, enough that he could do a few sums, read what he needed to, and sign his name. What use did he have for any learning beyond that? He wasn't destined for being a teacher or minister or any other line of work that required an education. He was a lightkeeper, and before that he'd worked on the tender crews delivering supplies to lighthouses.

She stood. "I'm starting an evening school next week for parents and students who aren't able to come during the day. Perhaps you'd both like to attend."

"I've gotten along so far just fine," Alex said. "I don't need any more education." That wasn't entirely true. He knew he'd be able to do so much more with his dog breeding if he were better at the business

97

aspect of raising purebred elkhounds. But he wasn't about to admit that to Tessa.

Her delicate brow wrinkled above her flashing eyes. "You'll come to my evening class, won't you, Michael?" she asked, all the while glaring at Alex.

Michael hesitated only an instant before nodding. "Sure, I'll come."

Tessa smiled at him. "Excellent. Then I'll look forward to seeing you there."

"I know you'll like having Miss Taylor as a teacher," Ingrid said, peering up into her daddy's face.

Michael looked directly at Tessa and responded with a small, rare smile. "I have no doubt I will."

Speechless, Alex stared at Michael. His brother had been like a dead man walking for the past five years. What was going on here? Was Michael finally waking up?

Under any other circumstance, Alex would have been thrilled. He loved his brother more than his own life. He'd watched his brother hurt for too long, and he'd been waiting for Michael to put the past behind him and move on with his life.

But move on with Tessa?

An anchor dropped in Alex's stomach. From the moment he'd seen Tessa, he'd been drawn to her in a way he hadn't been drawn to a woman in a very long time. Over the past couple of weeks, he enjoyed seeing her every morning when he walked the children to school, even if she hadn't paid him much attention.

He hadn't forgotten that he wanted to win her affection. Now maybe he needed to carry through with his plan and lay claim to her before Michael beat him to it.

CHAPTER 7

"Please, Nadine," Tessa said as she washed the table after dinner. "Please let Edward and Will Junior attend class tonight."

Nadine shifted the baby, moving the little one out of reach of the towel she was using to dry forks — the same dirty gray towel that everyone in the household used for wiping their hands and faces, and the Lord only knew what else.

Tessa tried not to think about the state of cleanliness of the plates and utensils during meals. Although that evening, Tessa hadn't thought about the lack of cleanliness even one time. She'd been too consumed with her revulsion of the giblets Nadine had served, especially when her hostess explained that the giblets were the feet, head, and bill of the goose they'd recently butchered. Apparently giblets were a special treat. Either that or the children had no taste buds. They'd devoured the waste pieces disguised with gravy faster than Nadine could serve them.

"Edward and Will Junior will benefit from the class," Tessa said again as she peered into the noisy front room where the children had raced after gobbling up the giblets.

"They're happy enough in the mine, that they are."

Tessa turned back to the table and swiped at a splotch of gravy that had congealed on the sticky plank. The floor, the walls, and the stove were just as sticky with a layer of grease and dust that was impossible to wash away, even though Tessa had tried. "But it's dangerous, dirty work. Wouldn't you like to see them have the chance to do something different if they want to?" Tessa had already had the same conversation with Nadine several times since she'd made the decision to have the evening school.

Nadine sighed, and her shoulders slumped under the weight of the baby. Her brownish-gray hair hung in stringy strands around her face. In the overcast October evening, the light from the oil lantern at the center of the table cast shadows upon the woman's face, adding another ten years' worth of wrinkles. "Today's not a good day for it, Tessa," she insisted. "Not with Mr. Rawlings in so much pain."

Tessa bit back a tart response. Those of the Rawlings family who worked in the mine were always coming home with injuries: cuts from falling pieces of rock, scraped knees and elbows, burns from the wax that dripped from the candles affixed to their hats. Will Junior had lost his thumbnail last week when a sledgehammer had nicked him. They'd all exclaimed how lucky he was not to have lost his whole thumb.

This time Mr. Rawlings was in pain from having his tooth pulled at the dentist earlier in the day, not a mining accident. As Tessa made her way through the house, she tried to mask her disappointment that she hadn't been able to convince Nadine to let the boys attend school in the evenings. She stopped next to the settee in the front room where Mr. Rawlings was resting and debated pestering him instead.

But with his arm draped across his eyes and a bloody wet rag hanging half out of his swollen mouth, she spun away and finished buttoning her heavy wool coat. She ducked to avoid being hit by a ball and was careful not to trip over the younger children racing toy horses around on the floor.

"Josie," she called over the galloping, bouncing, and screeching.

Josie sat on the edge of a chair, peeking

between the drab curtains. She let the curtain fall and gave Tessa her attention. With her long hair styled into a coil that Tessa had taught her how to arrange and her face freshly washed, Josie looked less like a girl and more like the woman she was becoming. Josie had been regular in attendance at school too.

Tessa smiled. At least she was having some influence on one member of the household, even if that influence came at the hand of some bribing. It seemed Josie was eager to do anything in exchange for learning how to style her hair, care for her skin, and add baubles to her clothing.

"Are you sure you can't convince your Robbie to attend the evening class?" Tessa asked.

"He's too busy," Josie said with a wave of her hand. "Besides, if he goes, we won't have no time to spend together."

Tessa shook her head, not surprised by another refusal. She was getting used to the resistance. But that didn't mean she'd give up easily. Michael Bjorklund was the only person in Eagle Harbor who'd made any kind of commitment to attend her class, even after all her efforts informing families about her new endeavor. At least one was better than none. She wouldn't give up hope

103

that with time and patience, the people would begin to see their need.

Tugging up her coat collar and lowering her hat brim, Tessa stepped outside into the fading evening. The day had been damp and foggy. A mix of sleet and snow had begun to fall. Josie had informed her it wasn't unusual to have snow in October, but Tessa had declared it was much too early for winter to begin.

Many of the trees were already bare or covered with a straggling of yellow leaves. She'd been told the boats would soon stop running from "below," the word used by the residents of Eagle Harbor when referring to the lower part of the state.

Mud squelched beneath her boots and splattered her skirt. She'd learned over the past damp days that most of the coast surrounding the harbor was a mucky sand-and-mud mixture, that there wasn't much clay. The clay the miners used to hold their candles onto their hats was brought over from Sault St. Marie.

Perhaps snow and ice would be a welcome change after all. If the ground was frozen, she wouldn't have to worry about spot-cleaning her skirts every night. Even though the schoolhouse was but a short walk, she was shivering by the time it came into view.

She stopped abruptly at the sight of the light emanating from the windows. She hadn't left a lantern aglow and had hoped to arrive well before any of the new students. Obviously someone was early.

With a burst of dismay, she hastened through the mud and wet grass. When she reached the front step, she hurriedly scraped at the soles of her boots and attempted to dislodge as much of the mud as she could, even though the effort was useless since the floor was hopelessly caked with it — both wet and dry — from the pupils who thought nothing of it.

They also thought nothing of the lice. She'd seen enough lice and their eggs on the heads of the children to fill a Cornish pasty.

Tessa pushed open the schoolhouse door and stepped inside, unprepared for the cozy warmth that met her. Kneeling on the floor in front of the open stove door was Michael Bjorklund, Gunnar and Ingrid's father.

He glanced over his shoulder in her direction, and at the sight of her, he closed the stove door and stood. His fair hair was parted neatly down the middle and combed so that every strand lay flat in submission. He wore a flannel shirt that was buttoned up to his chin and tucked into trousers that, although slightly wrinkled, were spotless.

Her heart warmed at the thought that he took his education seriously enough to attend her class neat and clean.

"Good evening, Mr. Bjorklund," she said. "It's good to see you."

"It's good to see you too," he said, darting a peek at her face before focusing on his boots that were covered in dried mud.

His peek, however, was enough for her to see the eagerness in his expression. Her heart warmed even further. After all the apathy toward her night school plan, she was delighted that she had at least one eager learner. "With the weather the way it is, I wasn't sure if anyone would want to come out tonight."

"I wouldn't miss it." His voice gave a tiny squeak, and he hurried to speak again. "Besides, the weather is still balmy compared to what's coming."

"So I've been told," she said, moving further into the room and shedding her coat. She took her time hanging it on one of the pegs and then straightened her hair and skirt.

When she turned, she found he hadn't budged from his spot in front of the stove and was staring at her with open admiration. He rapidly dropped his gaze and spun toward the woodbox, but not before she caught sight of the flush creeping onto his cheeks.

"I hope you don't mind that I came early to start the fire," he said.

"I'm very grateful, Mr. Bjorklund —"

"Michael."

"I'm very grateful, Michael." For some reason, using Alex's given name had seemed right. But saying Michael's first name felt unnatural and impolite.

He shook the nearly empty woodbox. "Looks like you're low on wood."

"Yes, well, I've been waiting and hoping for wood elves to come out every night and fill it while I'm away, but so far they haven't shown up."

She smiled at her own joke and waited for him to join her. Instead he opened the stove door and tossed in another handful of wood chips without cracking a grin.

"You don't know what I'm doing wrong, do you?" She tried humor again as she made her way to the front of the classroom to her desk. "Do the wood elves expect me to leave them an overpriced apple as a treat?"

Michael stirred the burning embers with a stick, tossed it in, and closed the door. Finally he turned to face her with raised brows as if he didn't quite know what to make of her rambling.

She apparently would need to use a more direct route of conversation with Michael. "I've asked the students to bring wood from home."

He nodded. "In past years, the teacher was always responsible for gathering wood for the stove. But then we've only had male teachers . . ." His voice trailed off at the realization of the current situation.

She inwardly cringed. Was he another one of those people who didn't believe females should be teaching? "I didn't realize it was my responsibility to gather wood. In that case, I'll begin to do so right away."

He frowned.

She hoped he wouldn't say that gathering and chopping wood was a man's job too. If so, she would have to give him a stern lecture about how she'd been chopping wood since she was a young girl, technically since her mom had died and she'd taken over the care of her younger siblings.

"Maybe we can figure out something," he started. But his words were cut off by someone rattling the schoolhouse door.

Another student? Her pulse leapt at the prospect.

The door swung wide, and amidst the whirling of wind and sleet, Alex barged

108

inside. He swiped off his flannel bowler hat and stomped his boots, dislodging mud.

For a moment, like Michael, she could only gape.

Alex raked his fingers through his untidy hair and shrugged out of an oiled cloak. "You haven't started class yet, have you?" he asked and tossed her one of his devastating, heart-stopping grins.

As he hung up his cloak, his shirt stretched across his broad shoulders. She couldn't stop herself from thinking back to the sight of him at the lighthouse last week when he'd been bare-chested and she got a leisurely view of his impressive physique.

Don't think about it, Tessa, she chided herself, as she had whenever her mind strayed to thoughts of him. Her disappointment at learning he was the assistant keeper was still too keen, although she knew it shouldn't matter in the least. "A very fine man completely ruined," she'd muttered to herself on more than one occasion since her discovery.

He rubbed his hands together and blew into them. His blue eyes sparkled as he looked between her and Michael. "Are we ready to start then?" he asked, winding his way through the rows of benches toward her.

109

"I didn't think you were coming," Michael said.

"I changed my mind."

"Why?" Michael's voice was hard.

Alex shrugged and continued toward the front row. "Maybe I realized how much I could benefit from Miss Taylor's attention."

Michael's brow dipped. "I'm sure you did."

Alex winked and said, "I'm eager to reap the benefits of her superior teaching skills."

Michael shook his head and started toward the front of the room too.

As Alex neared the first row, he stared at her openly and boldly. Even though she was tempted to glance away — and knew she should — she decided to stare right back. She didn't want him to think his presence in the classroom had any effect on her, though strange waves were rippling through her stomach.

He plopped into the spot normally occupied by Gunnar and Ingrid and smiled up at her innocently — too innocently. "So what are you going to teach me today, Miss Taylor?" His gaze dropped to her lips and lingered there.

The waves in her stomach rose and fell harder, and she couldn't think of a coherent response.

"Or maybe I'm the one who needs to teach you a thing or two," he said softly.

Oh, heaven. She swallowed hard. She had to think of something to say, and quick. But to her utter embarrassment, she was speechless.

Michael had made his way to the first bench. He sat down next to his brother and bumped Alex with a force that nearly sent him toppling off his seat.

"Sorry," Michael said. "Lost my balance."

"Sure you did." Alex righted himself, his grin only widening.

Tessa spun to face her desk. She reached for a paper and was tempted to use it to fan her cheeks, which she had no doubt were flushed. But she refrained.

"I thought you were watching the children," Michael whispered, none too quietly.

"They're responsible enough to be home without us, especially Gunnar."

"I told you I didn't like the idea of leaving the light unattended."

"And I told you I'm only staying for a little while."

Michael's long sigh told her his exasperation went deep. "It's your shift and you need to cover it."

"Everything will be fine," Alex said earnestly. "Gunnar's keeping his eye on it, and

111

if anything happens, he'll come get me."

"But you're the one who doesn't care about getting an education."

"Like I said, I changed my mind."

She smiled at their bickering, reached for the lesson plan she'd prepared, and walked to the blackboard. She couldn't fault Alex for changing his mind. In fact, she was glad he'd come to his senses and realized his need for bettering his education.

With careful strokes she wrote several words on the board. As she did, their whispering tapered to silence, and she could feel their stares burning into her back. She had the distinct impression they were looking directly at her and not at what she was writing on the board.

This new teaching experience wasn't going quite as she'd expected. She needed to pull herself together and start treating Alex and Michael with the same attitude she did all her other scholars.

She turned only to find that she'd been right. Two pairs of eyes were watching her with keen interest. She was sure neither had noticed anything she'd written on the board.

"Children," she said, "are we done with all the squabbling?"

The two men sat next to each other, their large frames completely out of place on the narrow bench meant for much smaller bodies. Michael was thinner and less stocky than Alex, but no less muscular, and he had a serious look on his face. However, Alex's lips were cocked into one of his lazy half grins, and his eyes danced with playfulness, obviously finding humor in her rebuke.

She tried to put on her sternest expression, which she knew wasn't all that stern. Nevertheless, she had to do something to hide the strange feeling of standing at the front of the classroom with two full-grown single men as her students.

They were lightkeepers, she reminded herself. Even if they were both handsome men, she would never interest herself in them if she were in a position to do so, which she wasn't. She'd rather strap her body to a large boulder and drop into the middle of Lake Superior before she let herself become enamored with a lightkeeper.

"If you're done with your discussion," she said again, "then perhaps you'll allow me to get started."

Michael nodded, his eyes offering her an apology. But Alex's expression contained nothing but mirth. How was she going to focus on teaching with him staring at her, watching her every move?

The schoolroom door squeaked on its hinges, and she breathed a sigh of relief when several more miners entered, a father and his two boys. When Henry Benney stepped inside a few seconds later with his father in tow, she all but forgot about Alex sitting in the front row watching her.

The line of grime at the edges of the miners' faces told her the men had made an effort to clean themselves before arriving, even if they were still attired in their mining clothes, their thick flannel pants and coats made of bagging and stained the color of copper.

The hour of lessons went all too quickly, and as the men stood to leave, she regretted that she hadn't extended the time to an hour and a half. Yet she hadn't wanted to discourage them from coming after a long day of work, and already several were stifling yawns.

"Henry's a quick learner," she said to Henry's father, a quiet, tall man who looked down at his son with pride. "I have a feeling he will make a good schoolteacher someday."

At her words of praise, Mr. Benney smiled and patted his son on the shoulder. "I would never have thought it possible for me kin to do anything but burrowing. But if anyone

114

can pass, it's me Henry here."

As the last of the men exited the schoolhouse, Tessa was surprised to see Michael and Alex lingering at the back, arguing with each other in harsh whispers.

"Class is over, children," she called to them. "Why don't you take your disagreement to the playground and fight there?"

Michael took a quick step away from Alex, chagrin flashing over his features. Alex, on the other hand, opened the door and waved her through with a flourish. "We were just waiting for you."

"There's no need —"

"We can't let you walk home alone in the dark," Alex said.

"Only one of us needs to go with her," Michael said in an irritated tone.

"Okay, that's fine with me. You head on back to the light."

"But it's your shift. And you're being irresponsible with it. You know as well as I do that anything could happen on a night like this."

Alex took off his hat and raked his fingers through his hair. He stared hard at Michael. Then he replaced his hat, his features growing somber with resignation. "You're right. I'll head back."

Michael nodded.

115

Alex tossed Tessa a last smile. "Thank you for sacrificing your time to teach a bunch of smelly men."

"It was my pleasure." And she meant it.

He ducked his head, hunched his shoulders against the wind, and disappeared into the dark evening.

She had to fight off a wave of dismay, because somehow she sensed that this was the first and last class Alex would attend.

CHAPTER 8

"I'll give you two dollars for the gloves," Tessa said, "and not a dollar more."

Samuel Updegraff's childlike eyes darted to the door of Cole Mine Company Store as if he hoped Jesus would return at that moment and rescue him. "The price is five dollars," he said again, just as he had a dozen times already, although his voice had grown softer, less insistent.

She was wearing him down. She'd learned that bargaining with Samuel was almost as difficult as eating Nadine's giblets. However, with persistence, she could eventually get him to lower the price of whatever she was buying.

She felt only slightly guilty that now every time she stepped into the store, Samuel would cower away from her. He busied himself with sweeping the spotless floor or polishing the pristine glass countertop, ignoring her for as long as possible.

117

But the guilt evaporated as soon as she took a look at the prices. Even if Samuel wasn't to blame for the exorbitant cost of the goods, she still couldn't stand by and pay such high prices.

"Very well," she said, pretending to heave an exasperated sigh. "You win, Samuel. I'll give you three dollars."

His round eyes widened with confusion.

Behind her, Nadine bounced the fussing baby. Tessa could feel the woman's scrutiny of her every move. She'd told Nadine to watch how she bargained so that she could learn to do it herself. *No one* ought to pay the outrageous prices charged by the Cole store, she'd insisted to Nadine.

Through the large glass that graced the storefront, she saw several of her students race past, along with the young Rawlings boys. The street was crowded with everyone who'd come out for the day's festivities. Through the throng she spotted Josie standing next to a tall youth with a pimply complexion, Robbie.

She didn't like the way Robbie looked at Josie. For a boy with only a few scraggly chin hairs, he was too young to be so enamored with Josie, always staring down into her eyes, putting his arm around her or holding her hand.

118

Tessa had tried to caution Josie not to take her relationship with Robbie so seriously. As usual, Josie had brushed off her gentle rebukes, and Tessa tried to remind herself that it would just take more time to wield her influence over the girl.

The sun had broken through the gloomy weather of the past week and brought a measure of warmth, a welcome change and just in time for the annual fall wrestling competition. Even so, after watching several wrestling matches, Tessa's fingers had grown stiff from the cold, and she'd decided to purchase a warmer pair of gloves.

"Three dollars," she said again. "Add it to my tab." Even though her salary was twenty dollars a month — higher than what she could make in Detroit — the high cost of living in the north had consumed her income far too quickly.

Samuel finally opened the ledger where he kept track of purchases. "Percival won't like this," he muttered. "Not at all. Not at all."

"You're not to blame, Samuel," she said, tugging the thick flannel-lined gloves on over her thin pair. "I know you're not the one setting such prices."

She had the feeling the Coles were to blame. She'd learned that the wealthy fam-

119

ily made their home in New York City and had purchased the mine the previous year. Apparently, many of the mines in the area were struggling with production and had resorted to laying off miners. The Coles' financial backing had helped to increase production again in Eagle Harbor. Although there were rumors that Mr. Cole personally visited his holdings from time to time, he hadn't come that summer or fall. Tessa supposed that like many of the Eastern millionaires who'd invested in the lumber camps and copper mines of the Midwest, the Coles only cared about turning a profit, not about the many people who depended upon them for their livelihood.

Samuel *tsk*ed at the back of his throat, but he wrote 3 DOLLARS in the ledger in his sticklike handwriting.

When he finished, she bestowed a smile upon him. Before he could move beyond her reach, she squeezed his fleshy hand. "Thank you, Samuel. You're a good man."

Deep red splotches formed on his cheeks. "You're all right too, Miss Taylor. For a woman teacher."

She patted his hand again and then started toward the door with Nadine trailing behind her. "Too bad there isn't another store in town to offer the Coles some competition,"

Tessa remarked as they stepped outside into the sunshine of the autumn afternoon.

"We had some men arrive in town and set up shop," Nadine said, "but they didn't last long. Mr. Updegraff won't let anyone step foot inside any place but his."

"Did I hear my name?" The tall, distinguished form of Percival Updegraff broke away from the group of miners he'd been talking with and strode toward them. In his dark pinstripe suit, bow tie, and round top derby, he cut a dashing figure. His face was freshly shaven, his salt-and-pepper mustache neatly trimmed.

Tessa wasn't sure why, but she had the urge to keep walking and pretend she didn't hear him. When Nadine froze, Tessa decided her ploy probably wouldn't work.

"Mr. Updegraff," Tessa said and forced a smile. "I didn't know that you'd returned."

"I arrived on the *Iron City* just this morning."

She followed his glance to the dock, where a steamer had anchored. Deckhands were unloading barrel after barrel into the warehouse, apparently more supplies to see them through the long winter. "I hope your visit with your family was pleasant. I'm sure it must be difficult to leave them behind."

"I console myself that my work here

provides a good and happy life for them." He smiled wistfully and cocked his head toward the store. "Besides, I don't like to leave Samuel on his own for too long."

"He seems to manage well."

"Apparently not so well in resisting your badgering him to lower prices." Percival's voice took on an edge, and before she could sling back a retort about how she wouldn't need to badger if the store had fair prices, he turned to Nadine. "How is your husband, Mrs. Rawlings? I heard he had to get a tooth pulled."

Nadine's haggard features were frozen, and she stared at the bonnet covering her baby's head. "He's been in some pain, but doing better now."

"He was beset with an infection, then?"

She nodded but didn't make eye contact with Percival.

"And I hear you've started an evening school?" he asked, turning back to Tessa.

Henry Benney's warning about Percival rushed back to her mind. *"A man can't relieve himself in the woods without Mr. Updegraff hearing about it."*

"Yes, I've had anywhere from six to ten coming every evening," Tessa replied. But not Alex. He hadn't come again after the first night. Michael, however, had continued

122

to arrive early. In fact, he'd started coming early enough to chop wood so that she'd have fuel for not only the evening class, but also for the next day of school. Even if he was one of her quietest scholars, he'd been one of her most helpful, including walking her home once the class was over.

"I'm not sure I approve of the evening classes," Percival said, narrowing his eyes.

"What's there to approve or disapprove of?" she asked.

His attention flickered to her bosom. "You're a young woman alone with a roomful of men. That's hardly proper for an innocent woman like yourself."

"I'm teaching the men." She didn't like the direction of the conversation or his eyes, and she had the urge to pull her cloak tighter. "They've been nothing but kind and respectful to me."

"You just never know what these men are capable of," Percival said with a glance toward the wrestling ring and the rowdy crowd. "We certainly don't want anything to happen to blemish your reputation, do we?"

There was something calculating in his eyes that made her wonder what he'd learned about her past. Had he made inquiries about her while he'd been in Detroit?

123

She had to stifle a shudder at the thought. "Why don't you stop by one of the evening classes next week and see for yourself all that the men are learning?" She was tempted to blurt out that then he'd sec she wasn't standing on top of her desk and dancing like a common barroom girl.

Thankfully, at that moment, before she said something she'd regret, she heard a young voice calling her name. "Miss Taylor! Miss Taylor!"

Ingrid Bjorklund hobbled across the rutted road with her cane, her father and brother not far behind. The little girl's eyes were alight with the pleasure of seeing her.

"If you'll excuse me, Mr. Updegraff," she said, then started away from him, relieved for the interruption.

"You won't be paid extra for the evening class." His hard tone stopped her.

Nadine stood unmoving next to Percival, still staring at her baby's head.

"I don't require any payment," Tessa said. "Except that my scholars reward me with enthusiasm for learning."

"How noble of you."

"Yes, it is. Now good day to you, Mr. Updegraff."

She didn't wait for his dismissal, but instead knelt and held her arms open to

124

Ingrid, who practically hopped the last distance to fall into her embrace with a cry of delight.

"I've been looking for you," Ingrid said.

"Have you?" Tessa hugged Ingrid tightly and smiled at Gunnar over the girl's head. The boy smiled shyly in return.

"She hasn't spoken of anyone but you since we arrived," Michael said, his hands tucked into his coat pockets. He glanced warily at Percival and gave the man a brief nod.

"How are things at the lighthouse, Michael?" Percival asked.

"We're managing fine, thanks."

"I hear you've joined Miss Taylor's evening school."

"That's true."

"I hope you're not shirking your duties as a result."

"I wouldn't dream of it." Michael's tone remained unruffled in spite of the obvious tension between the two men.

Tessa wanted to ask what kind of control Percival had over the lighthouse. She couldn't imagine it was much since all the lighthouses in Michigan were government owned and operated. But it was as clear now as it was the first day she'd met Percival that he thought he was king of the town.

As much as she wanted to ignore Percival and go on doing things as she had while he'd been gone, she had the feeling she wouldn't be able to — not if she wanted to keep her job.

Thankfully, before she had to say anything else in defense of her evening class, Samuel appeared in the store's doorway and called to Percival. With a frown, Percival disappeared into the store. After Percival was gone, Nadine finally moved, but only to scurry away as fast as possible, calling to Tessa that she was going home.

"Uncle Alex is *wrasslin'* next," Ingrid said, using the Cornish term for the event. "We hoped you'd come watch him with us."

"Alex is wrestling?" Tessa asked. "I thought only the Cornish were allowed into the matches." At least that's what Nadine had told her.

"They like to try to beat Uncle Alex," Ingrid explained.

"They've made an exception for him since he's a good wrestler," Michael added.

Tessa tried to peer past the crowd who'd gathered around a fenced-off area to watch the wrestling. Her pulse quickened at the thought of seeing Alex in the arena.

With Ingrid's hand in hers, they made their way toward the fence, past several bar-

126

rels of ale and the men already swearing and fighting as a result of too much drink. She wasn't sure if such an environment was appropriate for children, but no one else seemed to think anything of the children mingling among the revelers.

She'd been warned to cancel school on payday, and so she had. Her assistant had told her it was the one day a month, besides Sundays, when the men were excused from work. The mine operations were shut down except for the work of measuring the number of feet each miner had cut or drifted. Once the tabulations were recorded, the miners could go to the office and receive their pay — after deducting expenses. The rest of the day was spent tapering off.

Michael pushed them forward through the crowd until they reached the front. They arrived just as Alex was taking off his shirt and donning a loose jacket made of bagging that was tied closed with cording in the front. He was barefooted, like his opponent.

"Uncle Alex," Ingrid called.

He turned and glanced in their direction. Ingrid waved. At the sight of his niece, Alex grinned and waved back. The sun turned his hair to light gold. Underneath the loose-fitting jacket, his powerfully built chest radiated strength.

Tessa lifted her hand in a small wave and was rewarded with one in return.

"Make sure you win," she called.

"I'll do my best," he replied above the laughter and chatter of the crowd.

The referees took their places. As soon as the wrestlers were given permission to start, Alex and his opponent shook hands as was customary to start the bout. Then both went through the ritual of rolling up their jackets and tucking them under their left arms. Nadine had told her this was to prevent an opponent from gaining an early advantage by getting a quick free hold and an unexpected throw.

The bout started the same way as all the others Tessa had seen with both wrestlers getting into a hitch by taking a firm hold of the other's jacket at the left shoulder and right underarm.

From the previous wrestling matches, Tessa had already learned some of the rules. The wrestlers couldn't grab wrists, fingers, or any body part below the waist. But they could hold on to their opponent's jacket, arms, shoulders, and trunk, so long as they managed to throw their opponent onto his back. The goal was to make the landing flat so that all areas of the back touched the ground.

Tessa tensed as Alex circled around with his rival, a man who was equally bulky and stong-looking. As if sensing her worry, Ingrid's little hand squeezed hers. "Don't worry, Miss Taylor. Uncle Alex always wins."

As quick as a flash, Alex wrapped the crook of his arm around the man's neck. Then he hooked one of his legs through his opponent's, tripping him while simultaneously flipping him so that he landed on the ground with a thud.

The crowd cheered at Alex's swift move and the fact that he'd landed his opponent almost perfectly on his back. Alex straightened and looked to the referees, who nodded while raising their sticks in the air, signaling that Alex had indeed accomplished a "back."

A roar of approval rose from the crowd again. Tessa smiled with relief. Alex had won in the first move. By dropping his opponent flat on his back, he'd earned three pins. The pins consisted of the two hips and two shoulders, and as long as three of the four touched the ground at the same time, the wrestler automatically won.

Alex helped pull his opponent to his feet and shook the man's hand again. Then he turned in their direction and waved. Ingrid and Gunnar sent up cheers. Although Alex nodded at the children, he aimed his lop-sided smile at her.

Her heart nearly flipped at the thought that, with everyone else there, he'd singled her out.

"You did good," Gunnar said, staring up at Alex with pride after he'd finished his fourth and final bout.

Alex ruffled the boy's hair. "I don't think I broke any ribs this time."

"Broken ribs?" Tessa said, her eyes widening to reveal a concern that warmed his heart.

"You were worried about me getting hurt?" His back ached from where he'd been slammed several times. But other than that, he'd survived the wrestling contest with few injuries.

"I wasn't worried about you," Tessa quipped, tipping her face up and revealing cheeks painted pink from the chill in the air and eyes that sparkled with life. "I just didn't want the children to be exposed to anything too unseemly."

Unseemly? He'd show her unseemly. He'd kiss her pretty lips senseless in front of everyone. It would be completely inappropriate, but didn't the victor of the tournament deserve a kiss from the prettiest lady here? He sure thought so.

As if sensing his thoughts, especially since he was staring at her mouth, she averted her eyes and her breath hitched with a soft intake.

The crowd swelled around them, pushing them closer. Hands reached out to slap him on the back, and voices congratulated him on his wins.

Yes, a victory kiss. That would surely be all right, wouldn't it?

Now was his chance. Michael was gone, buying Cornish pasties from some of the wives who sold them during the contest to earn extra money. Not that they were alone; Ingrid and Gunnar were watching his interaction with Tessa with curious eyes. What would they think if he wrapped his arms around Tessa and gave her a kiss?

"So will you wrestle again today?" she asked somewhat breathlessly as she fidgeted with Ingrid's hair.

"Ah, I see," he teased. "You like watching me."

She started to shake her head.

"Don't deny it, Miss Taylor. You're enamored with my big biceps and Goliath strength."

"Why, Mr. Bjorklund," she said with mock indignation, "if you must know, I'm enamored by all the sweat, by the lovely smell of it."

He laughed. How was it possible that she could always make him laugh? He wished there was a way that he could spend more time with her. If only he could attend the evening school. Yet as soon as the thought entered his mind, he dismissed it as he had whenever Michael went on his way to the schoolhouse to attend class.

As much as he wanted to go along and make sure that Tessa paid him just as much attention as Michael, he'd known after the first class that he couldn't skimp on his responsibilities at the lighthouse simply because he didn't want to share Tessa with Michael.

He'd sensed Michael's eagerness, had watched him groom himself carefully for the first time in five years since his wife had died. Although Michael never showed much excitement or emotion, it had become increasingly clear that he was interested in Tessa. Just how interested, Alex couldn't judge. His brother had always been hard to read.

Nevertheless, the small amount of interest had been enough to worry Alex and make him wonder how he could spend time with Tessa too. His only chance at seeing her was when he dropped Ingrid and Gunnar off at school in the mornings. Usually she was already too busy with the other students to give him more than a friendly nod.

"I wish you'd consider coming back to evening school," she said. "I know the teacher is really mean and hard, but I still think it would be worth your while."

"You're right," he said. "She's a bear."

Tessa smiled. "Since when did you let a little old thing like a bear scare you?"

"She's actually a pretty *young* thing."

She tilted her face up to him with that sparkle in her eyes that made him wish more than ever that he could see her more often. Surely if he put his mind to it, he could think of something.

Michael shouldered his way through the bystanders until he was standing next to Tessa. He balanced two pasties on a piece of brown paper. "Have you had a Cornish pasty yet?" he asked Tessa, not bothering to give Alex a glance or word of congratulations.

"No." She eyed the pasty warily. "Nadine has given me the pleasure of many delectable dishes, but apparently not this one."

"Then you're in for a treat," Michael said. He held the pasties toward her.

Tessa stared at the thick crusted pastry

and raised a brow. "Does it have giblets inside? I'll only try it if it has giblets."

Michael shook his head. "I don't think so. I'm fairly certain these have venison."

"Tessa's being sarcastic, Michael," Alex interjected. Apparently Tessa had experienced something only a Cornish person could love. "Next time Nadine has giblets, make sure to eat it with Cornish Yarg. That way you'll enjoy the giblets even more."

"Yarg?" She quivered with revulsion. "I make it a practice to avoid eating foods that begin with the letter *y.*"

Alex laughed, but Michael only looked at Tessa with confusion.

"Try the pasty, Miss Taylor," Ingrid said, taking half of the one Gunnar had given her. "It's delicious."

Tessa broke off a piece of the pasty that Michael was holding out to her. She nibbled at the meaty side, which in addition to venison had chopped onion and potato. The Cornish miners usually took a pasty in their pocket down into the mine since they were unable to return to the surface at lunchtime. The pasty was easy to hold and eat, and the thick crust often kept the filling warm for several hours. It was the perfect miner's meal. And they were gaining in popularity among the locals.

134

Tessa took a bigger bite.

Michael watched for her reaction.

She finally rewarded him by popping a larger piece into her mouth and murmuring with approval.

He smiled.

At the sight of his brother's genuine smile, Alex couldn't begrudge Michael a moment of happiness, even if it was with Tessa. When Michael's wife, Rachel, had died and left him with two young children to raise, Alex quit his tender crew job and moved in with Michael to help his brother, thinking he would stay until Michael got through the worst of his grief.

After the funeral, Alex had assisted Michael in his job as a wharf supervisor down in Detroit. Then when a head lightkeeper and assistant position had opened up in Eagle Harbor, Michael asked him to move there with him. Alex couldn't say no, not when Michael could hardly function from day to day. He'd seen firsthand how his brother was struggling to take care of himself, much less the two children.

Jenny had said she'd needed him too. She'd already put their wedding on hold for the months he'd been gone with the tender crew, and she wasn't willing to delay any longer. At the time, he hadn't understood what her hurry was, why she couldn't wait another year. In hindsight, he could see her frustration hadn't been about the amount of time. It'd been about his unwillingness to commit. He'd put his family above her, and she didn't want to settle for second place in his life.

He had loved Jenny, and her rejection stabbed him painfully. He'd hurt for a long time after that.

He wasn't exactly sure when his deep wounds had started to heal, any more than he was sure when Michael's grief had started to subside. But apparently they were both beginning to feel the urge to be with a woman in a way they hadn't in a long, long time.

Tessa picked off another substantial piece of the pasty and slipped it into her mouth. As she chewed she made a murmur that sounded like a contented kitten. The pleasure rippling across her face sent a spurt of fire into Alex's blood.

Michael was watching Tessa too, and from the flare that lit his eyes, Alex had no doubt his brother was reacting the same way.

Alex let out a sigh, pushing down a swell of jealousy. He didn't want Michael to like Tessa so much. His brother's affection

would only complicate matters when Alex
finally swept Tessa off her feet.

CHAPTER 9

"Adoration," Henry Benney said. "A-d-o-r-a-t-i-o-n. Adoration."

Tessa nodded at her brightest student. "That's correct."

He was the last one standing at the front of the classroom for the spelling quiz she'd given to those students participating in her extra class in spelling.

Even though the spelling club met after school, she'd determined to offer the challenge to all her students. She wanted to foster a love of learning in them, to awaken an interest in studying by making each subject appealing. She knew that if her scholars fell in love with a subject, they would make more of an effort to learn and perhaps even do so on their own.

So far she had fifteen students who'd decided to stay after for the extra class. While several of the students were too young to participate, like Ingrid, she'd still promised the class that she would organize a special spelling bee with some of the other local schools during the winter. If they wanted to compete, they needed to start preparing right away.

"What does *adoration* mean, Miss Taylor?" Ingrid asked from her bench in the front row.

"Does anyone else know?" she asked, looking to the other students.

Henry raised his hand.

"Yes, Henry?"

"Does it mean strong admiration?"

She nodded. "Correct again."

"Kinda like my daddy feels for you, Miss Taylor?" Ingrid asked.

The class tittered. Tessa inwardly squirmed and tried not to glance upward to the general vicinity where Michael Bjorklund was even now repairing a spot in the schoolhouse roof.

He'd come several times that week after school to patch the roof, which had leaked during a recent rain.

Ingrid looked up at her with wide adoring eyes. Tessa was tempted to reply that Ingrid herself embodied the definition of adoration. But the expectancy on the little girl's face told her that she wouldn't be satisfied until she had an answer about her father.

"I think your father is very kind, Ingrid," Tessa said, choosing her words carefully. "I have the feeling he wants to make sure the schoolhouse is in good working order because he cares about your education."

That was only partly true. Michael did seem to genuinely care about Ingrid and Gunnar's education. But he'd also been looking at her with something more than scholarly interest. She'd sensed him appraising her on more than one occasion with an interest that went beyond the parent-teacher relationship.

She knew she needed to say something to him soon, so he understood that she couldn't involve herself with a man at this point in her life, not when she was determined to be a teacher — at least for a few more years. Since married women weren't allowed to teach, she'd crossed marriage off her to-do list for the time being. She certainly didn't want to lead Michael to believe she was eligible when she wasn't.

"Don't you think he's real nice, Miss Taylor?" Ingrid asked, not having yet caught on to the fact that she needed to raise her hand to ask questions.

Again the other students giggled. Gunnar blushed and shot Ingrid a censuring frown.

"He's very nice, Ingrid."

"And handsome too?"

Tessa fought back a smile. She couldn't deny that Michael Bjorklund was a handsome man, much like Alex. "Your father is fine-looking. And so are you."

Ingrid smiled. "Then maybe you can come out to the lighthouse and have dinner with us soon."

Tessa almost choked at the girl's audacity. "That's sweet of you to offer, Ingrid, but as your teacher I have to remain impartial — uninvolved, that is. I can't have personal entanglements."

Ingrid's unchanging wide-eyed stare told Tessa the little girl hadn't understood a single word she just said.

Tessa scrambled to find another answer that could explain why she wasn't romantically inclined toward Michael. But how could she possibly tell a six-year-old that even if she were open to the idea of marriage, she would never consider a man like Michael. He was a lightkeeper, and she wanted nothing to do with lighthouses ever again.

With all eyes watching her, waiting for further explanation, she glanced at the clock on the wall. Half past four. "Would you look at the time? Where did it go? Now we need to be done for the afternoon."

She encouraged the students to practice their word lists at home that evening and then dismissed them. As they filed out, she erased the board, hoping to avoid any more of Ingrid's questions.

"Uncle Alex?" Ingrid called out a greeting laced with surprise.

Tessa spun before she could stop herself. Sauntering down the center aisle was Alex, his hair wind-tossed, his smile carefree. He was wearing his blue-striped sweater, the one that made his eyes especially vibrant.

"You didn't need to come get us," Ingrid informed her uncle. "Me and Gunnar have been walking home by ourselves just fine."

"Gunnar and I," Tessa corrected.

"Gunnar and I," Ingrid said. "Besides, Daddy is here fixing the roof."

"I'm well aware that your father's here," Alex said, glancing up. "He's been here every blessed chance he can get."

"Aren't the two of you supposed to be sleeping during the afternoons?" Tessa asked.

"We should be," Alex replied wryly. "But apparently, one of us has been using that time to visit the schoolhouse every day while the other of us sleeps the afternoon away."

"Your brother has been a saint to make the repairs. He's obviously very dedicated to seeing that his children are taken care of."

"That's not all he's dedicated to seeing," Alex mumbled.

Tessa almost flushed at Alex's insinuation, but decided to pretend she hadn't caught the implication. "Your brother is a good man. A very good man."

"Whoa. You could have stopped with *good.* No need to gush over him."

Tessa smiled. Did she detect some sibling rivalry? "Well, I do appreciate his kindness. He's been generous to help around here without receiving any compensation."

As if sensing her goading, Alex grinned slowly. "Head on out now, you two," he said to Ingrid and Gunnar while staring at Tessa. "And make sure to tell your father that I think one of the gears on the lantern is stuck. He needs to take a look at it right away."

When the schoolhouse door opened and then banged closed after the children left, Alex said in a low voice, "You're right about Michael. He's much more thoughtful than me." He moved toward her and didn't stop until he stood directly in front of her. In fact, the presence of his towering body overwhelmed her so that she took a step backward and found herself at the edge of

143

the blackboard. "There's no way I'd help patch the roof without expecting some kind of compensation from you."

When his attention dropped to her lips, Tessa caught her breath and flattened against the blackboard. She knew exactly what kind of payment Alex had in mind. It frightened her to realize she might not want to resist him if he tried to kiss her. But certainly he wouldn't try, would he?

He slid an arm past her and rested a palm against the board near her head.

"You'd be disappointed," she said, wishing she didn't sound quite so breathless. "Because I don't offer any compensation." He was altogether too near. She caught the whiff of a fresh soapy scent and felt the warmth of his breath.

His cocked grin told her that he didn't believe her, that he knew the effect he had on women. "Not even for this?" He held up his other hand. He was holding a book, and the gold lettering on the spine read *The Courtship of Miles Standish.*

She smiled at the book. "Henry Wadsworth Longfellow."

"Your favorite, isn't it?" he asked.

She was amazed he remembered. She reached to take the book from him, but he moved it high above their heads.

144

"If I let you borrow this," he said softly, his attention again on her lips, "what will you give me in return?"

"What do you want?" She already knew, and her pulse began to race at the thought of actually kissing the handsome man in front of her.

"I think you know the answer to that."

Her stomach fluttered. "Maybe just a very brief one."

"Brief what?"

"Kiss."

"Kiss?" His tone lifted. "Miss Taylor, are you thinking of kissing me?"

She blinked rapidly, trying to make sense of what he was saying. "I thought that's what you wanted —"

"No," he said. "I was thinking of that pie you promised me."

"Pie?" She realized then she'd been staring at his mouth. She tore her gaze away and found herself looking into his eyes, which were filled with humor. "You big tease." She pushed at his chest, sending him stumbling back a couple of steps. "You're terrible!"

He bent over with laughter.

She couldn't keep from smiling. Even if she was embarrassed at being caught thinking about kissing him, she knew he'd been

145

thinking the same. Part of her was actually relieved that he hadn't coerced her into a kiss, although she had to admit there was a tiny part of her that was disappointed too. Her heart was still beating fast at the thought of what it would be like to feel his embrace and the touch of his lips.

He held out the book to her again.

This time she didn't reach for it.

His smile faded, and his eyes darkened with unmistakable desire.

She sucked in her breath.

"Here," he said. "I want you to read it. No strings attached."

Tentatively she reached for it, and when he let go, she found that she was almost trembling under his scrutiny. She hugged the book against her chest. "Thank you."

He nodded.

The schoolhouse door opened, and Michael poked his head inside. At the sight of Alex, he frowned. "What are you doing here?"

Alex shrugged. "What does it look like?"

All Tessa could think about was how Michael would have answered his brother's question if he'd arrived a minute earlier.

"I'm here to walk Tessa home from school," Alex said.

"I'll take care of that," Michael shot back.

146

"Didn't the kids tell you about the problem with the gears?"

"The gears were just fine when I went off duty this morning."

"I know for a fact that one of them is loose now."

Michael muttered something under his breath and then looked at Tessa. "I've got the roof patched up. Does anything else need fixing? I could come back tomorrow."

At the hopeful tone of his voice, Tessa couldn't say no. "Some of the students' benches are wobbly. I don't want to take up more of your time, but I'd be grateful if you could take a look at them."

"It would be my pleasure." He gave her a nod with the hint of a smile, and with a last frown at Alex, he stepped outside, leaving the door wide open behind him.

After Michael was gone, Alex shook his head. "Wobbly benches? That's a poor excuse to get alone with Michael."

She started stacking papers and books into a pile on her desk. "I'm not planning to spend any time alone with your brother."

"That's good," Alex said, standing directly behind her. He'd moved in close so that his breath tingled the nape of her neck. If she leaned back a fraction, she would have bumped his chest. "Don't you know you're

147

only allowed to spend time alone with me?"

"And who made that rule?" She fumbled at the papers, trying to act nonchalant, as though his presence didn't affect her so much.

"I did."

She had the urge to lean back against him. Would he wrap his arms around her, draw her close, and bury his face in her neck? The thought almost undid her.

Stop this instant, she scolded herself. *You have to be stronger. You have to resist temptation.*

Behind her, his breathing quickened.

She steadied herself and then ducked away from him. "Listen, Alex," she said while putting a safe distance between them. No matter how lighthearted he was, there was no denying that an attraction existed between them. She had to be honest and make sure he understood that she could never be anything more than friends with him.

"I don't want to mislead you," she started again.

He watched her with his infuriatingly lazy grin.

"I can't . . . We can't . . ."

"What are you trying to tell me, Miss Taylor? Have you been entertaining thoughts of

148

courting me? Is that why you told me your favorite book is *The Courtship of Miles Standish,* so that you could plant ideas in my mind about courting you?"

She laughed. "Yes, that's exactly what I was trying to do. How did you guess?"

"Well, you can put that thought far from your mind. I have no intention of courting you."

"Well," she repeated, "that's good, because I have no intention of being courted."

"There's no law against loaning you a book, is there? And last I checked, it was the polite thing for a man to make sure a lady made it home safely." His expression was so innocent, she wondered if perhaps she'd imagined the heat sizzling between them. Was she the one insinuating more than there really was, like she had with the kiss?

He waited for her to finish tidying up, all the while leaning against the doorframe and watching her. She was glad to step outside and let the cool October air soothe her overheated cheeks.

As they walked the short distance through town with Wolfie and Bear running ahead, the miners were pouring out of the hills, having ended their day shift. Others were waiting to descend the ladders and take their places. She nodded greetings to some of the men she'd gotten to know through her evening class. Their black soot-covered faces widened into smiles that warmed her heart.

"Why did you come to my evening class only once?" she asked Alex once they turned off Center Street and started down the grassy path toward her home. The shadows from the surrounding hills and the thick woods had lengthened, and the late afternoon sky was already turning darker.

"Do you miss me?" Alex teased.

"As a matter of fact, I do miss you. I'd miss any of my students if they decided not to come back."

"Michael doesn't want me to leave the light unattended," Alex said ambling next to her, carrying her bag of books and lesson plans. "Especially this time of year when the lake is moody. And I guess I have to agree with him. We need to stay on watch."

She nodded. She knew all too well the demands of the light. It had consumed her father's life for years before his arthritis had made it difficult for him to ascend the tower steps. Eventually the demands had fallen on her sister Caroline's shoulders. Everything had centered on making sure the lantern was lit every night. They'd never been able

150

to go anywhere, do anything, or have normal lives.

The lighthouse had taken much and had given little in return.

"Once commerce on the lakes halts for the winter, then I'll have more flexibility," Alex continued.

She knew too that they'd shut down the light for the winter, for there would be no need for it again until the spring. That was true of most of the lighthouses along the Great Lakes, including the one on Lake St. Clair where she'd lived. The long, lonely winter was just one more reason why the life of a lightkeeper was less than appealing.

"How many more weeks until you're free?" she asked.

He shrugged. "It all depends. Some years winter comes as early as November. Other years the ice doesn't form until December."

She calculated the number of days Alex would have to miss her evening class. Even if he was able to start attending in November, he'd be too far behind the others to catch up. "You'll have to miss too many classes."

"I guess I'm destined to remain ignorant," he said lightly.

"Of course it's not your destiny."

"I don't mind. I've always figured God

created me to do the kind of work that requires brawn, not brains."

"That's not true."

Alex stopped walking.

"Everyone deserves a chance at an education," she insisted, "including you."

He didn't say anything.

She turned to face him, not caring about the curious glances they were eliciting from the miners walking past them to their log homes.

"Having an education doesn't make me more or less of a man," he finally said, his shoulders stiff.

She didn't answer. The truth was, she did believe an education improved people, made them better citizens, better parents, and better workers. "How about if I tutor you?" she said without thinking.

His brow tilted up at the same time as his lips.

She could almost hear his playful accusation that she was trumping up an excuse to spend more time with him, which wasn't true — not in the least.

"I could give you the same lessons I'm giving my evening class," she hurried to explain. "Then when you rejoin the class in a few weeks, you won't be so far behind."

His grin widened, revealing his white teeth

in contrast to his tanned face. "How can I say no to your request to spend time with me alone?"

"I'm not requesting any time alone —"

"Just admit it. You like being with me."

"I'll admit to no such thing." He was an infuriating tease. But she liked it nonetheless. She bent and scratched the top of Wolfie's head, hoping to hide her pleasure.

He sauntered closer and lowered his voice. "So when can we get started? The sooner the better, right?"

She had absolutely no idea when she'd have time to meet with him. Her daylight hours were filled to overflowing. She was already teaching school six days a week, and her spelling class was meeting after school. She didn't know how she could squeeze one more thing into her schedule.

"I'm not sure . . ." Her voice trailed off.

"What about on Sunday afternoon?" he said. "I know it's the day of rest, but what if I promise that I won't make you work too hard?"

"Maybe . . ." She'd been attending church with the Rawlings family, who went to the Methodist Episcopal church. Out of the three churches in Eagle Harbor, it had the largest congregation, mostly Cornish people. She knew from Ingrid that Alex and

Michael joined the few Germans at the Lutheran church.

"And what if I promise to study on my own between times?" His expression contained an eagerness she couldn't resist.

"Maybe you should admit that *you* like being with *me*," she said.

"I can admit it. Easily."

She smiled at his answer. She wasn't sure that her suggestion to privately tutor him was the best idea, but suddenly she was looking forward to the coming Sunday more than she wanted to acknowledge, even to herself.

CHAPTER 10

"You're too young to think about kissing boys," Tessa admonished Josie in what she hoped was her kindest tone.

The young girl was taking off her special Sunday dress and had it halfway over her head. From behind the cotton muslin came a muffled giggle.

Tessa dug through the stack of pamphlets and books on the makeshift desk she'd organized in the attic room she shared with Josie. The desk was nothing more than a board balanced on two cut logs. But it sufficed, even if it was wobbly.

After finishing helping Nadine clean up the Sunday noon meal, Tessa still had several hours before meeting with Alex for tutoring. She knew her teacher's contract said she couldn't keep company with men, but she tried to silence the nagging voice of guilt by telling herself that the rule certainly didn't apply to tutoring.

They'd had to put off the tutoring last Sunday because a steamboat had hit a reef off the tip of Keweenaw Point and was torn to pieces by the powerful waves. Alex and Michael were busy all that afternoon rescuing passengers.

"Too late to tell me not to kiss boys," Josie said as she pulled the material away from her face and tossed the dress onto the double bed that took up the majority of the space. The girl's short-cropped bangs stood up from the static. Instead of chagrin, Josie's childlike expression radiated pride. "I've already kissed three boys."

"Three?" Tessa spun and planted her hands on her hips. "That's three too many."

Josie giggled again. "There's nothing wrong with kissing."

"Kissing only satisfies for a little while before you're ready to move on to more physical intimacy."

"What's so wrong with physical intimacy?" Josie asked while smoothing her chemise against her chest, rewarded only by hardly noticeable curves. "If we love each other, then why can't we express our love?"

"When you care for someone, you can express it in many ways," Tessa said. "But physical affection is designed to remain within the bounds of marriage."

156

Josie shook her head. "My mamm and dad sure didn't hold back or else I wouldn't have come along a few months after they got married."

For a moment, Tessa was speechless. What could she possibly say to counter the girl's bold proclamation? "You need to guard your reputation, Josie," she said, scrambling for something — anything — that might help. "It's a very precious thing, and once you lose it, it's very difficult to gain back." At least here in Eagle Harbor, Tessa had finally gone far enough away that her past wasn't trailing her anymore.

"Miss Taylor!" Pounding on the steps was quickly followed by banging on the attic door. It was one of the young boys of the household. "Gunnar Bjorklund is here for you."

Tessa's heart gave an extra thump of concern. Danger was inherent at lighthouses. As she clambered down the steps, all she could think about was that Gunnar had come to deliver bad news. But when she found him standing outside, his head hung low and his face flushed with guilt, her worry dissipated.

"Ingrid made me come," he said, hardly daring to meet her gaze.

Tessa hid a smile of amusement. "Is she

157

sick again?"

"No," Gunnar said, "but the birds are hitting the tower and she's scared."

Tessa glanced in the vicinity of the lighthouse. She couldn't see it from the Rawlingses' house, since it was situated farther out into the harbor. From what she could tell, the sky was clear with only a few high wispy clouds. It was a chilly Sunday, yet the sunshine and lack of wind added a mildness to the air.

Was this another of Ingrid's ploys to get her attention? "Are there really birds, Gunnar?"

Gunnar nodded. "Geese. And they've been hitting the tower windows."

Tessa hesitated. She'd heard of birds getting confused and smashing into lighthouse windows, sometimes knocking off lantern caps or even breaking windows. She wasn't sure, however, that she wanted to be the one dealing with the situation. "Where are your father and uncle? They'll be able to comfort Ingrid."

"Since the weather is fine, they've gone fishing."

Tessa crossed her arms and bit back a sigh.

Gunnar shifted. "It's all right, Miss Taylor. You don't have to come. I told Ingie we shouldn't bother you."

158

"You're not bothering me," she said, then reached out and touched his cheek. "You could never be a bother."

His flush crept higher.

"Let me gather a few things and I'll come with you." She didn't know what she could do to stop the geese from hitting the tower, but she couldn't leave Gunnar and Ingrid to fend for themselves. The least she could do was walk over and make sure they were both safe.

After donning her coat and hat, she hustled to keep up with Gunnar. Halfway through town she stopped abruptly at the sight of Percival Updegraff exiting one of the miner cabins in the process of buttoning his pants. His coat and vest were askew, his shirt only half tucked in.

"Miss Taylor," he said, glancing first at her and then at Gunnar. "Where are you heading? Certainly not out to the lighthouse again?"

"Again?" Actually it wasn't any of his business where she was going or why. He might be her boss, but he couldn't tell her where she could or could not go. He'd already visited her evening school twice over the past couple of weeks since he'd been back in Eagle Harbor. Both times he stood at the back of the room and watched every move

159

she made. Though she'd tried to ignore him, his scrutinizing made it difficult.

"I heard you visited the lighthouse while I was gone." He combed his mussed hair off his forehead.

"Is there anything you don't hear about, Mr. Updegraff?" she asked, clutching her coat against the afternoon chill that seeped through the wool.

"As chief clerk it's my job to know everything that happens in this town." He straightened his vest. "Lives depend upon me."

The cabin door behind him opened a crack to reveal a woman wrapped in a blanket. She held out a hat, Percival's round top derby. As she stretched out her arm, the blanket slipped away exposing a bare shoulder and daylight fell across her features. It was Hannah, the woman who helped the younger children at school.

"Hannah?" Tessa said and stepped forward, confused to see the woman wrapped in a blanket. "Is everything all right?"

At Tessa's voice, Hannah's eyes widened. Mortification poured across the young woman's pretty face. She cast her eyes downward. "Everything's just fine."

Percival took the hat from Hannah and placed it carefully on his silvery black hair.

160

"I was just stopping by to get an update from Hannah on her work at the schoolhouse."

Get an update from Hannah? Tessa almost snorted. On Sunday afternoon? Where were her husband and son? Were they out fishing too?

Hannah slipped backward and shoved the door closed. Tessa's heart sickened at the thought of what was really going on. With Percival's disheveled state and Hannah wearing nothing but a blanket, it was obvious he was doing more than getting an update from her.

Tessa was half tempted to open the door and confront her helper. Was she, a married woman, having an affair with Percival behind her husband's back? Why would she? And how dare she show up at school to help teach the children when she was living a life of sin?

Gunnar stood next to her, shifting from one foot to the next. What would the children think once they learned of Hannah's conduct? It was no wonder girls like Josie had so few morals, with the adults of the community having such low standards.

Tessa reached for Gunnar's arm to tug him along.

"I'd prefer that you abstain from visiting

161

the lighthouse, Miss Taylor," Percival said after her. "I won't allow female teachers to visit with single men."

"You needn't worry," she called over her shoulder. "Most of the men are out fishing. As you're apparently well aware." She sped along, having no trouble keeping up with Gunnar this time. With every step her anger fomented until it was a boiling cauldron. She despised men who held a double standard, rebuking women to remain above reproach when they felt they had every right to fornicate in plain view of others.

By the time Tessa reached the lighthouse, she was so incensed she had to take a deep breath before stepping inside. As she entered the front room, the sight of Ingrid's frightened little face peering out from under a huddled mass of blankets on the sofa left Tessa forgetting all about Percival.

"Miss Taylor!" Ingrid cried.

Tessa rushed to the girl, sat down next to her, and pulled her into her arms. Ingrid wrapped her bony arms around Tessa's neck and buried her face into Tessa's hair, which she was still wearing in loose ringlets to match her Sunday dress.

"Everything will be all right," Tessa promised, hugging Ingrid even closer.

Gunnar stood just inside the door, watching her hold Ingrid. Tessa smiled at him over Ingrid's head.

"Are the birds gone now?" she asked.

Ingrid nodded. "I think so."

Tessa listened and couldn't hear anything but the faint crashing of waves outside the lighthouse.

"How about if Gunnar and I go up and see?"

Ingrid scrambled off the sofa and reached for her crutch. "I'll go with you." Instead of fear, there was a sparkle of excitement in the girl's eyes.

Tessa sat back, both surprised and amused. If Ingrid had been afraid, she'd certainly gotten over it quickly.

"Come on, Miss Taylor," the girl called as she limped across the room.

She followed Gunnar and Ingrid past the kitchen which was as untidy as the front room, if not more so, with dirty dishes piled on the table, food stains and crumbs on the floor, and dried spills and grease coating the wood-burning stove.

They moved to the front hallway to a door that opened to a spiral staircase made of cast iron. She ignored the rising protest, the inner voice that urged her to flee. Instead she forced her feet to climb one step at a time. She soon realized that the staircase

163

served two functions. It led to the second floor of the house and also provided access to the lantern room.

The narrow steps twisted upward all the way to the hatch. Gunnar pushed up the metal hatch door and climbed through easily. Ingrid followed closely behind. Despite her deformed leg, the girl had learned to climb, even if it was slow and awkward for her.

Peering up through the hatch, Tessa couldn't contain a shudder. Hadn't she vowed that she wouldn't step foot into another lighthouse for as long as she lived? So what in heaven's name was she doing here?

Ingrid knelt at the opening. "What's the matter, Miss Taylor? Are you scared?"

Tessa hesitated. She very well couldn't tell Ingrid that she resented everything about lighthouses. To do so would crush Ingrid's spirit. She had to set aside the bitterness of the past and help Ingrid and Gunnar.

"It's all right," Ingrid said. "Once you're up, I'll hold your hand."

"That's good to know," Tessa said, then finished the climb with unsteady feet. "I'm sure I'll feel much safer with you right by my side."

"Watch for broken glass," Gunnar warned,

reaching out his hand as she straightened.

She found herself face-to-face with a fourth-order Fresnel lens at the center of the room. Its shiny glass prisms gleamed in the sunlight. The room was octagonal in shape with eight windows set in cast-iron frames. One of the glass panes had been smashed, and there in a pool of dark blood and shattered glass lay a goose, its eyes open, its neck broken at an odd angle, and its sleek body slashed in several places.

The wind coming off the lake blew through the broken window, sending chills up Tessa's arms and back. It pushed against her, telling her to retreat, to stay away lest she lose even more.

Ingrid's warm fingers slipped into hers. "Don't worry, Miss Taylor."

Gunnar popped open the latch on a half door and swung it open to reveal a wide gallery surrounded by a railing. He bent low and climbed outside.

Ingrid pulled Tessa onto the open catwalk too. As she stepped into the biting wind, she didn't bother to glance at the lake. She already knew what she'd see: the angry waves with their frothy caps seeking their next victim. The sound of their constant crashing was enough to endure without having to look at them too.

165

There on the iron galley lay several more dead geese. She guessed they'd hit the windows hard and broken their necks.

"There's nothing I can do right now with the window," Tessa said. "But we can at least clean up the mess."

Gunnar went to fetch a broom and a pail of water while Tessa gathered the geese on the catwalk. When he returned, he swept up the jagged glass and she scrubbed the blood from the floor. Finally they started back down with the geese.

"Gunnar, you run two geese over to Nadine to cook up," she said once she was standing outside in the yard behind the woodshed that formed the back of the house. "Ingrid and I will pluck this one and set it to roasting."

Gunnar obeyed without question. Tessa went to work clipping wings and plucking feathers. Though she hadn't dressed a fowl since starting her teacher training, the steps came back easily. After chopping off the head and feet and removing the entrails, she rinsed the blood away and placed the bird in the roasting pan Ingrid had located.

Once the goose was in the oven, she decided she may as well prepare something to go with it. So with Ingrid by her side, they peeled potatoes and carrots and set

166

those to boil on low heat. Ingrid's eagerness at helping warmed Tessa's heart. By the time Gunnar returned from delivering the geese, they were in the middle of making biscuits.

While the food baked and the kitchen filled with tantalizing aromas, she had the children go to work by helping her tidy up. They washed the dishes, swept the floor, and scrubbed until she finally stood back and crossed her arms, pleased at the progress. The children shared with her how their father and uncle wanted to win the Efficiency Star to help raise money for surgery on Ingrid's leg, but that they'd never once been able to earn the special badge along with its prize money.

"You're both old enough now to help your father and uncle with the cleaning," she said, walking with the children into the parlor with the broom and dust cloth. The Bjorklund brothers had been bachelors too long and it showed. "They both work hard to care for you," she added as they replaced the last of the rugs they'd shaken outside, "and one way you can thank them for all they do is to take some responsibility with the house. Maybe with your help they'll be able to keep everything in better condition and have a chance at winning the award."

Wiping an arm across her brow, Tessa plopped onto the sofa and patted the cushions on either side of her. "Now pick out a book and I'll read to you while we wait for the goose to finish roasting."

They dug through the crate that still sat next to the sofa, untouched except for the book Alex had loaned to her. Finally after much debate, the children settled upon *Treasure Island.* As they curled next to her, satisfaction wound through Tessa. Even if she'd spent the afternoon in a lighthouse, the one place in the world she most hated, and even though she was anxious to leave, she'd survived. And she knew she could do it again if she had to — for the children.

At the sight of the broken tower window, Alex picked up his pace. Michael was already running, a frown creasing his forehead. They still had two hours until darkness began to settle, but Alex couldn't keep disappointment from sifting through him. The broken window meant he'd have to put off his tutoring session with Tessa for the second week in a row in order to help Michael make repairs. Not that he cared all that much about the learning; it was just an excuse to spend time with her.

As he finished climbing the rocky ledge

that led up to the house, he tried to quell the frustration at his foiled plans. It was more important to help Michael, he told himself. In fact, their jobs, their livelihood, and the income that came from it — although not much — were more important than ever now. They had to keep saving so that hopefully by next year, Michael could take Ingrid to the surgeon.

It wasn't until just this past summer, when a new doctor had arrived in Eagle Harbor, Dr. Lewis, that they learned surgery was an option. Dr. Lewis took one look at Ingrid's leg and then gave them the name and address of a surgeon in Detroit.

Now they needed to save the money for the passage south and the surgery. But saving was going much slower than they'd anticipated. Alex needed Wolfie to have a large litter in the spring. Many residents on the peninsula relied upon dogsleds for transportation during the winter. His puppies were in high demand. The problem was that most of the men couldn't pay what they were worth, and he didn't have the heart to make them sacrifice any more than they had to.

He reached a hand down to pat Wolfie's head as the dog trotted alongside him. He'd left both dogs at the house to keep watch

169

over the children. But of course the minute their mackinac docked, both dogs were at the wharf greeting him with lolling tongues and wagging tails.

"What happened to the window, young lass?" he asked, crossing the yard toward the back door. "Did we get in the way of migrating birds again?"

He yanked open the door that led through the woodshed, well stocked with enough chopped wood to see them through the winter, and was surprised at the mouth-watering aroma that greeted him. His surprise turned to shock when he stepped into the kitchen. Not only was the room spotless, but a pan of golden biscuits was cooling on the sideboard. A pot was cooking on the range, and a heavenly scent emanated from the oven.

He could only stare for an endless moment. Then the sound of a cheerful voice from the parlor drew him in farther. He crossed the kitchen and peeked through the door. His heart stopped at the sight of Ingrid and Gunnar snuggled up to Tessa on the sofa.

She was reading with a delightful animation that would have entertained even the most hard-hearted. Not only that, but she was breathtakingly beautiful with her hair

170

hanging down in messy curls around her face. She usually wore her hair pulled back in a more severe fashion, as was befitting for a teacher, but the loose waves softened her expression.

He leaned against the doorframe, content to watch without their being aware of his presence. He couldn't deny that from the moment he'd seen her walk off the steamer, he'd been smitten with her. And every time he saw her, he liked her even more.

Gunnar was the first to notice him. "Hi, Uncle Alex."

At the boy's greeting, Tessa came to an abrupt halt in her storytelling. Her startled gaze flew to him.

"Hey there, young fella." He smiled at his nephew, next at Ingrid, then glued his attention back on Tessa.

Tessa extricated herself from the children and stood.

"Hi, beautiful. I see you're here early for our tutoring." He couldn't take his eyes from her. "You couldn't wait to be with me, could you?"

She tossed her wavy hair off her shoulder and gave him a withering glare. "Don't flatter yourself, pretty boy."

He grinned at her response. "Just admit

171

it. You were dying to be with me this afternoon."

"Actually, in the process of cleaning up bloody geese with broken necks, I'd completely forgotten."

He pushed away from the door and leveled a look at Gunnar. "Don't tell me you invited Miss Taylor over to do your dirty work."

The boy shook his head. "No, sir. I didn't mean for her to do it." When his attention slid to Ingrid, Alex knew exactly what had happened. His niece had devised another excuse to make Tessa believe she was needed and then had convinced Gunnar to call on Tessa again. Of course, Gunnar could never say no to Ingrid, and Ingrid knew it all too well.

"Miss Taylor let me help her peel potatoes and carrots and make biscuits," Ingrid said, sitting forward, her petite face alight with happiness. "And then we cleaned."

He had to push down that painful pinch again, the one that told him Ingrid needed a woman's influence. "I thought I smelled something tasty when I walked in."

"That's the goose," Ingrid continued. "Miss Taylor is roasting one for dinner."

Alex folded his arms across his chest. What would it be like to come home from

172

fishing every day to find not only a tantalizing woman in his house but tantalizing food too?

"Now that you're here," she said, "I'll head back home, gather the lesson plans, and meet you at the schoolhouse."

"I regret to say I'll have to cancel our session this afternoon again. Michael will need my help repairing the window before nightfall." Did relief flit through her eyes? Was she glad she didn't have to spend time with him? "Don't be too relieved, Miss Taylor. I'll be sure to make up for it next week. I'll expect your attention all afternoon."

He looked down the hallway that led to the staircase. He guessed Michael had already come in through the front door, ascended the tower, and was probably hard at work. He needed to go up and lend his brother a hand. But a few minutes' delay with Tessa wouldn't hurt, would it?

"Ingrid, Gunnar, go see if your father needs anything. Tell him I'll be up soon to help him with the window."

The two hurried to obey, Ingrid limping behind Gunnar. Tessa moved to the crate and tucked the book inside. While her back was turned, he strode over to her in three long steps.

When she straightened, he left her no

173

choice but to bump into him. And of course he *had* to take hold of her arm and keep her from wobbling. At the contact, she sucked in a breath. The air between them was charged. For a long moment he felt an almost irresistible urge to pull her into his arms.

She stared at his fingers clasping her. "I . . . I need to go," she whispered.

"You *can't* leave yet." He didn't care that his voice was laced with desperation. "Please, Miss Taylor, join us for dinner."

Slowly she pried her arm loose. "I've already overstayed my welcome."

He wanted to tell her that she could never overstay her welcome, that he'd never get enough of her. But there was something skittish about her, and he sensed he'd only push her away all the more if he voiced his desire.

Halfway through the kitchen she turned and offered him a smile. "I hope you don't mind that I gave Nadine a couple of the dead geese."

"Of course not."

"I couldn't resist," she said, her voice turning light. "You know how much I like her giblets. Now she'll have plenty of feet and beaks and heaven knows what else to make the delicacy."

Alex chuckled, relief loosening his taut muscles. With a last sassy smile, Tessa stepped through the woodshed to the back door. He knew at that moment he was falling helplessly in love with Tessa Taylor.

CHAPTER 11

Tessa rearranged the books on her desk for the hundredth time since she'd arrived at the schoolhouse, and she glanced at the door again.

The first day of November had brought a fresh dusting of snow that froze and covered the mud. The thermometer outside the school read twenty-four degrees, so that even after getting the stove roaring, the room was still cold enough that she could see the white cloud of her breath.

She'd come early because she had to confront Hannah about her conduct with Percival. She didn't want to. But she had no choice, not when impressionable young girls like Josie might hear of the situation — if she hadn't already.

The door opened, and Tessa took a deep breath of the woodsmoke that hung heavy in the air before turning to face her helper. Instead of Hannah, there stood Michael

Bjorklund. He stomped the snow from his boots and unwound a knitted scarf from his neck.

"Good morning." He looked around, his face relaxing at the sight of the deserted classroom.

"Why, Michael," she said, "what brings you out this morning?" Had he decided to walk the children to school instead of Alex? She glanced behind him, expecting to see Ingrid and Gunnar following him inside.

"It's just me," he said quickly, stepping farther into the room.

Outside, the sun had risen, though it remained hidden behind a thick layer of dark-gray clouds. He'd obviously already turned off the Fresnel lens, but surely he had other morning duties that demanded his attention, such as washing the glass, trimming the wick, replacing the oil, and all the other preparations to get the lantern ready for the next evening.

"Did you get the window repaired?" she asked, thinking back on the incident yesterday, unable to keep her mind from drifting to the moment Alex had arrived home. Every time she was with him, there was a spark between them that never failed to light a fire in her. She'd resolved that she had to keep her distance from the man.

"We have canvas nailed over the opening," Michael said. "Hopefully we can get a piece of glass to put in before it's too late."

She nodded. "I don't suppose a tender crew will come this late in the season?"

He shook his head. "Probably not."

"It's too bad the broken window is on the north side. I hope it won't interfere too much with the beam from the perspective of the bay."

"True." He cocked his head and studied her. "How is it that you know so much about lighthouses?"

She wished she knew nothing about them, yet she held back her rude comment. "My dad was a keeper. I spent my whole life in lighthouses."

"Where's your father a wickie now?" he asked, using the nickname that many people called lightkeepers because of the work they did trimming the wicks.

"He drowned in a boating accident."

"I'm sorry," Michael said. "I shouldn't have asked —"

"I don't mind," she replied. It had been over five years ago and it wasn't as painful to talk about anymore. "He was rowing our doctor back to Detroit when a storm whipped up the waves and capsized his boat. Both he and the doctor were swallowed up by the lake within a few minutes. My siblings and I had to watch helplessly from the shore. There was nothing we could do to save them."

"That must have been awful," he said softly.

"It was." She was struck by the similarity of the two brothers with each one having blond hair and blue eyes, and yet they were distinct in their build: Alex's bulky muscles in contrast to Michael's thinner, more angular lines. Still, there was no doubt that Michael was a handsome man.

He shifted his feet, and an awkward silence settled between them. She was tempted to fill it with her usual teasing chatter the way she did with Alex. But after seeing the differences between the bothers' personalities, she realized she needed to be patient with Michael. He was more deliberate and serious and would share his thoughts in his own timing.

He brought his hands out from behind his back, and for the first time she noticed that he'd been carrying something. He held out a pair of sleek-looking snowshoes. "I want you to have these."

In the lantern light, the hardwood gleamed. The rawhide lacings were clean and new and tight. They appeared to be the

179

right size for her feet.

"They're beautiful," she said.

"I made them." A shadow of sadness fell over his features.

Somehow she sensed that the snowshoes held value for him. "I couldn't possibly take them."

"I don't need them anymore." He held the snowshoes out. "They're just hanging in the shed collecting dust."

Who had he made them for? His wife? The question was on the tip of her tongue, but she bit it back.

"Besides, since the geese are all in a hurry to fly south, I'm sure we'll have several inches of snow by dawn tomorrow."

"Several inches?"

He nodded at the snowshoes. "You'll need these to get around."

"They're much too nice for me to accept as a gift."

He placed them on the bench closest to the door. "I'd like you to have them." Something in his tone told her he wouldn't take no for an answer.

"Thank you," she said quietly. If she accepted the gift, would he think there was more between them than friendship? She certainly didn't want to lead him to believe there was. "If I haven't told you yet, I want you to know how much I appreciate your friendship."

His smile faltered, and he looked as if he wanted to say more when the door opened again. This time a young woman bustled in with her son trailing behind. It was Hannah. At the sight of Michael, the woman stopped short. And when her gaze swung to Tessa, she visibly blanched and lowered her eyes.

"I best be going," Michael said, flushing again, no doubt embarrassed to have been caught talking with her alone.

Tessa could barely manage a good-bye to Michael, for her mind was preoccupied by the remembrance of the blanket sliding off Hannah's bare shoulder and her face ashen with guilt. After the door closed behind Michael, Tessa shifted her attention to Hannah's young son, Jeremiah, who was in the process of taking off his coat.

"Good morning, Hannah," Tessa said. "And good morning, Jeremiah. How would you like to be in charge of bringing in some extra firewood this morning? I have a feeling we're in for a very cold day."

The boy, about Gunnar's age, nodded and pulled back on his coat. Once he'd gone outside, Tessa faced Hannah squarely.

Before she could speak, Hannah's lips

began trembling. "Please," she whispered hoarsely, dropping her chin and staring at the floor. "Please don't say anything to my son. He doesn't know."

"I won't," Tessa reassured. "But, Hannah, I think we both know that your conduct is completely inappropriate. As a teacher's helper, you're supposed to model godly behavior for our young charges."

"I know . . ." The anguished admission was barely a whisper.

Tessa wanted to be angry, but she couldn't muster any emotion but pity. "I don't think you should help anymore, do you?"

Hannah's head shot up, and a new desperation rippled over her pretty features. "I can't stop. Mr. Updegraff warned me I had to continue working at the school."

Tessa frowned. "Why does he care?"

"He told me I have to report to him everything you're doing."

Percival Updegraff was spying on her? And Hannah was helping him? First astonishment, then anger rose within her. "I'm sorry, Hannah. I can't allow you in my classroom any longer."

"Please don't make me stop." She reached for Tessa's hands. Cold fingers gripped Tessa's. "If I don't do what he says, he'll fire my husband."

The agony in Hannah's eyes stopped Tessa's tirade. Something deeper was happening in this community. She'd known Percival was controlling, but surely he couldn't have quite so much sway. "So he makes you come to the schoolhouse every day?"

She nodded. "But I like helping the kiddies. I really do."

"What else does he make you do?" Tessa asked hesitantly, not sure if she wanted to know the answer.

Hannah let go of Tessa's hands and then twisted her skirt. The embarrassment on her face and the silence spoke more than any words could.

Revulsion swirled in the pit of Tessa's stomach. She nudged the closest bench to straighten it and fidgeted with the bench across from it. "Does he force himself on you?"

For a long moment Hannah didn't say anything. The only sound was the popping of the wood in the stove. Finally she said, "If I don't do what he wants, he'll not only fire my husband but he'll make sure Mr. Nance never gets another mining job."

Tessa swallowed hard, pushing down the rising indignation. "I'm sure your husband can find another job somewhere else."

Hannah shook her head. "Not in any mine around here. Most of them are struggling with production. They aren't hiring on anyone new."

"Couldn't he do something besides mining?"

"That's all he's ever done. It's the only thing he knows how to do."

This was exactly why the miners of Eagle Harbor needed an education. They were stuck in their jobs and poverty with no way out, and their ignorance was making them captive to men like Percival Updegraff.

"Surely your husband won't stand for Percival using you like this." If Mr. Nance loved his wife, how could he allow Percival to take advantage of her in such a perverse way?

"I'm not sure if he knows yet," she whispered. "Even if he did, there's nothing he can do. The last man who told Mr. Updegraff to keep his hands off his wife ended up dead in shaft number three."

"Percival murdered someone?"

"The man was crushed by falling rock. There's no way to prove that Mr. Updegraff was involved, but everyone knows what happened. Mr. Updegraff made sure of that."

Tessa stifled a shudder. Apparently Mr. Updegraff was more dangerous than she'd realized.

Through the frosted window they could see Hannah's son returning to the schoolhouse, his arms loaded with firewood.

"Please don't breathe a word of this to anyone, especially Jeremiah," she begged again.

"I promise I won't."

"You can't talk about it with anyone or Mr. Updegraff will find out."

"Don't worry. I'll keep it to myself." Tessa reached for Hannah and drew her into a hug before the woman could protest. "And forget I ever said anything about leaving your job. You have it as long as you need it."

Hannah sagged against her. A sob escaped before the woman could prevent it.

Tessa squeezed her hard. "We'll find a way out of this. I promise."

As the door opened, Hannah wrenched free, wiped at her cheeks, and then plastered a smile on her face. Tessa could see now that the smile was hollow, that the woman was slowly dying on the inside.

Tessa's chest expanded with a painful lurch. She'd been too quick to judge Hannah, just as so many people had been quick to judge her. Hannah was already punishing herself enough, and she didn't need anyone else adding to her misery.

185

CHAPTER 12

Alex blew bubbles into two-year-old Jimmy Rawlings's belly. The boy's burst of laughter warmed his heart. He reached for four-year-old Johnny Rawlings standing behind him on the sofa and grabbed him into a headlock, gently flipping him onto the sofa. Then Alex bent and blew bubbles into Johnny's belly, earning a chorus of giggles from him too.

"Time to get started with our tutoring session, Mr. Bjorklund," Tessa said, standing above him, her fists bunched on her hips.

"I told you it wasn't a good idea to meet here," he said as he tickled Jimmy. The boy darted to the other side of the front room, where the older boys were sprawled on the floor engaged in a game of marbles. Jimmy skidded into their game and sent the marbles rolling in every direction, earning a chorus of Cornish curses from his brothers.

Tessa cringed and glanced around the

crowded room in dismay. "Maybe we should go back to plan A and sit at the kitchen table." The hesitancy in her voice told him that she knew she couldn't very well order Nadine to move her sewing project off the kitchen table so that she could tutor Alex, not when Nadine already had everything laid out for lining trousers for winter.

"We could return to plan double A and meet at the school," he said. That was the original place she'd chosen, but after several thwarted tutoring sessions, she'd changed her mind. "We'll have plenty of quiet there. And no interruptions." He winked at her.

"That's exactly why we're *not* meeting at the schoolhouse," she said, cocking her head in that sassy way of hers.

He grinned. He'd determined over the past week to make more steps in winning her affection. Lately it had become increasingly clear that Michael was interested in her. What other explanation could there be for why he had given Tessa the snowshoes he'd lovingly crafted for his wife? Of course, Rachel had died before she'd been able to use them. Nevertheless, Michael had refused to part with them. Then he'd met Tessa . . .

And what other explanation could there be for why Michael continued to look for excuses to fix things at the schoolhouse? Just this past week he'd gone over to caulk around the windows so the cold north wind wouldn't blow into the building so easily.

Alex had decided he couldn't sit back and do nothing while Tessa fell in love with kind, sweet, sensitive Michael. He had to make her fall in love with him first. The problem was he didn't know how to win her. What could an unschooled man like him do to woo a young educated woman like Tessa? He couldn't settle for doing the ordinary things because she wasn't an ordinary woman. Somehow he had to find a way to sweep her off her feet and make her fall head over heels in love with him.

Jimmy jumped onto his back. At the same time Johnny came rushing to his front, attempting to tackle him. Alex roared and stood up, imitating a huge black bear. Both boys clung to him and laughed. He took several lumbering steps forward before he pretended they were bringing him down. Slowly, so that he didn't hurt them, he crumpled to the ground, until both boys were sitting on his chest and staring at him triumphantly.

Tessa peered down at him. She was trying unsuccessfully to hold back a smile. Suddenly all he could think about was how someday he wanted to have children with her. He wanted to have their little ones crawling over him and calling him Daddy.

He hadn't allowed himself to think about having a family of his own in so long that the thought caught him off guard. He'd always been content with Gunnar and Ingrid. He'd helped raise them since they were infants. But what would it be like to have his own children, his own home?

The thought sent such a sharp sense of longing through him that his breath hitched and his muscles tensed with the need to have her. Above him, as though sensing his thoughts, Tessa's half smile faded and she averted her eyes.

He rolled himself to a sitting position and silently berated himself for his intensity again. He had to stop scaring her. He was scaring himself too. He couldn't second-guess his decision to live with Michael and Gunnar and Ingrid. It had been the right thing to do, the thing his dad would have done.

His dad had lived a life of sacrifice. He'd not only sacrificed for his family to build a new life in America, but he'd also literally given the shirt off his back to strangers on more than one occasion. Alex couldn't think of a better man than his dad. Although he

189

respected the good Finnish man his mom had married after Dad's passing, no one could ever live up to the man his dad had been. Even though Alex knew he'd never be as loyal and strong as his dad, he'd vowed to try to be at least half the man.

Alex stood and shook his head, attempting to clear his mind. It wasn't that he was thinking of leaving Michael and the children. He wouldn't ever consider doing that, not when they still needed him. But certainly Tessa could join his life at the lighthouse with his family, couldn't she? It was the same question he'd asked himself before, one that kept recurring.

She leafed through a stack of papers and books she'd brought down when he'd arrived.

"Let's go," he said, not exactly sure where he would take her. "We'll find someplace else to do the lessons."

She spun and narrowed her eyes at him. "Someplace where we're not alone?"

He looked out the window to the low clouds and the muddy snow. After several inches of snow and arctic temperatures earlier in the week, the fickle November temperatures had risen above freezing and had melted most of the snow into mud puddles.

"How about if we take a walk? Maybe we'll find a place along the way."

She peered outside too, and her expression turned skeptical. Finally she nodded. Within a few minutes they were bundled up and outside. A fine mist hung in the damp air. Their boots squelched in the long wet grass, fallen leaves, and patches of remaining snow.

"I admire your commitment to my education," he said as they meandered nowhere in particular.

"I only wish you were as committed to it as I am."

He chuckled. "I think you're attempting to reform a lost cause."

She shoved his arm playfully. "No one's a lost cause. You have just as much potential as anyone else."

"You're on a mission here to change as many of us as possible, aren't you?" While he was jesting with her, he couldn't hold at bay the thought that perhaps she'd never be satisfied with an uneducated man like him.

"The longer I'm here, the more I see that needs changing." She glanced in the direction of Percival's big house towering above all the others.

He was sure she was thinking about Percival's abusive power, just as he'd done many

191

times over the past couple of years since Percival had taken over as chief clerk. Thankfully he and Michael could act independently without worrying about what Percival would do to them. But the same couldn't be said of anyone working for the Cole Mine. If any of the miners displeased Percival or refused to do what he wanted, the ramifications were swift and unpleasant. Of course, Percival bought the favor of a select few men, like Mr. Rawlings, who got the bigger homes and better pay.

As they walked, she told him about Percival's control over Hannah and her desire to do something to help the poor woman. And then he shared the lesson he'd learned the hard way with the last Cole Mine mechanic. He'd gone to Percival's office and had defended the family against untrue accusations that Percival was leveling. The next day the entire family had been thrown out of their home with only the few possessions they owned, jobless and penniless. Alex had used his meager savings to help them buy passage on a steamer headed to Detroit, along with enough cash to hold them over until they could find new employment.

After that, Alex had taken more care with how he helped the people in the community. He learned that if he or Michael interfered,

192

Percival only made things worse for the miner and his family.

"I want to give everyone the ability to move out of here and get better jobs if they want to," she said as they passed several dingy cabins.

"And who says they need better jobs? There's nothing wrong with being a miner."

"It's menial labor."

Though her words were spoken matter-of-factly, without derision, he couldn't keep from feeling a sting of embarrassment. His work was menial too. In many ways he was much like the miners, accustomed to working hard with his hands. If she thought the miners were ignorant and needed improving, what did she think of him?

"It's much more complicated than it looks," he said in defense of himself as much as the miners.

"There are many other jobs which aren't nearly as dangerous or demanding."

With a nod, he veered toward the east, knowing exactly where he wanted to take her. "You may not believe this, but some people actually like doing 'menial labor.' "

"You're right. I don't believe it." She followed alongside him as he steered her down a path that led away from town and toward the wooded hills. "I don't think people willingly choose mine work or other heavy labor. Rather, they fall into it because that's all they know how to do."

He mulled over her statement. Had he fallen into his line of work as a tender crew member because of his strength? Would he have chosen to deliver supplies to lighthouses if he'd had the opportunity to do something else? Like make more of a business out of breeding his elkhounds?

Perhaps there was some truth to what Tessa was saying. Even so, not everyone needed an education in order to have a fulfilling job. Many of the miners loved what they did and wouldn't change it even if they could.

"Why are we at the mine?" she asked when he stopped at the base of a bluff. Ahead was the stamp mill and a connecting side shack that housed a steam engine and boilers used to operate the engine. Once the miners removed the rock to the surface, wooden chutes transported the rock down the bluff to the stamp mill where it was crushed and washed, separating out the pieces of copper. From there the copper was placed in barrels and hauled by wagon to the harbor to be loaded onto steamers for shipment to ports in Detroit, Chicago, and Cleveland.

On a Sunday afternoon, the normal grinding from the stamp and hissing from the boilers were replaced with an eerie stillness. The tall stone smokestack next to the boiler room was void of the usual streak of gray that rose from it.

"Should we be here?" she asked, studying the huge mounds of crushed rock filling the land that had at one time been untouched and populated by a thick forest of evergreens.

"Come on," he said and reached for her hand. He tugged her along a path that led uphill. When he reached the top, a thump within the hoist building stopped him. The log shack housed the machine that was responsible for bringing up all the rock and material from the depths of the mine. He considered taking Tessa inside to show her the details of the machine and explain how the process worked, but instead he directed her toward shaft house number two.

The door was unlocked as he knew it would be. He stepped inside and she behind him, her eyes bright with curiosity. At the center of the building was the shaft hole where the miners descended into the bowels of the hill. The tip of a ladder rose from the dark cavern.

"Are we going down?" she asked, creeping

toward the gaping opening. The tap-tap of dripping water greeted them, along with cold damp air wafting up from the underground caverns. No matter the temperature at the surface, the underground chambers were always forty-five degrees whether in the dead of winter or on the hottest day in summer.

He hadn't released her hand and used the opportunity to tighten his hold. "Maybe some time we can go down, but we're not equipped for it today, unless of course you want me to tie up your skirt."

"Maybe it would help if I took it off altogether," she retorted.

He grinned. "Let's wait for that until after we're married."

The shaft house was windowless, the only light coming from the open doorway, but still he could see a blush creep into her cheeks and remorse crowd out the sparkle in her eyes. She tried slipping her hand out of his, but he wouldn't let her.

Instead he tugged her down to the edge of the shaft until they were both sitting with their legs dangling over the long steep drop that was at least a hundred fathoms. He wouldn't tell her, but he'd never allow her to climb down the ladder, especially this time of year when the damp ladders turned icy or sometimes broke.

There were usually several falls every winter that either killed or severely maimed miners. Even more dangerous were the accidents from broken cables that hoisted the large buckets of rock upward. The loose rocks cascaded down and fell onto unsuspecting miners climbing up from below. But he knew he couldn't tell her any of that now or he'd only prove her point that the miners needed a way out of their dangerous occupation.

Tessa sidled close to him, her shoulder brushing him. He was tempted to slip his arm around her waist and draw her even closer, but he resisted.

For a while he explained how the mining operations worked, how the men would sink the shaft twelve fathoms and then blast a drift that was four feet wide and six high along a vein of copper. They would timber up the drift and lay track for a wagon or cart that could bring rock to the shaft to be raised to the surface.

"I concede your point," she said. "Mining is more complicated than I realized."

"The men may not be book smart like you," he said, "but the Cornish are experienced in deep-mine operations. They know drilling techniques that cut the copper into

197

manageable-size pieces. They're experts in blasting. And they've mastered the ability of removing the ore to the surface from hundreds of feet below."

"Even if they are experts in copper mining," she said, "I still think more of them deserve the chance to do something better with their lives."

"Maybe this is the best it gets for them." He made the mistake of shifting so that his mouth was near her head. Wisps of her dark hair curled around the knitted wool hat she wore. The strands tickled his lips. He couldn't stop himself from leaning in, burying his nose in her hair and breathing in her enticing scent — one he couldn't name but that reminded him of spices his mother had used when she baked *Krumkake.*

Before he knew what he was doing, he'd slipped his arm around her waist and pulled her closer. He pressed his lips against her loose hair. She gave a soft gasp that only stirred his blood, and he relished the softness of her body leaning into him.

He let his mouth linger against her hair, not wanting to pull away and yet he knew he should.

"Alex?" she whispered, her tone wavering with both invitation and hesitancy.

He angled so that his lips brushed against

her cheek. "What, beautiful?" Without giving her the chance to answer, he pressed a kiss against the hollow part of her ear.

This time her intake was sharp and she trembled against him. "Have you ever been down in the mine?"

He smiled at her attempt to distract him. "Of course. Lots of times." His whisper fanned against her neck just below her ear.

"What's it like?" she asked, tilting her head and giving him access to more of her neck.

"Dark and damp." His lips made contact with the smooth skin of her throat, and at his touch she released a stifled moan.

"Miss Taylor?" A surprised voice came from the doorway.

Tessa jumped. Her rapid motion sent a spray of gravel over the edge of the shaft. Alex grabbed her arm to steady her and keep her from toppling down.

Shadows fell across them, blocking the light coming in through the door. "Is that you, Miss Taylor?" the voice asked again.

"Josie?" Tessa scrambled away from him, tripping over her skirt in her haste to rise to her feet. "What are you doing here?"

Alex swiveled to see Josie Rawlings next to Robert Hall. Their faces were flushed, their hair and clothes askew. Had Josie and

199

Robert Hall been in the hoist house? Was that the noise he'd heard? He narrowed his eyes on Robert, who lowered his gaze to his shoes but not before Alex caught sight of the guilt that told him all he needed to know. The boy had been doing a lot more than kissing Josie.

He'd heard rumors that the young people came up to the deserted mine buildings to find privacy, which was hard to come by in their crowded homes. Apparently the rumors were true.

Tessa smoothed down her skirt and brushed back her hair. The surprise on Josie's face transformed into a sly smile. "I think we were both up here for the same reason, Miss Taylor." She reached for Robbie and wound her arm around him, pressing against the boy's body in an all too intimate way.

"Josie!" Tessa's eyes widened.

Josie giggled. "We're just having a little fun. Aren't we, Robbie?"

Robbie didn't dare lift his head. Alex was tempted to cross to the boy and rough him up a bit so that he wouldn't lay another finger on Josie Rawlings for as long as he lived.

"Josie," Tessa said sternly, "you absolutely shouldn't be up here alone with Robbie.

You know what I told you about keeping proper boundaries with boys."

"If you can be alone up here with Alex, why can't I be alone with Robbie?"

"*Mr. Bjorklund* was showing me how the mine works. That's all."

"I suppose that's why he was kissing you."

"He wasn't kissing me."

"You looked awfully cozy to me," Josie insisted with an impish smile.

Tessa shook her head. Panic flitted through her eyes. She glanced at him, silently imploring him to speak up and help her explain the situation.

He shrugged and slowly pushed himself to his feet. He didn't understand why she was so embarrassed about being together with him. He supposed she wanted to set the right example for a girl like Josie. But surely Josie could see that he and Tessa were older, more mature, and ready for a relationship — at least he was ready for one.

"Don't worry, Miss Taylor," Josie said, reaching up to kiss Robbie's cheek. "I promise I won't tell anyone you were up here, if you promise not to say anything to my mamm. She thinks I'm visiting with Robbie's family."

"There's nothing for you to tell anyone," Tessa said, her expression darker than Alex

201

had ever seen it.

"Exactly," the girl quipped lightly. "And there's nothing for you to tell anyone about me and Robbie."

Tessa gave an exasperated sigh and then stalked across the shaft house and brushed past Josie. For a moment, Alex could only watch her in confusion as she stomped away down the hill. He needed to go after her and discover why she was so upset, but before he moved, he crossed his arms and stared hard at Josie and Robert. "As much as I like Miss Taylor, and as much as I try to steal a kiss or two from her every now and then, I respect her too much to do anything that is reserved for marriage."

Robbie's thin pimply face turned red, but Josie only smiled. "Well, since we know we're gonna get married, then that's all that matters."

Alex studied the girl's earnest face. "If a man really loves you, he'll show it to you by controlling his selfish urges and cherishing your purity." He leveled a look at Robbie. "Now head back to town and don't come up here again."

Under his breath, Robbie mumbled, "Yes, sir."

But Josie's smile turned brittle. "I suppose you're gonna treat me like I'm a baby too."

Hadn't she been ten years old last week? Wasn't she a bit young to think about marriage? "You're not a baby, Josie, but I think you should give yourself a few more years to grow up."

He didn't wait for her reaction. He strode past them out of the shaft house. Tessa was already far down the hill, and he had to run to catch up with her.

"Tessa," he called, slipping and sliding on the wet gravel in his haste.

She didn't slow down to wait for him. If anything she picked up her pace. She was almost at the bottom of the hill by the time he reached her.

"What's wrong, beautiful?" he asked.

"Just go home." Her countenance was as stormy as the winter sea. "And leave me alone."

Her walk across the rocky path past the stamp mill was choppy, but she didn't slacken her pace. He'd obviously done something to offend her. "Tell me what I did wrong so that I can plead for forgiveness."

She stopped abruptly and turned to face him, unleashing her wrath. "I told you I didn't want to be alone with you, that we needed to stay someplace public."

"The mine is public."

"Not today."

"We weren't alone. Josie and Robert Hall were there too." His attempt at humor was met with a scowl that made her features even prettier than usual.

"If you're not going to be serious, then I don't want to talk with you." She began to stalk away.

His start of a smile fell flat and he bolted after her. "Wait." He grasped her arm. "Tell me what I'm missing here. Why are you upset at me?"

He gave her no choice but to stop. From the stiffness in her shoulders he half expected her to try to jerk away from him. But after a moment, she sagged and her chin dropped. Resignation rushed in to replace her defiance. "I'm doing my best to protect my reputation here in Eagle Harbor. I don't want anyone to think of me as a loose woman."

"No one would ever think that. Not in a million years."

She focused on the crushed stones at her feet. "They might if I'm not more careful, or if Josie tells them that she saw us up at the mine together."

"She won't. But even if she did, there's

nothing wrong with us taking a walk together."

"As this community's teacher, I need to be above reproach. I shouldn't be pairing off with any men."

"I'm technically your student since you've offered to tutor me." He offered her a grin in his effort to lighten the moment, yet a part of him knew that after today he wouldn't pursue the tutoring any further, even if that meant losing out on spending time with her. He couldn't let her see just how ignorant he really was. He didn't want to chance her thinking any less of him because of it.

The uncertainty on Tessa's face made her appear younger and vulnerable. He wanted to pull her into his arms and comfort her. But he sensed that if he so much as tried to hold her, the storm would return with greater fury.

"I have to guard my reputation carefully, Alex," she said. "And if you care at all about me — as a friend — then you'll help me stay above reproach."

Her emphasis on the word *friend* disquieted him, but now wasn't the time to press her about it.

At last she looked him in the eye, and the wariness and pain in her expression stabbed his heart. He didn't know what had happened to put such pain there, but he could do nothing less than make sure he wasn't the one to cause her any more turmoil.

CHAPTER 13

December descended with a flurry of cold and snow. Tessa dismissed school on the Wednesday night before Christmas with a ten-day vacation to correspond with the mine closure. Church services were held on Christmas Eve, and afterward she joined others in the community who went from house to house singing Christmas carols in an attempt to combat the common practice among many Cornish to walk around singing for ale.

The Saturday evening after the new year she invited the students from the nearby Central Mine School to compete in a spelling bee. She'd spent several hours in preparation with the students over their vacation, and now as the last few students remained standing, she was pleased that Henry Benney was one of them. His family sat in the second row, watching him with pride. Tessa's heart warmed with satisfaction at the thought of just how much progress not only Henry had made in his schooling, but also Mr. Benney. At the first evening class he'd only been able to cipher and read a little, but now he was reading whole books as fast as Tessa could loan them to him.

Behind the Benneys sat Samuel Updegraff. At the delight filling Samuel's pudgy round face, Tessa knew she'd done the right thing to invite him. He watched each contestant with rapt attention. He clapped enthusiastically no matter how the child did. And he laughed with delight when one of the children spelled a word correctly.

He still gave her a hard time when she bargained with him at the store, but she didn't take it personally. Underneath his worrisome exterior, Samuel was like a child trapped in a man's body. He deserved as much of her kindness and consideration as any one of her students, even if he was Percival's brother.

Her gaze strayed to Hannah and Jeremiah sitting in a back corner. She'd overheard a rumor that Mr. Nance's drinking had worsened. When he wasn't down in one of the shafts, he was at the tavern. Tessa had no doubt that the man coped the only way he knew how — to drink himself into oblivion so he might forget the awful fact that he was sharing his wife with another man.

Hannah had shyly informed her just that morning that Percival hadn't visited her in an entire week. Apparently the women in Eagle Harbor knew this to be his sign that he was tiring of his current mistress and would soon be on the lookout for another. Tessa had sensed a growing tension among many of the women and now she understood why. They were worried which of them Percival would choose as his next victim.

Every time Tessa thought about Percival's control over the miners and their families, she wanted to march over to his house, tie him up, and lock him in a closet so that he couldn't hurt anyone ever again. At the same time she was frustrated that the miners were letting him hurt them. Mr. Nance didn't have to allow Percival to take advantage of his wife. He could stand up to his boss, no matter the consequences. Tessa didn't understand why the men didn't band together to fight for their rights and stop allowing Percival to have so much control over them.

She just prayed that if she ever found herself in a similar situation, she'd have the courage to do what was right and that her husband would love her enough to save her.

Inadvertently her attention shifted to Alex, who was sitting in the middle of the crowd with Ingrid on his lap and Michael next to him. While Gunnar had already missed a word and had to sit down, they still watched the contest with interest. The Rawlings family had come too. The town had few social events in the wintertime, and the spelling bee was a pleasant change from the monotony of cold and snow.

The wind rattled the stovepipe, and she was grateful again that Michael had taken such care to prepare the schoolhouse for winter. So far they'd had several snowfalls, bringing the accumulation on the ground close to a foot deep.

As the last of the students were eliminated, Henry Benney remained standing. With everyone else she cheered and clapped, nearly brought to tears by the beaming smile of her prized student.

She rewarded all the participants with the small stash of candy she'd brought with her, then treated everyone with the cakes she'd baked from the overpriced supplies she purchased from the company store. Since the Central Mine teacher and students had left early due to the snow that had started to fall, she had more cake left than she'd anticipated.

"It looks like the evening was a success," Alex said, approaching the desk she'd used as a serving table.

"Gunnar did really well," Tessa said. "I have a feeling he'll be challenging Henry Benney soon enough."

"That he will." Alex glanced through the milling crowd at his nephew sitting next to Michael. "It's obvious you're making school fun for them."

"What else do you expect from me?" She smiled. "I'm a fun person."

He didn't smile in return. Instead his expression was sincere, and the blue of his eyes shone with admiration. "Gunnar and Ingrid both told me you were a good teacher, but I didn't realize just how good."

His compliment wrapped around her and warmed her. "I guess you need to start believing everything they say." *If only you'd made an effort to come to my evening class, you would have found out for yourself,* she wanted to say. Now that commerce on the lakes had ceased and the lighthouse closed, he could have come.

But he hadn't come. And he hadn't made any further mention of tutoring either. It was just as well, she reasoned. After the incident in the mine, she couldn't encourage anything more between them, especially

211

because her stomach still did flips whenever she imagined the way his lips had felt on her neck.

"You work really hard," he continued with that same sincerity she didn't quite know how to interpret. She could easily banter with him, yet whenever he became too serious, her insides twisted into strange knots. "You've spent hours and hours with the children above what's required of your teaching duties."

"I don't mind. I like it." Her answer hardly sufficed, but she couldn't figure out what to say to Alex when he was acting sincere.

"Telling you thank-you doesn't seem like enough," he said, his smile showing off the slight dimple in his chin.

She couldn't make herself look away from him. She sensed he was beginning to understand her passion for teaching, that he not only accepted all she was doing but also appreciated it. That thought was enough to make her wish the desk wasn't between them.

He was the kind of man she could have easily cared for. He was everything any woman could ask for in a man — kind, sensitive, funny, and good-looking.

If she were in the market for a husband, he'd be a perfect candidate. But right now she loved teaching and couldn't give it up. Not yet. Besides, there was that other little problem. He was a lightkeeper. Even if she'd been able to consider letting more develop between them, it wouldn't be fair to either of them. She'd never be able to ask him to give up his job for her. And she certainly wouldn't consider shackling herself to life in a lighthouse.

She was relieved when one of her students interrupted the intensity of their moment and Alex returned to sit with his family. In the midst of the busyness of saying goodbye to everyone and congratulating her students, she didn't have the chance to talk to him again before he left. She was disappointed, though she knew she shouldn't be. She lingered for a while, talking with the Benneys and several other families before finally turning to Samuel.

"Thank you for coming, Samuel," she said, giving the short man a quick hug.

Flustered, he stuttered for a moment while he wrestled with his coat, accidentally putting it on backward before realizing his mistake and then having to take it off again.

"Sam, are you ready?" came a voice from the doorway behind them, a voice Tessa had learned to dread.

A gust of cold wind and a dusting of

freshly fallen snow blew in, along with the tall, distinguished form of Percival Updegraff, bundled in a finely tailored sealskin coat trimmed in thick fur.

The room was mostly deserted except for a few stragglers. At the sight of Percival, heads bent quickly and the room grew silent. A chill skittered across Tessa's flesh, but she lifted her chin determined not to let this man intimidate her.

"Percival is here to walk me home." Samuel fumbled at the buttons of his coat.

"Make sure you put on your gloves." Percival stepped inside and brushed off the snow that had collected on his coat. "The wind is kicking into a gale."

"Will we have a big storm?" Samuel asked.

"Yes, the snow is falling fast now." Percival stomped his boots. "I hope you had a good evening, Sam, because I don't want you to go out until the storm subsides."

Samuel grumbled his displeasure at the back of his throat but didn't object. If there was one thing Tessa could respect about Percival, it was his care for his brother. Many men would have considered a simpleton like Samuel an inconvenience or embarrassment, but she'd never seen Percival treat Samuel with anything but kindness.

As Percival's eyes adjusted to the brightness of the schoolroom, he took in Tessa standing near his brother and pulled himself up straighter. "Miss Taylor, I didn't expect that you'd still be here, not with the temperature dropping as fast as rocks down a chute."

"I was just about to leave, after I take a few minutes to tidy up the room and ready it for Monday."

"I suggest you leave now," Percival said. "I doubt you'll have to worry about school on Monday, not with this storm blowing in."

For just a moment, with the sensitivity he was showing his brother and her, Tessa could almost disregard all the horrible things she'd learned about Percival. She could almost believe this man standing before her was someone entirely different, someone who genuinely cared about his family and brother . . . until his cold eyes assessed her from her head down to her toes, like a man sizing up a woman in a brothel.

She shivered but refused to cower.

"In fact," he continued smoothly, "I'd suggest you accompany Samuel and me home since we're closer to the schoolhouse than the Rawlingses'."

"I'll be just fine, Mr. Updegraff," she said,

then glanced at her remaining guests, hoping they wouldn't leave her alone to fend for herself against Percival. None of them met her gaze.

"Please come, Miss Taylor," Samuel chimed in with childlike innocence. "I'll take good care of you."

She tried to offer Samuel a reassuring smile, but it felt stiff. "I'm sure I can manage."

"Now, Miss Taylor," Percival said as he reached for her coat on a peg near the door, "I won't take no for an answer. I can't in good conscience allow you to walk home alone in this storm. It's nearly a blizzard out there, and you could easily get lost."

"It can't be that bad yet." She thought of the Central Mine students and prayed that in their horse-drawn sleigh they'd had plenty of time to arrive home before the storm hit.

"Why take any chances?" There was something in his tone that told her he wasn't simply referring to taking chances with the snowstorm, that he was threatening her in other ways. "Besides, I've been thinking this week that I've neglected to get to know you. I think it's time we remedy that."

Hannah's whisper from earlier in the day came rushing back to scream at her. Percival

216

was tiring of Hannah. He hadn't visited her all week. Tessa gulped a lump of fear forming in her throat. Was he truly on the hunt for new prey, and was she to be the next victim he hoped to snare? She spun away from him and took long strides to her desk. "We know each other well enough, Mr. Updegraff," she said over her shoulder. "I bid you be on your way so that I can finish my work here."

She collected the cake crumbs on her desk and swept them into her palm. The soft creak of the door told her someone had left, and she prayed it was Percival and Samuel. After counting silently to ten, she glanced over her shoulder.

She gave a startled gasp and jumped at Percival's presence directly behind her.

A desperate look around told her that everyone else had filed out of the schoolhouse except Samuel, who stood by the door watching Percival with too much trust.

"Miss Taylor," Percival said in a low voice, "I'd really like to spend more time with you."

She shuffled back but bumped into the desk. "What about your wife, Mr. Updegraff? I doubt she'd approve of you spending time with me."

"She can't begrudge me a little companionship in this lonely place." He closed the gap so that his coat brushed her.

"You and I both know that my teaching contract forbids me to have male companionship."

"*You and I both know* that hasn't stopped you from spending time with certain men in this town."

She swallowed hard at his insinuation. Did he know about her trip up to the mine with Alex? She'd prayed fervently over the past month that no one would find out and so far she hadn't heard a single mention of it.

"You'll find that I can be very generous to those who are generous to me," he continued.

"No."

His mustache twitched. "I don't like anyone telling me no."

She had no choice but to arch backward over her desk. She was almost tempted to hop on top and crawl across in order to get away from him. "There aren't many who tell you no in this town, are there?"

"Not often." His body was rigid and unmoving like a wall hemming her in.

"Well, Mr. Updegraff," she said, inching sideways and trying to squeeze past him, "I'm not afraid to tell you no."

He slapped a hand on the desk, prevent-

218

ing her escape. Something violent flared in his eyes. A warning rang in her head, a warning to get away from him as fast as she could, that if she stayed she would get hurt.

"Percival, are you mad at Miss Taylor?" Samuel asked from near the door, his tone filled with anxiety.

Percival looked over his shoulder at Samuel. At the sight of his wide innocent eyes, Percival muttered under his breath and took a step back from her.

Tessa didn't wait for another opportunity to maneuver away from him. With her heart pounding, she hurried toward the door. She had to get out of the schoolroom. Now. While she still had the chance.

At that moment, a strong gust pushed the door wide and sent in a swirl of snow and wind. A white apparition stepped inside and shoved the door closed behind him. Shaking his head and unwinding the snow-covered scarf that covered his face, Tessa almost collapsed with relief to see Alex. His troubled eyes found her first. But a glance at Percival behind her turned the concern into frigid anger. "With the storm coming on so quickly, I came to make sure Tessa got home safely," he said firmly.

"No need," Percival said. "That's what I was doing."

"I have my dogsled," Alex said. "I'll be able to get her home the fastest."

Percival's nostrils flared and his jaw flexed.

"Even in these whiteout conditions, you know my dogs can get me anywhere I want to go." Alex went to Percival and grabbed Tessa's coat.

Percival didn't relinquish it, but instead glared at Alex. Alex stared back. All Tessa could do was hold her breath and pray the two didn't start swinging fists. After a long moment, Percival shoved the coat against Alex's chest.

Alex took it without another word. He crossed to Tessa, handed her the coat, and pulled an extra scarf from his coat pocket. "Put this on over your face."

She wasted no time. Within seconds she was bundled and Alex was escorting her out of the school. As she plunged into the dark night, the wind slapped the exposed flesh of her face with a sting that took her breath away. It was coming off the lake with a bitter dampness that was different from the land breezes she was accustomed to, and it was blowing the snow sideways with a blinding ferocity.

With the darkness and the snow, the world had disappeared. She stumbled forward, stretching out her hands to feel her way.

Thankfully Alex's grip on her arm was firm, and he guided her until she bumped into a curved sled. He maneuvered her to a narrow bench, then squeezed onto the seat in front of her.

His call to the dogs was lost in the wind, but apparently they still heard him because the sled lurched to a slow start. She grabbed on to Alex to steady herself. The howling and slicing wind made any conversation impossible, as did the scarves over their mouths. Even if she'd wanted to talk, she wasn't sure she could manage past the rattling of her teeth.

Within minutes the sled slowed and Alex was helping her to her feet. For an interminable moment he led her in what seemed like circles. Finally a door opened, and they stumbled into the Rawlingses' brightly lit front room.

All the rambunctious boys crowded around them. She peeled away the scarf and coat, which were frozen stiff.

"Are you all right?" Alex asked over the heads of the two little ones clinging to his snow-covered coat. His eyes probed her, and she knew he was referring more to her encounter with Percival than to the ride in the blizzard.

"I'm just glad you came when you did."

She dreaded to think what might have happened if he hadn't arrived. Or if Samuel hadn't been there to distract Percival.

"For now you'd better not be anywhere alone. Stay where you're surrounded by people. You'll be safer that way."

"I'll be fine," she countered, not willing to admit that something about Percival scared her to the core. "I'll start carrying a knife, and if that man touches me, I'll hack off his fingers."

Alex didn't laugh; he didn't even smile. "Did he touch you?" His voice sounded strained.

"No. He didn't."

Alex held her gaze as if testing the truth of her words. She had the feeling he would have raced over, blizzard or not, to confront Percival if he had touched her. And when angered, there was no telling what Percival might do.

Maybe Alex was right. Maybe she'd be safest for the time being if she kept herself surrounded by her students and other women. Then she'd be able to keep Alex safe too. She didn't want to think what Percival might do if Alex angered him.

CHAPTER 14

The storm lasted for three days. By the time the snow stopped falling, it had drifted in piles four feet high. Tessa had to cancel school for nearly a week because the snow blocked the roads. Some of the men with their teams of horses had begun to break paths to reach those families who ran out of firewood and had no way to stay warm.

Mr. Rawlings and his oldest boys had been among the men attempting to make the roads passable. Every evening they came back with tales about someone hurt by the cold, including one of the neighbors who was suffering from delirium tremens because he hadn't been able to get to the tavern. In his shaking and state of withdrawal, he'd gone outside for too long, had frozen his hands and would likely lose all his fingers as a result.

By the end of the week, Tessa was more than ready to return to her classroom. It was a great relief that the following Monday the roads were finally clear. The wind was still blowing strongly from the north and coming off the lake. Although the thermometer read ten degrees, it felt like minus twenty. The houses and school remained half buried in the snow, and the evergreens bent low under the weight of so heavy a burden.

Nevertheless, she reopened the schoolhouse. Only a quarter of the scholars came to class since the snow was too deep for the younger ones to walk through. By midweek, however, most of the students had returned and were studying diligently again.

The days off due to the weather only served to show her how much she'd grown to love her job and how much she missed it when she wasn't there. In spite of the demands of her work, the large numbers of students, the continued lack of school supplies, and the challenges of meeting so many different needs, Tessa realized that she thrived when she was in the classroom. She loved listening to the young eager voices attempting their recitations. She loved the faces that lit up after finally understanding a difficult arithmetic problem. And she was deeply satisfied when several of her older students who'd had trouble reading finally made progress.

After another week passed, she sent home word with the children to inform their parents and older siblings that she would resume the evening classes. When darkness fell and she arrived at the schoolhouse, Michael was already there as usual replenishing the wood supply and refueling the stove.

"I see you're getting around fine on the snowshoes," he said as she unlaced them at the door.

"I don't know how I would have gotten by without them," she said, wiggling her frozen toes. Her boots were hardly warm enough for the northern temperatures, and her feet were usually frozen within minutes of leaving home.

Michael watched her with a wrinkled brow. "You need sturdier boots."

"I'm not sure any kind of boot can keep my feet warm with temperatures like this."

Michael didn't respond. Instead he studied her feet as if measuring them. He'd always treated her with the utmost respect and consideration, yet she hadn't developed the same camaraderie with him that she had with Alex.

"Gunnar tells me you took him ice fishing last week when school was canceled."

Michael nodded. "The lake's frozen and

225

safe enough for fishing now."

She hung her coat and the scarf Alex had given her. "I'm surprised you don't freeze while you fish."

"We have a hut set up on the ice above the hole."

"That's what Gunnar said. But even so . . ."

"And warming boxes."

She shivered every time she thought about sitting out on the ice for any length of time, even in a tiny shack.

Michael moved away from the stove, brushing his hands and looking at her warmly. "I can take you ice fishing sometime, if you'd like to go."

"You're too kind to offer," she said wryly, "especially since I've just been dying to try it."

As she walked to the front of the classroom, she glimpsed the confusion on his face and she hid a smile. She had to remember to save the sarcasm for Alex.

She glanced at the clock and then out the window. In the darkness she expected to see the bobbing lanterns of the other evening students as they made their way to the schoolhouse. But there wasn't any light, not even a glimmer. "Where is everyone else?"

"Maybe they didn't get the news about

226

classes resuming."

"Maybe." Although she'd been emphatic with her students to relay the information to their parents.

Michael took his place on the front bench where he'd faithfully sat for the past several months, always punctual and never missing a night. He'd made good progress and was reading almost as well as his children. She only wished Alex had as much determination to improve himself.

She took a moment to reorganize the spellers and readers on her desk and was relieved when the door opened.

Henry Benney stepped inside. He was breathless, clearly having run the distance to school. His hat was askew, revealing one ear that was red from the cold. His face was splotched red too. When he moved into the light of the room, she could see that his eyes were puffy and his nose running. Had he been crying?

Her heart lurched. "What's wrong, Henry?"

He swiped at his cheeks and gulped a breath. "My father wanted me to send you his apologies for having to skip class."

"Skip?"

"Mr. Updegraff ordered twelve-hour shifts until further notice."

The eight-to-ten-hour shifts were already long enough. But twelve? "That's horrible, Henry. Can't the men protest?" But she already knew the answer to that. Most of the men unquestioningly obeyed Percival either out of fear or the favors he doled out.

"My father said that maybe I could teach him from time to time."

"Or maybe we could work out a different time for the class to meet." But after twelve long hours in the mine, she doubted the men would have the energy to attend school. It had already been difficult enough to get a regular turnout.

The sadness in Henry's eyes told her he'd reached the same conclusion.

"I don't understand." Frustration pooled in her stomach. "Why the extra hours now, in the middle of winter? It's not like the steamers are lined up waiting on the copper."

Henry's lip trembled. "I think Mr. Updegraff is punishing my father in some way."

Tessa frowned. "By making everyone work twelve-hour shifts?"

"If he makes him work longer, then he can't come to evening school."

"That can't be right. Why would Mr. Updegraff care if your father comes to evening classes?"

Henry sniffled and wiped his sleeve across his nose. "That's not the worst." His voice dropped and his shoulders sagged. "Mr. Updegraff told my father I'm too old to be in school, that I have to start work in the mine tomorrow."

Henry's declaration hit her in the chest and knocked the wind from her. For a long moment she couldn't speak.

Henry's eyes welled with tears, and he quickly swiped at them.

"He can't order you to work in the mine," she finally managed to say. "It's your choice, not his." But again, after all she'd learned about Percival, she knew it wasn't easy for grown men to defy him, much less a boy.

"Father already told him I'd be there."

It did indeed sound like Percival was punishing Mr. Benney. "What happened, Henry? Why is Mr. Updegraff doing this to your father?"

Henry shook his head. "I don't know."

"What difference will one boy make?" she asked, growing angry. "And why would he care if your father attends my evening classes?" As soon as the words left her mouth, it hit her. Maybe Percival wasn't punishing Mr. Updegraff. Maybe he was punishing *her*.

She'd started the evening class without

229

gaining his permission. And now, after refusing his advances the night of the spelling bee, after telling him no when he'd ordered her to accompany him home, was he sending her a message? Was he telling her that he would rip away the most important things in her life if she didn't do what he said?

Surely he'd heard from Hannah and others that Henry was her best pupil, her smartest student, that he'd won the spelling bee. She had great aspirations for the boy and had even recently talked with Mr. Benney about college options for Henry.

"I'm so sorry, Henry," she said, leaning back against the desk to keep herself from collapsing.

"It's not your fault, Miss Taylor. I figured I'd have to go to the mine soon anyway since my friends are already there."

Her throated tightened. "This isn't right. You shouldn't have to go. I'll speak with your father and I'll most definitely speak with Mr. Updegraff."

"Please don't do that," Henry said, his eyes wide with panic. "Mr. Updegraff won't take kindly to it, and he might find another way to punish my father. Something much worse than just a few extra hours of work."

Feeling helpless, Tessa stared at the boy.

He was right. If she tried to interfere, Percival would only find a way to make things worse for this poor family, just as he'd done when Alex had interfered with the family he tried to help. Only this time, in the dead of winter, there would be no steamer to take a homeless family south. And she would have no savings to give them.

"If you really must stop attending school," she said, scrambling to redeem herself, "then I'll meet with both you and your father for private tutoring." It was her fault, after all. She'd done this to Henry and Mr. Benney. And now she had to find a way to make it up to them. "I'll come to your home to give you lessons, and you can study in the evenings."

"Would you do that for us, Miss Taylor?" Henry asked.

"Of course I would. I'd do anything to help you continue your education." She tried to put aside the thought that perhaps Percival wouldn't approve of her doing that either. Surely he wasn't so controlling that he would forbid it.

Henry nodded. "I'll talk to my father about it, but I don't know if he'll allow it."

She remembered then that Michael was sitting on the front bench and waiting for the class to begin. She looked at him and found him regarding Henry with a gravity that made her heart sink further.

"Maybe there's a way you could pass lessons along to Henry secretly," Michael suggested. "Perhaps send them home with his little sister in her lunch pail?"

Tessa wanted to scream out her frustration at the unfairness of it all. Instead she swallowed the bitter anguish that was hurting her throat. "We have to figure out something," she said.

She wouldn't do anything to place Mr. Benney or Henry into more danger. She'd already done enough. But how could she let Henry go, not when he had so much potential?

If Percival could bring about such heartache after her rejecting him one time, what would he do the next time she told him no? Which family would he choose to hurt then?

"You're a good lass," Alex murmured. He snipped the last of Wolfie's front claws and then gently set her paw down. She rolled onto her back and looked at him with her big black eyes. Soon it would be time to breed her. Last spring she'd only had four pups. If she doubled that . . .

He sighed. Their savings was accumulating much too slowly. He glanced at the small wooden chest on top of the sideboard. Even with the longer hours they were putting in with ice fishing, come spring when they sold their catch, they would still end up short on the amount they needed to pay for Ingrid's surgery and all the expenses that went with it.

If only he could find a way to earn more money.

The front door opened and closed quietly. Michael was home and as usual was sensitive to the fact that Gunnar and Ingrid were already in bed. Alex had tucked them in, something he got in the habit of doing since Michael had started attending Tessa's evening school.

"Come, Bear," he said to the other big dog lying near the stove that was pumping out heat.

Bear raised his head, blinked at him, then gave a snort before lowering his head again.

"I know you don't like getting your nails trimmed," Alex said sternly, "but you're not getting out of it."

Bear's tail thumped once in protest.

"Come," Alex said again.

Slowly the dog rose and moved toward him. As Bear approached, Alex could sense more than hear Michael's presence in the doorway behind him.

"You're home early," Alex remarked.

Michael shifted. "She decided to cancel the class."

In the process of reaching for Bear's front paw, Alex pivoted and stared at his brother. A warning went off inside. Something was wrong, terribly wrong, if Tessa had decided to cancel her class. "What happened?"

Michael's brow was creased with the worry lines that had grown deeper in recent years. "Percival started mandatory twelve-hour shifts, and now none of the men are available to attend Tessa's class."

Alex pushed off the floor, dog hair floating in the air around his legs. "Tessa must be livid."

"And he's forcing Benney to send his son to the mine. Said he's too old to be in school."

"No." Alex could do nothing more than breathe a horrified whisper. Henry Benney was Tessa's pride and joy. And it was no wonder. The boy was a genius as far as Alex was concerned. He had no doubt Tessa was brokenhearted to lose him as her student.

Without waiting for further explanation, Alex bounded toward his coat hanging near the back door. He had to get to her before she did something rash, like stomp off to Percival's and give him a tongue-lashing.

"I walked her home already," Michael said.

Alex stuffed his arms into his coat and wrapped his scarf around his neck.

"You don't need to go," Michael insisted.

"I want to make sure she isn't planning to do anything stupid."

"I don't think she will."

Alex wasn't so sure. Tessa had too much spunk to sit back for long and do nothing. He had to go to her for himself and make sure she was acting level-headed.

"Do you think you're going to comfort her more than I was able to?" Behind him, Michael's voice was suddenly taut.

All fall and winter, Alex had tried to pretend he had nothing to worry about with Michael growing attached to Tessa. He'd rationalized that Michael couldn't possibly care for Tessa as deeply as he could. Michael was simply coming out of the fog he'd been in for so long, but he'd soon lose interest in Tessa and move on to someone else.

Apparently he'd been fooling himself.

Michael shoved away from the doorframe, and the sharpness in his gaze pricked Alex. "Or maybe you don't think she could find comfort in my arms?"

Alex spun toward Michael so fast that he almost tripped. "She was in your arms?"

"What if she was?" Michael asked. "I have every right to hold her that you do."

Alex wanted to protest but knew Michael was right. Tessa hadn't ever let him hold her, at least not willingly. If he'd slipped his arm around her once or twice, or if he'd touched her face or hands, it wasn't because she'd encouraged him.

She very well might like Michael more than him. What if Michael was having more success than he was in making Tessa fall in love with him? "I hope you haven't kissed her."

"It's none of your business whether I have or not."

Hot jealousy shot through Alex. Had Michael kissed Tessa? He studied Michael's face, searching for the truth, but his expression was smooth and suave. And dark with irritation. "I don't think you should even be attempting to kiss her," Alex said.

"I don't think you should be either."

Alex thought back on all the times he'd wanted to kiss her. Since the mine incident, he'd vowed he wouldn't put Tessa into a compromising situation again. And as difficult as it had been, he hadn't sought her out alone.

But maybe Michael was closing in. In fact, what if he was taking the lead in winning

Tessa's heart?

Alex had a strange urge to punch his brother in the gut. It was the first time in years, maybe even since they'd been boys, that he'd wanted to launch himself against his brother and have a fistfight. Of course, the last time they'd fought, Michael had been bigger and stronger and had easily subdued him.

Alex's biceps twitched. But now, though Michael was older, Alex was decidedly bigger. One punch to the stomach and another to the ribs and he'd knock Michael out in no time.

As if sensing the challenge, Michael straightened and puffed out his chest.

Alex tensed, and for a long moment neither of them said anything.

Guilt crept in and began to prod Alex. "Listen," he finally said. "All I'm going to do is make sure Tessa doesn't go over to Percival's house. Then I'll be back."

Michael pursed his lips but remained quiet.

Alex knew he should promise Michael that he wouldn't try anything with Tessa and that everything would be okay. But he couldn't, not when he had the overwhelming desire to stake his claim on Tessa before Michael could. He wanted to be the first to kiss her and ask her to marry him, and he couldn't stand the thought that Michael might already have done it.

With Michael's piercing gaze following him, Alex walked out of the house. He slid into his cross-country skis, and by the time he arrived at Tessa's home, he'd cooled considerably. His irrational anger toward his brother had been replaced with humor that he'd almost gotten into a fight with Michael over a woman.

In the darkness of the starless night, the light shining from the front window shimmered across the powdery snow that drifted high against the house, rising to the windows in some places. Through the thin walls he could hear the boys roaring or wrestling or something.

His gloved hand stalled above the door handle. Maybe he shouldn't have come after all. Maybe he was paranoid and needed to trust Tessa better. At his heels Wolfie growled low at the back of her throat. Alex put a steadying hand on her head, but she ducked and started to slink away from him toward the side of the house.

"Wolfie," he whispered. "Stay, lass."

But Wolfie acted as if she hadn't heard him, bounding around the corner.

Alex gave a low whistle to call her back.

When she didn't respond, he set his poles next to his skis and tromped through the deep snow toward where the dog had disappeared. He rounded the house to find Wolfie sitting in front of an apparition of coat and scarf illuminated only faintly by the glow of an upstairs window. The dog's head was raised eagerly against a gloved hand that was rubbing her snout and the spot between her eyes.

Tessa.

He didn't say anything. He was too overcome with relief that he'd arrived in time to stop her from running over to Percival's. He had no doubt Percival was waiting for Tessa to come to him, like a spider sitting in its web anticipating its next meal.

Her hand drifted to Wolfie's neck behind her ears.

"Michael told you about my night class?" she said, her breath a cloud of gray that settled in the air like a shroud.

He nodded, not trusting himself yet to speak.

"Did he tell you about Henry Benney?" Her voice caught on the edge of a sob.

He nodded again.

She patted Wolfie's side and then lifted one of her shoulders to brush at her cheek.

Was she crying?

239

He stepped closer. "I'm sorry, Tessa."

She sniffled. "It's not fair."

"I know it's not." He reached a hand toward her, but then stopped. He didn't want to cross the boundary he'd set, though he felt the need to comfort her.

When she finally lifted her face, her eyes glistened with unshed tears and her cheeks were streaked with the ones that had already run over.

An ache rose in his chest. He cast caution aside and reached for her.

She didn't resist. She fell into him and wrapped her arms around his waist. With a shudder she buried her face into his chest and shook with silent sobs.

He rested his cheek against the scratchy wool of her knitted cap.

She cried for a few minutes. Each of her shudders rippled through him and made him all the angrier at Percival Updegraff.

"Aw, beautiful," Alex murmured against her head. "I wish I could make everything all better for you and for them."

She gave a long sigh. "Can't we do anything, Alex?"

"I've already written to the owners of Cole Mine a couple of times to complain about Percival, but he runs this place well and turns them a hefty profit. I'm sure they'd be hard-pressed to find another supervisor as responsible and trustworthy."

"But don't the Coles care about how he treats their workers?" she asked into his coat. "How can they overlook such blatant abuse?"

"They're too far away and too busy to care what goes on with the workers here." Even with the layers of coats and scarves separating them, he relished the firmness of her body against his. He had the urge to press a kiss into her hair which fell out of her hat near her forehead, but he fought for the inner strength to hold her and nothing more. She certainly didn't need him taking advantage in her moment of weakness.

"Promise me you won't ever go to Percival's house alone," he said.

She rested silently against him for a long moment, then finally pulled away and replied, "I'd like to think I was braver, that I could stand up to Percival and fight for the rights of my students, and even though I wanted to go, I don't think I could have."

He drew her closer again, gratefulness welling within him that God had spared her this time. But what about the next incident? As sure as another storm would strike again that winter, Percival would strike again as well.

A shudder tore at her thin body, one that came from her core and signaled the cold had grown unbearable.

"You need to go back inside," he said, reluctantly pulling away. She didn't protest when he took her by the arm and led her around the house, following her footprints through the snow to the back door where she'd made her escape.

When her hand was on the knob, he released her and took a large step away so that he wouldn't draw her back into his arms like he wanted to.

She opened the door a crack and then paused. "Thank you for coming."

He nodded. "I'm always here for you."

"You're a good friend, Alex," she said, then slipped inside and closed the door behind her, leaving him standing in the darkness and staring at the place she'd just been.

There was something in her tone that issued a warning, almost as if she was trying to convince both of them that friendship was all that could ever link them together.

He smiled. Friendship was a good place to start. But if she thought that was all there would ever be, then he'd enjoy proving her wrong.

CHAPTER 15

"You sure have quite the collection of gifts," Josie said, studying the attic ledge where Tessa had started to keep the gifts Alex and Michael had bestowed upon her lately.

At her makeshift desk, Tessa was glad for the dimness of the attic that hid her embarrassment. Even though she'd told each of the men that she could offer them friendship only, that hadn't stopped them from seeking her out, giving her trinkets like beads or a leather bookmark or ribbons for her hair. The shelf was growing cluttered.

All throughout February and into March, the men had tried to outdo each other. They'd introduced her to cross-country skiing and fought over who got to teach her. Michael made her a pair of warm leather moccasin-like boots. Alex took her sledding with the children. Michael fixed the latch on the schoolhouse door when it was frozen. Alex brought her new books to read.

Another snowstorm had closed school again for a week and had given Tessa a reprieve from their interest, which she wasn't sure how to handle anymore. She'd wanted to deny that their attention was anything more than friendship, but she supposed she finally had to admit their pursuit of her had gone too far.

"Which one are you planning to marry?" Josie asked, fingering the copper-colored stone Alex had given her. It contained white crystal flecks dotted throughout, a beautiful and unique specimen like so many of the rocks she'd seen along the shore. "Alex or Michael?"

"I'm not intending to get married," Tessa protested. "At least not for a few more years, not until I've had the opportunity to teach a while longer."

She blew into her frozen fingers. Even clad in gloves and wearing her coat, the attic was cold. In fact, there were times during the winter when it had been unbearably cold, and she and Josie had to make their beds on the floor in the kitchen next to the stove.

Thankfully, for the past week the temperature had begun to creep above freezing, the sun had shone brightly, and the snow melted into enormous puddles. She wanted to disregard the naysayers who told her that spring was still a month away, that they could still have snowstorms for several more weeks until the end of April.

On days when the cold in the attic was bearable, Tessa liked to retreat there for a rare moment of privacy — usually interrupted by Josie.

Josie picked up a simple carved cross Michael had given her. Tessa had placed it next to the driftwood cross, the one her brother-in-law, Ryan, had given her. The brittle letter that had come with the driftwood cross was stored safely in her Bible. The letter was written by a lightkeeper's daughter, Isabelle Thornton, well over fifteen years ago during a time of desperation and heartache. Tessa loved reading Isabelle's story and the hope found by turning to the Giver of Hope.

Tessa had hung on to the cross for the past five years, since the time when she'd devised a foolish ploy to trap Ryan, the man her sister had loved, into marrying her instead. She'd been rash and selfish and desperate to get away from the lighthouse. When Ryan said he was leaving, she'd decided to force him to marry her and take her with him.

One night shortly after that, she'd tricked Ryan into taking his pain medicine. While he'd been under the influence of the opium pills, they'd gotten drunk together. After he passed out in bed, she'd crawled in next to him. That's where everyone found them the next morning. The lighthouse inspector, her sister, and even Ryan had insisted they get married, just as she'd hoped.

In the end, she confessed what she'd done and repented. But it hadn't changed the fact that everyone in Grosse Pointe and the Detroit area thought she was a loose woman. Even when she later explained that nothing had happened, her story sounded like the desperate attempt of a young woman to regain what was lost. Her reputation.

It had been lost ever since, until she'd arrived in Eagle Harbor in a place where no one knew anything about her past mistakes.

Tessa lovingly traced the dark grain of the shipwreck pieces that had been fashioned into a cross. Had she finally found hope here? Was it time to pass the cross along to someone else who needed it?

Isabelle Thornton's beautiful letter ended with an encouragement for the bearer of the cross to give it along with the letter to someone who needed hope. Tessa glanced sideways at Josie whose cropped bangs hung over her eyes in a crooked line. Should she give the cross to Josie?

"It must be wonderful to have two men who love you at the same time," Josie said, flopping back onto the unmade bed. "I can't even keep one interested."

Though Tessa was tempted to tell Josie *I told you so,* she refrained. "First of all, the men don't love me," she said while flipping the page of the arithmetic book in front of her. Maybe they were attracted to her, but that didn't equate to love. "Secondly, you don't need to have a boy who likes you in order to be happy."

"First of all, they both adore you," Josie said in a mocking tone. "And secondly, you're right. I don't need a boy. I need a man."

Tessa almost sighed in exasperation. Having meaningful conversations with Josie could be exhausting.

"I'm tired of boys. They're immature and don't know what they want," Josie babbled on. She wrapped herself in the thick comforter for warmth. "I think I'm going to start looking for a man. A *real* man."

"Miss Taylor?" A call came from the stairwell, one of the younger Rawlings boys. "Gunnar Bjorklund is at the door asking for you."

Tessa slowly closed her books and tidied her desk of the papers she was assembling

247

for Henry Benney's secret school lesson. She'd learned from Gunnar's previous visits that there was no need to worry or rush. Ingrid liked to make up excuses to get her attention, and poor Gunnar was simply the messenger.

When Tessa arrived to the front room where he was waiting, she put on her sternest teacher expression. "I suppose Ingrid is making up another excuse to have me visit?"

His face flushed as it usually did. "I'm sorry, Miss Taylor. I told Ingrid we shouldn't come for you." He stared at the wet snow dribbling down his boots and forming a dirty puddle. Even though it was nigh into the evening, the temperatures were still above freezing, warm enough to melt more snow.

"Perhaps this time you should go back home and tell Ingrid I can't come."

His chin dropped and he hung his head. "Yes, ma'am." He hesitated for a moment before turning to the door.

Tessa wished she didn't have to be so firm with him, but what kind of message would she send if she came running every time the girl called? She'd already encouraged Ingrid too much as it was.

Gunnar opened the door and, his lantern in hand, started to shuffle through the thick

248

fog that had been covering the bay and town all day and now made the evening even darker.

From the kitchen doorway Nadine called out over the noise of her children playing on the floor. "If your daddy and uncle don't come home tonight, you best let us know in the morning." There was something in Nadine's tone that made Tessa's pulse stutter to a halt.

"They're not home?" She tossed the question after Gunnar. "Where did they go?"

The boy stopped, and when he turned to face her again, this time she saw the worry tightening his features. "They went out ice fishing this afternoon. Said they'd be back by midafternoon, but they're still not home."

"I'm sure they're just running late," she said. "Don't you think, Nadine?"

Nadine brushed at the wispy graying hair that floated around her face. "Maybe. But those two aren't taken to leaving the kiddies by themselves for too long."

"I bet they're back right now, even as we speak," Tessa said evenly, trying to remain calm. Nadine was right. Alex and Michael were too responsible to stay out past dark knowing that Gunnar and Ingrid would be waiting and worrying.

She met Nadine's gaze, and the deathly seriousness there sent chills up Tessa's back.

Something must have happened.

The baby on Nadine's hip stopped sucking her thumb and let out a wail. She'd grown bigger over the winter, but she clung to Nadine wherever she went. Hoisting the baby to her opposite hip, Nadine said, "With the warmer weather, maybe the ice on the lake is breaking up. I heard some cracking earlier."

The look on Gunnar's young face told her he'd already come to the same conclusion. Did they think Alex and Michael had fallen through the ice and drowned?

"Or maybe they got lost in the thick fog," Nadine added.

Tessa's heart resumed its beating but at double the speed. "I'll go back with Gunnar and make sure the men are home."

"You'll stay with the children through the night, won't you?" Nadine asked, crossing the room.

Tessa prayed that she wouldn't need to, that when she arrived at the lighthouse, Alex and Michael would be there waiting. But what if they weren't? What if even now they were out on the lake, fallen through the ice and drowning? "Yes, I'll stay. But what about going out to look for them?"

"There's no use tonight," Nadine said. "Not unless we want to send more men to a watery —" At the sight of Gunnar's widening eyes, Nadine stopped. "It's too foggy," she hurried to finish. "We'll have to wait till morning."

Tessa could read what the woman didn't say, that if Alex and Michael had fallen into the lake, the freezing water would have killed them within minutes. There would have been no way for them to survive.

"Let's go," Tessa said to Gunnar as she slipped on her coat. "I'm sure everything's going to be just fine." She lifted a desperate plea that she was right.

"You send us word if they get home," Nadine called after them. "Otherwise we'll form a search party in the morning."

The very words *search party* made Tessa want to cry out in protest, but she forced herself to breathe and act normal. Hurrying through the darkness with Gunnar by her side, she prayed as she'd never prayed before.

When they stepped into the keeper's cottage and silence met them, Tessa's body threatened to buckle beneath her. The men weren't back yet. One look at Ingrid's tear-streaked cheeks sent a pang through Tessa's heart.

251

Who would take care of these two children if they were left orphans? Michael and Alex had both spoken of family living on a farm in Iowa. How would she find the relatives? If she did, would they want to take in two young children?

"Will they come home, Miss Taylor?" Ingrid asked later as she tucked the girl into the twin-sized bed in the smaller of the two bedrooms on the second story of the house. The room was plain, having no pictures on the walls, no rugs or frills. The children needed a mother, Ingrid especially. She'd gone so long without one, it was no wonder she craved Tessa's attention.

Tessa knelt next to the bed. She held Ingrid's hand and smoothed the girl's fine blond hair away from her forehead. "Let's pray again and ask God to keep them safe through the night."

Ingrid nodded and bowed her head, her fingers trembling in Tessa's. Standing in the doorway, Gunnar shut his eyes, but not before a tear escaped and trickled out.

For a long moment, Tessa's heart squeezed too painfully to find the words to utter. But knowing that Ingrid and Gunnar were relying on her, that she was the only one there for them, she finally found her voice — even if it was just a whisper. "God," she started, "we plead for your protection of Michael and Alex tonight. Wherever they are, bring them back to us."

Back to us. The words replayed over and over in her mind as she kissed both of the children good-night and then retreated to the kitchen.

Lying by the back door, Wolfie lifted her head while Tessa collapsed into a chair. Earlier in the week, the children had excitedly informed her that the dog was carrying pups. Tessa suspected this was the reason why Alex had left her home. The elkhound hadn't moved from the back door since Tessa had arrived. From the droop of her sad eyes, Tessa knew the dog sensed something was terribly wrong too. Bear must have drowned with the men. Otherwise why wouldn't he have come home by now?

Despair circled around Tessa, growing tighter and darker, threatening to cut off her breath. The hard spindles of the chair pressed into her spine. She couldn't give in to grief or worry. She needed to stay strong for the children's sake.

She stood and glanced around the kitchen, which was in need of a cleaning. She could see that the children had made more of an effort since she'd last been here, but nothing would help more than a woman's constant oversight of the home.

Reaching for a broom, she suddenly paused. Was that why Michael was intent upon wooing her? Was he in the business of finding a new mother and a woman who could manage his home?

She went from the kitchen into the parlor. Slowly her steps led her to the window where she peered out at the blackness of the lake, still frozen along the shore. The gaping mouth of the lake was closed. The gnashing teeth of the waves were silent. The biting sting of water was placid. But somewhere farther out, the sleeping beast was awakening. Its deep carnivorous jaw was opening and slowly making its way back to the shore, devouring all those within its path.

"I hate you." The loathing in her breath fanned against the window, steaming the cold pane. The monster. The murderer.

The sea had taken from her too many times already. Now it was taking from her again. Even though Alex and Michael weren't her flesh and blood, they'd become like family. The thought of losing them — or anyone else she cared about — to the lake was almost more than she could bear.

Anger rushed in hot and swift. "I hate you," she said again louder.

She spun around and glanced down the front hallway to the door that led to the tower. "And I hate you even more," she said to the lighthouse. "You're supposed to save lives, supposed to give hope. But all you've done is take from me everything I've loved."

Did she love Michael and Alex?

A sob slipped out before she could catch it. She sucked in a quick breath. The heat of holding in the rest of the sobs scalded her lungs and chest. Something deep and passionate was pulsing through her. She didn't know if it was love. But whatever it was tore at her soul until it was shredded and bleeding.

With an energy born of desperation, she attacked the kitchen, scrubbing it until it was spotless. Then she moved into the parlor and cleaned it with a fury. Finally she collapsed onto the sofa into a restless sleep where she dreamed about the ice cracking and laughing wickedly as it watched Michael and Alex plunge into the freezing water below, flailing helplessly with limbs growing numb, until finally their movements stopped and they floated on the icy water, staring sightlessly into the dark sky.

She awoke with a start.

"Miss Taylor?" Ingrid was perched on the

255

sofa next to her. The braids that Tessa had plaited the night before were mussed and fell over her shoulders. "It's light outside. Can we go look for Daddy and Uncle Alex now?"

Tessa sat up and wiped her own tangled hair from her face. She glanced out the window to see the faint streaks of dawn beginning to color the sky.

"Gunnar already left," Ingrid said.

Panic burst through Tessa. She shot up, the motion sending Ingrid tumbling to the floor. "Oh no! He can't go out there by himself!"

She whirled around, first toward the hallway that led to the front door and then back to the kitchen, tangling and tripping over her wrinkled skirt. "It's too dangerous to be out on the ice. He'll fall through just like them."

"Miss Taylor," Ingrid said from her spot on the floor, "he only went to the Rawlingses' to let them know that Daddy isn't home yet."

Tessa stopped struggling. A wave of relief rose up in her so strong that she fell back onto the sofa and buried her face in her hands. Hot tears wet her palms. She wasn't sure why she'd reacted so strongly to the thought of losing Gunnar too, except that

256

she knew it very well could have happened. He could have run out onto the ice, hoping to find his father.

She easily could have lost him too. So easily . . .

She shook her head. *Oh, Lord, I can't do this. I can't let myself love this family, only to lose them.*

Wasn't that why she'd vowed not to have anything more to do with the sea or lighthouses? She'd vowed she wouldn't step in one again. And here she was, right in the middle of one, caring far too much for this precious family.

Now look what had happened. She was getting hurt. Again. She couldn't keep letting this happen. She had to stop.

She took a deep shuddering breath. Of course, she couldn't abandon Ingrid and Gunnar now, not when they needed her most. She would stay and help them through this difficult time. But once she had them situated, she'd renew her pledge to stay away from lighthouses and the sea forever.

Chapter 16

When it was light enough and the fog less dense, a search party started out across Eagle Harbor Bay. Overnight they'd learned that two other men from the community who'd been ice fishing hadn't returned either. One of them was Hannah's husband. Although the teacher's helper had ashamedly admitted that she'd been unable to reconcile with her husband and that he was hardly ever home, Tessa knew the sweet woman wouldn't want her husband to suffer and was likely worried for his safety.

The search party loaded a sled with ropes, blankets, ice chisels, and other tools. Wolfie led the way across the ice. Tessa prayed the dog's keen sense of smell would track down the missing brothers and the other men. The grim faces of the rescuers told her it was probably too late. Though Gunnar wanted to go with them, Tessa held him back. She'd wrapped her arms around him and was relieved when, instead of resisting, he hugged her back. After watching the men disappear on the horizon, Tessa pressed a kiss against Gunnar's head and herded the children back inside the house.

She'd already put out a notice that she was canceling classes for the day. She decided that neither she nor Hannah would be able to concentrate. But as they waited for the search party, she wondered if she'd made a mistake. Perhaps they should have kept themselves busy at school. As it was, they had too much time to think the worst and run to the window at every shadow to see if the search party was returning.

Tessa was grateful at midday when Nadine came with her littlest one. She brought a jug of hot spiced mead to give to Alex and Michael once they were rescued. "It'll warm them down to their fingers and toes, it will," she said with a confidence that didn't reach her eyes.

Tessa nodded her gratefulness and glanced out the window to the dark clouds piling over the lake to the west.

Nadine followed her gaze. "We're in for a storm, that we are."

"Hopefully no more snow," Tessa said with a sigh.

"From the cold bite of the wind, I've a

mind those clouds are full of snow." Nadine turned from the window and sat down on the sofa where she began unbuttoning her blouse. The baby squirmed and released a wail, impatient for her next meal.

Ingrid sat pale-faced in a chair next to the fireplace while Gunnar stirred the embers and added more wood. Both had grown more silent and somber as the day progressed. Tessa guessed they were thinking the same thing she was, that if a storm blew in, the search party would have to give up and return to their homes. With each hour that passed, the chances of finding the men alive diminished. After being out all night, the chances were already slim.

"It's a good thing you closed school today," Nadine said, lifting the little one to her breast. The baby's whines were cut short as she began her greedy sucking.

"I'm not so sure —"

"Got news that scarlet fever took two kiddies yesterday over in Copper Harbor and three in Cliff."

"Do we know of any cases here?" Tessa was almost afraid to ask.

"None yet, and let's pray it stays that way."

Just the mention of the words *scarlet fever* was enough to cause a panic. The deadly disease spread without mercy and claimed

260

many lives every year.

"I say it's the change in weather," Nadine continued. "These warm spells in between the cold days always make the kiddies sick with one thing or another. Least mine are all running around with snotty noses."

Tessa hugged Ingrid. Above the girl's head, Tessa met Nadine's gaze. "Would you tell families with children to stay home for the time being? We'll cancel classes for the remainder of the week. At least until we make sure there are no children here in Eagle Harbor carrying the disease."

Nadine nodded. In spite of attributing most illnesses to old wives' tales and superstitions, Nadine appeared willing to cooperate with whatever Tessa might suggest.

"Make sure that parents check for rashes," Tessa said, "and also chills, body aches, loss of appetite, nausea, and vomiting. If any of their children exhibit these symptoms, they should be careful to keep siblings away."

Nadine finished nursing her baby and rose to leave. The wind had picked up and rattled the windows, the dark clouds rushing in with a galloping fury.

"The men are back," Nadine announced, her face pressed to the window.

Gunnar flew to the door and flung it wide. His eyes were wide with hope. But one glance at the lake deflated him. His shoulders sagged and the light disappeared from his countenance. He didn't need to say the words for Tessa to know the search party had returned empty-handed.

A gust of frigid north wind raced across the room and hit Tessa with a hard cold fist. She'd tried to prepare herself for the inevitable, but even so, the loss took her breath away. *Please, please let the men be there. Please,* she silently pleaded, breaking away from Ingrid and running to the window to see for herself.

All it took was one look at Wolfie, trudging along slowly with her tail listless and her ears down, for Tessa's throat to burn with the truth. Alex and Michael were gone.

Tessa couldn't do much more than curl up with Ingrid on the sofa as the little girl sobbed on and off during the afternoon. Tessa wanted to sob too. Her chest ached with the need, but all she allowed herself were a few silent tears from time to time when the children weren't looking.

She knew she had to stay strong for Ingrid and Gunnar, yet she couldn't make herself rise from the sofa to do anything. She was glad she had the excuse of holding Ingrid whenever Gunnar got up to add more wood to the fire or to check the flue. He was the one to feed Wolfie and to bring them hot tea late in the afternoon.

His sad eight-year-old eyes never once brightened, but he performed each task with the determination of a man. He retrieved her empty mug and then handed her a blanket for covering Ingrid, who'd finally fallen asleep next to her. Tessa wanted to weep at the boy's sweetness. When she met his serious blue gaze and saw both Alex and Michael in his expression, she had to close her eyes to block them out.

"Are you all right, Miss Taylor?" he whispered as he stood above her.

She swallowed hard and opened her eyes. "I just miss your dad and uncle," she said. It was the truth. She missed them much more than she knew she should. But at that moment she couldn't deny how attached she'd grown to this family and how much it hurt to lose the men. All she could think about was the time at the mine when Alex had held her and kissed her hair and how much she'd liked it.

"Thank you for all your help, Gunnar," she said. "Your dad and uncle would be really proud of you."

He nodded and didn't say anything for a long moment. Finally he cleared his throat

263

and said in a wobbly voice, "What will happen to me and Ingie now?"

"I don't know." Gunnar wouldn't be satisfied with platitudes. He wanted the truth, and she knew he would handle it like the man he was becoming. "For now, I'll stay with you. But once the lake opens to shipping again, then perhaps we can send word to your relatives, maybe your grandmother in Iowa?"

"Ingie wants you to be her mom," Gunnar said softly. "Maybe she can become your little girl."

His words choked Tessa and brought hot tears to the backs of her eyes. She looked down at the frail body next to her, the long lashes resting against tear-streaked cheeks. "She would make any woman the best daughter. And you'd make the best son." She reached for Gunnar's hand and squeezed it. "But I'm sure your grandmother will want you to come live with her."

"What about the surgery on her leg? She needs to have it done."

Tessa nodded. Alex and Michael had both shared with her their plan to take Ingrid to Detroit for surgery. But even if Alex and Michael had lived, they would have continued to struggle to earn enough money for the trip and the surgery.

The wind coming off the lake beat against the house. It howled through the windows and scraped against the roof shingles. Snow mixed with sleet had been pelting the glass for the past hour, but now it raged with the fury of a blizzard.

The sound of someone pounding on the door was almost lost in the wind.

Gunnar rushed across the room to the door. As he unlatched it, another gust threw it open to reveal a man dressed in a thick fur coat, hat, and heavy boots strapped to snowshoes. He was covered in a layer of snow so that he was unrecognizable. As he wiped the snow from his beard and scarf, she could see it was the doctor.

"Dr. Lewis," Tessa said. She stood slowly, trying not to disturb Ingrid.

The doctor didn't say anything. Instead he bent over as he struggled to catch his breath.

A shiver stole over Tessa and she hugged her arms across her chest. "What is it, Doctor?"

He motioned with his head outside and tried to speak, but he was still too winded to form the words. Gunnar stretched to see past the doctor. His eyes grew big, and with a cry he bolted forward. "Bear?"

Tessa's pulse jumped. She brushed past

265

the doctor too, the wind and snow shoving her sideways, stinging her skin. She had to shield her eyes to see through the blowing white to Bear.

The dog was hitched to a sled. At the sight of Gunnar, Bear wagged his tail and started barking.

Already shivering, Tessa was tempted to retreat back into the house. She swung around and called to the doctor, "Where did you find the dog?"

Without answering, the doctor shuffled past her.

It was then she caught sight of a second sled behind the first with two dogs hitched to it. Both sleds were heaped with blankets. Dr. Lewis must have run along next to his sleds rather than ride in them. As the doctor approached the first one, the blankets began to move. Then a gloved hand poked out of the mound and peeled back the layers.

The instant she saw the broad shoulders, her heart tumbled over itself and a one-word scream rolled out, "Alex!"

She couldn't make her feet run fast enough or her hands work swiftly enough to rip at the blankets and free him. In an instant, along with Gunnar she was hugging Alex, even as the snow hit her face and the wind threatened to blow her away.

She clung to him with all her strength. "You're all right. You're all right."

Gunnar was sobbing, and Alex kissed the boy's forehead. His face was half frozen and haggard-looking, but to Tessa it was the most beautiful face in the world, one she thought she'd never see again.

She started to pull back, to give him a moment with Gunnar, when Alex gripped her arm. He nodded at the second sled, where the doctor was already at work. "Gunnar, go see to your father. He's alive, but not by much."

Gunnar ran through the blowing snow toward the doctor and the other sled.

The wind battered Tessa's face and froze the tears she hadn't realized were on her cheeks. The temperature had dropped drastically since that morning. She knew she ought to get Alex inside and out of the cold, but when he turned his hungry blue eyes upon her, all it took was one glance to devour her and draw her back to him.

His tug was almost rough, but she couldn't resist as she fell against him. And when the cold brittle leather of his gloves cupped her cheeks and drew her face down to his, she knew she needed him as desperately as he did her.

He brought his lips to hers decisively as if he'd planned the moment. Even though an alarm in her mind warned her against kissing him back, she was too weakened by relief to pay it attention. Instead she slipped her arms around his neck and pressed against him with a franticness that contained all the worry of the past day, almost as if she needed to test the reality of his presence to know that she wasn't dreaming.

His lips found hers, fierce and demanding, taking her breath away. She responded just as strongly. She angled her mouth to fit against his more fully, needing more. But just as fiercely as he started the kiss, he broke it, leaving her breathless, her chest heaving.

His breath came in bursts too, and his hold on her arm was tight. "I told myself if I made it back alive that the first thing I'd do when I saw you was kiss you."

So he'd been thinking about her while he was gone? She threw caution aside and lifted her bare hand to his face and allowed herself to run her fingers over the bristle on his cheek and jaw, relishing the roughness against her skin and knowing that he was here and real and alive.

"I'll need help getting Michael inside," the doctor called above the wind.

Alex started to rise, but only got halfway up before collapsing, agony rippling across his face.

Gently Tessa pushed down on his shoulder. "I'll go help him." Though she didn't want to leave Alex, he nodded and released her.

With Gunnar, the doctor, and herself, they managed to carry Michael inside. They situated him on the sofa that Ingrid had deserted, the commotion having awoken her.

Tessa set about with rapid efficiency and with Ingrid's help to fetch blankets and to heat water. By the time she returned to the parlor, the doctor had assisted Alex inside and deposited him on the opposite sofa where he promptly lost consciousness.

"His joints are numb from frostbite," the doctor said, leaving Alex's side and taking his leather medical kit from Gunnar who'd retrieved it from one of the sleds. The doctor slid out of his heavy coat. The snow that had accumulated on it was already melting and dripping onto the floor.

Tessa began to lower herself at the end of the sofa, reaching for the laces of Alex's boot, but Dr. Lewis shook his head. "You best be helping me with Michael. He's suffered the worst and needs doctoring first. Alex made me promise to tend Michael

269

before him."

She assisted the doctor in removing Michael's boots and layers of socks, revealing toes that were hard, white, and waxy.

"He's got a severe case of frostbite," the doctor explained. "We'll try warming his flesh, but he's bound to get painful fluid blisters before too long."

For some time they worked on Michael, putting his fingers and toes in warm water and wrapping them in heated blankets. Gunnar and Ingrid were eager helpers, warming blankets, keeping the water heated, and fetching whatever the doctor needed.

When Alex began to stir again, Tessa and Dr. Lewis moved to him and repeated the warming process. As they worked, the doctor explained how he'd been riding home along Sand Dune Road after tending patients over in Phoenix when Bear came bounding up the rocky ledges and intercepted him.

It had already started snowing at that point, so he was able to follow Bear's tracks, which led him across the frozen surface of Great Sand Bay. He suspected they were getting close when Bear picked up speed. At the same time, from the cracking along the surface, the doctor knew the ice was thinning and that he would need to turn back before he broke through.

He was surprised when he came upon Alex dragging Michael across the ice toward him. Alex was barely conscious but had somehow managed to pull the two of them away from the edge. Alex had told him that after the ice had broken up around them yesterday, they'd stayed afloat on their piece of ice like a raft. The biggest challenge had been to keep the ice from moving out to deeper waters. It became difficult to keep their bearings in the fog. Alex had paddled all night with a few pieces of broken wood from their demolished shack and had kept as close to the icy shoreline as he could.

Once morning had come, a shift in the wind blew away some of the fog, allowing him to see where they were, near Great Sand Bay. They still had a treacherous walk across thin ice to reach land, but by that point Michael had drifted into unconsciousness from the cold. Apparently Alex had inched his brother slowly and painstakingly across the frozen bay before the doctor had found them.

Tessa tucked another blanket around Alex, then brushed a loose strand of hair off his forehead. Her fingers shook at the thought of how close he'd come to death.

"Luckily I had two sleds," the doctor said,

finishing his tale. "As it was, I had to leave most of my supplies behind by the dunes." The doctor looked out the window to the advancing darkness and blowing storm. "Looks like I won't be getting back to them right away. I'll need to get home myself before I'm snowed in here for the night."

She didn't want him to leave. She'd rather he stay through the night for Michael and Alex's sake. As if reading her thoughts, he said, "You'll do just fine doctoring them. Don't worry if the skin turns blue and purple. That's better than black. And there will be painful stinging when the feeling returns to their skin. Their joints and muscles will be in a lot of pain too." He handed her a bottle of laudanum. "Give this to them as needed."

She took it and nodded.

"If the storm blows over by tomorrow," the doctor said as he reached for his coat, "I'll stop by and check on the patients."

Gunnar had long since taken care of the dogs and brought them inside to warm and feed them. Tessa was as proud of Gunnar as if he were her own son, especially when he went outside with the doctor to hitch his dogs back up. She didn't protest when he stayed at his father's side long after she tucked Ingrid into bed for the night.

As the night wore on and the men began to awaken in excruciating pain from their thawing flesh, she was grateful for Gunnar's help. Alex's feet and hands finally began to soften and turn purplish red with blisters. He thrashed in pain even after a large dose of the laudanum.

Michael's skin hadn't fared as well. Even with continued warming throughout the night, he started to run a fever and some of his toes remained waxy and turned gray.

Tessa fought to stay awake, finally succumbing to exhaustion in the wee hours of the morning. With Gunnar asleep on the sofa next to Michael, she kneeled beside the sofa where Alex slept fitfully and wrapped her hands around his. She told herself she was only holding his hands to speed the warming, but for a reason she couldn't explain to herself, she had a deep unquenchable need to be with him and touch him and make sure he was really there.

And of course, there was that kiss . . .

She ought to feel mortified for how she'd thrown herself at him and kissed him so brazenly, but the heat in her belly flared more from pleasure than embarrassment. By the dim light of the fire, she watched his sleeping face, the handsome lines, the long lashes resting against his cheeks, and the

273

unshaven stubble that made him look rugged and irresistible.

Her attention shifted to his lips, and the heat in her middle spilled over into her blood. She may have been branded a loose woman, but the kiss with Alex had been her first. And she could understand now why the boys and girls sneaked away to the mine buildings to kiss. Kissing was entirely too enjoyable, at least it had been with Alex, and she wanted to kiss him again.

She studied the hard curves of his mouth and leaned closer so that he was only inches away. Surely she could brush her lips against his one more time. No one else needed to know, not even him. Her breath quickened at the thought of touching his lips.

No! The word clamored in the recesses of her mind. It was all too easy to get carried away. One innocent kiss would lead to another and would never completely satisfy. Instead the kissing would awaken a longing for what was reserved for marriage.

With a sigh, Tessa closed her weary eyes and laid her head down on the edge of the sofa next to his. As much as she wanted to kiss him again, she'd only hurt them both if she gave in to the temptation. She told herself that their earlier kiss was born out of desperation. It didn't mean anything more than that. If he hadn't been lost and half dead, they never would have kissed. And now she had to make sure they never kissed again.

CHAPTER 17

Alex yelled at Michael for the hundredth time, "Keep moving!"

Michael didn't raise his head this time. He'd stopped paddling again.

Alex dipped his scrap of wood deeper into the water. The more active they were, the better. They'd keep the blood flowing and hopefully stay warmer. Bear was lying on their boots, but even with the dog's warmth, Alex had lost all sensation in his feet.

"Paddle!" Alex shouted at his brother.

Michael sat motionless.

Alex couldn't see his brother's face, yet he could tell that Michael was staring out into the darkness. "Don't give up yet," he said, trying to keep the desperation out of his voice.

Michael's body tilted stiffly toward the edge of the floating piece of ice.

"We'll make it. You'll see —"

Before he could finish his sentence, Michael slipped off the ice.

"No-o-o . . ." Alex's throat tightened around his scream.

He jerked awake. Panic coursed through him. He'd spent the past five years pushing Michael away from the edge of the abyss. And now he'd failed. How could he?

He looked up to see a ceiling where the shadows of dying flames danced. His fingers made contact with the scratchy wool of a blanket. The weight covering his body told him he was buried in mounds of warmth on the sofa. The dull pain in his limbs and digits told him the laudanum was keeping the agony at bay.

He was home, he told himself. There was nothing to worry about now. They'd made it. Michael was alive. Even though Michael had wanted to give up, Alex hadn't let him, had forced him to go on, had promised him everything would be okay, just as he always had.

At a soft sigh next to his cheek, Alex glanced sideways. He sucked in a breath at the most beautiful sight. Tessa's sleeping face. She was kneeling next to the sofa with her head resting near his. Her face was pale, made even more so by her dark hair that hung loose and flowed in abandon all around her. Her wavy hair highlighted her delicate features, and the soft glow of firelight emphasized each curve.

During his worst moments over the past two days, the thought of seeing her again had pushed him to hang on. Now here she was. He'd told himself that the moment he saw her, he'd kiss her. He was done with waiting and with keeping a proper distance between them.

Renewed passion filled him at the memory of the brief but passionate kiss he'd claimed when she arrived at the sled. It didn't matter if she'd simply been hugging him as a friend, relieved that he'd been found. He hoped he'd made it very clear that he considered her more than a friend.

She released another sigh and her fingers gripped his harder.

Tessa was holding his hands. She'd chosen to lie next to him, not Michael. Surely that meant she cared for him more. In all the silly competition over the past couple of months, she'd never singled either one of them out with her attention. In fact, she'd made a point of hinting more than once that they were wasting their efforts if they wanted more than friendship from her.

He drank in her face, staring more boldly than he would have had she been awake. He'd fulfilled his vow to himself to kiss her the first chance he had, but maybe he needed to do so one more time to make sure she understood his true feelings toward her. He loved her. He wanted to marry her and spend the rest of his life making her smile. He loved that she was strong, witty, and beautiful. More than that, he loved how compassionate she was. She deeply cared for the children and the people of the community, and even if at times her passion for changing them was overzealous, he admired that she wanted to help them.

He shifted so that his nose almost touched hers. She didn't wake up. One more kiss, that was all it would take. To make it as clear as a summer day that he was claiming her for his own.

His lips grazed hers, lighter than a breath of air.

Still she didn't stir.

He brushed her lips again. If his kiss yesterday had been crushing and demanding, this one was the complete opposite. It was as gentle and tentative as a whisper. A whisper of his love for her. He let his lips linger and was rewarded within seconds by a returning pressure that was light, almost teasing.

Her eyes remained closed, and for a moment he thought she was still enveloped in the sweetness of sleep. But then she breathed his name, slowly, like a prayer. "Alex."

His entire being was overcome with a mingling of joy and desire. She hadn't expected Michael. No, she'd been thinking about *him,* even in her sleep. That had to mean she loved him too. If only she could admit it to herself.

He let his lips graze hers for a moment longer before pulling back. Without his touch, her eyes flew open and her lips chased after his. Of course, he gave in all too willingly and let her mouth capture his. She pressed into him with a passion that was almost his undoing. With a strength he hadn't known he possessed, he kept his own kiss gentle, although his muscles strained with the need to pull her against him hungrily as he had before.

As if sensing his reserve, she stopped abruptly. "I'm sorry," she whispered. "I shouldn't have . . ."

"Yes, you should have." To prove his point, he dropped a kiss onto her forehead.

"Alex . . ." Her voice was laced with regret.

He took in the wildness of her hair again, the sleepy droop of her eyes. "You're beautiful." He smiled, a smile he hoped would melt her heart.

The light in her eyes wavered before brightening.

"I missed you," he whispered. "From the way you kissed me, I guess you missed me too."

"I didn't mean to kiss you," she said, glancing at the opposite sofa to Michael and Gunnar. Neither moved. Her attention shifted back to him.

His grin widened and he arched a brow. "You didn't mean to kiss me? Twice?"

"I did it because I was relieved to see you —"

"You did it because you love me." While he was smiling, his tone demanded honesty from her. "Admit it. You're falling in love with me."

She pushed away from the sofa before he could stop her. "Apparently the time out on the ice froze your brain."

He chuckled. "That's the one thing that didn't freeze." Underneath the blankets his bare feet brushed against the wool, and the sting of the blisters cut off his laugh. As much as his limbs pained him, he was grateful for the sensation. It meant he'd survived intact.

She sat back on her heels. He caught a glimpse in her expression of the anxiety she'd suffered over the past couple of days.

He regretted that she'd had to worry so deeply. He could only imagine that she and the children had believed he and Michael had died.

"Thank you for staying with Gunnar and Ingrid," he whispered. "I'm sure it wasn't an easy time."

She visibly swallowed and replied in a thick voice, "It was incredibly hard."

He was tempted to tease her about missing him. But when she glanced at Gunnar, he knew she was thinking about what would have happened to the children. Their welfare was no laughing matter. The lake was dangerous. He and Michael had encountered life-threatening situations on more than one occasion. If something ever happened to them, what would happen to Gunnar and Ingrid? He'd never considered the fact that they would be alone here at Eagle Harbor.

If only they had a mother . . .

"I'm sure it was even harder for you and Michael," she said.

His nightmare came back to haunt him. He'd come so close to losing Michael again.

Her eyes were upon him and deadly serious. "The doctor told us about the rescue."

Alex lifted a silent prayer of gratitude as he had many times since Bear had come back with Dr. Lewis close on his trail. When Bear had raised his nose, Alex urged the dog to go find help. After Bear trotted off, Alex prayed the dog would find someone. He didn't know how much longer he'd hold up. After a freezing, sleepless night on the ice, he was losing the little bit of strength he had left. Yet he'd kept his sights focused on the distant tree line, slowly but steadily pulling Michael behind him as he slid toward land, praying with each step they wouldn't break through the ice again.

"Thank God, the doctor came when he did," Alex said, unable to keep the hitch out of his voice. "I don't know how much longer I could have gone."

A gust of wind rattled the window that overlooked the lake. In the darkness of the early morning, he couldn't see anything. But he knew a storm had blown in. He closed his eyes against the thought of how close he and Michael had come to being trapped in it.

A low groan rose from the other sofa. Alex tried to push himself up. Excruciating pain shot through his limbs, and he collapsed helplessly. Tessa was already on her feet and rushing to Michael's side.

Gunnar had awoken and was sitting up, watching his father, his young face filled with worry. When he saw that Alex was awake, his features softened only a little.

"Hey, old fella," Alex said. He cracked a grin at the boy.

Gunnar didn't return the smile. "Thanks for rescuing my dad."

Alex nodded and even that effort hurt. "That's what I'm here for." He tried to make his voice light, but the truth was that he meant every word he spoke. He'd sacrifice his very life for his brother if he had to.

Tessa pressed Ingrid's face into her chest and squeezed her hands over the girl's ears. The moans of agony coming from the parlor were half human, half animal. Ingrid's heartrending sobs couldn't drown them out. Tessa wanted to close her own ears against the unbearable anguish, but her first priority was shielding Ingrid from the horror of hearing her father have his fingers and toes amputated.

She rocked back and forth on the ice-cold floor of Ingrid's room, her tears sliding down onto the little girl's silky hair. While the stove in Gunnar's room pumped out heat to the second floor, nothing could take the chill out of the air, especially today.

"It's all right. It's all right," Tessa crooned, trying to reassure herself as much as Ingrid.

284

Exhaustion pushed in around her, making her shoulders and body sag under the strain of the past week. Alex's fingers and toes had fared much better than Michael's, yet he'd still suffered painful blisters the first few days. Worse had been the raging fever and cough he'd contracted. He'd been weak and delirious for days now.

When the storm finally abated, it left Eagle Harbor with several more feet of snow, preventing the doctor from visiting. She'd been worried sick about both men and had done her best to comfort them through their agony.

After four days, the roads had finally been cleared enough for everyone to start venturing out, and the doctor had come again. Although he had trouble maneuvering through the drifts, today he'd made time to visit Alex and Michael. His first proclamation after examining the men was that Michael would need to have four toes and two fingers amputated, the ones that had turned black.

Tessa knew they should count themselves blessed that he hadn't lost more. She should be grateful the men were home safe when Hannah's husband and his fishing partner still hadn't been found. But no matter how blessed they were, nothing could take away the pain of the moment.

Nadine and Josie had come by that morning to help with nursing the men. Tessa was relieved they were here to help with the amputation, so that she was free to comfort Ingrid. Truthfully the weight of responsibility of caring for both the men and the children had been heavy. Each day she stayed at the lighthouse her heart felt heavier.

She'd never wanted to be inside a lighthouse again, and yet here she was practically living in one, sleeping in the bed Gunnar had given up for her. Not only did she resent the lighthouse and the lake every time her gaze landed on them, but she worried for her reputation. She'd been snowed in with two bachelors for nigh to a week completely unchaperoned.

Of course, both had been lying on the sofas all week, too incapacitated to move. Nevertheless, she dreaded what people would say once word got out. People were bound to talk and question her.

The anguished cries and moans from downstairs finally ceased. Tessa leaned back against the bed frame and released a pent-up breath that came out white in the cold air.

The tapping of shoes against metal told

her someone was ascending the spiral tower stairway to the second floor. She swiped away the wetness on her cheeks just as footsteps creaked on the wooden floorboards in the hall outside the bedroom.

Nadine stepped into the room, wiping her hands on her threadbare grayish-colored apron that was now streaked with blood.

Tessa shuddered. "How's Michael?"

Ingrid lifted her chin, her red-rimmed eyes hopeful.

Nadine could only muster a weak smile for the child before turning grave eyes on Tessa. "He passed out, thank the good Lord."

Tessa nodded, grateful he was relieved of pain for a short while.

"He'll survive and be none the worse for it, that he will," Nadine continued. "And I've poured some of my special cod-liver oil down Alex's throat. He'll be better in no time."

Alex's rasping cough wafted faintly through the floorboards. "I'm sure he loved every last drop." Tessa wished she could have seen his expression when Nadine forced the liquid into him. It certainly would have lightened the mood.

"I'll leave Josie with you," Nadine said.

287

"You can't be staying here by yourself any longer."

"Are people beginning to talk?" Tessa had to ask, though she dreaded the answer.

"No," Nadine remarked. New lines of worry added to the wrinkles already creasing her face. "Not yet. Everyone knows how badly the wickies suffered from frostbite. So far they're only saying it's been mighty nice that you stayed to watch the kiddies and tend the men."

"Really?" Relief whispered through Tessa.

"But now that the men are recovering, it's just about time for you to come on back to the house. That way you won't give anyone the chance to start spreading rumors."

"I can come back tonight —"

"Not yet. They need you a couple more days. At least."

"Don't leave me, Miss Taylor," Ingrid said in a wobbly voice, not having left her side since she awoke. "Please don't go away."

How could she say no to the girl's request, especially when she peered up at her with her bright blue eyes so full of trust and love? Tessa squelched the desire to flee. She couldn't leave just yet. Michael and Alex still needed her and so did the children.

She prayed that both she and her reputation could survive a few more days.

288

CHAPTER 18

Tessa scanned the nearly empty shelves in dismay. The supplies in the company store had dwindled down considerably.

"Don't worry, Miss Taylor." Samuel paused in his dusting of one of the shelves. "The boats will be here soon with more."

She glanced out the wide storefront window to the big wet snowflakes that had begun to fall more rapidly since she'd entered the store a few minutes earlier. She was so tired of snow. No place on earth should be allowed to have so much snow, especially so close to April. "I wouldn't be so sure of that. This is the winter that won't end. I think it's tied spring up and put it in jail."

"Spring's in jail?" Samuel's eyes widened in his rounded flushed face. A glistening of sweat had formed on his bald head despite the frigid temperature in the store.

"What I meant is that I don't think spring

will ever arrive."

"Oh, it will," Samuel replied eagerly, as if revealing to her something she'd never before known. "It comes every year."

She gave a faint smile and eyed the bottom of the potato barrel where wrinkled potatoes sat among dirt with their overgrown eyes tangled together. They looked as unappetizing as about everything else in the bottoms of the other barrels. She wrinkled her nose at the moldy dirt scent. "Well, let's just hope that spring decides to come sooner rather than later."

The spring equinox had come and gone. April was almost upon them. Yet the ground was covered with layers of snow, the trees still barren. Everything was a dull grayish brown — the leafless trees, the log cabins, the boulders along the shore. Even the evergreens were looking pale, as if they too were in protest of the overlong winter.

Samuel anxiously eyed the back door that led to the company office. Then he leaned toward Tessa and lowered his voice. "Percival told me there's more in the storehouse. He just wants to make sure all this is used up first." Samuel gestured toward the barrels.

"That's good news, Samuel," she said, knowing he'd told her something he wasn't supposed to, even though she didn't understand what difference it made whether she knew or not. The company warehouse, located along the harbor, had been stocked full in the fall with enough supplies to see them through the winter. While much of the fresh food had frozen, it had still been edible even if it hadn't been palatable.

She forced a smile. "At least we won't starve to death before the new supplies come, right?"

Her attempt at humor fell flat whenever Samuel was concerned. In fact, instead of eliciting mirth, her words seemed only to stir anxiety within him. "We almost starved two winters ago. Percival had to divide up the remaining food carefully."

"I'm sure that won't happen again."

Samuel wrung the cloth in his hands, and his forehead puckered. "There's enough food in the storehouse. That's what Percival said."

"It must be true then," she said and squeezed his arm. She'd expected to eat more fresh game. But ice fishing was too dangerous now, many animals were still in hibernation, and the wild fowl hadn't yet migrated north. The fact was, even if there had been more game for hunting, the miners were still working twelve-hour shifts and too tired to think about hunting when they climbed out of the cold dark caverns of the mines every night.

"Even so, I'll be jubilant when the first steamer arrives." She moved on to the next almost empty shelf to find the flour she'd come to purchase. "I think I'll hold a party in its honor."

"What kind of party?"

She froze. It wasn't the question that stopped her and made her blood run cold. It was the voice. Percival stood in the doorway to the company office that adjoined the store.

"Maybe a box lunch picnic," she answered, wanting to keep her tone nonchalant.

So far, since the incident after the spelling bee, she'd avoided being alone with Percival. During the past weeks he'd been occupied and content with his new mistress and thankfully hadn't paid her much attention.

"A box lunch," Percival repeated cheerfully. "That sounds like a good idea . . . so long as I get to share the picnic lunch with you."

Was Percival once more on the hunt for a new woman to use? Was he about to prey upon her again? A sickening swell rose in Tessa's stomach. "Now, Mr. Updegraff," she said, wishing to race across the store and exit as fast as she could. "You'll have to bid upon the lunches fair and square and sit with the owner of whichever basket you pay for."

"Don't you think Miss Taylor should give us a clue beforehand, Sam? Then we'll know which one is hers so that we can eat lunch with her?"

Samuel nodded vigorously, his eyes bright. "I'd like to eat lunch with Miss Taylor."

Percival's well-groomed mustache twitched with the hint of a smile. "She's a nice lady, isn't she?"

Samuel smiled shyly and ducked his head while his cheeks flamed red.

Percival chuckled and then glanced at Tessa with what she could only describe as appreciation. Was he thanking her for being kind to Samuel? Although none of the townspeople dared to mock Samuel openly, very few made efforts to befriend the simpleminded man the way she had.

"I'd gladly share a box lunch with you Samuel," she said. "But I'm afraid at this point all I'd have to offer is shriveled potatoes."

"It's okay, Miss Taylor," Samuel said. "I don't mind. I like potatoes, especially mashed."

She shared a smile with Percival almost like two parents would over the antics of a child, but something in his glance turned suddenly more calculated. Time for her to go. She wrapped her scarf around her neck and started toward the door.

"You aren't leaving so soon, are you, Miss Taylor?" Percival's voice followed her. "You haven't made your purchase yet."

"I'd hoped to find flour and apples," she said, "but it looks like you're in short supply of both."

"I've heard you make a tasty apple pie."

Her skin crawled at how much he knew about everyone and everything in Eagle Harbor.

"If I find you flour and apples," he continued, straightening in the doorway, his intense gaze still upon her, "will you promise to make me an apple pie?"

"I can't make any promises, and I was planning to make one for someone else first." She knew she'd said the wrong thing when Percival stiffened.

"Don't tell me you were planning to bake a pie for Alex Bjorklund."

"And if I was?" She hadn't been. She'd planned to make one for herself and the Rawlings family, to try to bring some cheer into what had become a drab existence over

294

the past couple of weeks. Not only had she been forced to live through a never-ending winter, she'd had to watch Michael and Alex suffer after nearly losing them both.

Percival's expression had turned dangerous. "You're not allowed to purchase supplies to give to people who aren't employed by Cole Mine."

While she was anxious to leave the store and get away from him, she couldn't resist the challenge in his statement. "If I pay for the goods with my own hard-earned money, who are you to tell me what I can or cannot do with them?"

Percival took a firm step forward. "The lightkeepers get their supplies from the government. They have all they need."

"Yes, but if I purchase something, no one can control what I do with my belongings. If I want to give them away, I have every right —"

"The things in this store are for Cole employees only. It's my job to make sure the people in my charge are taken care of first and foremost." Percival's voice was taut. "If you don't like that policy, I'll make sure you're no longer a Cole employee."

The retort on the tip of her tongue died. Arguing with Percival Updegraff wasn't going to help her cause. She would only end up homeless and jobless. Besides, she didn't have to win the argument to continue to do as she wanted with her purchases.

His unyielding stance told her he was waiting for her concession.

"Very well, Mr. Updegraff." She had to yank each resistant word out. "You're the boss."

"He's the boss," Samuel echoed from where he'd resumed dusting a shelf.

"Now, if you'll excuse me, I'll be on my way." She pulled open the door.

"I hope you're not planning to go to the Bjorklunds'. You've spent entirely too much time there lately."

"Michael still needs someone to help change the dressing on his frostbite wounds."

"I'm sure Alex can do it."

She had the feeling Alex could do more than he admitted. He was usually on the sofa when she arrived in the afternoon after school, acting as helpless as ever. But from the appearance of things, she could tell he was getting around on his own.

Whatever the case, it was none of Percival's concern what she did or didn't do. "Good day, Mr. Updegraff." She opened the door wider. "Good-bye, Samuel."

Samuel's childlike good-bye followed her

296

as she stepped into the wintry mix of snow that was falling. She huddled further into her coat and lengthened her stride through the slushy gray mixture that covered Center Street.

She half expected Percival to follow her outside and demand that she turn around and go home to the Rawlingses'. But when she peeked over her shoulder at the storefront, only the gleaming, spotless glass of the window stared back at her.

Not taking any chances, she picked up her pace. When she arrived at the lighthouse, she didn't knock but entered through the back door into the woodshed. The dark lean-to was nearly empty of wood now, and a scattering of chips and bits of bark littered the floor. She unwrapped her scarf, breathing in the scent of balsam still strong in the air.

At an angry voice coming from the parlor, she froze and listened.

"You don't need her attention any more than I do," Alex shouted.

"I need it more than you" came Michael's terse reply. "You're the one lying around pretending to be helpless whenever she's here."

"I'm resting."

"So that she'll mope over you."

They were talking about her.

"And you're having a pity party for yourself," Alex countered, "so that she'll feel sorry for you every time she sees your sad face."

"You just don't want to admit the truth." Michael's voice was louder than she'd ever heard it before. "She likes me more than she does you."

"You're the one who won't admit the truth," Alex shot back. "She loves *me.*"

Michael gave a short barking laugh that ended up in a cough — the same cough that Alex had suffered through.

Tessa's entire body was riveted in place. Alex had accused her at one other time of loving him, and although she liked him and deeply respected him, she didn't love him. It didn't matter that her heart always picked up speed around him. It didn't matter that she was attracted to so many things about him. It didn't matter that she dreamed about the kisses he'd given her and that she longed for more.

She could never allow herself to love him.

"You're delusional if you think she loves you," Michael said in between hacking coughs. "But then again, you've always thought more highly of yourself than you ought to."

"I can't help it if women like me more than they do you."

"Oh yeah. Those hordes of women hanging all over you," Michael said, his voice dripping with sarcasm, "I'd like to see them."

There was a long silence. Tessa shifted her cold feet. Should she retreat slowly and quietly out the door and then come back in the front door noisily so that they'd know she was here?

"All that matters is that Tessa loves me," Alex finally said. "You might as well accept that and concede defeat."

"We'll see about that."

"I've kissed her. Twice."

"We agreed that neither of us would," Michael stated firmly.

"I never agreed to it. And I'm planning to kiss her again. Soon."

"Then maybe I will too."

"You better not." This time Alex's voice rose a notch.

"If you can, then I can too."

Tessa's muscles tightened in protest. She couldn't believe Alex had boasted about kissing her. Or that Michael thought he could kiss her too — whether she was a willing participant or not. Both men sounded like petulant children in need of a severe tongue-lashing.

"The reason I kissed her," Alex said even louder, "is because I'm planning to marry her."

Planning to marry her? She almost choked at his declaration. Alex *was* rather proud if he thought a couple of stolen kisses in the heat of the moment meant he had a right to marry her.

"You're wrong!" Michael yelled. "I'm planning to marry her!" His words trailed into a fit of coughing.

Tessa couldn't bear listening to another word. She strode out of the woodshed, crossed the kitchen, and stomped her way to the parlor doorway.

Her clomping through the house had drawn their attention. From their spots on the sofas, both men stared at her.

She fisted her hands on her hips and glared, first at Michael, whose cheeks flamed as he dropped his gaze to the knitted afghan covering his lean body, and then at Alex.

"Well, hello there, beautiful," he said, his lips curving into a half-cocked grin. The blue of his eyes sparked, but not with his usual mirth. Instead the sparks were sharp, remnants of his anger from his fight with Michael.

"You're both ridiculous," she said hotly. "I

300

can't believe you're lying here arguing over me like I'm a piece of cargo for barter."

"It *is* ridiculous," Alex muttered, tossing his brother a glance that seemed to tell Michael he was the loser and shouldn't have challenged him.

The look only stirred Tessa's ire. "You're insane if you think that just because we shared a kiss —"

"Two kisses," Alex interrupted. "And a half of one up at the mine, remember?"

She rolled her eyes. "That doesn't mean you're entitled to marry me."

"You're mine now —"

"No, she's not," Michael growled.

"Yes, she is," Alex responded in a steely tone.

She stood directly across from the big parlor window that overlooked the lake. For a long moment the view ensnared her. The jagged boulders poked through the crusty layers of snow covering the ice that still bound the shore. The gray afternoon with the low dark clouds on the horizon was ugly and ominous and taunted her. The clouds were partners of destruction with the icy lake. They rose up to laugh at her and remind her of all they'd taken and still planned to take.

She couldn't keep from glancing at the

swaths of bandages wrapped around Michael's hands and feet and thinking of the stumps that remained where his fingers and toes had once been. The nightmare of those couple of days of waiting and wondering what had become of the men rushed back to haunt her. It had been torture.

How could she spend the rest of her life wondering and waiting for danger to strike again? It was only a matter of time before something else happened. The next time the danger would take more than fingers and toes.

Michael lay flat on the sofa under an afghan. His handsome face was thin and pale from the past two weeks of illness and inactivity. He was staring at Alex, his anger at his brother flashing in his eyes.

She switched her focus to Alex sprawled on the opposite sofa, which sagged under his bulky frame. He'd folded both of his thickly muscled arms across his chest. His thin union suit stretched at the seams. His blond hair lay in disarray across his forehead, begging her to comb it back. The faint dimple in his chin, the strong jawline, the sandy bristles on his cheeks — his features beckoned to her, had become familiar and dear.

She loved the way his lips could so easily

quirk into a grin that never failed to make her stomach flip-flop. She loved his long lashes and the way his eyes lit up when he teased her. She loved the fierceness with which he defended and protected those he cared about.

Was he right? Was she falling in love with him?

Oh, heaven help her. Her chest compressed like a garment passing through a washer wringer. It squeezed hard and cut off the air from her lungs.

As if sensing her attention upon him, Alex turned to look at her. He stopped mid-sentence in a retort to Michael. The frustration and anger in his expression only made her heart hurt more. One word from her could halt the argument between the brothers.

His eyes pleaded with her to choose between them once and for all, to put an end to the misery that had been building between himself and Michael.

She found herself falling into the beautiful blue depths of his eyes. They drew her in irresistibly even as her mind screamed in protest. She couldn't — she wouldn't — allow herself to fall in love with a man whom she might lose in one easy breath of the wind or temperamental turn of the weather.

303

"No," she whispered hoarsely, taking a step back.

His eyes followed her, and the intensity in them begged her to pronounce the truth.

She shook her head, imperceptibly at first. But when he started to speak, she shook her head more forcefully and retreated two more steps. "No," she said louder, hating the tremble in her voice that rose from the painful emotions swirling in her chest.

"Please, Tessa . . ." he started.

"I can't." She held out a hand to ward off his charm and his effect on her. She could feel Michael's eyes upon her now too, silently urging her to choose him. "I can't," she said again with more force, needing to convince herself as much as she needed to convince them.

"You know you love me," Alex said softly, patiently.

Tears burned at the back of her eyes. "No!" she lashed out. She wouldn't give in to her tears or to Alex. "It doesn't matter how I feel about either one of you. I'm not the woman you need."

They both began to protest, but she cut them off. "The day I left Windmill Point Lighthouse, I vowed I'd never step foot into another lighthouse for as long as I lived."

"You're here." Alex pushed himself up.

"Which means some promises are meant to be broken."

"I've always hated living in lighthouses." Her voice cracked as her thoughts traveled back to the stormy night her mother had left their keeper's cottage for the last time. She'd dressed in her oil-slicked coat and hat. The lightning had flashed in the window, illuminating the anxiety and determination on her face when she stooped to kiss her two oldest daughters good-bye. Her kiss had lingered wistfully against Tessa's forehead, warm and gentle and fearful, as it was every time she went with her father to attempt a rescue. It was almost as if her mother had known that each time she put out in the little rowboat, she might not return.

Their father had come back hours later, his expression grief-stricken, his shoulders slumped, his eyes reflecting his broken heart. Mother wasn't with him. She'd never be with them again. Even if she'd given her life to save several of the survivors of the shipwreck, Tessa's hatred had taken root that dark night. Over the years it had dug into her soul deeper, until she couldn't uproot the hatred without ripping apart who she was.

Yes, there were other jobs just as danger-

305

ous — like working in the mines. There were wars and diseases and any number of factors that could take away the people she loved. But her resentment toward the sea and the lights ran too deep.

"I hate lighthouses," she said again, unable to keep the venom from her voice. "And I hate the lakes. After having no choice but to live in them all my life, now that I'm finally free, I won't go back. I won't marry a lightkeeper. I won't live in a lighthouse. And I won't allow myself to love someone who has any connection to them."

At her declaration, Alex sat back speechless, his eyes wide. Michael, too, looked at her in surprise. The silence was broken only by the crashing of the distant waves against the remaining ice. The slap of water was harsh and continuous, as if even the sea had risen up to agree with her.

"I'll never marry either one of you," she said with a finality that tore at her heart. Though the words were as harsh as the waves, she had to say them. She had to make the men understand once and for all that she meant them. "No matter how sweet you both are . . ."

Her voice cracked as her throat clogged with emotion. She had to get out of here. She couldn't let herself break down in front of them.

With her hand over her mouth to capture the sobs, she whirled away from the parlor, raced through the kitchen, and didn't stop in the woodshed to wrap her scarf around her neck. Blinded by tears, she shoved open the door and rushed outside.

The fat flakes of snow had changed to splattering drops of rain. They fell hard against her face and against the ground, making it slushy. She ran fast, needing to get away from the lighthouse, needing to escape the clutches it had dug into her, and needing to get away from the men who'd somehow, against her best efforts, managed to win her heart.

CHAPTER 19

Alex shifted on the sofa. Neither he nor Michael had spoken in the past hour since Tessa had left. Outside, evening shadows were beginning to lengthen. The only sound was the patter of rain against the window, a steady rain that would begin the job of washing away the snow and ice that still clung to the land.

He released a pent-up sigh. The constant rumbling in his stomach told him it was past time for him to get up and start dinner. Tessa wouldn't be there to make anything for them tonight. From the silence that shrouded the house, apparently Ingrid and Gunnar weren't planning to make anything either.

The two had shouldered a fair share of the housework and cooking during the past couple of weeks, but he was more than capable of doing the work now. Michael had been right about one thing. He'd lain on the sofa so that Tessa would fawn over him, so Michael wouldn't get all of her attention.

He pushed himself up from the cushions and forced back a groan. Only a few blisters remained on his fingers and toes, yet his entire body still ached from the fever and cough that had lingered and rendered him weak.

Once he was sitting he glanced at Michael, who was wide awake and staring at the ceiling, at a long crack that divided the room between them. His expression was grim. The emptiness in his eyes reminded Alex of the dark chasm that had existed for too long after Rachel's death.

A sliver of worry pricked Alex. "Tessa hasn't died," he said as he stood and straightened his stiff joints.

"I know that," Michael replied.

"Then stop acting like it."

"She won't be back."

"Sure she will."

"Didn't you hear her? She made it clear she doesn't want either one of us."

"She was caught up in the emotion of the moment." Alex lifted his arms above his head and stretched. "She didn't mean everything she said."

"Her father was a wickie and drowned in front of her eyes."

The news slammed into Alex's gut. He dropped his arms, his chest compressed as if he'd gotten the air knocked out of him. "She told you that?"

Michael nodded. "She lost her mom and sister too."

"How?"

"She didn't say, but I'm guessing in lighthouse accidents."

For an instant, Alex couldn't keep from wondering why Tessa hadn't shared about her past with him. Maybe she was closer to Michael than he'd realized. After all, his brother had spent more time with her, especially when she'd been holding the evening class and he'd walked her home every night.

"She won't be coming back," Michael said again, this time with a finality to his tone.

Alex didn't want to agree with him, didn't want to believe him. But she'd clearly been heartbroken. His own heart throbbed every time he thought about the anguish that had constricted her pretty features and had laced her voice.

After she'd run out of the house, his body had keened with the need to run after her, to reassure her that everything would work out all right and that they'd overcome the obstacles that stood between them. But he'd held himself back, sensing she needed time to herself. If he'd gone after her, he would have pushed her further away.

The urge to go to her welled up so strongly that he almost staggered. Now that he knew more about why she hated lighthouses, he needed to make her understand that her fears were unfounded.

But were they?

He had only to think of the times his and Michael's boat had capsized during rescues, of how close they'd come to losing their own lives on numerous occasions, not to mention the most recent incident of getting lost in the dense fog while ice fishing.

The life of a lightkeeper was fraught with danger. He couldn't pretend otherwise.

He blew out a frustrated breath. No matter the danger, they couldn't let that stop them from sharing their lives together, from enjoying and loving each other for whatever time God gave them in this fragile life.

He limped forward with renewed determination. He had no choice but to go to her and make her see reason.

"You can't run after her," Michael said tersely.

"Why not?" Alex swayed with dizzying weakness. He paused to steady himself. "You can't stop me."

"Accept that she doesn't want us."

"You can accept it," Alex said, "but I'm not giving up so easily."

Michael again looked up at the crack in the ceiling that stood between them as visibly as the crack that had grown in their relationship since Tessa arrived in Eagle Harbor.

Alex started to leave, but then guilt brought him to a stop. Slowly he pivoted. As much as he wanted to resist looking at his brother's sad face, his eyes were drawn there. Michael was pale and haggard, still suffering from the pain of his amputations. More than that, he wore an air of defeat.

Was Michael that enamored by Tessa that her loss would send him back into the abyss, the abyss Alex had labored to pull Michael out of the last few years?

Alex's shoulders sagged in a defeat of his own. He couldn't go see Tessa now, not when Michael was clearly falling into a pit of despair. A visit to Tessa might only serve to plunge him to the bottom. He'd have to put it off until later, perhaps after Michael fell asleep.

"Let's call a truce." Alex tried to infuse enthusiasm into his voice that he didn't feel. "I'll get the kids down here, and we'll make some dinner."

Michael didn't say anything. He rolled onto his side so that his back was facing Alex.

Alex stifled another sigh and shuffled to the front hallway that led to the winding iron stairway. "Gunnar. Ingrid," he called. "Come down and help me get dinner started."

His voice echoed upward against the cold brick tower. From the grates in the steps he could see the doorway to the second floor was closed. He waited a moment for the children to respond, but all he heard was the rain striking the nearby tower window.

"Gunnar! Ingrid!" he called louder, realizing he hadn't heard or seen them since he and Michael had started arguing. Lately all the children heard between him and Michael was fighting. He wouldn't doubt that the two had hidden to avoid it.

"You can come out now," he yelled up the stairwell. "Your daddy and I promise we won't fight anymore today."

He strained to hear their footsteps, but only the distant rumble of thunder responded.

He started up the narrow steps, one at a time, forcing his weak legs to climb. "All right, you two. You've awoken the big grouchy bear." He let out a loud roar that, if he could say so himself, sounded almost like a real bear's roar. "The bear's coming to get you."

Usually his pronouncement brought a chorus of giggles and a scampering of footsteps. Yet in the hollow emptiness of the tower, his heavy steps pinged eerily against the metal. When he reached the second floor, he opened the door in anticipation of them jumping out and attacking him. Nothing moved, no one there.

He poked his head first into Ingrid's room, then into Gunnar's. As he searched every corner and glanced under each bed, he soon realized the children weren't there. With a frown, he made his way back downstairs and searched his and Michael's bedrooms, the kitchen, and the woodshed.

"Have you seen the kids?" he asked Michael. "I can't find them anywhere."

"I haven't seen them since they came home from school," Michael said.

"Did they say they were going somewhere?" Alex peered out the kitchen window that overlooked the path leading toward town. The darkness was creeping in faster. It wouldn't be long now before it swallowed up the remaining gray light of evening.

"No. They didn't get my permission to

leave," Michael said, his face creasing with anxiety.

"I'm sure it's nothing." Alex tried to guess where the children might be.

Within the shadows of the room, the pallor in Michael's face was even more sickly than earlier. "Do you think they heard Tessa? When she said she wouldn't marry either of us?"

Alex thought back to when he was on the sofa before Tessa had arrived. The children were on the stairwell playing one of their favorite games. They pretended the tower was a mine shaft and they were descending into the earth to blast for copper.

"What if they heard what Tessa said?" Michael tried pushing himself to a sitting position but was too weak to hold himself up for long.

"It doesn't matter —"

"Yes, it does!" Michael cried. "Ingrid has been telling me every day how much she wants Tessa to become her mother."

Tessa become Ingrid's mother? He'd noticed Ingrid's affection for Tessa. But had she been playing matchmaker for her father? He supposed it only made sense, especially after the few times Ingrid had made excuses to invite Tessa into their home.

Unease pooled in Alex's stomach. "You

315

don't think Ingrid got upset, do you?"

"Tessa was adamant about not marrying us. If Ingrid heard that, then I'm sure she was devastated by it."

Alex looked outside again. The darkness was almost complete. He could only imagine Ingrid and Gunnar sitting on the metal steps, their eyes wide, listening to him and Michael yelling at each other again about who deserved Tessa.

He groaned at the thought. Why hadn't he been more careful with his words? Why hadn't he thought to rein in his frustration to protect them?

"Help me up," Michael demanded, trying to push himself off the sofa again. "I need to go find them."

Alex shook his head. "Stay there. I'll go look for them."

Michael sat up. His thin face was strained, and sweat broke out on his forehead. "I'm coming with." He shoved his body upward, but the moment he put pressure on his toes and feet, he gave a strangled cry and fell back into the cushions.

Alex crossed the room and swung Michael's feet back up on the sofa, returning them to the pillow that had elevated them. Michael's eyes were squeezed shut, his mouth clamped into a grimace. Alex was

316

tempted to berate him for getting up before he was ready, but he knew that would only frustrate his brother more. If the situation had been reversed, Alex would have killed himself to search for the children.

He quickly finished situating Michael on the sofa. As he started to move away, Michael's hand shot out and captured his. Alex glanced down and found himself gazing into Michael's stricken eyes, which revealed the pain that went all the way to his soul, the pain of having lost someone he'd loved once and the fear of losing again.

"Find them," Michael whispered hoarsely.

Alex squeezed his brother's hand. "I will." He prayed he was right.

He bundled into his waterproof slicker and rubber boots, drew up his hood, and started off with both Wolfie and Bear, hoping the dogs could track the children. He didn't have to go far before he saw the rain had washed away the children's footprints and any scent of them into the ever-increasing puddles of melted snow.

Nevertheless he plunged forward, praying as he went that he would find them before the blackness of night fell. Although he'd brought a lantern, the flickering light wouldn't give him much to search by.

His footsteps took him in the direction of

317

the Rawlingses' house. Part of him hoped that Ingrid had simply dragged Gunnar over to visit Tessa with the intention of getting Tessa to change her mind about marrying Michael. But even if Ingrid and Gunnar hadn't gone to see Tessa, Alex needed to share the burden of their disappearance with her.

The truth was he needed her. Amid the difficulty of the afternoon quarrel with Michael and now the disappearance of the children, he needed Tessa's strength and level-headedness to give him fresh courage. She'd become an integral part of his life, the first person he wanted to talk to when he was happy and the first person he wanted to talk to when he was sad. And definitely the first person he wanted to turn to when he was in a crisis. Like now.

He was breathing heavy by the time he reached the front door. It took only a few seconds after the door was opened and he was ushered inside for him to learn that Ingrid and Gunnar hadn't been there. Even so, he asked for Tessa.

"She said to tell you she's busy and can't be disturbed right now," Josie said, coming back down the stairs, flipping her hair over her shoulder and batting her eyelashes at him. He had the feeling she meant to be enticing, but she only managed to look like she was trying to dislodge a bug.

"Please tell her it's urgent," he said, eyeing the staircase behind the girl and hoping for a glimpse of Tessa.

Josie leaned one of her hips against the wall and widened her smile suggestively.

He frowned. If he'd had the time, he would have thrashed Josie soundly for trying to flirt with him, a full-grown man. But the knowledge that Gunnar and Ingrid were out there somewhere made his body tense with an urgency that superseded all else.

It wasn't that he didn't trust Gunnar. He knew the boy would never do anything to put Ingrid in danger. However, Ingrid could be strong-willed when she got an idea into her head, and Gunnar usually had a hard time saying no to anything the girl requested of him.

"Don't you want to tell her yourself?" Josie asked, eyeing the narrow spot beside her.

"Josie Rawlings," he growled, letting his anger rumble in his voice. The two younger boys were now clinging to his legs. They stopped trying to wrestle him to the floor and gazed up at him with wide eyes.

Josie stared at him a moment longer before lowering her eyes in embarrassment.

"Go tell Tessa that I need her help finding Gunnar and Ingrid."

The words had barely left his mouth when footsteps sounded on the stairs and Tessa appeared behind Josie. Her wrinkled forehead and worried eyes told him she'd been listening to his conversation with Josie.

"What happened?" she asked, brushing past the girl.

Her expression only grew more worried after he explained that Ingrid and Gunnar weren't at home and that he suspected they'd overheard the argument earlier.

"Michael thinks that Ingrid had her heart set on you becoming her new mother," Alex finished. "When she heard you say that you wouldn't marry us, she must have gotten upset."

"And so she ran away," Tessa said, rubbing her hands up and down her arms but unable to hide her shivering.

The boys had resumed their wrestling, but Alex had no heart for interacting with them today. He stood unmoving and let them pummel him.

Tessa's eyes grew wider with the implications of Ingrid and Gunnar being outside in the dark and the rain. Even if the temperature had risen above freezing, it wasn't warm enough for two young children to be outside for any length of time.

She sprang into action, hurrying toward the door and her coat. "We need to form a search party and go find them at once."

Nadine stuck her head out of the kitchen. "You two get a head start. I'll have William round up the older boys and some of the neighbors and join you."

Alex nodded his thanks. Within minutes he and Tessa were outside, walking through town and calling for the children. Wolfie and Bear stayed by their sides, so he knew the children were nowhere near. They checked the schoolhouse, the churches, the store, every building in town.

By the time they'd made a thorough search of the town, they'd been joined by several other families carrying lanterns and calling out the children's names. Night had descended, and the rain continued to fall. The ground was slushy and his boots soaked. Tessa fared worse, and even though he encouraged her to return to the house and change out of her wet garments, she was adamant about staying with him.

The men agreed that they should branch out to continue their search. Some of the men would check along the shore, others the surrounding hills. As Alex hiked around the base of the closest hill calling their

321

names, he had a sudden inspiration that filled him with dread. The children had been pretending they were at the mine. What if they'd really gone there?

"The mine shafts," he yelled to William Rawlings, who was combing the woods opposite him and Tessa.

William lifted his lantern and nodded. His long shift had ended only a short time ago. The dirty smears on his face said that he hadn't even had time to wash up yet. But William Rawlings was a kind man. Alex had no doubt his friend would keep looking until he dropped from exhaustion.

"I'll check shafts one and two," Alex shouted above the driving rain. "You take three and four."

William started down the road that led to two of the shafts with his oldest sons trailing behind. Alex grabbed Tessa's hand, and they climbed as fast as they could up the incline. They stopped at each of the mine buildings to peek inside and call out the children's names.

As he closed one door after another, the dread went deeper. He tried not to think about what could have happened if Ingrid had dragged Gunnar up into the mine. He knew with certainty that Gunnar would have brought Ingrid home by now. He wouldn't have stayed out this long with her. He would have carried her home if need be. He was too responsible and too caring to allow Ingrid to suffer the coldness and dampness of a rainy night.

Something must have gone terribly wrong.

"Gunnar!" he yelled, the panic growing with each deserted building he encountered. "Ingrid!"

Tessa echoed his calls, clinging to his hand as they stepped carefully over the rocks that littered the ground everywhere around the mine site.

As they moved into the number two shaft building and found it empty, he stumbled and fell, his body spent, his illness of the past week catching up to him. He wanted to bury his face in his hands and weep. He couldn't go back to Michael without the children. How could he face his brother and tell him he hadn't been able to find them?

He couldn't.

Michael had been devastated for months — no, years — after Rachel died. Alex didn't want to think about how losing the children would affect his brother.

A gentle hand rested on his back. "Alex?" Tessa kneeled next to him. "Are you all right?"

He shook his head, unable to get the

323

words past his heaving chest. How could things have gotten this far out of control? Why had he fought so much with Michael? In fact, he shouldn't have fought over Tessa at all. If she was so important to Michael, his own brother, if she was able to make him happy again and bring him back to life, how then could he stand in their way?

"Alex," she whispered, "tell me what's wrong."

He gasped for a breath. "This is all my fault."

She shook her head. "I was just thinking the same thing — that it's my fault."

"No," he said almost harshly. "I've been selfish. I've only been thinking about myself and what I want. Instead of what's best for Michael and the kids."

She rubbed her hand over his back like she might a sick child. "I shouldn't have been so forthright with my feelings this afternoon, especially knowing the children were close by and possibly listening."

"Don't blame yourself. If I hadn't been arguing with Michael, none of this would have happened." If he hadn't decided to pursue Tessa for himself, Michael could have quite possibly been married to her by now, and Ingrid and Gunnar would be safe and snug at home, with Tessa cooking them a hot meal and tucking them into a warm bed.

Shouts came from outside the shaft building. He sat up to listen, but Tessa was already heading toward the door. Across the hill at shaft three, the light of a lantern wavered in the darkness.

"We found them!" William Rawlings's faint shout hit Alex and brought stinging tears to his eyes. He surged to his feet and followed after Tessa as she rushed down the rocky path that led to the connecting shaft.

As they drew closer, the lantern illuminated two small children huddled next to William. He could tell Tessa had seen the children too because she picked up her pace until she was running toward them. When they finally reached the other shaft building, Tessa flung herself at the two, drawing them both into her arms.

The children threw their arms around her and buried their faces against her. Above the sound of his own ragged breaths, Alex could hear their muffled sobs and each one tore at his heart.

"They'd gone down into the shaft and hid in an abandoned stope on level one," William said, wiping a hand across his weary face. "When they thought to climb back up, the ice had formed so thick on the ladder that they couldn't make it up."

Gunnar released Tessa and swiped at his cheeks before standing to face Alex. His young features were lined with the copper-colored grime of the mines, but nothing could mask his shame. It radiated from every pore and every muscle. "I'm sorry, Uncle Alex," Gunnar said in a wobbly voice. "I shouldn't have let Ingrid talk me into coming here. I should have kept her at home."

Alex didn't have the heart to scold the boy. His relief was too overwhelming to do anything but grab Gunnar and fold him into a crushing hug. "You were wise not to climb the ladder," Alex said. He tried to block out the thought of what could have happened if Ingrid had attempted it . . . He couldn't keep from picturing her broken lifeless body at the bottom of the shaft, hundreds of feet down into the earth.

"I could have made it," Gunnar said as he pulled back to look up at Alex. Tears made trails down the boy's gritty face. "But I didn't want to leave Ingie. I was afraid she might try to climb up after I left."

Alex nodded and glanced again at Ingrid clinging to Tessa. "That was smart. I'm glad you stayed with her."

Tessa had pulled the girl down onto her

lap and was rocking back and forth, murmuring against Ingrid's loose, dirty hair. Ingrid's fists were bunched in Tessa's wet coat, and she clung to Tessa as if she'd never let go.

Ingrid needed a mother more than she needed anything else. How could he have been so callous to Ingrid's needs all these months? How could he have ignored the glaring messages that Ingrid had been sending over and over.

He'd always prided himself on being like his father, on being able to sacrifice, to put aside his own needs and remain loyal to his family above all else. What had happened to him? How had he allowed himself to put his own selfish needs and desires above those of his family?

Tessa stroked Ingrid's hair and pressed a kiss against her head. The light from William's lantern wasn't bright, but it was enough to show the tears that ran down Tessa's cheeks.

He squeezed his eyes closed to block out her image — her beautiful, loving image. His chest tore with burning hot pain at what he knew he had to do. He had to relinquish her to Michael. Not only did Michael need her, but so did Ingrid and Gunnar.

He hugged Gunnar tighter. No matter

what it would cost he had to sacrifice for them. He swallowed the inner protest that rose swiftly. As much as he loved Tessa, he had to stay loyal to his family and do what they needed.

For they needed Tessa more than he did. It was time for him to let go of her. As agonizing as it would be, he had to do it.

CHAPTER 20

Tessa took the mug of hot mead from Nadine and gave her a grateful nod. She hadn't been able to warm herself for the past two days, not since she'd gone out into the rain to help search for Ingrid and Gunnar.

"Drink it up now," Nadine said, shooing away one of the little boys from the sofa where Tessa reclined. "It'll help warm the blood, that it will."

Tessa drew the mug up, letting the wafting of spices and heat soothe her face. Her throat was scratchy, her nose running, and her head achy. She'd regretted that once again she'd had to cancel classes. But the chill ravaging her body had rendered her useless and tired. She'd done little else but sleep the hours away and drink the concoctions Nadine plied into her. And of course Hannah, her helper, was grieving the loss of her husband. It was possible his body might wash up onshore after the ice melted. But it was also likely he'd been swept far out and drowned in the depths of Lake Superior.

Two of the young children ran circles around the front room, one laughing and the other crying. Nadine had placed the baby among the toys scattered about the floor to play, but she sat unhappily whining to be picked up every time Nadine walked past her.

The temperature had once again dropped well below freezing, leaving a coating of ice over everything. Samuel Updegraff had stopped by earlier that morning on his way to the store. With his round face wrinkled with worry lines, he'd informed her that even though spring had been delayed again, the warehouse down by the docks still had plenty of food and that they wouldn't starve.

She'd thanked him for his reassurances, knowing he was trying to convince himself more than he was her. Nevertheless, she was touched that he'd taken the time to visit her, and that he'd brought her one of the few wrinkled apples from the bottom of the barrel.

Nadine tucked the scratchy wool blanket back over Tessa's feet and then straightened. "Stay put and don't you be getting up and trying to do any work." Nadine's tired eyes regarded her with a warmth that seeped into Tessa's heart and spread to her cold limbs.

She reached out and grabbed Nadine's hand, not caring that the woman's fingers were dirty or callused. "Thank you, Nadine." Her voice was low and hoarse. "You've been a godsend."

Nadine managed a half nod in reply. Smiling just wasn't a part of the woman's capability.

At a crash of a chair against the hardwood floor, Nadine spun away to grab the nearest of her children by the shirt. "I've told you kiddies a million times not to run in the house," she yelled as she dragged the child to the kitchen. "I don't want to have to tell you again."

Tessa leaned back and closed her eyes. She wasn't sure that she'd ever grow accustomed to Nadine's methods of scolding her children, and she'd become weary of trying to instruct her in gentler ways of mothering. Today, especially, she had no energy to issue any advice. Maybe once spring weather finally came, she'd muster the enthusiasm to form a gardening club or perhaps start a school for the mothers to give them tips on caring for their children.

While thankfully none of her scholars had contracted scarlet fever, many of them had missed school due to one illness or another that long winter. Though she continued to persevere and teach whomever showed up each day, she'd run out of paper and slate pencils. It was getting more difficult to ignore the ever-thinning faces and constantly grumbling stomachs of children who had too little to eat.

If only spring would finally come . . .

A knock on the front door interrupted her melancholy. Josie appeared seemingly out of nowhere to answer it. At the sound of Alex's voice, Tessa sat up straighter and swiped at the messy strands of hair that hung in her face. Against her will, her pulse pattered faster.

She hadn't seen him or the children since he'd left the mine carrying Ingrid in his arms with Gunnar following behind with slumped shoulders. Nadine had brought her reports and assured her the children hadn't suffered in the least from the escapade. Yet Tessa hadn't been able to stop from worrying about them, wanting the opportunity to talk to Ingrid and make things right.

She didn't exactly know what she'd tell Ingrid. She hadn't changed her mind about marrying either Alex or Michael. Even if they hadn't been lightkeepers, she still wouldn't have considered them, not when as a woman teacher she was prohibited from marrying. Perhaps a deeper part of her also wanted to prove that she could reclaim her lost reputation, that she could stay strong, and earn a good name as a single woman.

Whatever the case, she should have made clear all along that she wasn't ready for a serious relationship. At the very least she could reassure the sweet girl not to stop praying that God would bring along the right mother eventually, even though it wasn't her.

"Miss Taylor!" Ingrid cried as she entered the room. With her crutch under one arm, she shuffled across the floor, dodging the baby and toys. Her eager eyes were fixed on Tessa's face, a tremulous smile upon her lips.

Behind her came Gunnar, looking everywhere but at Tessa, his face pink with embarrassment. She was surprised to see Michael enter next with Alex at his side holding him up. Michael's face was taut from obvious pain, but his hair was neatly combed and his skin smooth from a recent shave. Although he was still suffering, Tessa was relieved that he was finally up on his feet again, that he wasn't letting all that had happened hold him down for too long.

Alex, on the other hand, didn't look as if

he was faring as well. His hair was unkempt, his face shadowed with several days' worth of stubble, and the circles under his eyes were dark. He steadied Michael and half carried him inside.

She waited for his ready smile, the carefree grin that never failed to melt her reserve. But he focused all his attention on Michael, talking to his brother gently, encouraging him toward one of the chairs near the sofa. He didn't give her even the briefest of glances, almost as if she wasn't in the room.

"We heard you were sick," Ingrid said, stopping in front of her. The little girl started to reach for her, then folded her hands in front of her.

"I just have a little touch of something," Tessa said in her scratchy voice. "It's nothing. I'm sure I'll be better in no time."

Ingrid took in the blanket covering her, the steaming cup of mead, and then Tessa's face, which she was sure was pale and gaunt. Any trace of Ingrid's smile faded. Instead the girl's eyes turned glassy, and her bottom lip wobbled.

"I'm sorry," Ingrid whispered.

"Sorry for what?" Tessa cupped the girl's cheek, needing to test for herself that Ingrid really was safe and well.

"I'm sorry for running away and making

you have to go out into the cold to find me."

"You shouldn't have run outside like that," Tessa said softly. "But it wasn't your fault that I got wet and cold. That was my own."

A tear spilled over and slid down Ingrid's cheek. "But if I'd stayed home, you wouldn't have had to look for me."

Tessa set aside her mug and wrapped her arms around Ingrid. "We all make mistakes sometimes." She thought about the rash words she'd spoken to the men about never marrying them. She'd only been thinking of herself. She hadn't considered their feelings or needs. And she certainly hadn't paid attention to how her words might affect Ingrid. "Even I make mistakes," she whispered against Ingrid's head.

Ingrid nuzzled her nose into Tessa's neck.

"And I'm very sorry if I hurt your feelings with the things I said to your father."

Ingrid nodded. The one small motion was all Tessa needed. Ingrid had forgiven her. Tessa released a long breath. As much as she wanted to lump Ingrid and Gunnar with all her other students, somehow she couldn't. She wasn't sure how it had happened, but Ingrid and Gunnar earned a special place in her heart. When she'd held Ingrid after finding her in the mine shaft,

335

she imagined that the depths of her feelings for the children mirrored what a mother might feel.

Tessa savored the bony arms around her neck and the soft cheek pressed against her. She closed her eyes, wanting to capture the moment because she knew it wouldn't last. Even if she had motherly feelings toward the children, she had to stay impartial. Eventually she'd have to tell the little girl that even if they were both sorry for what had happened, Tessa couldn't change the fact that she wasn't planning to become Ingrid's mother.

If she ever changed her mind about the men — which would be a miracle — she knew she wouldn't choose Michael. She couldn't deny that of the two, she was more attracted to Alex. There was something there between them that she didn't understand but that was undeniable.

She slid another glance at him, expecting him to be sneaking a look at her. But he had his back to her and was helping to arrange Michael in the chair.

Her chest pricked with unexpected pain. It didn't matter what was there between them, they simply didn't have a future together.

Ingrid squeezed her again. "Uncle Alex

said you didn't mean everything you said," she whispered. "He told Daddy to get another job someplace else besides a lighthouse and that then you'd marry Daddy."

Tessa froze and stared at Alex's broad shoulders and the muscles beneath his snug sweater as he spread a blanket across Michael's legs. "He told your daddy to get another job?"

Ingrid nodded solemnly.

Nadine had come from the kitchen and was fussing over Michael and Alex so she couldn't see either of their faces.

Tessa tried to picture Alex encouraging Michael to get another job so that he would be free to marry her. After the argument she'd overheard between them earlier in the week, she couldn't imagine Alex ever saying such a thing, not when he'd been so insistent about marrying her for himself.

She shook her head and turned her attention back to Ingrid. "Let's not worry about any of that right now. Why don't you climb here next to me and keep me warm. I'm freezing and I think you're just what the doctor ordered."

Ingrid complied with a delighted smile and snuggled next to Tessa as though she'd been made to fit there. Tessa took a sip of her mead and waited for Alex to comment

337

about her laziness, to say something funny or witty. When he straightened, he squeezed Michael's shoulder before turning to speak to Nadine again while the youngest children attacked his legs and climbed all over him as they usually did.

Gunnar had knelt next to his father's chair and was watching his uncle with amusement. Alex flashed the boy a smile. "You used to do this too, once upon a time. But I had to give up since you were always taking me down."

Tessa watched the light flicker in Alex's eyes and waited once again for him to turn his attention on her as he often did. She wanted to see the mirth in his eyes and feel the warmth of his affection. He bent to tickle the two boys, growling and pretending to be a big bear.

He was ignoring her. She frowned behind her mug. Was he angry with her for saying no to his appeal for her love? Certainly he wasn't that petty. They could still be friends, couldn't they?

After a few more moments of wrestling with the boys, Alex followed Nadine into the kitchen. After he was gone, the room turned strangely silent. Nadine had finally picked up the fussing baby. Josie had disappeared. And the two littlest boys had

338

trailed behind Alex.

She was alone with Michael and the children. They were glancing around the disarray of the room, at the toys and clothes on the floor, the muddy boots sprawled by the door, the overflowing ash pail next to the fireplace that needed emptying.

Michael cleared his throat and finally looked at her. "How are you feeling?"

I was doing better until Alex came, she was tempted to say. Now that he'd been here and had completely ignored her, she'd never felt more out of sorts. But she couldn't admit that. In fact, she didn't want it to be true. She didn't want to care what Alex did or didn't do.

"I'm feeling almost like new now that I have Ingrid by my side," she said, forcing cheerfulness to her voice. She had to focus on other things. She had to act as though she didn't care what Alex was doing in the kitchen with Nadine. Because she didn't care, did she?

"Ingrid, did you apologize?" Michael asked, giving Ingrid a pointed look.

She hung her head and nodded.

"Gunnar?" Michael turned to his son.

Gunnar stood and looked Tessa in the eyes, even though his red face said he'd much rather be doing anything else. "Miss

Taylor, will you please forgive me for not taking better care of Ingie and in the process causing you to get sick?"

"Of course I will." She held out a hand to him. When he stepped nearer, she reached for him and drew him into a hug. He didn't resist. His arms came around her and he hugged her back tightly.

"I'm not all that sick," she said when he finally pulled away. His face was redder than before as he resumed his spot, kneeling next to his father's chair.

Michael put a hand on Gunnar's head with a nod of approval to the boy. Then he turned his attention back to Tessa. While his face reflected the same shyness as Gunnar's, there was something in his eyes today that Tessa hadn't seen there before. Was it confidence?

No matter what was going on with Alex, Tessa was glad that at least one of them seemed to be improving in temperament.

Alex leaned against the kitchen wall and peeked around the doorframe into the front room just in time to see Tessa smile at something Michael said. Her lips curved up, transforming her features from pretty to heart-stopping.

The sight wrenched his chest again, as it

340

had whenever he'd sneaked a look at her. He only had to glance at the happiness on Ingrid's and Gunnar's faces, the rapt attention with which they looked at Tessa, and the adoration in Michael's eyes to know he'd done the right thing.

The night he'd brought the children home cold, shivering, and hungry, he'd cleaned them, fed them, and warmed them thoroughly. The first thing he'd done after he put them to bed was sit down across from Michael and tell him he was sorry for his selfishness. He relinquished all claim to Tessa and had given his brother his blessing on pursuing her in marriage.

Michael hadn't protested in the least. Instead, gratefulness had welled up to replace the melancholy that had overtaken him since Tessa's earlier declaration. The shadows had disappeared from Michael's face, and his eyes had come to life with new spirit.

Seeing the eagerness in his brother's expression only confirmed to Alex that he'd made the right decision, even if his chest felt as thick as three feet of ice. Every mention of Tessa's name since then had hammered him like an ice pick chipping, ricocheting, and battering to get beneath the surface.

341

Yet when Michael had sat up without help, and the very next day had forced himself to stand and take his first steps since the accident, Alex knew it was because he'd given his brother reason to hope again, reason to keep on going. The reason was Tessa.

Tessa.

Alex watched her tweak Ingrid's nose after the little girl had said something funny. Ingrid's smile was worth more than gold. When she snuggled deeper into Tessa's side, Alex ripped his attention away from the precious sight and returned it to the table where Nadine sat nursing the baby.

She'd yelled at Jimmy and Johnny for bumping into the table and had finally sent them outside to hunt for kindling, which was growing more scarce by the day as the snow refused to melt completely away. Now the kitchen was silent except for a pot bubbling on the cast-iron stove and the satisfied grunts of the baby gulping her meal.

At a burst of playful laughter from the front room, his heart ached with a pain that almost bent him over.

Nadine broke the silence. "I don't think I like what you're doing."

"I'm just standing here," he said innocently. "Would you rather I do a song and a dance?"

She narrowed her eyes like she did when she was about to scold one of the children. "Good thing you're not close by, young man. I've a mind to box your ears, that I do."

Maybe he'd let her slap his ears. Then he wouldn't have to feel the awful ripping in his chest.

"You're giving her up to Michael, aren't you?" Nadine's question was more of statement.

He wanted to pretend he didn't know what she was talking about, but he had the feeling Nadine would see right through his façade, just as she was seeing his pain right now. So he gave a slow nod, unable to speak past the knot in his throat.

"Maybe it's not your position to choose for her," Nadine continued. "Especially when she already loves you."

He'd wanted to believe Tessa loved him and shared the same attraction. He'd once thought that even if she didn't have the same fervor for him that he had for her, that it didn't matter, that he had enough for the both of them. Besides, over time he'd woo her and win her so that she'd have no choice but to fall in love with him.

But now it didn't matter what Tessa felt

for him. If she'd ever harbored any affection, she'd soon transfer it to Michael. Without Alex interfering, hopefully Michael would be able to make good progress in winning her love.

Alex swallowed hard and tried to formulate a coherent reply to Nadine's declaration of Tessa's love for him. "She cares for Michael too. If he works hard enough, he'll make her fall in love with him eventually."

Nadine pursed her lips and shook her head.

"He needs her more than I do." Alex's voice dropped to a whisper. "And the children love her. They need her for a mother."

"I don't like this one bit," Nadine muttered. "Not one little bit."

"It's not easy for me either." Alex wanted to close his eyes and shut out the sounds and images of Michael and the children enjoying Tessa's company in the other room. "But it's the right thing to do."

"The right thing to do is let Michael find his own way."

Alex shook his head in denial. Michael wasn't ready to find his own way. He was still floundering to keep his head above water, and Alex wasn't about to let him sink.

A hard, urgent knock came from the front

344

door. Alex pushed away from the wall before anyone else could make an effort to rise. As he made his way through the obstacle course of items on the floor, he tried not to look at Tessa even though he could feel her questioning eyes upon him.

He supposed she was wondering why he wasn't friendlier. But the fact was he didn't trust himself. If he looked at her or spoke to her, he doubted he'd be able to carry through with his resolve to let go of her.

He wasn't being entirely fair to her. He owed her an explanation. But for now, he reminded himself that *she* was the one who told him she didn't love him or want to marry him. Even if he wouldn't let a declaration like that stand in his way under normal circumstances, he could always tell her that was why he'd put a distance between them.

Fighting the urge to look her way, he swung the front door open to the mix of snow and ice swirling in the gray afternoon. Even if he was ready for the warmer weather of spring, the frozen ground allowed him to make use of the dogsleds a while longer. He wouldn't have been able to bring Michael to visit Tessa without the smooth ease of the ride. As it was, Michael had suffered over each bump.

When the door opened, he was surprised to see Hannah — the young woman who helped teach the younger children — standing there and panting, with tears streaking her cheeks.

"Hannah?" Had they found her husband's body finally? "What's wrong?"

"I came to see Miss Taylor." Hannah stood on tiptoe to see past him.

"She's not feeling well. Maybe I can help you in her stead." He wanted to tell her that he was sorry that he'd lived when her husband hadn't.

"I beg your pardon," Hannah said, her voice catching. "I don't want to disturb her, but I know she'll want to know —"

"I'm fine" came Tessa's voice. "Come in, Hannah."

Alex glanced over his shoulder to see Tessa rising from the sofa. The blanket fell away to reveal her shaking limbs. She straightened her shoulders, tossed her long dark hair over her shoulders, and took several unsteady steps forward.

Michael's forehead furrowed in concern and he started to rise from his chair. A grimace of pain halted him halfway, along with Gunnar's cautioning hand.

Alex hesitated. He didn't want to steal her attention away from Michael, but he

346

couldn't stand by and watch Tessa struggle, not when she needed help.

She stumbled over a discarded pair of shoes on the floor.

He bounded toward her and caught her arm. For an instant she held herself rigid. Her eyes turned up to his and gleamed with accusation.

Was she upset that he hadn't paid her any attention? He almost smiled in self-satisfaction but then caught himself.

He was certain she'd yank away and tell him she could take care of herself, but instead she shuddered and nearly collapsed against him. He frowned. She was weaker and sicker than she'd allowed them to see. "Let's get you back to the sofa."

She shook her head and tugged him forward. "No. I'm fine."

Hannah hadn't moved from the stoop outside the door. At the sight of the tears trickling down the woman's cheeks, Tessa's fingers dug into his arm and she trembled again.

He was half tempted to pick her up and carry her back to the sofa.

"Hannah," she said, inching forward slowly, "do you have news of your husband?"

"No, and I don't expect that I will." She

347

wrung her hands together in front of her. There was a sorrow in the woman's eyes that sent alarm through Alex.

Her tidings were devastating. Alex sensed it even before she said a word. "Miss Taylor isn't well today. I think you better wait to deliver your news until she's feeling better."

"Tell me, Hannah," Tessa insisted. "If not news of your husband, what tidings do you bring?"

Hannah glanced at Alex, her eyes rounding.

"Don't let him frighten you," Tessa continued. "He pretends to bark, but he's really only a kitten."

"A kitten?" One of Alex's brows lifted. In spite of the seriousness of the moment, he couldn't resist saying something. "I'm more like a giant lion."

Tessa raised one brow back at him, but then she turned her attention to Hannah and tugged Alex forward. He reluctantly assisted her to the door, though he wanted to put her back on the couch as quickly as possible.

"What is it?" Tessa reached for the woman's hand and grasped it in her own shaking fingers.

Fresh lines of tears trickled down Hannah's cheeks. "I'm sorry, Miss Taylor. I

348

didn't want to disturb you while you were sick, but I knew you'd want to know."

"Know what?" Tessa squeezed the woman's hand.

Hannah gulped back a sob. "It's Henry Benney."

At the mention of the boy's name, Tessa froze.

Hannah sobbed again. "He was in an accident at the mine."

Alex could feel Tessa's body beginning to sag against him.

"What happened?" Tessa persisted.

"The ladders have been icy recently," Hannah said haltingly. "He slipped and fell."

Tessa straightened and grabbed Alex with both hands. "Take me to him. Right away."

Alex's heart plummeted in his chest. He knew what Hannah was trying to tell Tessa even before she said anything further. He slipped his arm around Tessa's waist and drew her to his side.

"Please," Tessa said breathlessly. "I want to see him. I'm sure he'll want to see me too."

Hannah shook her head and turned her helpless gaze upon him, beseeching him to finish telling Tessa what she could not.

"Tessa . . ." he started gently.

"Take me to him," she said louder, almost

349

angrily as she struggled against him.

He didn't let go of her even as she grew more agitated. She shoved him and wrestled to free herself from his grasp.

Hannah began to sob openly.

"He'll be fine." Tessa's voice was heavy with panic. "He's young and strong and smart. He'll make it." She reached a hand toward Hannah, but the other woman just shook her head and took a step back.

Tessa strained for a moment longer, before finally releasing a strangled, "No-o-o . . ." He could feel every ounce of her strength seep out of her body, and then she collapsed against him. He caught her and easily lifted her into his arms.

She didn't resist, but instead buried her face against his chest and clung to him. Her body shuddered with silent sobs.

His entire being ached with the need to comfort her, to make her pain go away, to promise her that everything would be all right. But even as he carried her toward the steps up to her attic room where she could grieve in private, he knew there was nothing he could say or do to change what had happened.

CHAPTER 21

Henry Benney was dead.

She stared with dry eyes at the shallow grave covered with layers of soil, wet leaves, and damp twigs. After a week of warmer weather, the ground had thawed enough for some of the men to shovel aside the remaining snow and dig graves for all those who'd died over the winter. They hadn't been able to break ground while the temperature remained below freezing. Fortunately the bodies had mostly stayed frozen too. But now they needed to get the deceased buried before decomposition set in.

The low clouds of the spring day had begun to spit rain. Her cloak was damp and her boots wet. Yet she couldn't tear herself away. Even though everyone else had already left the cemetery, even though she'd promised Michael and the children that she would follow them back into town, she hadn't been able to make her feet move away from Henry's grave.

She could still picture his mother and sister with their slumped shoulders, their cheeks splotchy from crying. And she couldn't forget his father's face, thin and pale. His eyes were sunken and red-rimmed. More than that, they were empty, as dark and bottomless as the pits of the mine.

When she went to squeeze his cold fingers, she didn't say anything. She knew there was nothing she could say that would take away his pain, just like nothing would take away hers. The agony in his brief glance had told her everything. He would live the rest of his life with the regret of not keeping Henry in school where he belonged.

Tessa was sure she'd live with that regret for the rest of her life too.

As much as Mr. Benney blamed himself, she blamed herself more. It was her fault the miners had been made to work longer shifts. It was her fault Henry had been forced from the classroom and into the mine.

If only she'd done more to stand up for Henry's right to stay in school. Maybe if she hadn't angered Percival in the first place. Maybe if she'd figured out a way to placate him . . .

But how could she have done that without

selling her soul to the devil?

A twig snapped somewhere nearby and she raised her head. Barren branches formed a skeletal canopy overhead. Lifeless shrubs surrounded the wrought-iron fences separating one family plot from another. Wilted weeds from the previous year drooped over lichen-encrusted headstones. The granite slab next to Henry's grave read:

MARY
DIED DEC. 8, 1866
AGED 2 YEARS 3 MONTHS

She supposed the baby to have been Henry's sister who had also perished here in this godforsaken land.

She scanned the other grave markers nearby, some in the shape of beautifully scrolled iron crosses now black with age and the harshness of the elements, and others simple stone slabs. How many others, like Henry, had died needlessly?

The sharp throb in her chest radiated into her shoulders and head. She'd already wept all the tears she could during the past couple of weeks since Hannah had brought the news of Henry's fall. Since then she'd learned more details about his death, that he'd been on a ladder under a projection of the pump rod, which had caused that particular area to be full of ice. His feet had slipped, he struck his father who was behind him at the time, but his father hadn't been able to grab him.

Mr. Benney had been fortunate that the strike hadn't caused him to lose his hold, although Tessa had no doubt the man wished he'd fallen instead of his son. After plunging hundreds of feet, the boy was killed instantly. Her mind told her it was a blessing he hadn't suffered. Nevertheless, her heart protested that he'd had to die at all, not when he'd been so bright, not when the future held so much promise for him, not when he'd been so eager for learning and living.

"Why him?" she whispered to the empty graveyard.

She didn't expect God to answer. He hadn't answered when she'd asked the same question after her mother had died, or after her father had drowned, or again when Sarah, her little sister, had passed away. There were no easy answers to death, to why it took some and not others. Even so, she couldn't keep the anger from rising to mingle with the pain.

"He had so much potential," she said. She'd already penned a letter to Cole

Enterprises to let them know of the death, to inform them of the unsafe mine, to petition for better working conditions. She'd taken it to the company store to be mailed just yesterday, after a much-delayed mail messenger had arrived overland and delivered a backlog of mail.

The letter from home had cheered her only a little. Mostly it had reminded her of all that she was missing in spring, the return of the loons and monarch butterflies, and her sister Caroline's large flower beds that were likely beginning to bloom in earnest.

Tessa's shoulders sagged beneath her cloak. She wasn't ready to admit defeat, and yet everywhere she looked around Eagle Harbor, nothing had changed since she'd arrived. As far as she could tell, she hadn't made one bit of difference in anyone's life since she'd come here. She'd had such grand plans. She'd wanted God to use her to help the people better themselves. So far, though, her presence seemed only to make things worse.

With a sigh she turned away from Henry's fresh grave and shuffled toward the arched sign that stood over the gated entrance to the cemetery nestled among the evergreens. It read, PINE GROVE CEMETERY. It should have read, *The Resting Place of Those Who*

355

Died Unnecessarily.

As she began the short walk back toward Center Street, she huddled deeper into her cloak. While she was mostly recovered from her illness, she couldn't shake the listlessness that had plagued her all week.

"Miss Taylor." A voice nearby startled her. Percival was leaning against a fence post on the side of the road almost as if he'd been waiting for her. She hadn't noticed him earlier at the funeral, but then she hadn't paid much attention to who was or wasn't in attendance.

She stopped abruptly. A glance up the road toward town told her they were alone, that everyone else who had come out to bury their dead had already dispersed.

"Good day, Mr. Updegraff." She nodded at him curtly and forced herself to continue walking as she had been. She could feel his eyes upon her as she strode past. With her chin held high she stared straight ahead, refusing to let him intimidate her.

Once she was several feet past him, she allowed herself to breathe again. Maybe he hadn't been waiting for her after all. Even so, she picked up her pace.

"I received a letter from my Detroit agent yesterday." His voice came from behind her, from his spot by the post. Something in his tone made her footsteps falter.

"I'm sure you were as glad as I was to finally get mail," she replied over her shoulder.

"He had some interesting things to say about you."

A chill crept into her blood. There was no mistaking the insinuation in Percival's words. She halted and slowly pivoted to face him.

In his black trousers and matching vest and waistcoat, he was attired out of respect for those who'd lost loved ones. Yet the darkness of his clothes only highlighted the darkness of his eyes that were peering at her with too much familiarity.

What had Percival learned about her?

As if hearing her unasked question, his mustache shifted upward into a small smile. "It appears you haven't been honest about your past."

Her chest constricted. She tried to keep her voice level as she responded. "What may have happened in my past is none of your concern."

"As your boss, it *is* my concern." He pushed away from the post and straightened his coat. "You don't believe I would hire a teacher for this town's school without doing some investigating as to your background."

357

Why? she wanted to blurt. *So you could use every little issue you discovered as a way to blackmail the new teacher into doing your bidding?* "Regardless of my past, I hope I've demonstrated to you and this community my dedication and diligence to my job. I've been above reproach —"

"You've been lusting after those lightkeepers the whole time you've been here."

"I have not." Her back stiffened in protest even as guilt whispered that she had entertained too many thoughts of Alex.

"And now I know why," Percival continued, eyeing her in a way that told her he knew everything about her indiscretion. "You're not the pure lily-white woman that you want everyone to believe you are."

He was right. She wasn't that woman. She had nothing to say in her defense. Even if she hadn't had relations with Ryan that long-ago night, she'd been terribly wrong to trick him into lying in bed with her.

She'd prayed for God to forgive her and she didn't doubt that He had. But that didn't change the facts of what had happened. "I admit I'm not perfect," she said. "I've sinned dreadfully in the past. And now I'm trying to move forward by doing the right thing."

Percival studied her with the same open

358

hunger she'd seen there too often. "Very well, Miss Taylor. I'll keep your little secret."

She shivered, not sure if from the coolness of the air and the dampness of her cloak or from Percival's presence. She swallowed a rising sense of helplessness and lifted her chin again. She resented that she must ingratiate herself to this lustful man, but for now she saw no other way around it. "Thank you. I would appreciate you keeping this matter to yourself —"

"Under one condition." His voice had turned brittle, and he started to walk toward her. "I would like you to come to my house for dinner. Tonight."

"She won't be coming" came a stern voice from the woods to her left, followed by Alex's frame emerging from the thick evergreens that lined the road. He stepped onto the muddy gravel and stopped, his feet spread wide, his fists bunched at his sides. He glared at Percival with a deadly intensity.

He too was in his Sunday best — dark trousers and coat that contrasted with his fair hair. He'd lost the rugged look and instead had a clean-cut appeal.

Percival's eyes rounded, the man obviously taken aback by Alex's interference.

She didn't stop to think where Alex had come from, except to thank God that he was here.

"I won't allow you to coerce Tessa into going with you anywhere," he said, his voice almost a growl.

"Not your decision to make, Bjorklund," Percival said. "Go back to your lighthouse and do whatever it is you do all day."

"She's not going with you now." Alex stared at him with hard, angry eyes. "Or ever."

Percival's lips curved into a smirk. "It's time to share the wealth. You've had her all to yourself these past months. Now it's my turn."

"You're insulting Miss Taylor."

"I'm simply stating the truth."

"Watch what you say around the lady." Alex's biceps flexed beneath his coat, straining the seams.

Tessa couldn't look into his eyes. How much had he heard of Percival's accusations? If he'd heard everything, she doubted he'd be standing here defending her so nobly.

"She's no lady," Percival said. "In fact, I've learned she's little better than a whore."

Tessa cringed at his declaration, and shame flooded her soul. Alex would surely leave her alone now. He'd already done a good job of that lately anyway. The revelation about her past would only give him all the more reason to avoid her.

She lowered her head and stared at the hem of her black mourning gown. She wasn't surprised to hear the crunch of his footsteps. He'd run away from her for sure as fast as he could.

The crunch was rapidly followed by a whack and a grunt, then a thud and muffled cry of pain.

She glanced up in time to see Percival holding the side of his face and staggering backward, with Alex's fist making a line straight at Percival's belly. The punch doubled Percival over.

Alex raised his arm again, and rage contorted his features, turning the handsome face into that of a fierce warrior. "Don't talk that way about Miss Taylor ever again," he ground out.

With one hand on his face, Percival rubbed the other against his stomach. For a long moment he didn't say anything. He seemed to struggle to catch his breath.

Alex slowly lowered his fist and took a step back, all the while continuing to pin Percival with a deadly glare. Alex wasn't the local wrestling champion without cause, and she supposed Percival knew he didn't have a chance against Alex when it came to hand-

361

to-hand combat.

Percival tried to straighten, then grimaced.

"I hope I've made myself clear," Alex demanded.

Percival spit out a glob of blood and glared back. "You just bought a ticket to the graveyard."

"You might be able to bully everyone else in this town, but you can't touch me."

"Oh, I can touch you all right." Percival spat again. "I'll make good and sure you regret interfering with my business."

"If you don't stay away from Tessa, you'll be the one with the regrets."

Alex reached for Tessa's hand and tucked it within the crook of his arm and tugged her gently forward. She couldn't meet his gaze. She didn't know how she'd ever be able to look him in the eye again.

She could feel Percival's stare burning into them. As much as she tried, she couldn't stop her legs from trembling and was grateful for Alex's steady arm. She half expected the bang of a gunshot and the piercing pain of a bullet in her back.

Percival was angry enough to kill and that thought would have worried her, except she was too overcome with embarrassment. As she hustled along next to Alex, she couldn't find any words to ease her mortification. He

362

didn't say anything either, which only made her want to run away and hide.

Finally when they turned onto Pine Street and were hemmed in by a tall stand of pines, Alex stopped and gave her little choice but to halt next to him.

"I'm sorry Percival said those things," he said softly, his tone still carrying a hint of aggravation.

She stared at his shirt collar. "Thanks for coming to my rescue."

"He's lucky I didn't kill him then and there."

"I have the feeling you're going to get in trouble now because of me."

"He can't do anything to me and he knows it. It drives him crazy."

"But he'll figure out some way to punish you for coming to my rescue and for hitting him."

Alex shrugged. "I've been waiting a long time to give him what he has coming. I only wish I'd punished him earlier. Maybe then things wouldn't have gotten so out of control in this town."

"Just be careful." She started to slide her hand away from his arm, but he grabbed onto it and held it firmly in place. "Those things Percival said about me . . ." she started.

"It doesn't matter, Tessa."

"It *does* matter," she said, unable to contain the anguish in her heart. "I made a horrible mistake in the past —"

He put a finger to her lips to silence her.

Suddenly all she could think about was being in his arms, holding him, and letting him embrace her and comfort her. It was the one place in all the world that she wanted to be more than anywhere else. She swayed toward him. She'd missed him over the past couple of weeks with the distance he'd put between them.

He leaned closer to her and dropped his finger from her lips. "Tessa," he whispered.

Was that longing in his voice? Did he miss her as much as she missed him? But how could he? Not after what he'd learned about her today. Maybe he'd only heard part of the revelation. Or maybe he assumed Percival was lying.

She had to clarify. "I'm not lily white."

"I don't care." His response was quick, almost as if he'd anticipated her words. "Whatever your past mistakes, I've seen the godly woman you've become. That's all that matters."

Her heart warmed at his praise. "But I have a tarnished reputation."

"You're making for yourself a new reputation, one that everyone here admires and respects."

"Not if Percival tells what he knows."

"If people are stupid enough to listen to his opinion, then they're not worth having as friends."

She wanted to believe him, wanted to find hope in his words, but she'd already faced too many rejections from well-meaning people.

His blue eyes regarded her with a compassion that brought a lump to her throat. She wanted to tell him what a fine man he was, how considerate and wise.

He brought both of his hands up to her cheeks and tenderly held her face. The kind look in his eyes filled her with a reassurance that no matter what, she'd always have a friend in him.

"Thank you for believing in me," she whispered.

He smiled, and the warmth in her chest expanded. Her whole body seemed to melt as sweet longing coursed through her veins. She'd never felt this way about a man before. She'd never been so entirely attracted or so utterly enraptured. The past days without his presence had awakened her to a need for him. It was almost as if she'd been parched and thirsty but hadn't known how much until she was with him again, talking to him, and drinking him in.

Did she love him?

She searched his face, the strong angular jaw, his chiseled chin. He'd become dear to her. But love?

Could she allow herself to love him even though he was a lightkeeper?

She raised her eyes to his again and stared deeply into his soul just as he stared into hers. There was no point in pretending anymore, no point denying the truth, no point fighting against it. Yes, in spite of her efforts not to care about him, she had fallen in love with him.

She'd vowed never to have anything to do with a lightkeeper, but here she was in love with one. Heaven help her. What should she do?

As if seeing that love reflected in her soul, his smile faded and was replaced by an intensity that made her stomach quiver in anticipation. Then his gaze dropped to her lips, and he cocked his head as if angling himself to kiss her.

She didn't pull away. Instead she lifted her face, all too eager for his kisses.

He bent forward until his mouth almost brushed hers. "Tessa," he whispered. The yearning in his voice mingled with something else. What was it? Regret? His lips hovered near hers, and his breath was damp against her skin.

"Alex?" she asked, almost grazing him.

With a strangled groan he wrenched back and dropped his hands from her face.

"What's wrong?" She tried to catch his attention again, but he averted his eyes and stepped away from her. He tugged his hat from his head and raked his fingers through his hair.

"Michael believes in you too," he said.

"That's good." She hugged her arms across her chest, a chilly breeze enfolding her and replacing the warmth of his presence.

"He respects and admires you."

"And I respect and admire him." Michael had stood by her side during Henry Benney's funeral, had even slipped his arm around her when she'd trembled with weakness. He was one of the kindest men she knew — next to Alex. Michael had wanted to walk her home after the funeral, but from the strain on his face she'd seen that all of the standing had taxed him. Even with a cane, he was still weak and cumbersome on his feet, still having to adjust to walking with missing toes. He hadn't protested when she sent him ahead with the children.

"Tessa . . ." Alex's tone was laced with exasperation. He jabbed his fingers into his hair again and stared down the road toward the slanted roofs of identical miner cabins that showed in the clearing.

Something urged her to lighten the moment, to tease him, to direct the conversation toward something else. But her throat constricted around her words.

"Listen," he started again, "Michael loves you."

But I don't love him, she wanted to shout back. *I love you.* But she had the feeling she'd only humiliate herself if she said anything.

"He loves you," Alex said again. The drizzle had begun to increase and was dampening his hair. "And Ingrid and Gunnar love you."

Understanding dawned then, and Alex's recent aloofness began to make sense. He'd been deferring to Michael, allowing his brother to be with her at every opportunity. It was almost as if he'd given up the competition that had been ongoing all winter, and for some reason he'd decided to let Michael win.

Not only was he stepping aside, he was actually pushing her to be with Michael. In hindsight she could even see that he'd made a point of getting the two of them together, like that morning. He'd positioned Michael by her side and then disappeared.

"So you don't want me anymore," she stated as evenly as she could.

Alex refused to meet her gaze. "It doesn't matter what I want. What matters is Michael and the kids. They need you more than I do."

He didn't need her? The thought stung. Although he'd accused *her* of loving *him* many times, he'd never spoken the words to her. What if she'd been mistaken in thinking that he did? If he could relinquish her to his brother, then perhaps she'd been wrong to assume his feelings ran as deep as hers. She'd seen the way some of the husbands in the community had handed their wives over to Percival. They'd given in to the pressure all too easily.

Alex wasn't giving her up to Percival, and she doubted he ever would. Still, she'd determined that she wanted the kind of man who wouldn't ever be willing to let go of her, not for anyone or anything. If Alex could give her up for his brother, if he didn't treasure her enough to fight for her, then he wasn't the kind of man she wanted.

"I know you don't want to marry a light-keeper," he continued. "So I'm trying to

369

convince Michael to move back to Detroit so that we can be near the doctors who can help Ingrid."

"I'd never ask a man to give up his job for me." Anger began to churn within her. "Besides, do you really think you can plan my life? Maybe I don't want to move away from Eagle Harbor. Did you ever think that I want to continue to teach school? Did you think that maybe I want to wait to get married?" Her voice had risen, and each word came out sharp.

"They need you." Alex's words were just as clipped. "Since Michael met you, he's been happy again. I haven't seen him like that since Rachel died."

"I'm glad he's happy again. I really am. But that's a heavy load for any one person to bear, taking responsibility for someone else's happiness. And I won't do it."

Alex scowled. "You know what I mean, Tessa. It's a mutual happiness. You make him happy, and he'll do the same for you."

But would he? "I'm sorry, Alex." She started to leave. "Maybe you've decided to spend the rest of your life doing whatever it takes to make your brother happy, but I'm not going to do the same."

He didn't respond. She could sense his frustration burning into her back as she strode away.

She didn't want things to end between them like this. She wanted him to tell her he'd been wrong, that he wouldn't let her go, that he wouldn't hand her over to his brother like she was some prize in a wrestling match to give away to whomever he pleased. She wanted him to love her enough to chase after her and do whatever it took to make things work between them.

The mud sticking to her boots weighed down her stride — at least that was what she told herself as her footsteps slowed.

Would he really let her walk away? Her chest ached, as if someone had plunged a knife into it.

"Wait, Tessa," he called. Finally.

She spun to face him, too quickly. He hadn't moved from where he stood. His wet hair stuck to his forehead and his shoulders sagged. In his dark suit, against the grayness of the leafless shrubs and trees, he was a striking figure — as handsome and strong as the day she'd met him.

"Promise me you won't push Michael away because you're mad at me."

Her heart sank at his words. She'd hoped for his declaration of love, but from across the distance his eyes regarded her with a

371

sadness that snuffed out any remnants of hope.

She was tempted to yell at him and tell him she never wanted to see him or Michael ever again. But she swallowed the bitterness, spun around, and walked away.

Her body tensed with the need for him to rush after her, to stop her, to tell her he'd been a fool to let her go. But when she turned onto Center Street and glanced over her shoulder, he was gone.

CHAPTER 22

Tessa lay on her back in the dark and rolled the cross in her hands. The grainy texture of the wood wasn't reminding her to hope in the Lord this time. Instead, all she could think about was the steamer the piece of wood had once belonged to and how her life in Eagle Harbor was starting to resemble a shipwreck.

Henry Benney's death. Percival's threats. Alex's rejection. How could she bear it all?

She rolled to her side, careful not to let the covers slide away. Even though the temperatures had continued to rise all week and melt more snow, the nights remained cold in her attic room. She grazed the empty spot where Josie should have been sleeping. The girl was gone, just as she'd been most nights of late, meeting with a young man.

Tessa had talked to Josie about sneaking out of the house after dark, but Josie only giggled and brushed off her concerns. Just that night, when Josie was tiptoeing out of the room, she told Josie she would have to inform her parents about the clandestine meetings if she didn't bring them to an end.

Josie had glared at her and threatened her in return. "Remember that time I caught you kissing Alex Bjorklund at the mine? Well, I can tell my parents I've only been following the example of my teacher."

Josie's accusation barreled into her like a ton of falling rocks. Tessa sank back into the sagging mattress and said nothing more. What could she say?

Tessa sighed and ran her fingers over the cross once more. "God," she whispered into the silence, "I thought you wanted to use me here in Eagle Harbor. I thought I could make a difference. But it seems like I've only caused more problems."

A flurry of shouts from outside stopped her prayer. She sat up and listened. In the room below, voices and the clomping of footsteps told her the commotion had awakened Nadine and William.

What if something had happened to Josie? What if she'd been accosted, hurt . . . or worse?

"Heaven help me," she whispered, whipping back the covers and jumping out of bed. If anything had happened, it would be her fault. She could have done more to help Josie. She should have been a better role model. She should have gone to Nadine and William about what she knew, no matter Josie's threats.

Her heart pounding in her ears, she slid a gown over her nightdress and raced down the stairs. William was already striding out the door, his two oldest sons behind him. Nadine was standing at the front window, peering in the direction of the shore.

"What is it?" Tessa asked as she went to stand next to her.

Nadine clutched her shawl. "There's some sort of fire down by the lake."

Tessa stared at the night sky. It was glowing bright near the harbor. "Is anyone hurt?" Her thoughts charged ahead to Josie trapped somewhere in the flames with no one knowing she was there.

She didn't wait for Nadine's response and instead ran outside. She ignored Nadine's calls to stay home and away from the danger. Desperation clawed at Tessa, forcing her toward the harbor. All she could think was that Josie was in danger and she was the only one who knew about it.

At the edge of town alongside the rocky beach she stopped behind the others who'd gathered, the dismay on their faces evident

375

by the light of the fire that was consuming the warehouse. Some of the men, including Mr. Rawlings, were organizing a bucket brigade from the lake to the burning building. But the flames were already leaping high in the air out of the roof, and Tessa had a feeling any effort to douse the fire would be wasted.

"I don't think they'll be able to put it out!" she called, striding toward Mr. Rawlings. "We should work instead on salvaging whatever we can."

He stopped and sized up the fire. He took only a moment before coming to the same conclusion. Their meager buckets of water wouldn't begin to touch the roof. It was only a matter of time before the building was completely engulfed in flames, and the least they could do was try to rescue as many of the remaining food stores and supplies as they could.

While the ice on the lake was melting, they were still locked in with no telling when the waters would be thawed and safe enough for fresh supplies to reach them. If they didn't save the food, there was the very real possibility they could starve.

"We can form a line and pass the supplies to one another," she said, starting toward the building.

Mr. Rawlings shouted to the others, an almost frantic ring to his voice. She was sure that he too was thinking about how difficult it would be for their community to survive if they lost the remaining food stores.

As they neared the open front door of the building, a large figure emerged from inside. He stumbled outside onto the rocky shore with his arms laden with supplies.

As the firelight shone upon the man, Tessa's breath caught. It was Alex.

"Get away!" Alex shouted as he rushed toward them. His face was streaked with soot and sweat. Smoke rose from patches of his coat. "The whole thing is going to blow."

She glanced behind him. "We have to save the supplies!"

"There's no time!" He dropped what he'd been carrying and motioned at them with his arms. "Move back! Now!"

Like the others she stopped, but indecision wavered through her. What if they had time to make the trip in and rescue everything?

Alex moved nearer, his arms outstretched. He directed the townspeople to step farther back. "Help me clear the area!" he shouted to Mr. Rawlings.

The older man nodded and began to urge the people away from the burning building.

At several loud pops the crowd turned on their own, and Tessa had no other choice but to do likewise.

"The fire reached the cellar," Alex called in explanation to Mr. Rawlings. "And there are still several kegs of powder in storage."

At the mention of the powder that was used in blowing up rock in the mines, many took off running. Just as Tessa picked up her pace, an explosion rocked the harbor. The blast was deafening, and the rush of heat and flash of flames reached out to grab hold of them.

The force pushed Tessa to her knees in the soggy grass and leaves.

"Tessa!" Alex called. He covered his head to shield himself from falling debris. In an instant he was beside her, grabbing her arms and forcing her to look up into his face. "Are you all right?"

"I think so —" she started to say but was cut off by another explosion, this one louder than the first.

Alex pushed her down and threw himself on top of her. Under the shelter of his body, with her cheek pressed into the damp earth, she squeezed her eyes closed and sucked in uneven breaths that smelled of soil and smoke.

Alex's chest rose and fell rapidly against

her back. His bulky arms moved over her head to shield her. "You'll be okay," his voice rumbled near her ear. "Just don't move."

Strangely she felt completely safe. Within the strong confines of his chest and arms, she knew nothing could touch her. Even as a third blast rent the night air, she didn't flinch. The screams and cries around her seemed distant. When at last the night grew quieter, she made no effort to move. With Alex's weight on top of her, she couldn't even if she'd wanted to.

As if realizing the possibility that he could crush her, Alex slid halfway off to lie in the grass beside her, his arms still surrounding her and his face pressed into her hair.

They lay unmoving, listening to the popping and crackling of the fire. As dazed voices began to murmur around them, Alex pulled back a fraction. "You're not hurt, are you?"

She twisted to see his face. In the light of the flickering flames, his eyes were filled with concern, his forehead furrowed. "Really, I'm fine," she insisted. "How are you?"

"None the worse for wear."

Before she could stop herself, she smoothed a hand over his cheek to assure herself that he was unharmed. When she reached the tip of his chin, his body stiffened and his breath quickened. His hand splayed across the small of her back, and his warm breath brushed her forehead. He wanted to kiss her. She could feel it in every tight muscle of his body.

No matter how much distance he tried to put between them, no matter how much he deferred to Michael, and no matter how much he tried to deny his feelings for her, apparently Alex still couldn't resist his attraction to her. One little touch was all it took to turn him into mush in her hands.

Although her heart had ached with the pain of his rejection over the past few days, she'd tried to tell herself that she ought to be grateful he didn't need her. It made her choice to avoid entanglement with a lightkeeper all that much easier. It made her choice to remain a teacher easier too. Even so, she couldn't deny that she relished being in his arms again.

He turned his mouth to her cheek and then her ear. Her blood stirred. For a long moment he didn't move and she waited for him to do something — anything — to reassure her that he still wanted her, that he'd been mistaken in letting her go.

Abruptly he shifted and gave a soft groan.

She wanted to cling to him and hold him in place, but he was already putting distance back between them, and his expression turned to one of frustration. "If you're all right," he said in a tone that told her their intimate moment was over, "then I need to make sure everyone else is okay."

She sat up and didn't say anything. He rose, brushed flecks of sooty debris off his shoulders and clothes, and looked around at the small fires that had started here and there where burning pieces of the building had landed. Thankfully, because of the dampness of the earth, the fires didn't have much strength.

He glanced back at her and held out a hand to help her up. Once she was standing, he let go of her, almost as if she were one of the flaming boards. "Go back home, Tessa," he said roughly. "Stay where it's safe."

He spun and strode away in the direction of the warehouse, which was now completely engulfed in flames.

"There's Alex Bjorklund!" someone shouted from the growing crowd at the edge of the bay. "Arrest him."

Alex halted in his tracks. The glow of the flames highlighted the confusion that rippled across his face.

When Percival stepped to the front of the gathering and pointed at Alex, Tessa's heart started racing. She wasn't surprised by his accusation, but she *was* surprised that he was attired in his usual immaculate suit, suave and perfect except for the bruise on his cheekbone beneath his eye.

Compared to the rest of the crowd, most wearing boots with coats thrown over night-clothes, how had Percival found the time to dress so well — unless he'd never gone to bed in the first place?

"Arrest Alex Bjorklund," Percival called again, this time motioning to William Rawlings and another supervisor of his mine to do his bidding.

The men looked at Percival but didn't move.

"What reason do you have to arrest me?" Alex crossed his arms over his chest as though daring them to come near him.

"You destroyed the warehouse," Percival answered.

"What?" Alex roared, rising to his full height and puffing out his chest.

"I've got several witnesses who saw you enter the building before the fire started," Percival continued, his face a mask of steely calm. "And everyone here saw you leaving right before it blew."

"I went in because I saw a fire," Alex said, his eyes widening. "I'm the one who sounded the alarm. I actually managed to make several trips out with supplies before the explosion."

Tessa nodded. Alex's explanation made perfect sense.

"No one is out this time of night unless they're up to mischief." Percival locked glares with Alex.

"I was up in the tower and noticed a strange light in the warehouse," Alex said. "I came down to investigate."

"In the tower? This time of year?"

"As a matter of fact, yes, I was."

"You're expecting us all to believe that you were sitting up in a completely dark tower tonight?"

Alex released an exasperated sigh as if realizing his explanation did sound rather suspicious. "Tell me, why would I blow up the warehouse, Percival? What motivation could I possibly have for doing that?"

Percival pointed at the swollen purple bruise beneath his eye. "Because you want to hurt me in whatever way you can. When you couldn't beat me the other day, you decided to make me suffer another way."

Alex snorted. "You deserve to suffer long and hard for the hardships you've brought to this community. But how is blowing up a warehouse punishing *you*?"

"Because you want to undermine me in the eyes of the new owner, Mr. Cole. You've never liked me and have always tried to diminish my authority here. You even tried to write a letter to my boss to get me fired."

"Tried?" Alex asked.

Percival's thin smile made Tessa's stomach lurch. Had Percival intercepted Alex's letter to Mr. Cole? Maybe Percival had done the same with her recent letter of complaint about the working conditions that had a part in killing Henry Benney. She wanted to believe that if her letter had reached Mr. Cole, he would have done something to help their community, although she suspected the business magnate would have responded only with silence.

The flames consuming the warehouse cast a ghoulish light over the harbor, which was half covered with ice. If only the fire would melt the ice the rest of the way so that the ships could resume their transport and bring them food and supplies, something that was needed now more than ever before.

"I'm not the only one who doesn't like you," Alex said. "No one else does either."

"Then you're admitting your guilt. You started the fire to get back at me."

"Absolutely not —"

"Maybe you started it because you didn't want to take turns."

"Take turns?"

Percival's gaze flipped to Tessa. She fisted her hands on her hips and narrowed her eyes at him. Now that he knew about her past, she'd been waiting for him to come to her again and threaten to tell the news to the town if she didn't do whatever he wanted.

So far he hadn't made any further mention of the incriminating information he'd discovered. Or if he had shared the news, no one had treated her any differently.

The moment Alex grasped Percival's insinuation, fury clouded his face. "I already told you to be careful what you say about Miss Taylor."

"Why?" Percival's brow rose. "If her past is any indication, she's quite proficient at sharing her favors —"

Alex started toward Percival, probably to teach the man another lesson.

"Alex, no!" Tessa shouted as she rushed to intercept him. Percival wanted Alex to attack him publicly. It would only add evidence to the case he was trying to build against Alex. And if the gasps behind her were any indication, Percival's tactic was working.

Before Alex could reach Percival, Michael broke through the crowd and grabbed his brother just as Tessa approached. He wrestled Alex's arms behind his back and jerked up on one, which brought a quick end to Alex's struggle to free himself.

Even in the dark, Tessa could see Alex's coat strain against his muscles. Michael's face contorted with the effort it took to keep Alex under control. If Alex freed himself, Tessa doubted Percival would walk away this time.

Percival turned to those around him. "Do you need any more evidence? Isn't it clear that Alex Bjorklund wants to harm me? And isn't it clear he set this fire to try to destroy me?"

No one nodded. But neither did anyone disagree with Percival. The light of the fire reflected the fear on their faces and in their eyes — the fear that held them captive to his control. They were all likely thinking of what Percival would do to them if they stood up for Alex.

"Rawlings. Carter," Percival barked. "Take Bjorklund back to the company office and lock him up in the cell."

William Rawlings took a step backward and started to shake his head.

"Do as I say, Rawlings. The man is a safety hazard to our town and needs to be locked up so that he can't cause any more trouble."

"Now wait a minute," Michael said, pulling Alex back a step. "You can't arrest him without proper evidence. And there's nothing here that says Alex started the fire except a whole lot of speculation."

"That's right," Tessa said. She wasn't afraid of Percival, she told herself. Percival couldn't arrest Alex, could he? "Everyone knows that Alex is a good man. He's kind-hearted and helps those in need." Including his brother, she realized. No, most of all his brother. Alex lived to help his brother.

She swallowed the revelation to mull over another time. For now, she had to get the townspeople to defend him. "Each person here can testify to some way Alex has come to their aid," she went on, raising her voice. "He's a man of integrity and above reproach —"

"I suppose that's why he took you up to the mine," Percival said, "to share intimacies with you."

A murmur arose from those surrounding her, and suddenly she wanted nothing more than for the ground to open up and swallow her. How had Percival learned about her indiscretion? She should have guessed he'd find out eventually since he knew everything. But who had told him?

Her eye caught a movement on the edge of the gathering — a thin girl with short-cropped bangs. Josie.

Tessa's first thought was relief that Josie was safe. She hadn't been hurt or anything. Her second thought was that Josie must have told someone about seeing her at the mine with Alex.

"Everyone around here knows what goes on when a couple goes up to the mine," Percival added.

Tessa was too horrified to defend herself. In truth, she had no right to defend herself. She'd been wrong to be alone with Alex there.

Alex shook his head, his frustration etched in every line of his face. "Nothing happened between Tessa and me. She's innocent —"

"Neither of you are innocent!" Percival said with disgust. "And now I have no choice but to fire her from her job."

A fresh wave of murmurs circled her. Yet she was so shocked that she didn't hear what they were saying. Instead all she heard in her mind were the words *fire her, fire her, fire her . . .*

Alex and Michael called out their protest, but she couldn't think straight, not when her life was unraveling before her.

Percival's harsh response broke through the haze. "I won't allow a woman of her questionable reputation to teach the children of this community any longer. And anyone who provides her shelter or help will be guilty by association."

"You can't do that!" Alex shouted.

"Where will I go?" Tessa asked at the same time, trying to control the panic bubbling up in her chest.

Percival shifted his hard eyes upon her. "It doesn't matter to us where you go, Miss Taylor. That's up to you. We simply don't want a woman of your loose morals in this community any longer."

"I won't let you do this." Alex yanked to free himself from Michael.

"You have no authority to stop me," Percival said. "Besides, you'll be in jail. Right where you belong."

"You can't take him," Michael said. His features were taut with pain. Without his cane, and in the exertion of trying to contain Alex, Michael had put too much pressure on his wounds.

Percival nodded to Mr. Rawlings and Mr. Carter again. "If you men don't arrest him right now, you'll find yourselves and your

389

families in the same situation as Miss Taylor."

Reluctantly the two men shuffled forward, their faces wreathed in apology. Over the past months she'd learned that Percival earned loyalty from a small circle of miners by the favors he bestowed on them, and William Rawlings was one of his best workers. Although Mr. Rawlings was a decent man, Tessa had early on realized that he was also very passive. He did everything Percival asked. As a result, Percival allowed him to remain in his big house along with a decent salary. Percival knew that if he had a man on his side whom everyone respected, a man like Mr. Rawlings, then he'd gain control over the others by default.

Michael began pulling Alex backward away from the men. "I won't allow this. You won't be able to arrest him without arresting me."

"Oh," Percival said, his voice echoing over the strange silence of the gathering. "So you're admitting that you had a hand in the warehouse fire too? Very well, we'll arrest you both." He motioned to several other miners.

Both of the brothers protested and defended each other at the same time.

"I'm sure you don't want to cause any

390

trouble for my men," Percival said, raising his voice. A warning edged his tone. "As long as you cooperate, you won't cause problems for anyone else."

Alex strained against Michael's hold only a moment longer before his muscles slackened and his shoulders slumped. Though his eyes still glittered with anger, resignation rolled across his face. He said something to Michael about leaving him and going back to the lighthouse, but the miners had already surrounded the two, preventing any attempt to escape.

"This is ludicrous!" Tessa found her voice. "You can't arrest them!"

Percival's smirk told her he could and there was nothing she could do to stop him. The words he'd spoken to Alex after the funeral came back to haunt her. *You just bought a ticket to the graveyard.*

Percival wanted revenge for the way Alex had struck him and humiliated him after the funeral. She had no doubt that Percival had somehow orchestrated the warehouse fire so he could blame Alex, have him arrested, and then make him suffer for it, slowly and painfully.

She scanned the gathering and searched the now-familiar faces, the men and the few women who'd come out of their dingy

391

cabins to witness the warehouse fire. Some were parents of her students. Some had been in her evening class. Still others she'd met at church. "Are you all just going to stand there and let Percival Updegraff throw these innocent men in jail? Why don't you stand up for yourselves and your rights? You don't have to do everything this man commands you to do."

At her request, most dropped their gazes, refusing to meet her challenge. They stood mutely, their apprehension and shame as life-sized as the fire still burning the remains of the warehouse.

"If we stick together against Percival," she continued, "if we all refuse to do as he asks, then what power will he have?"

Again no one said anything. Out of the corner of her eye she could see Percival's smile crook with satisfaction. Her insides churned with a rising helplessness. Was there nothing she could do to save Alex and Michael or herself?

"Mr. Rawlings?" she said, seeking him out. But he kept his focus on the rope he was tying around Alex's wrists. She turned to Henry's dad. "Mr. Benney?" He lowered his head, stared at his boots, and said nothing.

A fresh wave of shame coursed through

her. They wanted nothing to do with her now — now that they knew about her stained past.

When Percival issued several more orders and the men didn't hesitate to obey, Tessa's body sagged in defeat.

"Tessa!" Michael yelled as a couple of the men finished binding his hands behind his back.

Through the bodies surrounding him, she caught a glimpse of the desperation on his face.

"Take care of the children," he said.

"You have my word," she called back.

He nodded his thanks before he was shoved forward. She waited for Alex to turn and look at her one last time. But he hung his head and allowed himself to be led away behind his brother.

She wanted to sink to the ground and weep. In just a matter of minutes she found herself jobless, homeless, her reputation in tatters. Worse, she was watching the man she loved being taken to jail with little hope of seeing him ever again.

Chapter 23

Tessa opened the little door at the back of the lens. Its brass hinges squeaked from lack of use over the winter. With the extinguisher she reached carefully inside the tall lantern and covered the flame. The flicker disappeared without even the tiniest amount of smoke.

Gunnar stood by and studied everything she did. She'd told him she wanted him to learn how to operate the Fresnel lens so that he'd be able to take care of the lighthouse if anything happened to her. But the truth was she didn't want to do it at all. She wanted Gunnar to run the lighthouse so that she wouldn't have to.

"There," she said, trying to still the trembling in her limbs that hadn't gone away all night as she'd operated the light. "Now we just need to clean everything and we'll be done."

"I know how to polish the prisms," Gunnar said. "And I can wash the windows."

"That would be very helpful." Tessa retrieved the small pair of scissors she'd tucked into her apron pocket. She reached back into the lantern and carefully trimmed the cotton wick.

"Do you want me to refill the oil too?" Gunnar asked.

Tessa straightened and peered out over the lake. After a week of fifty-degree weather, the ice was almost gone. The rising sun shone over the silver water and illuminated the remaining ice floes that floated in clusters near the rocks. The waves had finally reached the shore again, and through the thick glass panes she could hear their steady rhythm.

She sighed and leaned against the cold window. She'd made it through the first night tending the light.

"Why don't you go on down to bed," Gunnar said gently behind her. "I can finish up."

She nodded but didn't make a move to leave. Last night, when she ascended the tower to light the lantern, she'd dreaded every step up. She'd cringed at every noise. She'd resisted every movement.

She'd almost talked herself out of doing it. But after reading Alex's hastily scrawled message for the hundredth time, she hadn't been able to say no. Not after he'd pleaded with her. Someone had to manage the lighthouse now that the lake was thawed. They couldn't leave the lantern dark, not with the possibility of steamers arriving any day.

As much as she wanted to ball up his note and throw it in the fire, she'd kept it like the few other messages he'd smuggled to her through Samuel. After reading the note, she'd closed herself in the oil house and had cried and pleaded with God to find someone else to take care of the lantern. Hadn't she already done enough by staying in the keeper's cottage? Hadn't she done enough by managing the house and caring for the children over the past week while Michael and Alex had been locked away? God couldn't possibly be asking her to take the position as lightkeeper, not when she loathed the very thought.

But when Ingrid had knocked timidly on the oil house door and asked her if everything was okay, Tessa hadn't come up with any other solution than to walk up the tower steps at dusk and light the lantern.

She wanted to claim ignorance. Truthfully she didn't know all that much except the little bit her sister Caroline had shown her over five years ago. Her sister had been locked in a cellar, and the Windmill Point Light remained dark for two nights as a result. After that, Caroline insisted Tessa be prepared for taking over should anything happen to her again.

And now because of Caroline's training, it turned out she was the only one in the community, other than the Bjorklund brothers, who knew the slightest thing about how to work the lighthouse. Besides, even if anyone else knew, they wouldn't help her. Very few people were speaking to her. In fact, anytime she walked into town, no one even dared to look her way.

Only Samuel talked to her. He didn't understand that he wasn't supposed to. She was grateful for his childlike acceptance of her. He didn't care or know about her past. She doubted he even understood anything about what had transpired during the past couple of weeks.

As it was, the responsibility of the lighthouse fell on her shoulders, at least until she could clear up the arrests. She'd written an additional letter to Mr. Cole and one to the lighthouse superintendent, praying Percival hadn't intercepted her mail like he had in the past.

"I've watched my dad do all the cleaning

plenty of times," Gunnar said from behind her.

She turned back to the lantern room and studied the now-dark lens. She was surprised that the resentment she experienced last night when she'd turned it on had dissipated into a strange calm.

"You did a good job, Miss Taylor. I know how much you hate the lighthouse, so I promise I'll learn quickly so that you don't have to do it much longer."

His words stabbed her with guilt. She didn't want the children to think that she didn't want to be here. She wouldn't have left them to fend for themselves, not even if she had to kiss the tower floor a hundred times a day.

"I'll stay with you and help you as long as it takes," she assured him.

Gunnar nodded and glanced down, but not before she saw him swallow hard.

Ingrid and Gunnar had been surprised to see her the morning after the warehouse fire. They'd been even more shocked to hear that their dad and Alex had been accused of setting the fire and subsequently arrested. But even though they'd been worried, they handled the stress with a maturity that had nearly broken her heart.

She hadn't told them her news, that she'd

been fired from her job and banned from living with any of the miner families or at any of the company-owned hotels and establishments. But they learned soon enough when the schoolhouse remained closed with a notice posted on the door that classes were canceled until a new teacher could be hired.

The lighthouse had been her only refuge. The one place in the world she'd never wanted to live had turned out to be the only place she could live.

"God sure has a sense of humor," she said with a half smile. "I've always tried to stay as far away as possible from lighthouses, and here I am the acting lightkeeper."

Gunnar smiled, and the crooked tilt of it reminded her of Alex and sent a pang through her chest. "Maybe God is trying to make you less afraid of lighthouses," Gunnar offered.

She started to protest, to tell Gunnar that she wasn't afraid of lighthouses. But she stopped and stared first at the lens, then at the lake. Was she afraid?

For so long she'd blamed the lighthouse and lakes for all the deaths and problems in her family. She didn't deny that she'd been angry and bitter. But maybe she was afraid too.

Had God placed her here at the Eagle Harbor Lighthouse time after time this year so that she'd have to face her fears? If so, she'd resisted His plan all along. She'd dragged her feet, determined not to have anything to do with the lighthouse or the men who lived in it.

After resisting all this time, had God decided to give her one last chance to face her fears? One last *big* chance?

She closed her eyes. *"God hath not given us a spirit of fear; but of power, of love, and of a sound mind."* The verse resounded in her mind. Part of her knew that one of the best ways to overcome any fear was to face it head on and walk through it, instead of trying to run away from it. Once she persevered and made it to the other side, the fear would be less menacing and less controlling. It was just the process of getting there that was so difficult.

"I think you might be on to something, Gunnar," she said, opening her eyes and smiling at him again. "Maybe God is trying to teach me to stop running away from the things I fear — starting with this lighthouse."

After all, she couldn't blame the lighthouse or the lake for her lost loved ones any more than she could blame the mine for

400

losing Henry Benney or illness for taking lives. If so, then she'd have to stay away from everyone so that she never got hurt again, and that was unrealistic.

The truth was she could lose those she loved at any moment, anywhere, and under any circumstance. She couldn't let her fear of losing stop her from loving.

Gunnar nodded shyly as he picked up one of the cloths used for cleaning the prisms. She reached for one too. He started shining the bull's-eye at the larger middle part of the lantern. She rounded to the opposite side and started wiping the prisms across from him.

"I don't mind doing the cleaning, Miss Taylor," Gunnar said.

"I know you don't. But the only way I'm going to stop being afraid is by doing the things I don't want to do."

His smile widened.

Even though her heart and body protested having to touch the lantern, and even though everything within her urged her to finish quickly and make her escape, she forced her hand to keep wiping.

"Will they ever be back?" Gunnar asked, his voice hoarse with emotion.

She didn't have to ask who he meant by *they*. Gunnar hadn't asked many questions

401

about what had happened. As with most things, he seemed to accept the situation and work at making the best of it. He was turning into a fine young man with the best qualities of both Michael and Alex. And he deserved an honest answer.

Her notes from Alex hadn't given her much information, but she'd gathered enough to know that Percival was waiting for travel to resume on the lakes. Once the first steamer arrived, he was planning to escort the two brothers to a prison in Detroit. Apparently he'd even arranged for two of his miners to accompany him to testify against the brothers.

She didn't know how she'd be able to defend Michael and Alex. Still, she'd have to go with them, find them a lawyer, and do whatever she could to plead for their innocence. It would be hard, especially since Percival had developed a case against them, and no one was willing to contradict him.

Her heart grew heavy every time she thought about her part in their arrest. Percival had never liked Alex, but if Alex hadn't come to her defense and beat up Percival after the funeral, she suspected that things wouldn't have spiraled so far out of control.

Now Percival was not only punishing her

by firing her but by locking up Alex too. Percival had probably guessed how much she'd grown to care about Alex and knew that he'd cause her the most pain by hurting Alex.

She paused in her cleaning and met Gunnar's serious gaze. "I'm sorry, Gunnar. I wish I could promise you that they'll be released once the judge hears the truth, but I just don't know."

Gunnar's shoulders slumped, but he continued wiping.

She wouldn't voice her worry that Alex might not even make it to a trial. Percival was a dangerous man. If he'd killed before, she had no doubt he'd do it again. Already she'd learned through Samuel that the prisoners weren't getting much food, and for the past couple of days she'd managed to sneak some provisions to them through Samuel.

Yet everyone in the community was hungry. The last of the food had burned up in the warehouse fire, and now they had almost nothing until the first steamers arrived from the southern ports.

Percival had apparently rationed out the remaining food in the store, which hadn't been much. The miners had organized into groups for hunting and fishing, but so far they hadn't been able to keep up with the needs of the community. The game was scarce, and what they did find was thin and meatless after the long winter. Even the wild animals were suffering.

Tessa had been careful with the remaining food in the lighthouse pantry, and although she'd been stingy, particularly with herself, she'd started to scrape the bottoms of the barrels.

"Miss Taylor?" Ingrid's voice came from below the hatch.

Tessa stepped over to the hole in the floor and peered down the stairway to see Ingrid slowly limping her way up. Dismay settled on her as it did whenever she thought about how Ingrid might not get the surgery she needed, not with all the expenses they would incur with traveling and hiring a lawyer.

"Good morning." Tessa forced a smile.

Ingrid's eyes had dark circles around them, and her bones poked through her clothing. The girl couldn't afford not to eat. She was thin enough to begin with.

"Someone is here to see you," Ingrid said in a small voice without returning Tessa's smile. With each passing day that the men were locked up, Ingrid was having a harder time keeping up a brave front.

"Who is it?"

"It's Josie Rawlings."

Tessa started down the stairs, her heartbeat rushing in rhythm to her footsteps. She hadn't seen any of the Rawlingses since the night of the fire, after she'd packed her belongings and walked to the lighthouse.

Before she'd left, Nadine had whispered angry curses against Percival. She'd even muttered some against her husband once she learned of his role in arresting Alex and Michael. But she hadn't made an effort to stop Tessa. In fact, she told Tessa that she wished she could help her, but to do so would only bring swift and severe repercussions on their family.

Tessa had squeezed Nadine's hand and told her not to worry, that she would be all right. She hadn't wanted anyone else to get hurt on account of her.

So why was Josie here now?

Ingrid led Tessa through the kitchen to the woodshed. There in the dark shadows of dawn, Josie stood inside the back door. She shifted nervously and glanced through the crack of open door toward the lighthouse yard.

"Josie?" Tessa ducked into the lean-to with its low roof.

Josie jumped and pressed a hand against

405

her chest. "You startled me."

"I'm rather surprised to see you here as well," Tessa said, unable to muster the anger she knew she should feel toward the girl for telling Percival about her time at the mine with Alex.

As if thinking the same thing, Josie lowered her eyes and rubbed the tip of her boot into the dust and wood shavings that covered the floor.

"It's good to see you," Tessa said, realizing it was true. No matter Josie's faults, she appreciated that the girl was here at that moment, that she'd been brave enough to come see her when no one else had.

"I didn't think you'd ever want to see me again." Josie's coat hung too loosely over her frame.

Conditions were worse than Tessa had realized. Fresh worry flooded her at the thought of how hungry Alex and Michael must be if everyone else was suffering so badly.

Tessa squeezed Josie's shoulder, the bones underneath protruding against her fingers. "I forgive you, Josie." The words came easily, and Tessa felt free once she'd said them.

"I didn't mean for Mr. Updegraff to find out." The words rushed out as Josie lifted her guilt-ridden eyes. "But he threatened to tell my mamm about my new beau if I didn't answer his questions about your relationship with the lightkeepers."

"He didn't hurt you, did he?"

Josie shook her head.

"Good, because if he did, I would have had to blacken his other eye." She wanted to lighten the situation, to show Josie the grace she herself hadn't received long ago after her mistake.

Josie didn't smile, but instead hung her head further. "You don't have to be nice to me, Miss Taylor. I don't deserve it."

Tessa reached out and touched Josie's chin and lifted her face so that the girl had to look into her eyes. "I made mistakes in my past too, Josie. The important thing is to learn from them and to move forward and do better the next time."

Josie nodded. After another silent moment, she brought her hand out from behind her back and held out several glistening trout that were still wiggling on the line strung through their gills. "These are for you. Dad and the boys caught them this morning."

Tessa shook her head. "No, you take them to your family —"

"Mamm will slap me senseless if I return with them."

"But you're hungry too."

"She's worried about you and the children."

"Tell her we're surviving." Tears rose quickly at the thought of Nadine's concern. She hadn't expected it, but thanked the Lord for Nadine's willingness to reach out to her and reassure her that she cared in spite of learning about Tessa's past.

"She said if you don't need them," Josie said, peeking out the crack in the door again, "that maybe you could find a way to get them to Alex and Michael."

Tessa nodded. "I'll cook them up and take them to Alex and Michael today."

Josie hesitated as if she wanted to say more but didn't know how to start.

Tessa waited patiently.

"I have to go," Josie finally said. She opened the door slowly and looked around.

"Be careful, Josie," Tessa warned. "Don't let anyone see you."

"You don't have to worry about anyone seeing me. Remember, I'm the expert at sneaking around."

Tessa smiled, but Josie had already slipped outside where she disappeared among the shadows.

Alex stared at the bars that covered the lone

window in the door. He'd already tried a hundred times to find a way to escape. But apparently Percival had built the cell more compactly than a copper penny. The brick walls didn't budge. The door was a solid unshakable slab. The ceiling was hard and plastered.

The room was dank, the only light coming from the window in the door. The stench from the chamber pot mingled with the odor of mildew growing on the floor and walls. At the moment, however, the constant gnawing ache in his stomach had taken his mind from the foulness of the place. He could think of little but his hunger, which hadn't been appeased by the few small morsels Samuel had handed them through the window. The water bucket in the corner was nearly empty now, and he'd begun to ration it for fear that Percival wouldn't refill it.

Michael lay on a pallet on the floor, his eyes closed, his chest barely rising and falling. Alex had tried to give Michael the greater share of the water and food, but Michael had stubbornly refused until finally last night they'd had another fight. Alex berated Michael once again for getting involved the night of the fire. If only Michael had stayed back at the lighthouse. If only Michael hadn't stepped forward to stop him from hitting Percival. If only Michael hadn't said anything at all and stayed out of the whole affair.

Alex heaved a sigh and leaned his head back against the wall. The *if only*s played through his head numerous times every day, a futile litany. He couldn't change anything now. The only thing he could do was make sure Michael survived, and then once they finally had some semblance of law besides Percival, he'd plead Michael's innocence.

"You're worrying again," Michael said in a hoarse whisper.

"I've got to think of some way to save you."

Michael opened one of his eyes a crack. "Stop trying to be my savior."

Anger and frustration wound through Alex's gut. "Maybe if you tried saving yourself, then I wouldn't need to."

Michael closed his eyes again and resumed his shallow breathing.

Alex shifted his legs away from the cold floor and brought them up to his chest. He wrapped his arms around them to keep himself from reaching out to Michael and yanking him up. He wanted to yell at his brother, hit him, and force him to agree to fight for his survival.

Instead he had to sit back and watch Michael waste away. For once, there was nothing he could do to help Michael. He was utterly powerless to rescue his brother this time.

"You can't always make things better for me." Michael's voice was stronger and startled Alex with its clarity. "I've relied on you a lot since Rachel died. Maybe too much at times."

"I've wanted to be there for you," Alex assured him. "That's what family's for."

"You've been a blessing to me, Alex." Michael opened both eyes and shifted his head sideways so that he was looking directly at his brother. "I can't thank you enough for all you've done for me these past years."

Alex swallowed a sudden lump of emotion. "There's no need for thanks —"

"Yes, there is. I've been a cad for not letting you know how much I appreciate all you've done. You've sacrificed a lot for me and the children."

"You've told me thanks plenty of times."

"But not like this. Not for putting your life on hold so that you could help fix mine."

For a moment, Alex couldn't think of a suitable response. He had to admit, he was touched that Michael was acknowledging all his sacrifices. Of course, he hadn't done

411

any of it for accolades. He'd meant what he said about not needing any thanks. It was satisfying, though, to know that everything he'd done had meant something to Michael.

"The thing is," Michael continued, "I'm not the same man I was when Rachel died."

"You're not?" Alex didn't see much change.

"No. I'm working on changing," Michael said as if reading Alex's mind. "I'm making more of an effort. And now I think it's time for you to stop putting your life on hold for my sake."

"I'm not putting my life on hold," Alex said quickly. "This is where I want to be." He grinned and glanced around the cell. "Well, I don't actually want to be *here,* but you know what I mean. I want to be with you — with family. I don't want to be anywhere else."

Michael pushed himself up on one elbow and his expression tightened. "I also think it's time for me to stop relying on you so much and try to make it on my own."

Alex felt his grin fade. "Why would you want to make it on your own? We make a great team."

"I rely on you too much. Sometimes I wonder if I can even make it now without you."

"You've got two kids and a full-time job. Of course you need my help. That's only natural."

Michael's brows furrowed above sad eyes.

"Like I said," Alex continued, "family helps family. That's the way God intended it. That's what Dad always did, and that's what I'm going to do."

"And like *I* said, I appreciate it. I'm grateful for all you've done these past years. But . . ."

"But what?"

"But I've got to start standing on my own two feet."

Alex shook his head. "So that's why you've been flat on your back all week, Michael? Sprawled out on that pallet like you're about to die."

"I'm conserving energy."

Alex snorted.

Michael grinned and fell back against the floor with an *oomph.*

Alex sat back and tried to ease the tension from his shoulders, the tension that had been building with each passing day of watching Michael grow weaker and more listless. He didn't quite know what to make of everything Michael was saying. Was Michael rejecting him, or was he finally starting to think and feel again instead of going

413

through the motions of life?

Unsteady footsteps in the hallway outside the cell alerted him to Samuel's approach. After several more seconds, Samuel's bald head and fleshy face filled the window. "Are you still there?" he asked.

Hidden in the shadows, Alex supposed Samuel had a hard time seeing inside the cell. For a second he debated pretending that they weren't there anymore. Maybe then Samuel would open the door to investigate. Alex could wrestle Samuel down, and they could break free.

One glance at the worry in Samuel's innocent eyes made Alex put the thought out of his mind. He couldn't hurt Samuel.

"We're still here, Samuel," he said as he would to Ingrid.

Samuel turned and spoke to someone behind him. "They're still here." His voice was raspy, as though he'd tried to whisper, yet it was as loud as his normal speaking voice.

The other person whispered back, but Alex couldn't decipher the words.

"Percival told me that the prisoners couldn't have any visitors," Samuel said in that same voice, which told Alex he was indeed trying to whisper. "He said absolutely no visitors."

"I'm not a visitor," the return whisper was louder. "I'm a friend."

The voice belonged to Tessa. Even in a whisper, he could tell it was hers.

His heart gave a leap, and he bolted off the floor. In two strides he was at the little window in the door. "Tessa?" He gripped the bars and peered through them, needing to see her face and hear her voice.

She wriggled in front of Samuel, pushing his bulk out of the way. In an instant her face replaced his at the window. "Alex?" At the sight of him, a smile filled her green eyes and radiated throughout her face, making her more beautiful than he remembered.

He couldn't stop from reaching through the bars and touching her cheek. Her skin was soft and fresh, unlike his grimy face that hadn't been washed or shaved in over a week.

She leaned into his touch, her eyes searching his face, eagerly taking him in.

"You can't do that," Samuel said from behind Tessa, the anxiety in his voice making it even louder. "You have to keep your hands inside the cell."

Alex moved his fingers to her hair, to the dark wavy strands. He skimmed the silkiness, unable to get enough of her, starved for far more than food. For a few seconds

415

he forgot all about Samuel's fretting. It was just the two of them again. And this time he wanted to tell her that he loved her, that he couldn't stand the thought of his life without her and would do anything to be with her.

"You have to hurry!" Samuel's voice had grown frantic. "You have to hurry before Percival comes back."

Tessa glanced over her shoulder. When she looked back at him, sadness and worry had replaced the joy of their reunion. "How are you, Alex?" she asked.

"I'm fine. How are you and the children?"

"We miss you." There was something bright and intense in her gaze, something there that sent ripples through his stomach. Was it love?

"We miss you too." Whether or not she loved him, he couldn't deny that he loved her. He loved her more than anything else in his life. He didn't care if she could see it in his eyes at that moment. Not when he might not see her again. Not when he might not live through another week.

"Hurry, hurry, hurry," Samuel chanted.

Tessa frowned as she retrieved some items out of a basket she was carrying. "Here," she said, holding them up to the barred window. "Nadine sent me some trout this morning to give to you and Michael."

"You and the children eat it." He refused to take it from her, even though the scent of freshly baked fish wafted up and made his knees go weak.

"We're getting along fine with the supplies in the pantry," she insisted, pushing a small package between the bars. When he didn't take it, she let it fall to the floor and then pushed another package through.

"We can't take it —"

Ignoring his words, she shoved another bundle into the cell, then another. Finally she looked at him again. Her eyes were fierce with determination, the determination he loved about her. "Don't give up." She reached through the bars and cupped his cheek. "Please don't give up."

He grabbed her hand and pressed his lips into her palm. The taste of her was sweet and smelled of lilac soap. He breathed her in, let his lips linger in her hand. This was all he needed. *She* was all he needed.

Her fingers trembled against him, and he wished he could reassure her that everything would work out fine, that he'd be home soon. But he couldn't lie to her.

"Uh-oh, uh-oh," Samuel said, sounding near to tears. He was pacing behind Tessa and throwing his arms up in the air. "We have to go now."

417

She took a reluctant step back, giving him no choice but to release her. She studied him for a long moment, as though she were trying to memorize every line and feature. Then Samuel nudged her toward the office door.

She stumbled away.

Alex clutched the bars with both hands and wished he was strong enough to tear them away and go after her.

She glanced at him over her shoulder. "I lit the lantern last night."

He knew he should be relieved that the lighthouse was in operation. Michael had fretted about it when he'd learned the lake was mostly thawed, and he'd begged Alex to write a note to Tessa asking her to turn the lantern on. Alex hadn't wanted to bother her, not when he knew how much she loathed lighthouses and how it would stir up painful memories for her.

However, as usual, he hadn't been able to say no to Michael.

"How are you?" he asked, searching her face for the agony she was sure to be feeling.

"I have to admit I wasn't thrilled about doing it." A pained smile formed on her lips. "But I know God is using it to work in my life where I most need it."

He wanted to ask her more, but before he could, Samuel propelled her through the door. Long after she was gone, he stood staring through the window, trying to envision her, savoring the memory of her face and the touch of her skin.

"You really do love her, don't you?" Michael finally croaked, the sound breaking the silence and startling Alex.

He turned slowly, bent and picked up the bundles of food she'd delivered. "It doesn't matter now."

Michael didn't respond.

Alex tossed the packages of food toward his brother — four bundles altogether. They landed near Michael's hand. "Eat up," he said, sliding down the wall to the spot on the floor he'd occupied for most of the week.

Michael didn't move a muscle or open his eyes even to look at the food.

The smell of the trout caused Alex's stomach to rumble loud enough to echo off the cell walls. "If you don't get going, you'll force me to start."

"Go ahead." Michael turned his face toward the opposite wall.

Anger spurted through Alex. He sprang forward and said, "Come on, Michael! You just got through telling me that you need to stand on your own two feet."

Michael's back stiffened.

"If you're going to stand on your own two feet, then prove it to me right now. Prove it to me by eating the food." Alex fumed. If Michael didn't make an effort, he'd open up the bundles and shove the food down his throat.

"She loves you," Michael said so quietly that Alex almost didn't hear him.

For a minute he was tempted to pretend he hadn't heard. But something told him they were going to have this conversation about Tessa whether he wanted to or not. He sighed and then finally spoke. "You don't know —"

"It was very clear." Michael rolled over and looked at his brother, resignation in his eyes. "She loves you, Alex. Not me."

"Don't jump to conclusions."

"I'm not."

"She cares about both of us."

"She didn't ask how I was doing." Michael's voice was flat and stopped Alex's retort. "She didn't look in the cell to see me. She didn't talk to me. I doubt she even realized I was here."

"That's because I was the one who came to the window first."

"No. It's because she loves you," Michael said. Alex started to shake his head, but Michael cut him off. "I need to stop fooling myself into thinking she could ever care for me."

"Well, she won't care about me either. I'm too uneducated for her."

"Tessa doesn't care if you can read or not. She's too kind to let something like that stand in her way."

Deep inside, Alex knew Michael was right. But that didn't stop him from wishing he had more to offer her.

"Just give her time," Alex insisted. Even though he couldn't keep from feeling a measure of relief that Tessa had been excited to see him instead of Michael, he knew he had to convince his brother that Tessa still cared about them both. He couldn't risk Michael falling into a melancholy, not now while he was barely hanging on as it was.

"I could give her a lifetime," Michael said, "but she'll always love you more than me."

"It doesn't matter how much she loves me. We're not meant to be together and that's all there is to it."

Michael gave a short, scoffing laugh. "Stop it, Alex. You're not going to convince me that Tessa will ever love me more than she does you."

"You and the children need her —"

"What I need is for you to stop trying to

421

fix my life and make everything all better."

Michael's words stabbed Alex and flattened him against the cold cell wall. For a long minute he couldn't speak past the pain. It almost sounded as though Michael resented him and his involvement.

"I'm sorry," Michael said, his tone less harsh. "I didn't mean that the way it came out."

Alex wanted to call Michael a liar, to tell him that he had meant every word. But he was suddenly tired — tired of fighting, and tired of attempting to save Michael from every problem he faced.

While Michael's declaration stung, maybe it was the truth. Maybe Alex had to stop trying so hard to make Michael's life better and let his brother do it for himself.

Chapter 24

Tessa forced herself not to look at the oranges in the bucket near Percival's feet. A sign written in Samuel's childlike print marked them at the outrageous price of fifty cents apiece. But like everyone else, she was willing to pay a month's salary if need be for the fresh food. Unlike everyone else, she wasn't allowed to shop in the company story anymore, and even if Percival had allowed her to buy the newly arrived produce, she didn't have any money.

She pressed a hand against her stomach and quelled a rumble of hunger. "You've jailed them unlawfully for over two weeks," she said. "What you've done is illegal. The American Constitution guarantees a fair trial."

Percival hadn't moved from where he leaned against the doorframe of his office. "Out here on the frontier of civilization, sometimes we have to take the law into our

423

own hands so that people stay safe."

Tessa repressed a cry of frustration. She'd tried numerous times to gain an audience with Percival since he'd locked Alex and Michael up in jail. But he'd turned her away every time.

Until today.

Samuel stood behind the counter wiping the glass top with vigorous circles. From the way he'd been sneaking glances at her and Percival, she guessed he'd been listening to every word. She didn't know how much he understood about why the Bjorklund brothers had been locked up. She'd attempted to explain it to him on several occasions, hoping he'd have more sympathy and allow her to see Alex again.

But after the first visit, Samuel had been adamant that she not go back to the cell again. No matter what she said or how she bribed him, she couldn't get him to change his mind. However, he'd been more willing to continue to deliver the food she brought.

Percival smoothed his hand over his mustache. "They'll get the justice they deserve once we head down to Detroit and they stand trial for their crimes."

"And when will you stand trial for *your* crimes, Mr. Updegraff?" The words slipped out before she could stop them, but once they were out, she didn't care. He'd already fired her. He'd ostracized her within the community, and now he was preventing her from buying the food that had just arrived by wagons from Copper Harbor only yesterday.

The *Iron City* had tried to sail into Eagle Harbor but couldn't make it in on account of a severe wind. Instead it had sailed back to Copper City and docked there. Men had gone over to retrieve as much as they could, including the oranges, a few cattle, and fresh salted pork.

Even if the steamer hadn't been able to dock in Eagle Harbor, the sighting had given the townspeople hope. Their days of starvation were nearing an end.

Unfortunately that didn't include her, the two children, or Alex and Michael. She'd used up the last of the food stores in the lighthouse pantry, and they desperately needed the new food supplies as much as the rest of the community. Since she'd prohibited Gunnar from going in a boat out on the lake by himself, he'd taken to fishing inland on some of the streams where there were still snowbanks and the water was ice cold.

Most days he had what the men in the area referred to as fisherman's luck: a weary leg and a hungry gut. But all it took was one good day, like the morning he caught fifteen trout. She'd taken a feast to Alex and Michael that afternoon.

Thankfully, Josie continued to sneak provisions to her, usually in the early morning or at dusk when the shadows hid her. Tessa had been surprised by how many of the townspeople had begun to reach out to help her, albeit as secretly as possible. On one occasion she'd bumped into Hannah walking down the street. The young woman had slipped something into Tessa's hand. Once she returned home, she discovered a wedge of old cheese. On another occasion, Mrs. Benney had given her two wrinkled apples. And several other students and their parents had left items outside the lighthouse door.

Maybe the townspeople weren't brave enough to fight against Percival, but she was grateful for the small things they were doing to show they still cared about her in spite of her tainted reputation.

"Miss Taylor, *you* asked to see *me*," Percival said, sliding a hand up to his necktie and loosening it. His expression was impassive, although something dark lurked in his eyes. "I don't appreciate you coming in here and slinging insults at me."

Insults? She almost laughed. He hadn't heard any insults yet. Just wait until she really got started. Then he'd learn the true meaning of an insult.

"Why don't you get to the point of why you came here today?" He stretched his neck, pulled out his bow tie, and unhooked the top button of his shirt.

"You know very well why I came." She forced herself not to inch toward the door in case she needed a quick escape. She couldn't run away like a scared rabbit every time she was around this fox. This was perhaps her last chance to plead for Alex's release and she had to stay strong. "I want you to release Alex and Michael. Today. Right now."

Percival tossed his bow tie onto the counter, disrupting Samuel's wiping. Samuel looked up at him with curious but trusting eyes.

"You know as well as I do that neither of those men started the fire," she continued. "You're getting back at Alex for hitting you. And you're punishing me by hurting the men I care about."

"You should know, Miss Taylor, that since the night of the fire we recovered an oil container from the ruins that's stamped with the words *U.S. Lighthouse Establishment.*"

All brass lighthouse ware was either stamped or had official plates affixed to them. Because she'd grown up in lighthouses, she was accustomed to such labeling. There was no ignoring the stamp. "That doesn't mean Alex was there or that he was the one who started the fire with the oil." She knew in her heart that Alex was innocent, no matter what kind of evidence Percival came up with.

"We also have two witnesses who stepped forward, claiming to see Alex and Michael going into the building well after dark."

Tessa shook her head, the frustration tearing at her insides. How would she ever prove their innocence? Percival was making it impossible, and they both knew it. "Why don't you just tell me what I need to do in order for you to drop these ludicrous charges?"

Percival perused her slowly, and as he did a sickening heaviness settled over her. Would he really demand that she hand herself over to him as he'd wanted all along? Was that what this was all about?

When he began to walk toward her with calculated steps, she almost shrank backward. How far was she willing to go to save

428

Alex? She shuddered at the thought.

Percival stopped in front of her, and she caught the whiff of tobacco and oranges lingering on him. Again he studied her, as if deciding whether she was worth the bargain.

Was this why Hannah and the other women Percival victimized had gone along with him? Maybe their husbands hadn't allowed or supported their choice after all. She'd been so sure that the men had been weak and unloving to sit back while Percival used their wives. But maybe, like her, the other women had decided the sacrifice was worth it in order to save the men and families they loved. Maybe they'd been willing because they so desperately wanted to protect their families.

He took a step nearer so that his body almost touched hers. "If you want to work out a deal," he said in a low voice, "then you can meet me back at my house in one hour."

What should she do? If she didn't give in to Percival, Alex might die. If she did, she'd truly become tainted. She would become the loose woman she'd tried so hard to run from. Yet if everyone already thought she was loose, what difference would it make if she really was?

Percival lifted his hand to her cheek and

stroked along her jawline.

At the touch she couldn't hold back another shudder. Before she could stop herself, she slapped his hand away.

He struck her back, swift and hard, his palm smashing into her nose.

She cried out in pain as blood dribbled from her nose onto her lips. She lifted a hand to her mouth and pulled it away, the bright crimson smeared on her fingers.

"Percival?" Samuel's voice from behind the counter wobbled. "Why are you hurting Miss Taylor?"

Percival scowled at her. She'd defied him and now he'd punish her even more. She had to run. She had to get away from him while she still could. She couldn't go through with his demands, not even for Alex. As much as she loved him, she wanted to do the right thing before God. She had to stay strong and pure and then trust that God would honor her choice.

"Is Miss Taylor bleeding?" Samuel came from around the counter, his eyes round, his face horrified.

"This isn't your concern, Samuel," Percival said. "Go back to your work."

Samuel stopped, but tears welled in his eyes. "Percival, please don't hurt Miss Taylor. She's my friend."

430

Blood dripped from her lips onto the floor, making a splattering of dots near the oranges. She cupped her hand over her nose to prevent any more mess. She didn't want to make this more traumatic for Samuel than it already was.

Percival glanced at Samuel just as a tear rolled down his flushed cheek. Percival swore under his breath and took a step away from her.

Tessa didn't wait for another opportunity to make her escape. She slipped around Percival and hurried toward the door. Stepping outside, the early May sunshine blinded her. A few of the trees had buds beginning to show. She'd even heard birds singing when she walked the path from the lighthouse to town earlier. In spite of her hunger and the problems she faced, she'd allowed herself to rejoice that spring was finally arriving. At long last maybe she could say good-bye to winter. But now, as she stumbled down Center Street, her vision blurred. The dingy gray of the buildings and surrounding woodland brought her no comfort. The chill breeze blowing off the lake sliced through her garments as if to remind her that even if spring had come, this northern land was still cold, harsh and unforgiving.

431

"Miss Taylor, are you all right? What happened?"

Tessa's footsteps faltered at the sight of Mr. Benney coming down the mine path. He was staring at the hand covering her nose. It was covered in blood.

Several other men stopped behind Mr. Benney. They were attired in their dusty miner's clothing and wore their miner's caps. Mr. Benney looked around before stepping back into the shelter of brush and beckoning her to join him. Once they were secluded, he gazed with concern at her face. She guessed he could see the remnants of fear left in her eyes and knew that what had happened to her was no accident.

"Did someone hurt you, Miss Taylor?"

"Percival Updegraff hit me."

The words were barely out of her mouth before Mr. Benney turned and muttered angrily at the men behind him. They argued in whispers for a moment before Mr. Benney's voice rose. "That cack's murdered enough folks here, including me son. We have to stop him before he hurts more."

A spark of hope lit inside Tessa. She grabbed Mr. Benney's arm. "Will you help free Alex and Michael Bjorklund?"

When he looked at her again, she glimpsed sorrow in his eyes, the same hollow look

432

he'd worn the day of Henry's funeral. But just as quickly a hot, almost wild, anger surged in to replace the sadness.

"We might not have the fitty means to save the lightkeepers," he said, "but a steamer has just docked with the owner of Cole Mine."

Tessa nodded at the news, already devising a plan. She would go to Mr. Cole, tell him everything that had happened, and beg him to release Alex and Michael. Surely he'd have the power to make Percival listen to reason, especially if Mr. Benney and the other miners went to the owner with all of their complaints.

"Why don't you go to Mr. Cole first," she said. "Tell the owner all of Percival's misdeeds. And then I'll go after you. He'll be more willing to listen to my complaints if he's already heard yours."

Mr. Benney glanced at the other men. "Stop the gawky indecision, you," Mr. Benney pleaded. "The daft Cole is our only hope."

They shook their heads, their faces wreathed with worry.

Once again Mr. Benney turned and argued with the men, but from the stubborn shakes of their heads, Tessa could see they were too afraid to do anything. She could

433

almost read their thoughts. What if they failed to convince Mr. Cole of Percival's crimes? What if Mr. Cole was every bit as evil as Percival? What would happen to them then? If Mr. Cole didn't fire them, then surely Percival would. They couldn't take that chance.

After the men continued on their way, Tessa followed after them at a distance. Even though she knew she should return to the lighthouse and clean her hands and face, she couldn't resist the pull to gather near the docks to watch the *Illinois* and Mr. Cole. As the crowd swelled, it seemed half the town had the same idea.

She didn't cheer with the rest as the gangplank came down. The boat was low in the water, which meant more supplies for the famished community. She watched expectantly as the passengers began to disembark. A middle-aged man dressed in a tailored gray suit was one of the first to descend the gangplank. A young girl walked next to him, her gloved hand in the crook of his arm. She looked to be about Josie's age yet decidedly prettier. Her lavender skirt had layers of ruffles, and her matching bodice was cinched at the square neckline by a ribbon. The girl took dainty steps and carried a parasol above a fancy hat that was

434

perched on her perfectly coiled blond hair.

As soon as the man and girl reached the end of the gangplank, Percival stepped forward and greeted them. The ingratiating smile on the mine clerk's face told her that the man was important, most likely the mine owner, Mr. Cole himself.

They strolled the dock together, Percival doing all the talking with Mr. Cole nodding now and then. When they stepped onto land and began to pass the group of assembled miners, including Mr. Benney, Tessa inwardly shouted at them to rush up to Mr. Cole and expose all the atrocities Percival had committed in their community.

She willed Mr. Benney to jump into Mr. Cole's path. But her heart shriveled in her chest when he and the other miners stood silently by, unmoving as Percival and Mr. Cole passed them.

Only after Percival had gone several feet beyond the miners did he turn and address them. "Bring Mr. Cole and his daughter's trunks and bags up to the company house once they're unloaded."

"Yes, sir," Mr. Benney said with a slanted gaze that radiated hatred. Thankfully, Percival had already resumed his conversation with the mine owner and hadn't noticed.

Tessa's blood went cold with all the pos-

435

sibilities of what else Percival would do to punish Mr. Benney should he discover the man's true feelings. She shouldn't have asked Mr. Benney to go to Percival. The other miners were right. Mr. Benney would only bring more danger and disaster into his life.

She stared after Mr. Cole and his pretty daughter walking the path toward town. Resolution rose within her. She knew what she must do. Perhaps this was the reason God had brought her to Eagle Harbor all along. She must go before Mr. Cole and plead not only for Alex's life but on behalf of the entire community. She was the only one left who could do it. Any man who was connected to Cole Mine, like Mr. Benney, would only endanger himself if he did.

Of course, she might bring more danger upon herself as well. But she couldn't leave before attempting to expose Percival for the tyrant that he was.

From her hiding spot behind the privy, Tessa watched as Percival exited the company house and strode back toward the center of town. She dug her fingers into Bear's thick coat, grateful for his companionship during the past couple of hours of waiting. Percival had finally taken his leave of the Coles. Just in time too, for the evening was growing darker.

The Coles were staying at Percival's home, although she supposed that technically the house belonged to Mr. Cole. As the biggest and finest house in Eagle Harbor, she wasn't surprised the Coles were lodging there. It just made her plan to see Mr. Cole alone more difficult.

The moment Percival turned the corner she stepped out from behind the privy and ran across the yard. She had no time to waste. She didn't know how long she had before Percival returned and she had to make the most of every second he was away.

At the front door she knocked urgently and prayed Mr. Cole would answer and not the housekeeper. When footsteps sounded in the hallway from within the house and then the door rattled, she motioned for Bear to lie down.

The door swung open to reveal the girl that had come ashore with Mr. Cole. From an interior room, a male voice said, "Victoria, don't open the door."

The girl, however, opened the door wider. Curiosity lit her delicate features and danced in her honey-brown eyes. She glanced first at Tessa and then down at Bear. When Bear lifted his head to stare back, Victoria jumped back with an "Oh my!" before breaking into a grin.

"I'm Tessa Taylor, Eagle Harbor's schoolteacher," Tessa said, unable to resist a glance in the direction Percival had just disappeared. "I'd like to see Mr. Cole right away."

If Victoria had heard her, she gave no indication. Instead she kneeled and held out a hand to the dog. Bear sniffed the outstretched fingers before putting his head back down on his paws. Victoria leaned in and scratched Bear's head. "Is this a tamed wolf?"

"No, he's a Norwegian Elkhound."

"He's beautiful." Victoria ran her hand along his body.

Bear thumped his tail, pleased to receive the attention.

"He says thank you for the compliment," Tessa said with a smile.

Victoria lifted her face and returned the smile. This time she studied Tessa. "Where did you get that bruise?"

Tessa touched the tender spot on her cheekbone beneath her eye. She'd washed away the blood and reassured Ingrid and Gunnar that she was fine. But she couldn't hide the blackish-purple bruise from where Percival had hit her.

"As a matter of fact," Tessa began, "Mr. Updegraff himself gave me this precious gift just this afternoon. That's what I'd like to talk to your father about. I would appreciate it if you'd take me to him."

"Victoria!" the voice coming from a room down the hall sounded exasperated. "I told you not to open the door."

"It's just the schoolteacher, Father," Victoria called back. "I told you, you're only being paranoid." The young girl sighed and scratched Bear's neck before whispering to Tessa, "We got a threatening letter a few weeks ago from someone saying my life was in danger, and now my father won't let me out of his sight."

"I can imagine that would be rather scary," Tessa replied. Up close, the girl was even prettier. Without her hat, her sandy hair hung freely in ringlets, loose and wispy. Going by the girl's maturing figure, Tessa guessed that perhaps Victoria was sixteen or seventeen, a year or two older than Josie.

"What's his name?" Victoria asked, her eyes back on the dog.

"Bear. And he's about to become a father any day now." Tessa had made Wolfie stay at home, though her big black eyes had pleaded to come along.

Victoria's face lit up. "You mean you're

having puppies?"

Tessa nodded, but her attention was diverted to Mr. Cole entering the hall and striding toward them, a frown furrowing his forehead.

"Victoria Elizabeth," he said, "what would your mother say if she knew you were talking to strangers?" The man's shiny black shoes tapped ominously against the floorboards. The gold chain of his pocket watch attached to his vest gleamed in the light of the hallway lantern, as did his gold shirt studs and cuff links.

He stopped behind Victoria. The angular lines in his aristocratic face were hardened with frustration. For a few seconds he watched Victoria pet the dog and he seemed to be reining in his temper.

Tessa waited for him to acknowledge her. She had to say her piece before Percival returned and tried to contradict her. But she also didn't want to start off by making a bad impression on the man, a man who could determine Alex's fate.

"Bear is about to become a father," Victoria said, smiling up at Mr. Cole.

The smile was all it took to soften the man's expression. The lines melted away and love oozed from his eyes.

"Could we get one of the puppies?" Victoria asked.

"I don't know about that —"

"Pleeeease?" She batted her exquisitely long eyelashes. Surprisingly there wasn't a hint of manipulation in Victoria's sweet demeanor. Her smile was genuine, her eyes guileless. Nevertheless, the girl seemed to know how to wrap her father around her pinkie.

Tessa almost laughed. What man could resist such a plea?

Not Mr. Cole. From the tilt of his head, Tessa could tell he was seriously considering Victoria's request. He finally looked at Tessa, and she was surprised by the kindness in his eyes. "When will the puppies be ready to leave their mother?" he asked.

"They're not born quite yet."

His lips quirked with the hint of a smile. "Not born quite yet?"

She had the feeling she'd like Mr. Cole if he'd been anyone other than the owner of Cole Mine. "The mother is due any day, but she hasn't had the pups yet." Part of her hoped that Wolfie was waiting to have the babies until after Alex came home.

"Then I don't think that's going to work for us, Victoria," Mr. Cole said gently to his daughter. "We're only staying for a few days, and the puppies won't be ready to leave

441

their mother until they're at least seven or eight weeks old."

Victoria rubbed Bear's head again and was rewarded by a lick. She laughed. "I'm sure we can figure out something, Father."

"Maybe once we're back in New York, I can have my manager track down a puppy for you there."

Yes indeed. Victoria Cole had her father wrapped around her pinkie. Tessa smothered a chuckle and then cleared her throat. "Mr. Cole, I need to talk to you about your mine clerk, Mr. Updegraff."

Mr. Cole had shifted his attention back on his daughter. "I'd rather not talk any more business tonight, Miss . . ."

"Miss Taylor. I'm the schoolteacher here."

"My clerk told me we no longer have a teacher in Eagle Harbor, that he had to fire the current teacher due to . . . indiscretions."

"That's right. He fired me." Tessa gulped down the rising consternation. If Percival had already spoken ill of her to Mr. Cole, then was she doomed before she even had the chance to begin?

"And you disagree with his decision?" Mr. Cole asked, weariness crossing his brow.

She ought to leave him and his daughter to rest. She had no doubt he was a busy

442

man and that his travels had left him tired. Yet her heart pressed for her to speak the truth about Percival, so that Mr. Cole would know once and for all the character of the man he'd hired, who treated the people of Eagle Harbor with cruelty and intimidation.

"Mr. Updegraff took away my job because . . ." She stopped and glanced at Victoria, deciding to hold back the ugly truth that he'd wanted her for a mistress and instead tamed her words. "Because I refused his advances."

Victoria raised her head and again took in Tessa as if weighing whether or not she was genuine. "I already told Father that there's something about that man that makes my skin crawl."

"Exactly," Tessa said, relief flooding her at Victoria's declaration that added support to her cause. She wanted to explain to Mr. Cole that Percival had abused many of the women in the community, but again she didn't want to go into specific details in front of a young girl like Victoria. "Mr. Cole, you need only ask the students and parents of this community about my conduct. All of them will testify that no matter my past mistakes, I've been a hardworking teacher and have lived a godly life."

"Very well, Miss Taylor," he replied. "Why

don't you call tomorrow and you may present your side of the story to me then."

"I'm sorry, sir." She had to stay strong. She couldn't back down now. "The matter is urgent. I really must speak with you now while Mr. Updegraff is absent."

"I'm sorry too," he said. "Unfortunately, everywhere I go, matters are always pressing —"

"Father," Victoria interrupted, "I'm sure you can take a few minutes to listen to what Miss Taylor has to say." She gazed up at her father with trusting eyes. "Mr. Updegraff hit her. You're always saying that men should never hit a woman, not for any reason. Ever."

Bless you, Tessa wanted to say to Victoria. *Bless you for understanding and for taking my side.* But Tessa forced herself to remain silent as Mr. Cole considered his daughter's words.

At last he reached over and rested a hand on her head. "You're compassionate just like your mother."

Victoria grasped his hand and squeezed it. "Don't worry. I know you miss her terribly, but we'll be with her again soon."

Mr. Cole rubbed a hand across his eyes and then nodded at Tessa. "I'll give you five minutes, Miss Taylor."

Hope leapt in her chest. "Thank you, sir. That's all the time I need."

"And I can't promise anything except that I'll listen and try to understand."

"That's all I ask."

He waved for her to precede him down the hallway. As she passed Victoria, she silently mouthed *Thank you.*

The girl smiled. "I'll watch Bear while you talk with Father."

After Mr. Cole ushered her into Percival's office, Tessa launched into a brief summary of all that had happened over the past year, starting with Hannah, as well as what had happened to Mr. Benney and Henry as a result of rebuffing Percival. She ended with the warehouse fire and how Percival had locked up Alex and Michael and then fired her.

"He hit me this morning when I refused his offer to become his mistress in exchange for releasing the lightkeepers."

From behind Percival's tidy desk, Mr. Cole studied her, his elbows resting on the desktop, fingers steepled under his chin. The only sound for a long moment was the ticking of the large brass clock resting on the mantel above a cold hearth.

"I would like to believe you, Miss Taylor," he finally said with a deep, weary sigh. "But

445

Mr. Updegraff has been working at this mine much longer than I've owned it. He knows a great deal more about it than I do." He motioned toward the shelves of ledgers that had been meticulously labeled and organized. "From what I can tell, Mr. Updegraff is efficient, hardworking, and honest."

"Honest?" Tessa choked over the word.

"Believe me, I've had clerks who attempted to line their own pockets at the expense of Cole Enterprises, and Mr. Updegraff has so far proven that he is no such man. He operates my mine with an integrity I only wish I could find in all my clerks."

Tessa sank further into her chair. The hope she'd carried through the conversation quickly deflated.

"Mr. Updegraff admits he can be hard-handed at times," Mr. Cole continued apologetically. "But he keeps order, which is more than I can say of some of my holdings in the Midwest."

"He's a tyrant and a bully." Tessa shook her head. "He intimidates everyone around him in order to get what he wants."

"No one else has come forward to complain."

"That's because they're all scared to death of what he'll do to them once you leave."

446

Mr. Cole's kind eyes crinkled at the edges with age. Even so, he was still a handsome man with the kind of looks that had probably once turned the heads of many a woman. "I don't wish to disregard your concerns, Miss Taylor," he said with a glance at the bruise on her cheek. "So before I leave Eagle Harbor, I'll interview a number of people to validate your concerns."

"No," she said quickly, her lungs constricting in fear for her friends. "If you talk to anyone else about this, Mr. Updegraff will find out who spoke against him and then punish them for it." She'd already caused enough trouble, and she wouldn't be able to bear knowing anyone else was suffering on account of her meddling.

Mr. Cole cleared his throat. "Perhaps I can speak to the residents discreetly then."

"Nothing happens in Eagle Harbor that Percival Updegraff doesn't eventually learn about." She had no doubt he'd learn about this secret meeting with Mr. Cole too. But it didn't matter. She'd soon be gone, and he wouldn't be able to hurt her anymore. At least she hoped that was the case.

"If you don't allow me to question anyone, Miss Taylor, then how am I to investigate the matter any further?"

"Speak with the lightkeepers," she said. "They'll confirm everything I've just said."

"I hardly think I can trust the word of two criminals."

"They're not guilty, Mr. Cole." She leaned forward in the chair. "No matter what Mr. Updegraff has told you, they didn't start that fire."

"Then I suppose you have facts to refute Mr. Updegraff's?"

Percival had already presented his side of the story to Mr. Cole, and with all the evidence piled against Alex and Michael, what could she possibly say to defend them? They had no alibis. Alex had been caught coming out of the burning warehouse. Now apparently an oilcan from the lighthouse had been found among the charred remains of the building.

"I don't have any proof," she said. "I just know both men wouldn't ever do such a thing."

Mr. Cole pushed back from the desk and stood. "I'm sorry, Miss Taylor. Without any proof, I really must agree with Mr. Updegraff. The men must be brought to Detroit to stand trial."

She knew that was her signal saying she needed to leave. He'd graciously given her his time and was now dismissing her. But she couldn't make herself stand. Her body was stuck to the chair as surely as frost to a window.

"I need something more than just your word to go on," he continued more gently. "Otherwise my hands are tied." Something in his eyes and tone told her that he also knew about her past, that Percival had made sure to defame her in order to undermine her trustworthiness. How could she blame Mr. Cole for not believing her, not when she had a tainted reputation already?

A rush of bitterness cut off her words. She didn't know how to respond without sounding angry or without breaking down and crying and pleading. She'd tried so hard to bring life to the community here, to make changes, to help the people, but in the end her past mistakes had once again been her downfall.

He walked toward the office door and opened it.

Dignity, she told herself, fighting the urge to fall on her knees and beg him to listen to reason. *Leave with dignity.* Slowly, almost painfully, she peeled herself from the chair and rose. She tried to hold her chin high as she crossed to the door.

When she entered the hallway, Mr. Cole spoke one last time behind her. "If you'd

449

like, I can write a letter of recommendation that you can take with you to secure a new teaching position elsewhere."

You can take your recommendation and toss it in the lake, she was tempted to tell him. Instead she swallowed down the bitterness and nodded. "Thank you, Mr. Cole. I would greatly appreciate such a gesture."

She'd have need of it to secure another job. She had Ingrid and Gunnar to think about and take care of until she could make arrangements to send them to their grandmother.

"I'm sorry," Mr. Cole said again. "I wish I could have been of more help."

She didn't blame Mr. Cole. She was the one who'd failed, utterly and miserably. Somehow she had not only let down Alex and Michael, but she also failed the entire community she'd grown to love.

CHAPTER 25

It was over. She was leaving Eagle Harbor with as much shame as she'd left every other place she'd lived.

Tessa stood near the dock and gripped her emerald skirt, the same one she'd worn the day she arrived here. It was no longer as crisp and sharp. After the long winter, the hem had begun to fray, some of the ruffles had loosened, and the brightness had faded.

It was only fitting that her outward apparel matched the tattered condition of her heart. After the past three days of packing and saying good-bye to as many of her friends and students as she dared, her heart — or what was left of it — was indeed in shambles.

The shouts of deckhands and the cries of sea gulls rose above the slapping of waves against the *Illinois*. Her trunks and bags sat on the rocky shore next to crates containing all the worldly possessions that belonged to

451

Michael and Alex. Ingrid and Gunnar stood next to her, watching the crew load the Coles' trunks. The men would load theirs next.

Tessa glanced to the lighthouse on the bluff that overlooked the harbor, and a pang of guilt resounded in her chest. When she first arrived, she'd refused to acknowledge the lighthouse or go anywhere near the brick tower and keeper's dwelling. How was it that over the past three weeks she'd become the acting keeper, operating the light and growing more accustomed to being in the tower? Nevertheless, she'd slowly begun to shed the bitterness and the fear that once consumed her. Although she was ready to leave the lighthouse and never look back, she hadn't expected to feel remorse.

"It's not my responsibility," she muttered under her breath. "It never was."

Both the children and the dogs turned to look at her, eyes full of questions, just as they had been all week since she told them they were leaving Eagle Harbor on the same steamer that would transport Michael and Alex to Detroit.

"Are you sure about this?" Gunnar asked, holding Tessa's orange carpetbag that contained all the things they'd need during the four-day voyage.

"I'm the only one who can help your father and uncle," she said again. "First, I need to find them a good lawyer. Then I'll seek out my sister's friend, Esther Deluth. Her father is a state senator and might be able to intervene."

But who would take care of the lighthouse, if not her? Gunnar didn't ask the question aloud, but it was in his eyes every day, every minute. The question also burned on the note Alex had penned to her earlier that morning. He and Michael had asked her to stay with the children and watch over the lighthouse until a replacement keeper could be found.

The glass windows glinted in the sunshine, winking at her, as though beckoning her to return. She shook her head and shoved aside the guilt. The lighthouse wasn't her concern anymore. She'd done her duty, she'd faced her fears, and now it was time for her to move on. Hopefully the inspector and Lighthouse Board would find a replacement soon. She'd sent a letter on yesterday's steamer and prayed it would reach the inspector before she did.

Victoria Cole and her father were making their way toward the docks with Percival by their side. It was payday for the miners and so the mine was closed. But instead of the

453

Cornish wrestling match that everyone had been looking forward to — the first of the spring — the miners lingered along the waterfront to watch the departure. A somberness replaced the usual festivities. Tessa guessed they were curious to see the mine owner and his daughter, as well as interested in seeing the Bjorklund brothers being taken away in chains.

"Have you seen Josie or Nadine?" she asked the children as she glanced at the driftwood cross she'd placed on top of the closest trunk. She'd wanted to say good-bye to the Rawlings family one last time, had hoped Josie would sneak down to the docks to see her off. But so far Tessa hadn't seen her anywhere.

The last time Josie had come to deliver food, yesterday morning, she'd been neatly dressed, her face scrubbed clean, and her hair brushed into a mature knot. She'd told Tessa that Hannah had gained permission to reopen the school for the young children and had asked Josie to assist her.

"I told her I would," Josie had said shyly.

Tessa praised Josie for the decision. Secretly she prayed the work would help Josie just as much as it would the children. Tessa had decided she would give Josie her cross. It was time to pass it on to someone else, and who better than Josie to be given a beacon of hope in this hopeless place?

As Mr. Cole and Victoria came closer, Ingrid shrank into Tessa's skirt. Ingrid's face was pale, her body not much more than skin and bones. Though they'd had enough food to survive, it hadn't been nearly enough for the children.

Tessa was grateful to have found a stash of money in a small wooden chest on top of the sideboard in the kitchen when she was packing. She suspected it was the money Michael and Alex had been saving for Ingrid's surgery. The greater need at the moment, however, was to use the money to pay for passage on the steamer and also to hire a lawyer. As much as she wanted Ingrid to be able to walk and run normally, she wanted the girl to have her daddy and uncle back more.

Ingrid had braved the past few weeks without too many tears, yet each day the men remained in jail had taken its toll on her. Her sparkle and zest for life had slowly begun to ooze out of her, with fear and sadness creeping in and taking up residence in its stead. The girl burrowed against Tessa as the Coles approached.

Victoria Cole walked arm in arm with her father. Once again she wore a beautiful matching skirt and bodice of dazzling magenta that made her stand out in the dull landscape like a ruby in an ash heap.

"Good morning, Miss Taylor," Victoria said, pulling her father to a stop in front of Tessa and the children. "Am I to have the pleasure of your company during the remainder of the voyage?"

"Yes, I understand you're cutting short your trip around the lakes and will be returning to Detroit."

Victoria cast a glance at her father, who was speaking with Percival, and with a conspiratorial smile she leaned toward Tessa. "He misses my mother terribly. He can't bear to be apart from her any longer. Lucky for me, he's decided to postpone the remainder of the trip."

"Then you're headed back to New York?"

Victoria shook her head. "My mother is visiting with her father. He's a lightkeeper on Lake Erie near Toledo."

Victoria Cole's grandfather was a lightkeeper? Tessa never would have guessed it, not of a young lady as wealthy as she. "My sister is a keeper at a lighthouse north of Toledo. Which light does your grandfather operate?"

The young girl shrugged. "He's been a keeper for so long and moved around so

456

many times that I can't keep track. My mother is always pleading with him to retire and come live with us in New York. But he's too stubborn to give up his seafaring ways." Victoria's attention moved on to Ingrid and Gunnar. "And who are these children, Miss Taylor?"

Before Tessa could reply, Mr. Cole drew in a sharp breath, then stepped forward and grabbed the driftwood cross off the trunk. His eyes widened and his face drained of color. He turned the cross over in his hands, examining it as if he were seeing a ghost.

"What is it, Father?" Victoria asked.

Thankfully, Percival had finished his conversation with Mr. Cole and was heading back toward town. Tessa decided she'd be happy if she never had to speak to Percival ever again.

Mr. Cole studied the cross carefully before turning to Tessa. "Is this yours?"

"Yes, I —"

"Where did you get it?"

It really was none of Mr. Cole's business where or how she'd gotten the cross, and she wanted to tell him that. But something in his stare was so intense that it caused a shiver to travel up her backbone.

"Did it come with a letter?" he asked.

It was Tessa's turn to be surprised. "How

457

did you know?" She pressed her hand against the letter tucked in her pocket. She'd planned to give it to Josie along with the cross, just as the instructions in the letter indicated.

"May I see it?"

Slowly she pulled out the letter and handed it to him.

He unfolded the yellowed paper with shaking fingers. At the sight of the faded ink, he gasped and took a quick step backward as though struck.

"Father?" Victoria's delicate features creased with worry, and she put a steadying hand on his arm. "Are you all right?"

Mr. Cole didn't say anything. Instead his eyes moved from line to line as he read the letter.

"Father?" Victoria persisted.

He lifted his eyes to his daughter's, and Tessa was surprised to see them welling with tears. He handed her back the letter and pointed to the signature at the bottom of the page.

"Isabelle Thornton?" Victoria's voice rose in confusion. "Did Mother write this letter?"

Mr. Cole simply nodded, a stunned look on his face.

Victoria skimmed the page before turning

to Tessa with a frown. "How is it that you have possession of one of my mother's letters?"

"Your mother is Isabelle Thornton?" Tessa asked, trying to make sense of the situation.

"Not anymore," Victoria said. "She's now Isabelle Cole. But she was once Isabelle Thornton, daughter of the lightkeeper, Stephen Thornton. And this is her handwriting."

Tessa's knees grew weak as she stared at the faded letter and the cross Mr. Cole clutched in his hands. "Your mother wrote the letter?"

Victoria looked to her father and raised her brows, waiting for his explanation. She was obviously as confused as Tessa, perhaps more so.

Mr. Cole again turned the cross over in his hands, running his fingers along the dark coarse wood. "Isabelle wrote the letter . . . and I made this cross."

Tessa sucked in a breath, too shocked to speak.

"I made it seventeen years ago," Mr. Cole said softly, "when I was shipwrecked at the Presque Isle Lighthouse on Lake Huron."

"That's where you met and married Mother," Victoria said.

Mr. Cole nodded. "I fashioned the cross

459

out of pieces of the ship as a reminder never to give up hope."

They all stood in silence, staring at the cross that had somehow made it through the passing of time and distance to intersect with them at that exact moment. The mystery of it overwhelmed Tessa.

"Miss Taylor! Miss Taylor!" A childlike voice called to Tessa from the rocky beach, jarring the beauty of the moment.

She glanced up to see Samuel, red-faced and breathless, waddling at top speed behind a group of miners who surrounded Alex and Michael as they came down the beach.

At the sight of Alex's hatless blond head, her heartbeat slammed against her breastbone with a pain that almost sent her to her knees.

Percival led the entourage, with the miners enclosing Alex and Michael. They moved slowly, and after a moment she could see why. Alex and another man, Mr. Rawlings, were carrying Michael.

Tessa started forward, forgetting that Ingrid was attached to her skirt. "Alex!" she shouted, straining toward him as desperation erupted within her. She needed to see him, needed to hear him, to be with him even if only for a few seconds to reassure herself that he was alive and well.

At the sound of his name, he straightened and raised his head above the crowd. His blue eyes met hers, and they lit up at the sight of her. His face was thin and pale after the days of hunger and captivity. His hair was unkempt and he had the beginnings of a beard, but he'd never looked more handsome to her than at that very moment.

Tears sprang to her eyes. She wanted to call out to him that she loved him, that she'd do everything she could to save him.

"Daddy!" Ingrid cried. Her gaunt face creased with the need for her father.

Michael lifted his head and strained to see in their direction.

Ingrid called his name again and would have run forward, except that Tessa caught her and held her close. This was neither the time nor place for a reunion with her father. Once they were aboard the ship, she would speak to Mr. Cole about arranging visitation with the prisoners. Surely he wouldn't prevent them from seeing the men.

"Miss Taylor," Samuel said, stumbling over the rocky shore in his haste. His rounded eyes flashed with the need to reach her.

Tessa had the urge to hide. She wasn't in the mood to reason with Samuel, not with

461

her being forced to leave Eagle Harbor, not when she had to witness Alex and Michael being treated like common criminals, not when Ingrid was falling apart at the sight of her daddy whom she loved and missed.

Samuel broke from the group and made his way toward her as fast as his short legs would carry him. She strained for another sight of Alex, but once again he'd been swallowed by the crowd.

"Miss Taylor," Samuel said, his voice ringing with distress. Sweat rolled down his forehead and cheeks, and his breath came in gulps.

"Calm down, Samuel, and tell me what's wrong," she said as Ingrid buried back into her skirt, sobbing now. Tessa hugged the girl closer, wishing she had the forthrightness to send Samuel away so that she could comfort Ingrid in private.

"Aren't you my friend?" Samuel asked her.

"Of course I am, Samuel," she reassured while smoothing Ingrid's hair and patting her back. "You're one of my favorite friends."

She'd hoped her comment would placate him, but it only seemed to agitate him all the more. He studied the bags and trunks behind her and wrung his hands. "If you're my friend, then why are you leaving me?"

"I told you good-bye yesterday, Samuel," she gently reminded him.

"You can't leave!" he cried, his voice rising.

Maybe yesterday he hadn't understood that her good-bye meant she was leaving Eagle Harbor for good. Maybe he'd assumed she was saying good-bye like she did every time she left the store. "Samuel," she said calmly, "I have to leave Eagle Harbor —"

"No, you don't!" he shouted. "You don't have to leave if you don't want to."

Samuel's agitation was beginning to draw the notice of those around them. Tessa glanced with embarrassment at Victoria and Mr. Cole, who were watching her exchange with raised brows. She returned her attention to Samuel's profusely sweating face and tried to think of some way to calm him. "Maybe someday I'll come back to visit —"

"No-o-o!" he howled, stomping his feet and sounding altogether like a two-year-old having a tantrum.

Percival was passing nearby with the company of men and prisoners. At Samuel's cry of distress, Percival held up his hand and stopped the group. "Sam," he called. "Calm down or you'll need to go back to the store at once."

463

Samuel took a deep shaky breath and lowered his voice, clearly trying to obey his brother. "Please don't go, Miss Taylor."

She wanted to brush past Samuel and reach out to Alex, who was now less than a dozen paces away. Instead she squeezed Samuel's arm. "I know this is difficult for you to understand, Samuel, but I have to go with Alex and Michael."

"Then let them stay too."

She caught sight again of Alex's face but only briefly. Weariness pulled the muscles in his face taut. She had no doubt he was weak from his days of near starvation and inactivity. And now here he was carrying Michael.

"They can go back to the lighthouse," Samuel said, as if that solved all the problems. "And you can go back to being the teacher."

She sighed. If only things were that easy. "Remember, Alex and Michael have been accused of causing the warehouse fire? They have to go to Detroit for their trial, and I have to go to help find a lawyer to defend them."

Samuel shook his head, obviously not understanding. She couldn't explain the injustice of it herself. Sadness washed over her, and she didn't want to prolong her

464

good-bye to Samuel any longer than she had to.

"Good-bye, Samuel," she said. "You've been a good friend and I'll miss you." With that, she spun away from him.

Then a shriek rent the air — Samuel's shriek. The sound of it was long and loud enough to wake up any animals still in hibernation. As it continued on, Tessa's heart dropped. She'd had no idea her parting would be so hard on Samuel.

"Sam!" Percival yelled.

Samuel's shrieking ceased abruptly and was followed by an eerie silence.

"Go back to the store. Now." Percival spoke to his brother in his firmest tone.

"I know how Miss Taylor can stay!" Samuel said, a thread of excitement coloring his voice. "Michael and Alex don't have to go!"

"Yes, they do," Percival said.

"No, they don't! They didn't start the fire —"

"Of course they did." Percival's frown deepened into a warning.

"I saw you leave the store with the oilcan from the lighthouse," Samuel said almost happily, oblivious to the murmurs that arose at his declaration.

"You saw no such thing!" Percival retorted.

"Yes," Samuel insisted. "It was the same oilcan you had hidden away in your office."

More murmurs and gasps punctuated the air.

Tessa was too stunned by the revelation to breathe. Instead she could only stare at Samuel with an open mouth. He smiled at her in obvious delight. "So you see, Miss Taylor, Michael and Alex didn't start the fire. And now they don't have to leave Eagle Harbor."

"Samuel Updegraff, go back to the store this instant." The harshness of Percival's words bit into the air and went straight into Samuel. His smile disappeared, his shoulders slumped, and he began to drag his feet toward the rutted path.

A rush of panic pulled Tessa out of her daze. "Wait!" she shouted. "That's the evidence we need to set Alex and Michael free."

Several ayes rang out among the crowd. She wanted to shout out her thanks because she knew how much courage those ayes had cost the men who'd voiced them out loud. But she didn't want to draw attention to anyone in particular.

Percival gave a scoffing laugh. "You don't mean to tell me you're going to believe Samuel? He's a good man, but he doesn't

466

know what he's talking about."

Samuel hung his head and didn't attempt to contradict his brother.

"Sounds like he knew well enough," Mr. Cole said, searching Percival's face as though it contained a map that would help lead to the truth.

"He's just trying to keep Miss Taylor from leaving," Percival said smoothly. "She's obviously got Samuel under some kind of spell."

"It's called friendship," she said. "Something you wouldn't know anything about since you have no friends."

"My men will support me."

"Only because you bribe them with favors."

"Face it, Miss Taylor, you're the one who doesn't have any friends." Percival glared at her and added, "No one wants to be friends with someone having your soiled reputation."

Embarrassed heat rushed to her cheeks. She was sure his intent was to humiliate her in front of everyone again, especially Mr. Cole and Victoria. And it was working.

"You're dead wrong about Miss Taylor not having any friends here," said someone from among the group of miners.

Tessa stood on tiptoes and scanned the

crowd, hoping to thank and also caution the speaker at the same time.

Mr. Benney was already shouldering his way through the men until he stood in front of everyone. He spread his feet and crossed his arms over his chest. His jaw was set with a determination, which told her she was much too late to warn him. She could only swallow the lump of fear for what Percival would do to Mr. Benney later, after he returned from Detroit.

"Miss Taylor has a heap of friends here in Eagle Harbor," Mr. Benney said. "No matter her past, she's a fine lady."

The words washed over her like a sweet honey poultice soothing the deep burn in her soul. She smiled her thanks to him.

"Yes, sir, she's a real good lady." Gratefulness shone from Mr. Benney's eyes. "She taught me son even when that cack, Mr. Updegraff, forced him to minch school."

"Minch?" Mr. Cole stepped forward and raised his brow at Percival. Tessa was tempted to interpret the Cornish word that meant to skip school, but before she could explain, Percival spoke up.

"He was old enough to work in the mine," Percival explained matter-of-factly. "And we had a shortage of labor."

"Miss Taylor didn't just do extra to help

468

learn our cheldren." Mr. Benney's voice rose higher in strength. "She cared about the rest of us folks too. She gave up her time to start the evening class that Mr. Updegraff eventually stopped too."

Mr. Cole's forehead furrowed into a deeper scowl, but again Percival had a ready answer.

"I had to institute longer shifts," he said.

The mine owner studied both men as though weighing their words. Tessa held her breath and prayed he'd see the truth for what it was.

Even when Percival shot a dark look at Mr. Benney, the tall miner didn't look away or back down. Tessa's heart quavered at the thought of the consequences he'd likely face for speaking up, yet she was thrilled that someone was finally willing to take a stand against Percival, regardless of the cost.

"It wasn't right to fire her from her teacher job," Mr. Benney said, turning to Mr. Cole. "Every folk here will agree with me."

"I completely agree," Alex said.

Mr. Benney didn't look to the miners behind him. He didn't move either to encourage or shame them into saying anything. If the others would oppose Percival, they must do it on their own — because they wanted to, not because they were coerced. They, like Mr. Benney, had to be willing to face whatever punishment Percival would mete out. For there was no doubt about it. He would make them pay severely.

For endless seconds no one else spoke. The men stood mutely, staring at the ground. The chatter of nearby deckhands combined with the slapping of the waves, filling the awkward silence.

Percival folded his arms across his chest and glowered at Mr. Benney with a look that said he was a dead man. Tessa didn't blame the other men for not agreeing with Mr. Benney. The risk was too great for them to defy Percival. She started to guide Ingrid toward the waiting steamer when a shaky voice sounding a lot like Mr. Rawlings spoke up. "I agree."

"Me too," said someone else more loudly. "I agree. Miss Taylor shouldn't have been fired."

"I agree" came another, and then another, until all of the men were voicing their opinion to Mr. Cole.

Tessa pivoted around. Her gaze bounced from face to face as the miners stepped forward and listed out loud their complaints about Percival in his presence. There wasn't a man among them who stayed silent. Soon their voices escalated until they were almost yelling their frustrations and calling for Tessa to be given back her teacher job and Percival to be fired instead.

Percival shook his head vigorously and began shouting back his excuses, the same excuses he always offered for why he dominated Eagle Harbor with such a heavy hand. He was doing it for their safety and well-being. Someone had to make sure the community ran smoothly. If he didn't discipline them, then they'd have anarchy on their hands.

Tessa could only watch him with a sad kind of amazement. How could he not see how awful he was and how damaging his methods were? How could he offer excuses at all for the atrocities he'd committed among these people?

Several of the miners strode past Mr. Benney and began to close in on Percival, anger chiseled into every line of their faces. Alex called out a warning, cautioning the men not to do anything they'd regret.

"Hold on now, everyone," Mr. Cole yelled, but his voice was drowned out in the commotion.

Not an ounce of remorse came from Percival as he continued his tirade at the miners opposing him.

One of the miners was about to pounce

on Percival when Alex crashed through and yanked the man aside before he could put his hands around Percival's throat. The miner was left with no choice but to stumble away.

Alex stood before Percival, his breath coming in gasps from the exertion in his weakened condition. He held up his chained hands, the chafed skin at his wrists showing beneath his dirty shirt sleeves. He waited for silence to descend.

When the gathering finally tapered to a hush, he said, "If we take justice into our own hands, then we're no better than Mr. Updegraff. What's to separate us then from the same crimes he's perpetrated?" Slowly Alex looked from one miner to the next, piercing them with his gaze. "I know what it's like to suffer injustice and mistreatment at Mr. Updegraff's hand. But I also know that as tempting as it is to wrap these chains around his neck and choke him, I can't do that. I can't repay evil with evil. We have to let justice be served the right way. If we have any hope of turning our community into a law-abiding and safe place for our families to live, then we have to start now by being law-abiding ourselves."

Several nods and grunts of agreement swept over the gathering.

Mr. Cole stepped next to Alex and clasped him on the shoulder, gratefulness and relief etching his features. "It appears to me that I need to delay my departure and investigate the situation here further."

A murmuring arose again from the miners.

Mr. Cole spoke quickly. "I'll make myself available to anyone who wishes to express their concerns regarding Mr. Updegraff's conduct or any other issues. And I'll stay for as long as it takes to hear everyone and to see that justice prevails."

Tessa's heart swelled as she saw the hesitant yet hopeful smiles begin to form on the smudged, weathered faces of the miners. They'd done it. They'd taken a stand against Percival and broken the chains that had bound them.

"And it would appear that we have chained the wrong man," Mr. Cole continued, squeezing Alex's shoulder again before turning to Percival. "Would you like to tell us all how you came to have the lighthouse oilcan in your possession the night of the fire?"

An ache pushed at the back of Tessa's throat, and tears stung her eyes. Overwhelming relief pulsed through her, making her legs weak. She wanted to crumple to the ground and sob but instead pressed a fist to her mouth to stifle the outburst.

Ingrid had already left her side and was limping her way through the men to where Michael lay on the ground. He stretched out his arms weakly toward her, unable to manage more than raising himself a few inches from the ground. What he lacked in strength, however, he made up for in his smile. It was bright and overflowing with love for the little girl who tripped and stumbled her way toward him.

When Ingrid reached her father, she dropped to her knees, threw her arms around him, and buried her face in his chest. Tears trickled down Michael's cheeks as he wrapped his arms around the frail body of the little girl who adored him.

"What's wrong with her leg?" Victoria stood next to her, watching Ingrid and Michael's reunion.

"Nothing that surgery won't cure," Tessa said, wiping at the wetness on her cheeks.

"Then why hasn't she had it?" Victoria asked.

But Tessa couldn't respond. Her gaze had collided with Alex's. Bear and Wolfie were at his side, licking his hands and rubbing against him. Though he was still chained, that didn't stop him from scratching the heads of both dogs.

His eyes were filled with tenderness for his niece as she embraced her father. But there was something more there, something directed at Tessa — a desperate, almost agonizing need for her. He studied her face as if feasting on every feature. Her heart nearly stopped at the love that radiated in his expression.

Then, in that same moment, he glanced at Michael. Tessa watched as his shoulders sagged, his head dropped, and he didn't turn to look at her again.

Chapter 26

Alex leaned against the trunk of the red maple, letting its low branches and new leaves hide him. The school yard was full of families who'd come to celebrate spring with the box-lunch social Tessa had organized.

New life finally came to Eagle Harbor again, with the grass, the trees, the flowers, even the weeds all adorned in green. After the bleakness of winter, the colors of spring always struck him as so much brighter than any other place he'd lived. And Tessa in her green dress looked vibrant and full of life as well, mingling among the families. As the men purchased the box lunches as instructed by their wives and sweethearts, families and couples had begun to spread out blankets in preparation of eating.

Only two boxes remained on the makeshift table next to the schoolhouse. Both boxes were the prettiest of the day, and it was no secret to whom they belonged. One was Tessa's, the other Victoria Cole's. They were almost identical in size and style, and Alex didn't doubt that Victoria had a hand in helping Tessa put hers together.

Victoria stood next to her father, who sat in the desk chair that had been brought out of the school especially for him. The ribbons on her hat fell down past her shoulders and flapped in the breeze coming off the lake.

Tessa stood near Victoria, a smile gracing her beautiful face. In the last week, after sorting through all the statements and evidence, Mr. Cole had reinstated Tessa to her teaching position. Not only that, but he'd fired Percival Updegraff and had him locked up for starting the warehouse fire, as well as a dozen other crimes against the miners.

Samuel's statements would have been enough to convict Percival of setting the fire, but in the end others had come forward and testified against Percival. Several had seen him at the warehouse not long before the fire. Alex was grateful so many had stood up for him and shared examples of the many ways he'd served the community over the years. He supposed the celebration today was one of freedom — freedom from

477

the tyranny and oppression that had reigned over the town for as long as Percival had been the mine clerk. Mr. Cole had appointed Mr. Benney as the new supervisor and Mr. Rawlings as his assistant, and already there was a renewed sense of gladness and peace that hadn't been in the community in a very long time.

After a week's delay, Mr. Cole and his daughter were leaving tomorrow with Percival in tow. Alex had to admit, he'd always resented the mine owners for their distance and superiority. But he was learning that Mr. Cole was different. He had conducted himself with integrity and fairness, showing that he truly cared about the people who worked for him. For that alone, Alex respected him.

"Let's start the bidding on this lovely box," called Mr. Benney from behind the table. He held up a white box covered with big green polka dots and tied with an enormous green bow.

At the announcement, Tessa ducked her head almost shyly, easily giving away the fact that the box belonged to her.

Alex straightened, almost bumping his head against a branch. His mouth turned as dry as fish bones baked in the sun. Although he'd told himself a hundred times since he'd

478

arrived earlier that he wouldn't bid on her box, the need to be with her had carved a deep aching hole in his soul that wouldn't go away no matter how hard he tried to fill it with thoughts of other things.

Several of the other single men tossed out their good-natured bids.

Alex glanced nervously toward Michael, who was relaxing on a blanket with Ingrid and Gunnar. Michael smiled down at Ingrid and laughed at something the girl had said. He didn't seem to be paying any attention to the bid for Tessa's lunch. In fact, Hannah and her young son, Jeremiah, sat on a blanket adjacent to Michael, and Alex had noticed his brother talking to the pretty widow from time to time.

"I could give her a lifetime," Michael had told him, *"but she'll always love you more than me."*

All week long, Alex had wanted to approach Tessa, to ask her if she loved him more than Michael, to find out if she could really love him, even though he wasn't nearly as educated as she was. But they'd both been busy trying to put their lives back together. She'd returned to the Rawlings house and had commenced classes again for both students and adults. He'd been occupied with running the lighthouse while

479

Michael attempted to regain his strength. And Wolfie finally had her pups, so Alex had his hands full tending to the eight newborns.

Deep inside, though, Alex knew those were all excuses. The truth was, he'd seen something in Tessa's eyes on a couple of occasions. He was afraid to call it love, yet he was convinced that she felt something for him. Too bad he'd spurned her and turned away from anything she might offer him so that Michael could have her.

And now he was afraid to approach her for fear that she'd reject him all over again. It would serve him right for having neglected to win her when he'd had the chance, though part of him knew he'd make the sacrifice for his brother again, if Michael showed even the slightest inclination toward her. But all week Michael hadn't mentioned her name once. He'd poured out all of his attention on Ingrid and Gunnar, spending more time with them in one week than he had since before Rachel had died.

As another young man with a toothy grin called out his bid on Tessa's box, Alex took a step away from the tree. Now was his time. He needed to capture her undivided attention and, while he had it, make his declaration of undying love.

He stuffed his hand in his pocket and

fingered the wad of bills he'd brought with him. Twenty dollars. It was everything he'd saved from offering sled rides over the winter, plus the deposits some of the miners had put down on the pups.

It wasn't enough to pay for Ingrid's surgery, but they were getting closer to the goal. With the way Tessa had cleaned up the keeper's cottage during her stay, they had a good chance of winning the superintendent's Efficiency Star and the cash reward that came with it. Only another month's wait. By summer's end they should have enough money saved for the surgery.

He shoved the wad deeper in his pocket. He couldn't spend any of it now, not when they were nearing the point of having enough.

"I'll pay twenty-five dollars" came a voice Alex knew all too well.

Gasps arose from the crowd at the exorbitant amount. When most of the other boxes had sold for mere pennies, twenty-five dollars was a serious amount.

Alex jerked back under the tree and stared at the speaker — Michael. His brother was standing and handing an openmouthed Mr. Benney a roll of cash similar to the one Alex had in his pocket. Michael must have cleared his half out of the canister in the

481

cottage and brought it today too.

The smile of delight that lit Michael's face sent Alex's pulse skittering on a wild downward spiral. Speechless, he could only watch as Michael took the elegantly decorated box from Mr. Benney and then made his way over to Tessa.

Tessa smiled at him with a relief that cut through Alex's heart. He fell back against the tree trunk. He wanted to pull out his money and outbid his brother. On second thought, even if he'd had more than twenty-five, he wasn't sure he could walk over and claim Tessa away from Michael. He longed to have her for himself. He loved her and needed her. But if Michael needed her more, how could he selfishly stand in his brother's way?

Burying a cry of despair, Alex ducked away from the tree. And without a backward glance, he started down the path that led away from town.

"Father, you should have let someone else have a chance to bid on my box," Victoria said with a smile.

Mr. Cole chuckled. "What, and give up the opportunity to enjoy lunch with the prettiest lady and the prettiest box here?" Tessa was still too shocked to speak. Mr.

Cole had bid one hundred dollars for Victoria's box. One hundred dollars that would go toward a new house the community had agreed to build for the Eagle Harbor schoolteacher. In fact, they'd already drawn up plans and had a plot picked out for the house just a block away. All the proceeds from the box-lunch social would go to help defray the costs.

Her heart swelled with thankfulness at all that had happened over the past week. She gazed with satisfaction at the families seated on blankets all around the yard, then at the children playing Fox and Geese in front of the school. All of them had come out to support her and raise money for her new home.

Thank you, God. Again her heart whispered the prayer that had been ongoing all week.

Mr. Cole had given the miners several days as paid holiday, so that everyone would have the chance to speak their piece about Percival if they wanted. The line to meet with Mr. Cole had stretched out the front door of his house for three days straight.

Percival was locked up in prison, awaiting his transport downstate, which Mr. Cole had promised to personally oversee. She was sad to see Samuel readying himself to accompany his brother. He was confused and worried and certainly had no idea that he'd been the one to set the changes in motion with his simple confession about the oilcan.

Nevertheless, Tessa was proud of all her friends for finding the courage to come forward. She'd never cried, laughed, or hugged so much as she had that week with Nadine, Hannah, and all the others who'd finally been able to find forgiveness and release for all the hurt they'd experienced over the years.

Although they thanked her for bringing about Percival's demise and for instituting some long overdue changes in their community, she thanked them for showing her the true meaning of grace. They'd accepted and loved her even when they'd known the worst about her. She realized she had as much to learn from them, perhaps even more, than they had to learn from her.

"Are you ready?" Michael asked as he stood patiently by her side, holding her boxed lunch. His smile was gentle, somehow different. Tessa could tell that the weeks in jail had changed him, had given him an inner strength that hadn't been there before.

She nodded and tried to push down the disappointment before he could take note of it. She hadn't expected Michael to bid.

He'd seemed content on his blanket, talking with Hannah next to him. In fact, she'd even noticed Ingrid sitting on Hannah's lap at one point and wondered if perhaps Hannah would ever consider trusting a man again. Certainly she'd find no one better than Michael.

Tessa had prayed and hoped for Alex to step forward and bid on her lunch. She'd noticed him hovering at the back of the crowd in the shade of a tree, watching the festivities with an amused smile.

When the bidding had started for her box, she'd held her breath and waited for him to shout out his claim. She hadn't wanted to share the lunch with anyone but him. Of course, he hadn't made a peep. She shouldn't have been surprised or disappointed that he'd let her go again. Not after the way he'd resisted her all week.

But she was disappointed anyway, even though she knew it was for the best. She'd have to give up her teaching job to be with him. And even at the present she missed him enough that she might just do it, she couldn't keep from wondering if eventually she'd resent the sacrifice.

She stifled a sigh and forced a smile for Michael. At least Michael had given the highest bid. If she had to eat with anyone else, she much preferred Michael. After paying so much money for her boxed lunch, he deserved a nice meal with her, not one where she was distracted and thinking about Alex the whole time.

"Are you sure you don't want Ingrid and Gunnar to join us?" she asked.

Michael glanced to where the children were running and playing games. Ingrid was hobbling on her crutch but was giggling along with the other girls. Tessa had never seen Ingrid so happy and carefree. A lump formed in Tessa's throat. Michael's love was the best medicine for his daughter. Even if she was never able to have surgery, she'd be happy as long as Michael was there showering his love on the little girl.

"I'd like a few minutes alone with you, Tessa," Michael said. "If you don't mind."

Victoria's smile widened knowingly. "Father and I will keep an eye on the children," she offered with a wink at Tessa. "Now be on your way and enjoy yourselves."

She wouldn't dampen Michael's or Victoria's enthusiasm now by telling them she wasn't interested in Michael. She couldn't today, not with all the excitement and happiness that surrounded her. But she would need to break the news to Michael at some point, and soon.

It wasn't that she resisted the idea of marrying a lightkeeper anymore. In some ways, she sensed that God found some humor in taking her *I won't ever*'s and turning them into *I will*'s. She wasn't about to say no to God again. If He wanted her to be a lightkeeper's wife, she'd do it. Just not with Michael, for she wasn't in love with him.

Tessa took several steps after Michael, then stopped. "Wait," she called to Victoria as she hurried to a supply basket she'd stashed under the table. She lifted the cover, and her fingers brushed against the rough grain of wood.

All week she'd thought about the cross and the startling revelation that Mr. Cole had been the one to carve it. Mr. Henry Cole had been the same Henry that Isabelle Thornton had fallen in love with, the man she thought she'd lost. In the end, Isabelle placed her hope in God rather than dwell on her circumstances and the frightening prospect that she might go blind someday just as her mother had. The letter had never explained whether she'd married Henry. And it had never explained what had become of her, whether she'd eventually become blind.

It was clear now that Isabelle had married Henry, and that they had a beautiful daughter as a result of their union. But had she gone blind?

Tessa caressed the cross one last time before straightening and walking back to Mr. Cole and Victoria. She handed it to Victoria. "I'd like you to have this." Even though Tessa had debated giving the cross to Josie, somehow she felt the cross needed to go back to the Coles.

Victoria's light brown eyes widened. She reached out to take the cross, but then hesitated and glanced at her father as though asking his permission before touching it.

Mr. Cole looked Tessa in the eyes. "You don't have to give it to Victoria. It's yours."

Tessa shook her head. "No. It's never been mine to keep. It's given me hope when I needed it most, and now it's time for me to pass it along."

Mr. Cole nodded. "Thank you. I'd like to pass along that same hope to Victoria. Who knows, but maybe she'll have need of it someday."

As Victoria's fingers closed around the wood cross, a look of wonder and delight filled her eyes.

Tessa had the urge to ask her more about Isabelle. But as Victoria smiled and bent to kiss her father's forehead, Tessa knew with sudden clarity that it didn't matter. Blind or not, Isabelle had shown them all how to make God their beacon of hope.

Tessa strolled off with Michael. She paused for only a moment at the thought of being alone with him. Perhaps it was time to stop worrying so much about what other people thought about her. God had forgiven her for her past, and now she was doing her best to live uprightly with integrity. That was all that mattered, all that she could do.

Michael led her down the road away from town, a blanket over one arm, her box in the other. A companionable silence surrounded them. With each step, Tessa breathed in the sweet scent of the budding leaves and grass and newly awakened bloodroots. The tiny white flowers poked between the withered leaves left on the ground from last fall. They were stout, hardy plants that had weathered the harsh winter. If they could flourish in this land, why couldn't she?

She'd thought she would need to leave Eagle Harbor, that the long winter had defeated her, but perhaps she'd been wrong. She didn't want to leave anymore.

As Michael directed her to a path that led uphill the sunshine streamed through the branches overhead, bleaching his hair. The color and texture was so much like Alex's

489

that longing for him swelled in her chest.

Michael glanced at her over his shoulder and smiled almost mysteriously. "Are you doing all right?"

Once again she tried to hide her disappointment. She forced a return smile and nodded. "Where are you taking me?"

"Copper Falls. I hope you don't mind."

"Not at all." She lightened her voice. "You paid twenty-five dollars for my lunch. I can't complain in the least." Except that he wasn't Alex.

Almost as if Alex had heard her, he came bounding down the trail in front of them. His footsteps were heavy, sending dried leaves and twigs cascading along the path.

Michael stopped so quickly that Tessa almost bumped into him.

"Don't go a step farther," Alex boomed, closing the distance like a charging bull. He didn't halt his rapid descent until he was mere inches from Michael. His face was flushed, his hair mussed, and his eyes flashed wildly.

Michael didn't move.

"I have a few things I need to say to you." Alex towered over his brother. Although his expression was grave, his strong features appeared more striking than ever. He nodded to the upward path. "In private."

490

Michael shook his head. "Whatever you have to say to me, I'm sure Tessa needs to hear it too."

Alex glanced at her briefly, but it was enough for her to see the agony in his eyes.

"Fine," he ground out. "If that's the way you want to do this."

"Yes, it is."

Alex sucked in a breath. He jammed his fingers into his hair and stared at the canopy of leaves above them. For a moment he didn't say anything. Finally he blurted, "You can't have Tessa. I love her. I always have. And I can't sacrifice her for you, no matter how much I want to. I'm sorry. I just can't do it."

Tessa's heartbeat tapered to a halt. He loved her? He wasn't giving her up after all?

Michael shrugged. "I know that already."

Alex's lips stalled around the response he'd had ready to sling back. Instead he stammered, "Then why did you pay half of our savings to have lunch with her?"

"Because you weren't bidding, you dolt," Michael said wryly. "And I didn't want any other man to monopolize her."

"So why are you coming out here with her?"

"I saw that you headed out this way and figured you'd hiked up to the falls to pout."

Michael's tone was laced with humor. "I was bringing her out here to be with you."

For long seconds neither of the brothers said anything. Tessa couldn't think. Her muscles wouldn't move. Only her heart seemed to be working, and at twice the normal speed.

Then Alex's lips cracked into a lopsided grin. "You mean to tell me you used half our savings to get me together with Tessa?"

"That's right."

Alex gave Michael a playful punch in the arm. "You're crazy."

"No, you're the crazy one," Michael said, punching Alex back. "You keep trying to make me happy, and I told you that you need to stop it."

"I am stopping. I can sacrifice many things for you, brother. But I can't sacrifice the woman I love. I won't do it. I'll fight you for her if necessary." Alex's eyes met hers above Michael's shoulder. The love within them shone as brightly as the lighthouse beam on the darkest, stormiest night. It broke through her confusion and heartache and filled her with a warm glow. He'd come back for her. He hadn't given her up. And he'd been willing to fight for her.

"You don't have to fight me," Michael said. "Although once I get back from Detroit, you may fight me when I insist that you leave the lighthouse."

"Back from Detroit?"

Michael nodded. "Mr. Cole is paying for Ingrid's surgery." His voice broke as he shared the news.

"He's what?"

"He knows a specialist in Detroit, and he's making arrangements to have the surgery done. He wants to cover the entire bill, including the steamer passage and housing while we're in Detroit."

Tessa's throat clogged with emotion. No wonder Michael had been willing to spend his savings to bid on her boxed lunch.

Alex's Adam's apple rose up and down, and he wiped his hand across his eyes.

"I need you to stay here and run the lighthouse while I'm gone," Michael continued. "And I'd like to name Tessa as your assistant keeper."

Alex glanced at Tessa and started to shake his head. Michael cut him off. "Just until we return. Then I'm firing you both."

Tears welled in Tessa's eyes, and she had to blink them back before she embarrassed herself. She could see that Michael wanted to protect her from the lighthouse, and she loved him for it. But she'd have time later to explain that she didn't mind anymore,

493

for God had helped her overcome her fears.

"You can't fire me," Alex said, though rather weakly.

"You've helped me long enough," Michael said with a tender smile. "In fact, I've taken advantage of your kindness, and it's time for that to stop as well. Ingrid and Gunnar need me to be a strong father. They need a man who can stand on his own two feet. And I won't be able to do that if I'm always relying on you."

"That doesn't mean you have to kick me out," Alex said, attempting to add mirth to his voice.

"It's time for you to be free to pursue your dreams, to start the dog-breeding business you've always wanted."

Alex didn't respond except to swallow hard again.

Michael only smiled.

"I guess that means Alex will be free to take my evening class," Tessa said with a laugh.

Alex shook his head. "No way. I'm not taking your evening class."

Tessa tilted her head and studied him, seeing past his teasing. "You know that I admire you for who you are, not for what you can or cannot do." She hoped he could see that she'd come to respect the mining community. While she still believed education was important, she'd grown to realize it didn't define a person.

Alex grinned. "What I mean is that I'm not taking an evening class with a bunch of other men when I can have private lessons. Very private."

Heat speared her stomach. The dimple in his chin combined with his strong jaw and perfect nose made her think again as she had when she'd first met him that he was much too attractive for any one man. "I only give private lessons to good scholars," she teased. "Not naughty ones."

"Well, I'm very naughty," Alex warned with a rumble in his voice that made her insides ripple with pleasure. "I'm pretty sure I can convince you to change your mind."

Michael chuckled softly. "Time for me to go and let the two of you work out all the details. After all, I can't make Tessa your assistant unless you marry her first." He started to push the green polka-dot box into Alex's arms.

Alex's gaze landed upon her with a desire that let her know he loved her, that he'd never stopped loving her. There was nothing more she wanted at that moment than to be in his arms and hear him whisper his love again and again in her ear.

But she couldn't make it quite so easy for him. She tugged on Michael's arm. "Alex will have to wait until later to *work out all the details,*" she said nonchalantly. "You paid good money for my lunch, Michael, and I can't in good conscience let your money be spent for nothing."

Both men's eyes widened, and she had to work hard to keep from laughing.

Michael's brow began to dip and he pulled the box back. Of course, Alex gave her that slow, devastating half smile of his, which never failed to make her heart melt. He shoved the box back into Michael's arms, spun his brother around, and gave him a gentle push that sent him back down the trail. "Michael can have the boxed lunch with a certain pretty lady sitting on the blanket next to his. And we'll consider the money a wedding present, a contribution toward our new house."

Our new house. Tessa's smile faded, taking the hope with it. "The house is for the teacher. I won't be able to teach anymore if . . ." She didn't finish her sentence. After all, he hadn't officially proposed to her.

Some of the light had disappeared from Alex's expression too. "I don't want you to give up your teaching. I know how important it is to you. I'll wait for you as long as you need. Even years."

She didn't want to wait years. She couldn't wait years. But how could she give up teaching?

"It won't be easy to wait," Alex added, "but I'll do anything for you, Tessa."

Michael let out an exasperated sigh. "There you go again doing the noble thing. Sacrificing yourself and your life for someone else."

"Tessa's worth the wait."

"I know she is," Michael said. "Luckily, though, you won't have to put your life on hold."

"What do you mean?" Alex asked.

Michael's smile grew wider. "I already took the liberty of speaking with Mr. Cole. He's agreed to letting Tessa keep her job, even if she's married."

Tessa drew a shaky breath, unsure if she'd heard correctly. "He'll allow a married female teacher?"

Michael nodded, his chest puffing out.

Tessa squealed and threw herself at Michael, hugging him with all her might. His face turned red, and he extricated himself quickly and took a step back. "It's not that I don't appreciate the hug," he said. "It's just I don't want to put my life in peril."

Alex was grinning broadly. "I'll allow the

hug this once. But if you touch her again . . ." He punched his fist into his palm playfully.

Tessa laughed at the teasing between the brothers, relieved that after all the fighting that year, the two would still be friends.

"Now it's my turn for a hug," Alex said, moving past Michael so that he stood on the path before her. Before she could offer a rebuttal, his grin faded. He reached for her, slid his hand behind her neck, and tangled his fingers in her hair. In the same motion he bent his head to hers. She couldn't have uttered a protest even if she'd wanted to, as his mouth crashed against hers with the ferocity of a stormy sea. He took her under, his lips swirling against hers, clinging to her, promising that he'd never let her go, that he would always fight for her.

She eagerly responded back, matching her lips to his, pressing her need into him. But at the sudden remembrance of Michael watching them, she broke the kiss and pulled back. "Alex," she whispered breathlessly, "we have to wait."

A glance at the path told her Michael was gone. Even so, she knew she had to stand strong with integrity even when no one was looking.

Alex didn't let go of her. His lips grazed

498

her cheek and made a soft trail to her ear. "I love you." The words were a caress that echoed down to her soul. "I'm sorry I didn't tell you sooner."

"Just don't let it happen again," she teased.

"Oh, don't worry . . ." He planted a breathy kiss against her neck. "I won't."

"You're rather sure of yourself, aren't you?" she said, tipping her head back and smiling as he tried to chase her lips with his.

"What do you expect? I just swept the woman of my dreams off her feet."

"I don't think so." She continued teasing him by moving her lips out of his reach.

"Yes, I did." And with that he scooped her up into his strong arms, just like he did the first time they'd met when he carried her back to shore after she'd nearly drowned. She was helpless to do anything but wrap her arms around his neck and let him claim her lips again. This time the kiss was soft and sweet and ended all too soon.

"I love you," he whispered again, his eyes growing serious.

"I love you too. More than you'll ever know."

"I can't think about going another day without you being my wife."

"Then don't."

His smile was heart-stopping and steady as he carried her down the path that led back to Eagle Harbor.

"Where are we going?" she asked.

"To get married."

"Today?"

"Right now."

She held him tighter and buried her face into his neck.

"I don't want to miss out on another moment of enjoying and loving you for whatever time God gives us together on this earth."

Tessa pressed a kiss against his jaw, her silent agreement and her benediction.

Although her heart quavered at the thought of losing Alex to some unforeseen danger in the future, she also knew that she couldn't let fear control her again. She had to accept God's gift — this incredible man — for as long as He willed it. Since there weren't any guarantees, she would love and enjoy Alex with every heartbeat, every moment of their lives.

AUTHOR'S NOTE

As I wrote this third book in the Beacons of Hope series, I had the wonderful privilege of visiting Eagle Harbor and the lighthouse that serves as the setting for the story. In fact, I was able to stay for a whole week in the assistant keeper's cottage that now sits next to the original lighthouse.

Though the book isn't based on the real lightkeepers who lived and worked at the Eagle Harbor Light, the details regarding the lighthouse, the keeper's cottage, and the surrounding harbor are all as true to the actual setting as I could make them, including the climate. The lighthouse is located in the far north of Michigan's Upper Peninsula. When I visited at the end of June, I brought short-sleeve shirts but had to wear sweatshirts almost every day instead.

The real Eagle Harbor didn't have a copper mine within its town limits, so I took the liberty of adding one for the sake of the story. However, the entire area was once a bustling copper-mining community, a rough and wild settlement that resembled the Old West. Except for a few tourist towns, the area today is a graveyard of ghost towns and abandoned mines. During my research trip, I was able to explore deep underground into one of the old mines and get a firsthand look at just how dark, damp, and dangerous the mining life was.

Most of us gravitate toward the stories that glamorize lighthouse life and honor the women who served in them. That's only natural. And I hope that in my other books in this series, I gave those women the laud due to them. However, I didn't want to neglect the women who served in lighthouses whose experiences weren't quite as glamorous, who served even though they disliked the duty. One woman in particular inspired this book. Her name was Cecelia Carlson McLean. She was married to Alexander McLean, a keeper who worked at various lighthouses around Lake Superior. When she was interviewed later in her life, Cecelia was very forthright in stating that she hated lighthouses, that they were lonely places, and that she'd had to sacrifice a great deal to live in them. She claimed that if she had to do it over, she wouldn't choose life in a lighthouse.

Of course, her story made me think about the many hardships that light keeping entailed, especially for women — the extreme isolation, the lack of conveniences, and the constant threat of danger. So out of Cecelia's hardships, I created Tessa and tried to imagine the underlying motivations for what might cause someone to hate lighthouses. Although I had Tessa work through some of her fears and dislike of lighthouses, I'm sure most women like Cecelia took their resentment of lighthouses with them to the grave.

Although the main characters of this book are fictional, the villain, Percival Updegraff, is based on a real rogue from Michigan history, Albert Molitor. Molitor lived in Rogers City and ruled as "king" over his wilderness lumbering community. He controlled who was hired and fired. He had a company store and held a monopoly on all food and merchandise. He was also a sexual predator. Since he had so much control over the people who worked for him, if he took interest in a woman, he would walk into the woman's house and order her to go to bed with him. If she refused or resisted, he'd fire her husband and force the family to leave their company-owned home. He ruled this way until the people in the community finally revolted. They held secret meetings to plan to overthrow him. And while it took a couple of attempts, they set out to assassinate him. He was mortally wounded and eventually died, finally freeing the town of his cruelty.

Another resource I used in writing the story was a diary of a schoolteacher, Henry Hobart, who lived and taught in Clifton, which was a few miles down the road from Eagle Harbor. He wrote a detailed account of his life as a teacher to the mining children, including his holding evening classes and special spelling bees. He boarded with a Cornish family by the name of Rawlings. Mr. Rawlings was a prominent mine engineer and mechanic. I loved reading Hobart's diary and drew a great deal of inspiration from the many hardships he faced, from bedbugs and lice to scarlet fever and much more. He had a bright, promising student named Henry Benney, who left school at the age of thirteen to work with his father in the mines. Not long after Henry started working, he fell to his death while climbing up a slippery ladder. It was my hope to model Tessa after Hobart, a compassionate and caring teacher, and bring to life some of his experiences.

Eagle Harbor has an old one-room schoolhouse now known as the Rathbone School House. While it's no longer in use and instead serves as a museum, during my research trip I was able to visit the old school and used it as the inspiration for the schoolhouse in *Undaunted Hope.*

As with all my books, I pray this story encouraged and filled you with renewed hope. Just like Tessa, I pray you'll find the strength to face your fears, to know that God is there to walk beside you through them, and to come out on the other side stronger as a result.

ABOUT THE AUTHOR

Jody Hedlund is the bestselling author of multiple novels, including *Love Unexpected, Captured by Love, Rebellious Heart,* and *The Preacher's Bride.* She holds a bachelor's degree from Taylor University and a master's degree from the University of Wisconsin, both in social work. Jody lives in Michigan with her husband and five children. Learn more at JodyHedlund.com.